SPLINTERED

Enjoy !.

Lizzy Elliott

Published under licence by Brown Dog Books and
The Self-Publishing Partnership Ltd, 10b Greenway Farm, Bath Rd,
Wick, nr. Bath BS30 5RL

www.selfpublishingpartnership.co.uk

ISBN printed book: 978-1-83952-306-9
ISBN e-book: 978-1-83952-307-6

Cover design by Kevin Rylands
Internal design by Andrew Easton

Printed and bound in the UK

This book is printed on FSC certified paper

SPLINTERED

A psychological thriller seeping from
the bones of a family saga

LIZZY ELLIOTT

Dedication

I would like to dedicate this book to all parents, who, despite their constraints, believe and hope they are doing the right thing for their children. Also, we must never forget the scars of all wars and veterans who have kept evil at bay. We thank you. Strong voices have encouraged me and I thank you all, especially Michael. This book is just the beginning.

CHAPTER 1

1969
BASTARDS BEGET BASTARDS

Mentally she pressed down hard on her shoulders, concentrated fiercely and made her voice soar to reach that often elusive top A note. Tonight, with spellbinding precision, her mystical silver thread of sound showcased Mozart effortlessly, sending reverberations into her head and the audience.

Not many opera buffs amongst the parents though, the embarrassingly weak applause barely skimming the rafters of the school hall. Few would understand the difference between a note from the head or the throat. Four years of classical singing lessons had drummed this expertise into Berenice. Thanks to her scheming mother.

From the age of twelve she'd been thrown into a world of opera when all she'd desperately wanted was to whizz around the Waltzer in the Spanish City amusement arcade. Whitley Bay, a Northern seaside town, was a magnet for excited, adventurous youths in the 1960s.

Tonight, in the audience, her mother's eyes were misty, interested only in whether her adopted daughter was the best.

She was. Only because Berenice knew there would never ever be another night like this again. She had a secret.

Her daughter's reality eluded Edith. Silk purses may have been laboriously and expensively made, but the stench of maternal ambition eclipsed all as it wafted nauseously around the panelled oak of this private school.

If the girls were not all upper class, then at least they became well enunciated and knew where to place their cutlery and hopefully, how to cross their legs. Parents were mostly pleased.

Berenice rushed off the stage unaware that the zipper on her school uniform, box-pleated green wool skirt, had started its descent. The button of her white nylon Marks and Spencer school shirt was straining across her blossoming cleavage, narrowly hidden by a ghastly purple and white tie.

Alone for her singing solo on the school stage she had had some company. A tiny beating heart within her heard her song. She had felt an inner joy as she had mastered the top notes and she had wanted to sing out loud of her future imagined bliss. The sight of her mother's face had put a sudden stop to such silly thoughts.

She could not wait much longer though.

As Berenice sat down with those fellow students who had finished the concert at this excellent city school, she cocooned herself calmly. She felt soothed and sure of herself. She sank back into a very different world from that which her mother had mapped out for her. She felt serenely sure of her future. The only hurdle being the open truth and the awful look of bewilderment, hate and disgust that she knew she would see when she finally confessed to her mother.

Her mind raced back to that moment when she had first discovered the beating pain of sex. Rushed and frantic, yet in that moment inevitable. Then the horror of hearing her parents' car, a Marina Coupe, rev up into the drive and park. The womb-like darkness of the room, lit devilishly by the glow of gas fire, would imminently be no haven for the naive young lovers. Fear ripped Tony up, out and away. As quickly as he'd entered, he left. Darting through the kitchen into the garage and then down the side passageway.

He opened the gate adjoining the garage wall just as Edith and William entered the front door to check on their only daughter, Berenice.

Excellent getaway timing, he had thought.

As the textured-glass front door slammed shut the gas fire in the dining room flickered eerily. Her mother bowled into the house ahead of her father, always ahead of her father, and thrust open the door from the kitchen into the dining room. She was curious as to why Berenice was sitting in the dark. She would have been furious if she'd noticed the underwear curled up tight between her daughter's calves as Berenice sat with her feet up on the armchair in the corner of the room.

The light clicked noisily on and her mother questioned her about the darkness, perhaps only vaguely accepting the excuse that her daughter had nodded off after a strenuous bout of A- level revision. As her mother turned back into the kitchen to ask William to make a cup of tea Berenice slid quickly out of the chair and through the glass doors to the lounge then up the stairs and into the bathroom. Thankfully her underwear had partially disappeared under the chair.

Edith fussed through the dining room switching on more lights and missed Berenice's underwear by a whisker. The thought of Edith careering through the house with her daughter's knickers snagged onto her stiletto made Berenice giggle nervously as she gave herself a hasty swab-down in the bathroom. William called her down for a cup of tea and Berenice rescued her hidden garment just as William handed her the steaming mug. His tea always tasted of nicotine from his yellowing fingers and she sipped slowly whilst simultaneously stuffing the evidence in her skirt pocket.

William sank down onto the red plastic stool in the corner of the yellowing kitchen and lit his sixtieth cigarette of the day. It had been a good day. No fights. No nagging. No obvious stress. The subliminal tensions in this family ran as deep as the darkest pits of hell. But by Christ, if the outside world got to sniff out any trouble, then the tranquillisers came marching out of the bathroom cabinet of their own accord.

It was as if the quaking of the floor-boards and the slamming of doors dislodged them from their home and they marched off to work again. They were a patch-up team known to quell the thunder and quench the fire. As the tranquillisers were placed back in the cabinet they never once looked over their shoulders at the broken souls they left behind.

Later that night, as she bathed, with eyes tight shut, Berenice slid her fingers down to test the freshly turned flesh and found a swollen mound that ached and throbbed as if it had a life force of its own. She barely had time to snatch her hand away before her mother marched in on some pretext.

Edith fussed in the cabinet, secretly staring down at her

daughter and wondering for the zillionth time who the sturdy birth parents of this child must have been. Then just as swiftly she left.

Berenice sighed and in bed that night the exquisite pain finally abated and in its place alarm and doubt took hold. She fell asleep to the echoes of what if.

The next morning, she sat next to Tony on the freezing platform of West Monkseaton railway station waiting for their respective journeys to school and work in Newcastle. Both silently wondering if they had done the right thing the night before as they had hurriedly journeyed into sexual adulthood. Tony groaned inwardly because despite being six years older than Berenice, he too had been a virgin last night. A friend of his had lent him a book called *The Joy of Sex* and Tony had quoted a newly learnt fact to Berenice. She had never heard of coitus interruptus and questioned whether he was telling her the truth. He groaned again. Explanations were given and just as the electric train pulled in, he was saved by a noisy full carriage.

As he sank back into what seemed like an accusatory prickly seat, he rubbed his knees as the moquette- covered chair caressed his calves through his grey work slacks. Last night he'd suffered friction burns from the nylon mix in the carpet. Today he was being reminded of that. His nerves silently howled. His mind managed to make his voice work and as he looked sideways at the underage schoolgirl in her green school uniform, he managed to whisper to Berenice that it had been his first time too.

The alluring girl at his side reached for his hand, twisted his chubby fingers around hers, just as cells within her continued to bud. Berenice found her future in that moment. She did not dread a second of what might lie ahead. In her innocence she felt calmly resigned. The train pulled into Jesmond and the grind started again. A clear new day had begun.

Three months later the urine sample, hastily transferred to Tony's pocket by Berenice in the very same train carriage, was deposited at the hospital. A week later, Berenice made the phone call from a public call box around the corner from the traffic lights in the centre of Whitley Bay. She hung onto the rusting red-panelled edges of the sides as she absorbed the news. Clearly Tony's rather Catholic taste in contraception had not been enough to stem life's flow.

Strangely her favourite teacher at school was also pregnant, by almost the exact same number of weeks. In school Berenice sank further into herself as this teacher walked bump first into class to teach A-level history, wearing new maternity dresses and always sporting a huge smile. These lessons were painful. Berenice sought refuge in her music. That was why she had sung at the concert. It was over now.

Clearly over now.

As the last echoes of someone's piano recital hung limply in the air, she was nudged into awareness by her music teacher shooing her chicks along the dismal oak-lined corridor and into the enveloping dark night. Berenice was startled by the glare of her parent's headlights and like a cat her eyes dilated and she moved stealthily forward. She saw her father's clenched white knuckles on the steering wheel and her mother's white pearls glistening like dew on cemetery marble. The mood was epidemic, as Tony sat in the back looking ashen when the lights of passing cars caught his cowering frame. Berenice slid into the back seat and his comforting hand sought hers. Everyone was waiting for the official verdict before commenting.

'The violinist in the second row was not with you, did you notice?'

'No Mummy, I didn't.'

That's the style, Edith. Blame someone else and if possible two or three others but never your own family.

'However, you sang very well tonight – I am pleased.'

Her father's sigh was just audible. As if the camp commandant had released him from a hole in the ground, above which his eyes scanned the territory for scorpions. William loosened his grip on the steering wheel. The vision of a calm sleep ahead of him spurred him into a premature sense of wellbeing.

'Not too fast, William, the road is not well marked.'

How true.

As Tony was dropped off at his parents' house he whispered to Berenice, 'I love you.'

Bernice caressed his face as he reversed awkwardly out of the coupe. She knew the time was getting close. Today was Friday; all school concerts were held on a Friday and this was to be her last. She prayed in silence.

Sunday was the designated reveal day she and Tony had chosen and she wished the intervening hours away. She longed now for openness and the freedom to cast off what she appeared to be. In her eyes she was a schoolgirl imposter. A young expectant mother busying herself with crib choices, nursing bras and baby bouncers was to be her future.

'Berenice, Berenice,' came a distant whisper she could not hear.

The car stopped and she held her breath as she walked in. Her zip finally plunged down to the last rung and her father, who was behind her and glanced at it in the porch light, whispered that she had better do that up before her mother saw it.

He knew.

She climbed the stairs to bed and wept silent, bitter tears. If only she could talk to her Daddy. Berenice was soon to find out about the power of her parents' marriage.

William's love for Edith had blossomed as a child of nine when they attended junior school together in Fleetwood. It was that love which had irrationally sustained him through a Japanese prisoner-of-war camp, endless tortures and degradations. It had finally been consummated in a barren marriage, rescued by the adoption of a dear child that Edith swore she had dreamt of long before Berenice had arrived. The bond between Edith and William was unbreakable.

However hard William tried.

However hard Edith pushed him away.

Berenice loved her Daddy but felt conflicted about her mother. They just didn't seem to have anything in common. Obviously not looks, but nurture had not even included temperament. Edith seemed an outwardly cold woman, caring overly for image above all else. The neighbours laughed at her haughtiness behind her back whilst chatting to her father over the garden fence.

On shopping days, she insisted on being dropped off exactly outside each shop so as to avoid the riff-raff on the street. This meant that Berenice was left in the car with her father as he desperately sought car-parking space. She longed to make him tell her mother to walk like everyone else. He never did and the shopping charade churned on.

On Sunday she put the lead on the dog and took her scruffy black mongrel for a walk along the Links Promenade at Whitley Bay. She had agreed to meet Tony at two o'clock and she had half an hour to wait. She walked past the beach huts, down through the unused pitch-and-putt and up to the cliffs to look out at St. Mary's lighthouse. Standing at that spot she could imagine the restraints of her deception being blown away from her and felt cleansed as if the hand of something Holy had erased her guilt and fears. She saw a clear and honest vision of her future self.

Her mantle of depression always lifted as she turned the corner away from her home, a conventional bow-fronted, pebble-dashed semi-detached house on Grasmere Crescent. Lately she was having to move further and further away from home in order to recapture her sanity, her soul.

Today she just about managed to breathe evenly as she hurried back towards the cold café on the front and she felt a spit on her. Turning her face upwards she saw the darkening clouds mocking her in hoots of laughter and sudden droplets. The dog stopped abruptly and she tied his lead to a cracked black drainpipe outside the Rendezvous Café. She went in, ordering an espresso and her favourite biscuit, a Wagon Wheel, as she moved towards a window seat to await Tony's arrival.

He strode towards her. Through the rain-jewelled windows of the café she saw him, his tousled blonde hair whipping frantically around his head, as if looking for escape.

Whitley Bay Promenade in the 1960s was a cool hangout for youngsters.

In each explored alleyway between the beach huts there lurked an ever more frenzied gust, intent on unleashing if not his hair from its roots, then at the very least the toggles from his duffel coat.

Early spring on a North East coast was like that. Raw and savage. There would be no escape. Berenice ordered another frothy espresso and a biscuit whilst waiting for Tony to enter the nearly deserted café. The rusty hinges fought him as he opened the creaking old metal door. It managed to shut out the waiting world. That was only temporary, though.

Berenice sought his hand under the table, as if just holding it would somehow help. It was clammy with fear, sticky with sea salt, and rough. Tony drifted through that moment as unspeakable images of skewered foetuses, maternal demons in twinsets and pearls slithered through his mind. His Wagon Wheel rolled away from his touch and gathered dirt on its journey.

Later that day, after the tell, Berenice's adoptive mother Edith slouched uncharacteristically against the kitchen wall. Not for some sodding second-generation foreign evacuee jumped-up insurance clerk was she going to allow her daughter to waste herself.

Sacrifices had been made. Edith had bartered her soul early on. In exchange for flapping academic black gowns and the rich jewel of the right match. She dimly heard her husband William call her back into the lounge. Her quintessentially British sofa of cabbage-rose print resembled gargoyle heads contorting in jest at her discomfort. Future glories were to be fought and won on the battlefield of Berenice's character. Nothing was going to stop Edith.

Nothing at all.

Those two sitting on her couch, in her shrine to Sanderson Interior Design and desperate supposed middle-class good taste, had better believe that. Edith pulled herself up straight, centred her pearls between her collarbones as she simultaneously smoothed the outline of her wool Jaeger suit. As she left the kitchen to enter the lounge a chill descended almost imperceptibly upon the collective group. The devil had accepted his invitation.

'I really am pregnant,' said the nervous schoolgirl.

Bastards beget bastards was the last thought Edith had before the fraying tightrope of her sanity finally unravelled in front of her and she plummeted into an abyss, partly of her own creation. She lay frothing and churning in the hell fires of stigma. What a pleasing sight for the elusive guest from hell.

'She's nearly five months pregnant,' said Tony.

All the heartbeats that had stopped beating started again as the tide of their collectively dysfunctional lives shifted.

Sometime later, after the doctor had arrived and Tony had left, the doctor looked determinedly and piercingly into Edith's eyes. The National Health was not going to agree to a termination at this stage of a pregnancy. He had already seriously sedated a traumatised Berenice and he was not going to have two lives on his conscience. Edith had no such conscience and urged him to do it then and there. Nobody would know, she had implored.

As the frosted glass rattled when the departing doctor slammed shut the front door behind him, William met Edith's slightly bulbous stare and searched for any remnants of the carefree young girl he had left behind before he went to war, decades ago. He found no resemblance to the laughing, lovely, Lancashire lass he'd dreamt of whilst in unimaginable places.

He said, rather resignedly, 'The doctor intimated it may kill her, to abort right now. I mean, we don't want to do anything that might endanger her life, do we?' There was no reply from Edith.

William drifted away again as Edith plotted. In his tortured mind he found himself opening doors previously well sealed. Images flooded into the twisted tangle in his head of times not talked about too often. Swamps and stakes, bayonets and butchery. The gates of Changi had indeed clanged shut behind him as he had marched painfully away at the end of World War Two, in September 1945, towards his imprisoned freedom. But who could ever be truly free? Maybe the dead.

But worse, perhaps not even them!

Dimly he heard Edith get up and start to organise things. A second opinion was to be sought. Edith instructed William to call his old chum from the POW camps, a doctor called Rupert who now worked at Bristol River Infirmary. Edith had very little time for Rupert and his drunken weekends with William, designed to slay the demons. The morals of the man were questionable and that was all Edith needed to know. William obeyed her clipped instructions.

He always had.

There was really no fight left in him now.

It had all been fought out of him many years before.

The road trip to Bristol was interrupted as Berenice roused slightly when her baby kicked and she screamed, 'My baby, it's moved!'

William swerved the car violently, narrowly missing the pavement and a startled mother pushing her new-born son in his smart Silver Cross pram. Edith winced, ordering William to stop and dish out two of his tranquillisers to Berenice, to be swallowed down with hastily made lukewarm tea from a half-filled Boots Thermos flask.

Berenice then slept on.

William, depressingly, drove on.

Edith was rigid with self-control.

The devil, however, knew that there was still some hard work for him ahead.

Afternoon tea in the maternity ward at the Bristol hospital was served at a large and most inappropriately round table, at the furthest end of a long thin room. The French windows were open and a light breeze wafted through. For Berenice, the view across the veranda to the budding flowers and nesting birds was choking. The expectant mother next to her seemed unaware, intent as she was on balancing a cup of tea on what appeared to be her vastly over-inflated stomach.

Berenice's tears would just not come.

Her emotions had been sanitised by sharp syringes.

She felt a very long way from Tony. Her last memory of him was as he squirmed out from under the grip of her father as he had pinned him to the upright piano in the corner of the bay-fronted room in Whitley Bay. Then he had fled, this time through the front door.

Edith had made the right phone call. William had executed a fast car journey. Doctor Rupert, his old war buddy, had affected a paperless hospital admission.

It was nearly over.

Or perhaps this was where it all began?

Endless words and actions merged in Berenice's mind as she fought to make some sense of the last two days. The jigsaw of her life would just not come together, the pieces kept on falling out of place. She would never realise until much later that the pieces were not ever designed to fit.

The Devil was aware of her efforts to make sense of it all so he obligingly flicked an errant piece her way, lulling her into thinking everything would be fine. It stayed put long enough for Berenice to doze off into a troubled sleep. A nurse came and took her hand, leading her towards her bed. Doctor Rupert was doing his rounds. The nurse glared. No words were spoken. The nurse had seen it all so many times before with this doctor. She stayed quiet, took the money, kept her job and so did he.

Berenice was told many things she did not understand, partly because of her immaturity, partly because she was drugged. She lay in her bed, a slumped soul. She was hooked up to something designed to drip her baby away. But she did not think about this. No thoughts came at all. The pills made sure of that. She unhooked herself sometime later and collected a bedpan on the way to the loo, as the nurse kept reminding her to do. She was told they had to examine her urine.

For what, she naively thought?

As she perched on the bedpan on top of the loo there was a worrying shift to the left underneath her. She peered into the swirling mass inside the bedpan, alarmed at the congealed lumps. An orderly came and took the offending bedpan away.

'Is it over?' Berenice whispered to his retreating back.

The orderly turned, stared at her, laughed, then walked away. The Devil found her innocence sustaining.

By four o'clock the next day the pains were so severe that Berenice felt she was being dismembered. Visiting time came around and her adoptive parents walked cautiously into the ward, led by Edith. William shared many unspoken memories of four years of captivity with Rupert, slow painful deaths, suffered in the absence of medication. In a heartbeat William understood the wrong being done and backed out slowly, not giving his daughter eye contact. He left Edith to walk on alone. As she always had.

Rupert brushed past an exhausted William towards Edith, who was footing the bill from her personal bank account. She was not encouraged by his assessment. Little progress had been made and Berenice was on the brink of total exhaustion. Rupert made the very worst of suggestions. Edith replied quickly.

'Let me make this clear. She is not to have a scar. No visible evidence,' said Edith.

His patient was twenty-one weeks pregnant and Rupert was at a medical loss. Berenice's child was just not interested in leaving its mother's womb. There were some contractions. They never increased though. Nothing was shifting. Her strength was ebbing away. Edith would not listen and nobody heard Berenice's screaming soul.

Not yet anyway.

Edith, dressed in her Sunday best for visiting hours, felt inspirational.

'Let's go to the chapel and pray.'

Berenice moved with a crouched clutching gait as if trying her hardest to hold her child inside from the forces of evil around her. She started to cry. Edith grasped her punctured hand firmly and marched her down to the chapel altar.

'Pray!' she ordered.

Berenice began to focus now, hate crystallising her swirling thoughts, but with Edith at her side no prayers would be heard. No thoughts worthy of that Holy place would come and instantly Berenice wished she was dead. Right now, dead on the floor in front of her mother.

Edith sat with her eyes tight shut, thinking up excuses for the neighbours as to why they had gone on a road trip in the middle of a school term.

'Well, I don't think praying did much good!' screeched Edith.

Berenice snapped open her eyes. Her mother was wrong. Even though she was bent double with pain and her stomach was undulating like a demon was wreaking havoc within her, she had seen some things very clearly. She would be back. She needed to go to the chapel alone. Maybe someone would hear her.

Edith left the hospital praying to herself that perhaps by her next visit she could take Berenice away, spend some money on new clothes for her and return her to base all buffed up and squeaky clean.

It had been done before, in other situations, why not now, she thought?

William was out of step with his wife as she hurried to the car. His soul, eternally twisted from a heinous captivity, was tortured into silence from years of unresolved inner turmoil. The only thing he consistently wished for was death. He was so bloody cross that it had eluded him in the camp, on the railway line, in the pits. Perhaps in Edith's bed one day.

He'd work on that.

By the time Berenice returned to the small chapel by herself the sun lay low behind the exquisite stained-glass window depicting a Holy scene. Strangely jewelled beams of coloured light wove their way towards the altar cross and danced around the candlesticks, simultaneously mesmerising and seductive. Clouds dulled the chapel for a moment only to scurry away, and in their wake, Berenice saw a distorted version of Madonna and Child.

As she stumbled forward with outstretched hands, she clipped her toes on the altar step and fell face forward. Berenice's time had mercifully arrived. So did Rupert and the nurse, alerted by her screams. She was led back to the ward. They worked on her and were busy.

'I'll leave the rest up to you now, nurse,' said Rupert as he turned and walked away.

The nurse felt her hate welling up inside her again. It was just not fair to leave her with another young girl like this. The last time she had helped him with an illegal abortion so late in a pregnancy, she'd had to take time off work afterwards. She dreaded the thought of another baby crying out as it was thrust into the incinerator; was she expected to kill it first?

Nobody ever talked of these things to her.

'I want to shit!' screamed Berenice, not understanding that her child was arriving. She was distressed beyond words that she felt like this at this moment. She stared into the hardened eyes of the nurse. All around her the expectant mothers slept on, their babies safe and warm inside of them.

In the distance Berenice thought she could discern someone laughing. It got louder and louder inside her head until she felt an enormous pressure to bear down. The head of her child appeared between her thighs. A beautiful pair of blue eyes blinked for a second into the eyes of the waiting nurse.

She choked, 'Oh God, please don't look!' and turned away to avoid the horror of another live and illegal abortion. At that moment Berenice sat up and did indeed look awkwardly down into the bloody space between her legs, and stared into the eyes of her son.

And yes.

The little boy did cry out as the incinerator door flapped open.

The Devil was waiting with open arms.

CHAPTER 2

1871–1953
UK – SWATHES OF FATAL SILENCE

A baby was just something that Edith had to have. At the age of thirty-five, with a failed secret pregnancy behind her and a string of medical problems thwarting further attempts, she was sure that a baby was all her marriage to William needed to make it work. In 1953 few successful gynaecological interventions were available. Perversely, other women had babies. Those who should not have them had them.

Her sister-in-law, for instance.

She often wondered why she was being punished in this way. But not for long. Thoughts of urgent couplings in empty operating theatres, darkened wards and elsewhere brought joy to her heart. Then they were banned instantly, along with the other procedure. All of this was then hurriedly encased once more in the recesses of her mind.

Yet there was a catch to this longing for a baby.

A girl was required. A simple request perhaps. A baby girl born on a certain date with a particular colouring. Not so simple. In her darkest moments Edith understood this need but it was hardly surprising that she masked these facts in swathes of fatal silence.

Her scheming sister-in-law understood her obsession very well.

In Scotland, the owner of an Adoption Agency was an old friend of Edith's and between them there were few secrets. Sister Hart had covered for Edith as the Nazi bombs wreaked their havoc upon Glasgow and Nursing Sister Edith had sought the confusion of these raids to soothe a recently arrived Jewish doctor as he wept for his homeland. Edith gave her heart to him whilst his was breaking.

Meanwhile the German Luftwaffe continued to release their bombs early over Glasgow in order to avoid persistent and heavy anti-aircraft fire from the nearby shipyards on the River Clyde. The German air crews, who then climbed high into the night sky, scarpering back home to refuel and reload, were envied by the doctor. The sound of their whining engines on retreat was regularly eclipsed by Edith's pleasurable moans.

Edith had been born into a family of Scots living 'in exile' in the somewhat forlorn heart of Fleetwood in Lancashire, a once bustling fishing town on the north-west coast of England. This port town still boasts a tramline running from its heart all the way to a much more prosperous Blackpool. Transport weaves and dodges on the main road as tram drivers ring bells heralding their approach. The covered market, running almost down to the sea from the grey heart of Fleetwood, entices those brave enough to face the wicked damp sea mists to hide in the belly of its heated warmth. Crag-faced pensioners stare blankly from the elevated tea shop within and really have to take the spoon out of their tea sharpish. Ten minutes longer in the chipped, off-white heavy mug and it would have dissolved anyway. Northern tea is toxically tainted and substantial.

From the 1920s and for quite a few decades onwards, locally owned Icelandic trawlers had departed from Fleetwood to the chilly soulless world of the North Atlantic, only to return three or four weeks later with enough cod and plaice to keep the Northern fish and chip shops stocked to bursting.

Edith's father-in-law, Jack, had owned four such trawlers. He was a man of compact stature with gritty determination and dogged endurance. He and the other nine thousand or so who worked the local fishing industry in its heyday made the short walk every morning, out of a two-up two-down terraced home, past the Mount and along to North Euston Quay to start the daily search to provide food for the region. His metal-soled clogs clacked on the cobbles and echoed their wake-up call to his crew as he marched past their homes. On the way to work football was discussed. Jack was equally passionate about the local team as about his work. Fleetwood Windsor Villa Club, as it was then known, surpassed themselves in the 1930s by winning three county tournaments and Jack had campaigned for and helped finance their successes. His Masonic Lodge connections helped enormously.

The combined symphony of his workers' clogs on the cobbles vied only with the squawking seagulls and thus the rhythm of the day started anew in Fleetwood. Once on the dockside, clogs were replaced with rubber boots and the work began. Jack's oiled jacket gleamed with droplets from the sea frets. Beads of salty pearls clung on to his weathered, yet resolute brow.

His heart was in his small fleet but he was eventually forced to sell his boats to the giant company called Ross. Canny man as he was, though, he did not sell the company name, and to this day, a company in his name delivers around 250 tonnes of fish around the world.

A canny man, Jack Wright.

But the Cod Wars to come were the final end to Fleetwood's elevated port status. Small, privately owned fleets were no longer viable. They were bought and then leased back to these once proud men. Many fishermen took to drink. Some gave up altogether. They did so in various ways. Calculated carelessness swept some overboard. This ensured a sizeable pension from Ross to a grieving or otherwise widow.

For who could endure a broken man night after night who needed mothering, when what you'd been waiting for was a bout of dominance?

Jack took to drink. When he sold out altogether, he'd often hide in the pavilion of the Mount, the iconic structure on a hill, from which all streets originally radiated. He would muse, on a clear day, as he stared across the Irish Sea to the hills of the Isle of Man, some sixty miles away, of the things he had not accomplished. He wished that he had actually been able to take his wife Faith there, rather than just having sailed past it alone. The rolling fells and mountains of the Lake District were visible too. He'd heard of the beauty of Tarn Hows. Faith would have enjoyed the pleasant amble around the water and perhaps even have been encouraged to sit at the viewpoint as he tried the longer summit of nearby Black Crag.

He dreamt of Fleetwood football club's future glories and would have been astonished to learn of Fleetwood eventually playing and winning at Wembley, something he could only close his eyes and imagine, with joy in his heart.

Violent coughing fits and clenched fists reminded him of his inability to achieve either of these whimsical dreams and he clutched his coat around him as he lit a new fag from his silver engraved lighter. He would time his homecoming just after his clever son William darted home from school. He kept silent, and the lad would never know of his father's shame at not being in regular work anymore.

Gordon, Edith's father, was the only dentist in town. The foreign crews spilling out of the bellies of the container ships flocked to his practice. They wanted golden smiles to charm the local lasses. They left the dentist's simultaneously scratching their jaws and their crotches. A walk along Fleetwood's impressive promenade at the end of a night of carousing took the sailors away from the port. At the far end, when they could wait no longer, they pushed open the unlocked black iron gates of the cemetery. Many an ice-cold Carrara marble or Scottish granite grave was then abused in a way that would probably cheer the Lancashire dead if they could have had their say. Gordon's father was cursed from land to land as sailors' wives wrung their hands in despair at the lack of money their husbands brought home. A dose of the clap was their reward, plus a twinkling smile.

Gordon knew that the heart of Fleetwood was bleeding and he too bled his own portion. But he was owed, he reckoned. He was proud of the fact that he was one of the first locals to own a car. His only daughter Edith was the first girl of her age to drive. Gordon had been one of the original R.A.F. pilots in World War One. A pedigree like that rendered him unbearably insufferable. He'd survived a fall from the open cockpit of his Airco DH2, a nimble and sturdy fighter plane. He had been flying too low over no man's land, on a reconnaissance mission, when he had tumbled out.

He had survived.

He did not see Wilfred Owen's far-off lights but he lived to receive medals and a special pension, following his softly cushioned landing in a quagmire of churning mud and decaying corpses. His wartime life had been exciting and dangerous. A slight deafness in his left ear and extreme arthritis were the only scars. The mental toughening that had taken place kept him on a steady path later in life and those around him went in fear of his strength of character.

Edith was initially in awe of him. Her father was a war hero and a respected member of the local community, a strict Scottish Presbyterian who naturally loved his sons more than he did his daughter. A boy had been born into the family. At last Edith had a brother. Gordon and his wife May felt they had achieved something special when the boy was born. Edith sank imperceptibly further into the shadows of the oak panelling of the home as her brother grew, her intolerance of the male of the species perhaps attributable to her father's attitude.

Gordon himself came from a clutch of boys born to a wealthy Scottish chemist. Edith's grandfather was one of the first chemists employed by Alfred Nobel's British Dynamite

Company situated in Ardeer on the River Clyde estuary, about 19 miles south of Glasgow in Scotland in 1871. The company was later to become part of the once mighty ICI engineering conglomerate. This stubborn Scot argued over ammunition formulas and left. Ironic really when it was ordinance from this very factory that had shot down Gordon.

However, shares were kept, treasured and built upon. The family would talk about this for generations to come. What if he had stayed and been part of the hugely successful chemical company that this firm was to become?

Listening to this kind of talk became very tedious, even to Edith.

She knew that her grandfather had been rich. She also knew that if he had stayed at ICI her family would have been an awful lot richer. About this there was a bitterness in her father which had turned him into a workaholic. She rarely saw him, or for that matter her mother. The dentist's surgery was situated in the front right-hand living room of their sturdy double-fronted detached house. Theirs was a privileged existence in a relatively prosperous Fleetwood at that time. The richly patterned tartan carpet of blue and green with red stripes, which covered every floor in the house, reminded Edith somewhat of the tramlines she was forbidden to cross on Lord Street. The leaded windows were always kept sparkling especially after the toxic waste from the seagulls splattered and obscured the view of the then bustling port town. The family shared their house with two live-in maids, and Edith's mother, May, worked alongside Gordon as his dental assistant and receptionist.

This was a rather bold step in the late 1920s but May

felt that she had to assert herself in a household where women outnumbered the men. She was a comfortably rounded woman of proud Scottish heritage. Always dressed immaculately and coifed to perfection, she was distanced from her daughter in subtle ways. Although May loved Edith dearly, she sensed that her daughter was not quite what Gordon had hoped for in a firstborn. His implicit rejection of Edith was all too obvious. When a son was born, both parents felt that all was at last correct. Edith loved her baby brother Campbell, not least of all because he loved her back unconditionally. He was fun and once upright never stopped moving, darting from room to room to play hide and seek with whomever was around, and he was fearless. When he died in 1927 at the age of five, she was never to forgive her parents for clearly blaming her for his death.

Campbell and Edith had been playing in the oak-panelled living room. One maid was busy in the pantry, cleaning the stone-flagged floor of the residual stains from the milk churn. The other maid was sorting the soiled linen into household and surgery piles ready for the boiler. Earlier in the week one maid had noticed a piece of skirting had worked its way loose and needed nailing. Nobody had nailed it flush to the wall. As Campbell rushed around pretending to be a Red Indian, he stubbed his big toe, right foot, on the offending sharp edge of the skirting board.

In the following few days, he succumbed to septicaemia. Edith's life was also in the balance. Youngster Campbell had been in sight of penicillin but not within reach. The following year it was to be discovered. Too late for Campbell. Far too late for Edith. As Campbell's tiny white coffin was lowered into the damp grave a mantle of guilt settled itself effortlessly upon Edith's shoulders. The cemetery at Fleetwood is an unforgiving place.

Within sound is the rough churning sea, and freezing damp winds whistle inshore, whipping with unrelenting fury round the edges of whimsically designed monuments to the frozen dead. Winds there have the power to topple mourners if not directly into the gaping hole in the ground, then at least into bed with an almost lethal dose of pneumonia.

Edith stared at the grave as her parents wept. Nobody thought to comfort her. The night before the funeral she had been unable to sleep. She'd crept down the curved staircase and edged up to the ornately carved double drawing-room doors. Her intention was to seek some comfort from her parents within. A cuddle perhaps. As she had been about to open the heavy doors, she had realised that they were slightly ajar. Her name was mentioned and the words she overheard made her realise there would be no comfort.

She climbed back up the stairs to her bedroom in a house that suddenly looked and felt quite different. Colours were less brilliant, sounds a shade muted and love, a fading feeling. She stayed in Fleetwood long enough to see the life-sized, white marble replica of her little brother lowered into place at the head of the grave. He looked like a little angel. His head was bent slightly to the left as he looked at the lamb he was stroking. Edith could not remember Campbell ever looking that peaceful or serene. The statue was a monument to the craftsman and his knowledge of children's illustrated bibles. It had little to do with Campbell and his boisterous, rampaging short-lived childhood. Edith supposed that

Campbell was in heaven with his lamb and this thought gave her comfort when she visited the cemetery.

May beseeched otherwise, but Gordon was adamant that Edith be sent away to live with his ageing mother in Scotland. Gordon's father, Murray, had died two months earlier. Edith's presence would give her grandmother a reason to live. Gordon and May would then have a period of calm to assess their feelings. It was all arranged with indecent haste and Edith was packed off to live in West Kilbride in Scotland for an indefinite period of time. It seemed to Edith that she had never stopped weeping since the night that she had overheard her father saying that Edith should have taken better care of Campbell.

In her haste to escape that night, she had failed to hear her mother's reply. May knew she was not to blame. It had been a tragic accident, especially when both parents had known about the loose skirting.

As Edith alighted from the train carriage, she was enfolded into the agreeably large arms of her recently widowed Grandma Ruth. So began a time in her life that Edith would constantly look back upon with warmth and fondness. At last, she had found a relative who wanted to cuddle her. They both dreaded the day when the summons would arrive to send her back to Fleetwood. Each other's grief comforted and assuaged by the other.

Edith waited seven loving and stress-free years. West Kilbride was nothing like Fleetwood. No noisy trams to dodge on Main Street. The nearby Firth of Clyde was nothing like the uninviting, tempestuous Irish Sea. Grandma Ruth did everything by hand, no maids around at all. Edith scurried home from the local school attached to the West Kilbride Parish Church and willingly helped her grandma with the chores.

During that time her parents had made even more money, given birth to another son and finally thawed enough to let her return. She did not want to leave her ageing grandma. But as she had arrived, she also left, in a fog of tears and confusion.

Grandma Ruth died the very next day. Edith was never told.

Greeting Edith on the platform at Blackpool North train station was a strange young lad, not unlike wee Campbell but called Douglas. He was stunningly attractive with dark Gaelic looks and a quirky character. After seven years Edith had grown up but her parents seemed the same. Her mother kissed her lightly and her father shook her now adolescent hand. Young Douglas pulled his mother away and insisted upon being escorted to the train station's toilet. Edith was left alone with her father, for the first time in seven years.

'Douglas is old enough to look after himself now, that's the reason we brought you home.'

Edith felt very, very cold. She did not cry, she secretly unleashed her slowly mounting hate and nourished it with each glimpse of her father. Her grandma had taught her how to love and she missed her warmth and embraces terribly. Edith managed to keep her anger in check as she followed the family of three out of the station and into the waiting black Ford Model A. She sat in the back on the shiny leather seat and slid herself into the far-left side, gluing herself to the doorframe. Douglas eyed her suspiciously from the far right-hand side.

The journey back into her old life in Fleetwood was not quite as she had imagined it to be. Classmates had matured yet her memories of them had not. New friendships had been forged and she was now the outsider, both at home and at school. In her first week back, she floated through life on a blossoming tide of loneliness and tedium. Nothing roused her melancholic frame and no drop of life sparked her awakening sensuality and spirit.

Until she saw William.

Most of the young lads at Fleetwood Grammar School longed to leave school at the earliest opportunity and go to sea, as generations before them had done, in order to bring home a decent wage. Then they dreamed of wedding the girl they'd been doting on since junior school, who in all probability lived on the same street as they did. Some longed to leave school, go to university, get a safe job and marry the smartest girl with an equally good job and never ever return to Fleetwood. William fell into neither category

He had blossomed late.

Edith could hardly remember him but he remembered her. From a thin small boy, he had grown into a wiry, brilliant academic. He was to win the coveted Bailey Memorial Medal of 1936, a scholarly honour so rich in tradition in Fleetwood that the medal itself was cast in pure gold and kept in a purple velvet box by each recipient. The medals were handed down from generation to generation, to be either worn or displayed but always to be treasured as a recognition of someone who had the highest Joint Matriculation exam marks attainable in that region.

As a puny youngster William had been laughed at. Girls his

own age were cruel and teased him remorselessly behind his back. His innate cleverness could not convert his diminutive size into stature in their eyes, so he gave up wishing for a girlfriend. What was even worse was that he went to dance classes. His mother, Faith, hoped that all the stretching and leaping about would help him to grow. He had not complained about going as he liked to be close to a young girl called Edith. Then for years Edith had stopped coming. The town spread rumours, but he chose to hear nothing.

For seven long years he stretched and leapt about in the hope that if she ever did return, he would be tough enough to warrant a second glance. William's dentist was Edith's father and on one visit to the surgery he had plucked up courage to ask about her whereabouts. The maid, who was closing the heavy front door by the time he had guts enough to enquire, looked at him strangely and said that she supposed Edith would be back one day. This gave him immense hope but also perplexed him as he had no idea why she had left in the first instance. He went home determined to be the young man of her dreams by the time she returned.

It was late October and William was on his way to his regular Saturday afternoon dance classes at the Marine Hall seafront theatre on the promenade. As a frustrated teenager he always felt, as he trudged past the shape of the domed theatre, that the roofline reminded him of something he was yet to encounter. He often felt uncomfortable these days when his dance partner pressed too close and he was forced to move away sharpish.

One day, as he arrived, he noticed a familiar Ford parked outside the entrance. His heart thumped as Edith stepped out and made her way inside. As he approached the car, he noticed a young boy inside stick his tongue out at Edith.

Edith had been back at school for just one week and, in that time, he had not had the courage to talk to her. She seemed very lonely. He was too. He decided that now he had the confidence to catch her up and talk to her.

Edith barely recognised William out of his school uniform. William's father was quite well off for a fisherman. Edith's father called them all fishermen. William was as tall as Edith, but then she was quite short. They stood looking at each other and then finally, after William had reminded her who he was, they reached a level of understanding as William remarked upon Douglas's behaviour in the car. Edith liked the sympathetic note in his voice and she recognised the look of love in his eyes, eyes that reminded her of her relationship with Grandma Ruth from Scotland. The two youngsters skipped dance class and went for the first of many walks along the promenade. Walks that would cement their relationship and bind William together, forever, with the prettiest, wealthiest young lady in town.

William wanted to go to university, come back and be somebody in Fleetwood. He wanted to marry Edith and be the best ever teacher at Fleetwood Grammar School. To achieve all of this would mean that he had arrived socially as well as professionally, and the deepening gloom his father was sinking into and believed William could not comprehend would be relieved by the successes of his only son.

William offered Edith a chance to escape from the constraints of her otherwise tightly controlled life. They walked home from school together every day. He was awed by the splendour of her house. She was initially unaware of this, caring only for the friendship of a boy who was not dominated by her father.

On Saturday afternoons, in the darkening gloom of autumn days they would wander down the prom and hide in the cemetery amongst the tombstones. Something always held Edith back from the fullness of a relationship that William desperately desired. The giggly teenage girl, freed for the afternoon and clasping her boyfriend's arm to the side of her breast, slowly shrank back from the presumption of more intimacy. No matter how close they may have been to wee Campbell's statue, it was always too close for Edith.

Their love was found to be flawed. Tested to the limits. Frayed at the edges. The bond nearly severed. But not quite. A war was looming.

At his school leaving ceremony, with the Bailey Memorial Medal in his hand and the girl of his dreams in the audience watching the presentation ceremony, William could hardly contain his pride. Edith sat next to his parents, Jack and Faith. They too were proud, Faith more so of the medal. However, Jack doubted the ability of his son to convince Edith's parents of the suitability of the match. But the couple could not be stopped. Although unbeknown to them, both sets of fathers wished that the damn romance would just burn itself out.

William was staying on at school to swot for his entrance exam to read History at Bristol University and Edith was going off to Glasgow Royal Infirmary to train to be a nurse.

As the medal ceremony ended, all eyes seemed to be on the couple as they barely spoke to anyone else.

During the harrowing weeks before Edith was due to leave for Glasgow, William was anticipating all sorts of exciting plans with her. Tram rides through town and along Blackpool's Golden Mile. Fun in Blackpool Tower, perhaps a tea dance or two to show off their skills in the iconic ballroom. Visits to Gypsy Rose Lee to have their certain fortunes told and afterwards sticky candy floss consumed on the lower promenade hiding from the Scottish day trippers. And so very much more!

But it seemed that daily May found Edith something to do: a visit to the seamstress necessary for another fitting of her probationary nurse's uniform or tea with relatives that she would actually be glad to see the back of. The worst thing of all for Edith was the hell of escorting Douglas back and forth to school; an odious task as he tried in vain to escape and hide in the hedges along the route. A firm grip of his jacket and a strangely satisfying clip round the ear usually sorted out his antics and confirmed their mutual love–hate relationship, which would endure until death. Douglas did love his sister Edith but was now old enough to realise that she had been treated unfairly by their parents. He enjoyed his favourite sibling status whilst also recognising Edith needed to get away to start her new life in Glasgow really quickly.

Edith sensed the upheaval in her life that her nursing training in Glasgow would herald. All of England was on the brink of change but in their innocence Edith and William had no clue as to the horrors that would unfold so shortly after that hot summer in the ninety thirties. Edith swept thoughts of the future aside as she very nearly gave herself to William one balmy night under Blackpool's Central Pier at low tide.

But she didn't.

William wept tears of anguished frustration and disbelief as they then strode along the shore towards North Pier, William venting his tension upon the soft ridges of the sand and kicking great holes in the beach that would soon to be filled. The tram journey back to Fleetwood was agonisingly silent for the young couple.

In September, at university, he was finally to find sexual relief beside the water as he rose from making love for the first time, on the riverbank, below the 330-foot Clifton Suspension Bridge in Bristol that spans the River Avon. The Latin inscription on the bridge 'Suspensa Vix Via Fit', he translated to mean that not only was the bridge, but also this encounter, made with difficulty. He had immensely annoyed the woman who still lay on the grass searching for a cigarette to calm her fraying temper, by calling out Edith's name. He had not even asked the girl hers. Yet for a brief moment, as the course of the second half of the twentieth century was set in slow motion, two people had found comfort, when all else around was beginning to destabilise. During the next three years at university, he would annoy many more in the same way. Climaxing to the sound of Edith's name became a routine.

On September 3rd 1939, Britain and France had confirmed their entry into the theatre of war. His chums from school were joining the Blackpool Regiment and a year later joined the Royal Engineers.

William had enjoyed his halcyon days of study and social

successes. Travel was beginning to be restricted and his time with Edith was almost non-existent, except that is, in his head. He still craved her. More so as he had been so cruelly denied her. He was just as determined to marry her one day. Meanwhile, William had studied and copulated as if the end of the world was in sight.

Edith was so very busy in the first year of her five years of training that she could not even remember sleeping. All nursing probationers were given an unfair amount of night duty and she seemed to stumble from week to week with exams every three months. She passed her final exams to the backdrop of heavy bombing of the ports on the River Clyde.

That William still wanted to marry her was clear to her from the frequent letters he sent. He wrote of returning to Fleetwood and buying a large detached house, galaxies away from his parents' terrace. His father would actually have been able to buy something bigger as he prospered in his early days as a trawler owner, but because William's mother had extremely serious cataracts in both eyes, she had stubbornly refused to leave the home she knew and could navigate almost blindly. That terrace in Harris Street had finally become an embarrassment to William. Before he left for university, his mother had had the habit of sending him to the chippy on the street corner every Saturday night for six pennies' worth of tripe and batter bits. His father would reject his portion when he staggered in drunk from the football and it was left to William and Faith to sit in weary silence and eat whilst his father retched in the yard. William would then eagerly wash the smelly plates in the stone-flagged scullery, the very floor Faith was later to fall and crack her head open upon, and die. William had always hated to share these Saturday night slippery, sickly offerings with his mum. Following the meal, Faith would wipe her fingers on the greasy apron she could not properly see and adjourn to the front parlour to listen to the radio. It was a blisteringly chilly room, used infrequently and suffering from mould that even found its way into the pleated edges of the pink satin cushions on the brown velvet sofa.

William would reluctantly perch on the edge of the upholstery and listen to the radio. On the mantel of the chillingly barren marbleised fireplace was a picture of William as a child in his iron-soled clogs. As far as William knew, many other people rarely ate tripe and never wore clogs. His longing to be away was tangible.

Edith recognised that William was obsessed with bettering himself. She despaired for him.

Later, at university, William schemed and plotted his path forward in life.

How would he be able to claim Edith as his own?

At work Edith hardly dared to open William's letters. She was, after all, exceedingly busy.

Busy during the day.

Busy during the night.

How could she explain?

How indeed?

CHAPTER 3

1938–1939
A QUESTION OF WHEN AND WHERE

After considerable pondering, Edith had happily opted to specialise in midwifery at Glasgow Royal Infirmary. As she was telling her co-worker and best friend Sister Hart this, both women silently recognised that the decision was almost certainly connected to the fact that Doctor Jonathon Weiss was in residence at the same hospital, specialising in that field. Sister Hart had heard the rumours about this dejected émigré who pined for his beautiful wife and adoring son, both of whom he had been forced to abandon in Munich.

In early November 1938 he had been away seeing to his sick sister-in-law in Berlin when suddenly news of Joseph Goebbels' revenge for the killing of the German ambassador in Paris reverberated throughout the Jewish community. 'Kristallnacht' or 'the Night of Broken Glass', saw many Jewish shops targeted and looted between November 9th and 10th 1938 in Munich. Esther, Jonathon's wife, lived with her family and her father above their antiquities shop in the medieval heart of Munich. On November 9th 1938 Esther had been helping her father, Franz, to balance the accountancy books downstairs in the closed shop.

A crazed officer of the 'Sturmabteilung', or Nazi Storm Troopers, had crashed through the heavily carved spruce shop door and eyed a startled Esther as she sought to shield her ageing father from the butt of an E-11 blaster rifle. Her father was felled without mercy and died slowly at the foot of the stairs as he tried to escape. Esther was then savagely hurled to the ground, her red woollen dress ripped and her sturdy undergarments frantically torn off. Her frightened young son, Klaus, had trembled as he hid behind the hand-turned banisters at the top of the stairs, wondering why the soldier was on top of his mother. At four years of age, he knew not of the horrors unfolding before him. But his heart beat wildly, as so it ought. He was soon to be in mortal danger. As the stormtrooper offloaded, his comrades burst in through the open door and continued as he had left off. Perhaps luckily, Klaus had passed out, unable to process the sight below him and desperate to block out his mother's agonised cries of torture and humiliation.

By the fourth soldier she too had passed out. The tenth soldier stared down as the blood of her mutilated body mingled with the fabric of her similarly ripped dress. He put away his manhood and decided to give it a miss. As he left the once stylish and respected Jewish shop, he smashed the front window in frustration and threw in a match to light the petrol that had already been sloshed inside.

Jonathon never heard these exact details. He would perhaps have benefitted from knowing that the burning bodies of his family had been unconscious before the flames sucked the flesh from their bones, the crackle and pop of their burning a mere footnote to the sounds that echoed in Munich that night. So many of his Jewish friends were not unconscious when the Nazis inflicted death upon them.

In Scotland Jonathon lived quietly at 225 Wilton Street, Glasgow. This was the city that had taken him in when he and his brother had escaped on board the SS *St Louis* sailing from Hamburg on May 13th 1939. Following a torturous and convoluted journey on the high seas the ship eventually disembarked its passengers in Antwerp, Belgium. Jonathon had been lucky to get a place on the ship. His weeping brother had comforted him during the five months in hiding since the Night of Broken Glass. Sadly, even Jonathon's expertise had not been able to save his sister-in-law from a laboured and horrific breach birth. The baby never took breath.

Many a night Jonathon had wanted to hike back from Berlin to Munich to find his beloved family. His brother had locked him in what had been planned to be the nursery and, in the morning held him as the nightmares subsided with the dawning of each new day. Money, bribes and sheer good fortune secured them both a berth with the nine hundred and thirty-five other Jews on the last boat to sail out of Germany before the concentration camps did their worst.

As the boat docked, immigration officers from Britain, the Netherlands, Belgium and France boarded and divided up its occupants. Jonathon lost sight of his brother before this even took place, as he had gone in search of water because he was seriously dehydrated, perhaps the more so from all his crying. Jonathon was escorted into a waiting British ship and sailed to Glasgow as his brother started a new life in Antwerp.

It took several weeks before the British could establish the credibility of Dr Jonathon's medical claims. When they did, they put him to work in Glasgow Royal Infirmary where he startled them with his expertise. Work was his escape from thought.

Edith recognised Jonathon's brilliance and ached for his embraces.

The couple of times that Edith and William had met in the last few years had been unsatisfactory and wearisome, surrounded as they inevitably were by watchful relatives in mockingly gay festive spirits. Hugs and stolen kisses under mistletoe or railway arches did nothing to help. Their relationship seemed to survive on a surfeit of Royal Mail, the contents on William's side being hot enough to sear holes in the weathered canvas bags of the postman.

It was beginning to feel like a fantasy romance; perhaps it had always been so. William elevated Edith to heights no mortal woman could attain and Edith turned away from the memories of William, as Dr Jonathon entered and left her life more frequently.

Sister Marigold Hart watched it all unfold. She was ten years older than Edith and challenged physically to the extent that men avoided looking too closely. She had been brought up in Fowey, a picturesque fishing village in Cornwall. She had attended the local school until hurriedly leaving for Truro to train at the nursing college there. Her teenage years had been difficult. She was the ugly sister to a vibrant and daring older sister named Violet. Like the symbol of the purple flower after which she was named, Violet's thoughts were constantly occupied with love. Sister

Hart had never had her sister's power of attraction. Named Marigold after her mother's obsession with flowers, she was less golden than reddish and fared badly in the heat of Fowey's epic summers

Usually, she was to be found under an umbrella, shielding her freckles from the sun, and she was always the butt of teenage laughter in the village. They watched her freckles steadily join up, culminating, by the end of August, in a vision akin to large rambling age spots.

Briefly, in the summer of her nineteenth year, she had believed herself to be in love. Her sister Violet had a new boyfriend named Gregory, a tanned god of the sea who plied his motor launch up and down the estuary with Venetian aplomb, believing his smile was all he needed to attract any females it fell upon. It usually did. Violet was smitten as soon as she set eyes on him. He had arrived one night from Bodmin and had instantly disgruntled the other local lads who worked the tourist trade on the estuary. A stranger, how romantic, thought the sisters. He's mine, thought Violet, who was unused to rejection. Marigold overheard her sister making a date to meet Gregory on Saturday night, on the steps leading down from the harbour wall to the estuary. There he would transport Violet out to a romantic sea-going picnic and who knew what else?

At home on the said Saturday Violet fussed and primped herself, as did Marigold. She shared her sister's gorgeous eyes. Leading down from the eyes it went badly wrong. Marigold's nose was bent and bulbous and her lips too thin. Her skin was a riot of freckles and summer sunburnt blotches. As her sister skipped gaily to each new beat of her life Marigold stumbled awkwardly after her, her thighs chafing in their fullness and her calves seemingly welded directly into her feet as if God had forgotten to give her ankles. Her hands were delicate and soft, not unlike Violet's, and their mother often said that Marigold would make a caring nurse as she was always taking care of her sister. Her last name was Hart after all, her mother was fond of saying that Marigold indeed had a heart of gold. Mothers can often be that blind.

Ahead of her plan Marigold had sent a message to Gregory, as if from Violet, that she would be half an hour later than arranged as she first had an errand to run for her father. Gregory had not minded as he was happy to wait half an hour for another local conquest as his long-suffering wife sat by herself, yet again, on a Saturday night. With four children under six years old she was lucky if she would get a night out on her own any time soon. As he left, their front door slammed. She did not realise then what an interminable wait it would be before she saw him again.

Marigold was prone to clinging to her sister at every turn: shopping together, walks along to the harbour wall to watch the ferry to Bodinnick, and most importantly shadowing Violet throughout the annual Fowey Regatta and Carnival Week in August in the desperate hope of wallowing in her brilliance, dazzling by default and securing a lover before she turned twenty-one. Sister Hart was truly a sister…but an unattractive sister…and it annoyed her.

With her plan set in motion, the ugly duckling who had never been kissed, stroked or loved set about following her sister through the cobbled streets. The gentle lapping of the river on the estuary wall drawing both sisters towards their fate. Violet stopped to check her appearance in the front window of the chemist's. Ironically it was the same chemist's where earlier in the day Gregory had popped in to ask the pharmacist quietly for 'a little something for the weekend'. Frowning his Catholic displeasure, the pharmacist had handed over the condoms rather than contemplate what the muscles on Gregory's arms might do to him should he challenge his request. Anyway, August was a bumper month for such sales and his wife wanted a trip to London soon. He had sighed as he'd heard the till ring in tune to the door closing on another happily prepared customer.

Violet sat on the bottom of six cracked and sloping stone steps leading down to the river from the harbour wall. Gregory was late. She was frowning. Being stood up was not about to happen to her, surely.

Marigold had come prepared. Scarf in hand, she would wind it around her hair and lower face and in the dim light Gregory would catch a glimpse of the near identical pair of eyes and invite her on board. Marigold was seething with uncontrollable jealousy, which had evolved into hate.

She leant over into a moored fishing boat on the jetty and removed an unsecured oar. Violet was still searching the estuary for Gregory's returning boat. From the safety of the harbour wall, Marigold peered over, with oar in hand and suddenly, alerted by the scraping of the wooden oar on the rugged stone wall above and behind her, Violet spun around. Her fashionable high heeled shoes caught in a crack on the surface of the step. She stared up into familiar eyes, gasped, flailed backwards and as her feet popped out of her shoes, she executed a near full turn, rotating wildly in the air to grasp at a rail that was not there and a footing which was lost. Marigold's eyes were transfixed and the oar seemed to move by itself as it gave Violet the fatal shove.

Violet somersaulted into the water, catching the back of her head violently on the submerged bottom two steps, her neck snapping with a resounding crack which reverberated up through the harbour wall and into the palms of Marigold who was still clutching the oar and staring manically below her. She recoiled backwards. Replacing the oar quickly as she heard a boat chugging up the estuary, she rushed down the steps to see Gregory approaching from upstream, waving encouragingly at what he thought to be Violet.

Marigold hurriedly wound the scarf around her; the wind was conveniently picking up, so Gregory would not be surprised at her headgear. He was not interested in her head. As he barely slowed the motor next to the steps Marigold jumped in and the moon hid in fear behind some clouds. Seconds later they were midstream and Gregory hastily dropped anchor. Her head was jammed against the wood of the small boat as he fumbled with the condom, whilst prising her legs open. She was wedged into the triangular bow of the boat, daring to hope that her dream was about to be fulfilled. In her madness she had become her sister and as Gregory called out Violet's name, she arched her back to welcome his entrance. Inexplicably to Marigold, he hesitated. Stopped altogether and she opened her eyes to see his blanched face staring into the water beyond the bow.

Nothing seemed to happen. Time was frozen in a tableau of disbelief. Gregory kept screaming Violet's name as Marigold was aware of the anchor being raised beside her and as she twisted to look over the edge, the glittering wet face of her dead sister appeared, impaled upon its three-pronged spokes. Gregory eerily silent.

She dived into the water. The cold sea snapped her back to reality. Her sturdy limbs, for once an asset, meant she made it to shore in minutes. She ran sodden to a call box and alerted the police to an unfolding situation in the estuary. She told them how she had witnessed a young girl entering a small pleasure craft. The craft had moored and a struggle followed as the girl tried in vain to reject the sudden and furious advances of the skipper. She had fallen into the waves, only to be hauled back into the boat dead, on the end of his anchor.

Then she hung up.

Then she ran.

The village of Fowey turned out in full for the funeral. Marigold used the same scarf to obscure her face and large sunglasses to hide the lack of tears in her eyes. Her mother was comforted by her sister from Falmouth who arranged everything.

Marigold accepted the nursing training in Truro and her mother let go of the lease on the cottage and moved in with her sister. In the months that followed Marigold lost a lot of weight and was usually to be found in her sister's clothes. As before, she languished in the shadows of other, prettier women and very occasionally men took pity on her and took turns with her, their exploits always recounted on the nights when she was not with her friends. Horrid stories of her grateful touch were swapped around the doctors' hall of residence.

After finals, one nurse, feeling sorry for Marigold, told her the stories being bandied about and Marigold was so incensed she strangled the girl in a heartbeat and left her limp corpse in the sluice room of the hospital, locking the door firmly on her way out. Within days she had transferred to Glasgow. Sister Hart was truly reborn. She vowed never to make quite the same mistakes again.

Edith had been sorely homesick when she had first arrived in Glasgow. Sister Hart took her under her wing and encouraged her in her studies and her lust for Jonathon. They both lusted after him. This time, though, Marigold Hart would be just the voyeur. She waited eagerly for that.

Back in Bristol, William recovered from the excesses of finals and late-night studies in the arms of various willing females. As soon as he was free of the burdens of university he would go to Glasgow, surprise Edith and take her before she could even utter a word. Such were his fantasies. Right now, the depth of his carnal knowledge was going to be more important than the breadth of his First-Class Degree and he plotted his advances upon Edith's unsuspecting body with relish. He had balanced his studies with various sports and although small of stature he was muscular and tested. He sunned and sinned his way through that summer.

Jonathon and William heard the fact that Edith had moved into 226 Wilton Road at roughly the same time. Both were pleased. The doctor looked upwards through the faded lace curtains of his basement flat at 225 Wilton Street as Edith and Sister Hart moved into a flat in the house opposite. Jonathon was so very heart-weary. The lack of news out of Germany was agonising. What was left of his wife's family had written to him whilst he had been in hiding with his brother, urging him to escape. They could not bring themselves to fear the worst and always ended the few letters they had managed to send with hope that his wife and son were alive somewhere. Then the letters stopped coming. It was this more than anything that had convinced him to escape. Yet the guilt was always with him.

Much against his head's advice, Jonathon's heart was entranced by Edith, a petite fulsome young woman so eager to learn his skills on the ward. So desperately beseeching with her eyes and body. The hospital authorities frowned upon doctor–nurse relationships and he didn't want to jeopardise their jobs. Yet he lusted for Edith just as her heart skipped a beat whenever they were close to each other. Already, without saying a word on the subject, both knew, in the deepest shrines of their beings, that soon they would be together.

It was only a question of when and where.

William had been to Bristol station that morning. He was now the proud owner of a second-class sleeper ticket through to Glasgow. His landlady's husband worked as the Stationmaster and this had been his only stroke of luck in obtaining the ticket. As William rushed back to the flat to tell her of her husband's help in fulfilling his dreams she stepped forward into the gloomy hallway and invited him into her kitchen. An unheard- of invitation previously.

She told him to sit down. He presumed there had been a death. Her own son was, at that very moment, helping to escort Allied convoys across the Atlantic. William braced himself for her bad news and was prepared to give comfort.

Perhaps her son had been lost at sea.

What had been lost was more tragic to William.

He wept as he read the familiar government letter which she hesitatingly handed to him. The Army had waited for him to finish his degree long enough. His country needed him.

He needed Edith just as badly.

He had to set off and see her and make love to her before he went to war. Of this he was absolutely sure, or else he risked his sanity.

But it seemed that right now there was to be no more time. The recruiting sergeant was quite sure that Lieutenant General Yamashita would not put the war on hold so William could reassure himself of his sweetheart's intentions. Lieutenant General Percival required Royal Engineers. He was given his orders to report the very next day. What William did not realise was that his landlady's husband, a World War One veteran, had been reporting to his old regiment regularly and identifying young graduates from Bristol who had the right mental attitude to be sworn into the Intelligence Service. That accounted for the haste.

As William packed his kit for war training Edith unpacked her belongings in her new flat. Her new life was beginning just as William's old one was ending and neither ever quite realised the significance of that date.

On the ward that night Jonathon called in to see his patients. Edith was on duty. He then called her into his small curtained office and silently they came together as if moulded from the same clay. Bombs were breaking overhead and sirens blaring loudly. Never had Jonathon experienced such a rush of passion to his groin and Edith suddenly found the oiled key necessary to unlock her body for a man. They sprawled over the desk, knocking files and his treasured German stethoscope to the ground. There was an urgency coupled with tenderness, which was unusual. Neither dominated, they flowed into and through each other in an act of consummate passion and love. They gasped at their fire and clung in their delight. They were oblivious to the all-clear.

They were equally oblivious to Sister Hart as she watched the whole lustful episode through a gap in the curtains. She had been tailing Edith, sensing the moment was soon to come. She gasped as the lovers cried out and dug deeper into each other. Her nails raked up her thighs as she clenched her jaw shut in a breathless parody of sensations. She turned silently, leant against the wall and closed her eyes as she inserted a handy speculum.

Before her eyes she saw Gregory. Not the confused Gregory who had stared at her intently all the way through the trial. Nor the Gregory who had been led screaming and cursing as the judge in Bodmin Court sentenced him to hang until he was dead. His was one of the very last hangings at Bodmin jail. Marigold Hart had bitten her stumpy nails to the quick that day, praying to what God she was not sure, but hoping that there would be no last-minute reversal of the judgement. There was none and Gregory had gone to his death very much not at peace with the world, his limp dead body seemingly still twitching in disgust at the wrongfulness of it all.

Edith and Jonathon were so involved in each other they failed to see the voyeur in their midst. Sister Hart lived her life in shadows and her mind slipped further and further into darkness.

After three months of basic training, and some special intelligence briefings at night when others were asleep, William was due to sail out of Liverpool with the 18th Division of the Royal Engineers in October 1941. His First-Class Honours degree had ensured his entry into the secret world of surveillance. He made a friend on the course called Paddy Heynan. Together they had great fun learning how to make rodent bombs by filling dead rats with explosives. The best part was the cunning ways they were taught to make everyday objects work like a radio and a camera. It was drilled into them all that communications and recordings, once in the theatre of war, would be vital, especially behind enemy lines. They were issued with compass buttons on their uniforms and learnt how to conceal their boot prints with rubber over soles in the shape of bare feet.

Those three months of rigorous hard work had rendered William as taut physically as he was mentally. Before leaving he was given a special pass to travel to Glasgow on a train. He was unaware that his former landlady's husband had ensured this privilege; they had felt so bad for him when he had been denied his earlier trip to see Edith. Working behind the scenes they had cajoled a rather reluctant senior officer to issue William with a travel pass.

There was only one more thing William had to do. With a wad of money sent to him by his father, he was determined to buy Edith an engagement ring she would cherish and gaze down upon as a constant reminder that she was his. It would also serve as a warning to anyone else.

War-torn London was awash with barriers, smoking, gaping holes where rows of houses used to stand proud and tall. Surveying all of this made him only more determined to fight the enemy and return the war hero. Eventually he found a small jeweller's shop and upon entering was assailed by the sight of four hunched and bearded men whispering in tears. They paused as he stepped in, wiping their eyes slowly and carefully. He was in full uniform. One by one the men came forward and shook his hand silently, then departed, finally leaving him alone with just the shopkeeper.

'I'm looking for an engagement ring,' he said quietly to the old man.

'Certainly, young man, I can see that in your eyes,' said the shopkeeper.

'Why did your friends shake my hand?' asked William.

What words could possibly speak of the news filtering out of Germany.

'They are just proud of you, my son, that's all. Will this ring do? It's quite the best I have right now.'

Before William was a ring of superior brilliance, symmetrical and polished so that the impact of the jeweller's cut had not obscured any of its splendour. Set in rare platinum it screamed of elegance and was petite enough to fit Edith's finger, of this, he was sure.

'For the brave soldier a special price.'

William held his breath. He had nowhere near that amount in the envelope sent from his father. He turned to walk out of the shop broken-hearted. The old shopkeeper watched his sale shuffle away and as the door opened saw the stubborn faces of his four friends who looked quizzically back at him through the open doorway. And then he softened.

'It's yours, my son.'

William did something very uncharacteristic then and jumped for joy, followed by shaking the shopkeeper's hand vigorously.

The deal was sealed.

The ring bought.

The train journey was tedious.

He arrived at the hospital where Edith worked just as she was leaving.

Edith last remembered being truly alone with William under the pier at Blackpool. She shuddered at how far she had come since then. William put his arm around her, fearing she would catch a chill in the raw autumn air. Like a hammer blow, his touch made her realise exactly why William was there. Often in his letters he had written of his frustrations at not being able to come up and see her. She had sympathised, and thinking he would never get the chance to visit, played the game and reassured him that she was indeed waiting for him.

William's eyes burnt with a passion beyond reason.

She couldn't go through with this, but there seemed no way out. They walked down Castle Street away from the hospital. Holding hands, holding breaths almost. Each praying for something wildly different to happen. As they rounded the corner to Wilton Street and her flat the air-raid sirens sounded. Air-raid wardens propelled them and others into a makeshift shelter in the basement of a bombed-out house. William had exactly four hours in Glasgow until he had to race back to base on the train.

William groaned with pain and disappointment as they crouched low, their backs against the damp cellar walls. On the other side of the wall, Jonathon was preparing his dinner hoping that Edith would come around and share it with him, share his food, his love, his body, his heart. He was in love. He ignored the air-raid sirens. He was immune, so much suffering in his life; Edith, he had finally decided, was to be the antidote.

In the cellar, amidst the whimpering of children and the sobbing of the war-weary, Edith agreed to wear William's engagement ring. The collective sighs of the fellow inhabitants of the cellar when he had twisted around to try and face her in order to propose had heartened everyone to the goodness and love rightfully belonging in their world. Momentarily this declaration of love by William had raised the spirits of so many smoked-streaked faces of unwashed children and the smiles on the lined faces of the adults melted her resolve to resist William at all costs. The nurse in her looked around and she saw spirits raised, heard the cheers and accepted the handshakes of congratulations. William was ecstatic. As Edith closed her eyes when he slipped it on her finger she felt as if it immediately burnt a hole in her heart.

At that very same moment Jonathon, just next door, turned away to look out of the window to see if Edith was racing down the street to see him. As he returned, disillusioned, to his cooking a large spit of fat leapt out of the pan and burnt a hole in his jumper, on the left, just below his collarbone. He looked down at the hole in his jumper and saw his shirt beneath beating wildly.

Oh, how his heart longed for Edith. Jonathon had recently stopped fighting his conscience, succumbing to Edith at every given opportunity. If he thought about his wife Esther, then he blocked it out with an embrace from Edith. If the screams of his son came to him in his dreams, he woke in a sweat and reached over to smell the side of his bed where Edith had left her scent. He had to quell his fevered imaginings. Edith was his life, his love and seemingly his future. Munich seemed a very far-off dream. His old life as a respected doctor at the Clinic Belle Maison in Munich was obliterated by his desire for Edith. But still he dared not openly share a flat with her.

The bombing lasted four hours exactly.

As Edith and William left the air-raid shelter, he looked at his watch and gasped. He felt desperate that he should have to race to the train station in Gordon Street at this moment. His train was about to leave, in just twenty-five minutes. For the rest of eternity, he knew that he would never forget those four hours in the shelter with Edith. The two of them had been in a world of their own. They had been close, but not close enough. Now had not been the time for Edith to mention her fears. William squeezed her so hard on the street that she felt her fragile body buckle under his strength. She fought for air as he took her head in his hands, stared longingly into her eyes and said, 'Wait for me!'

How could she? She already belonged to another.

And then he was gone, off to fight.

CHAPTER 4

1939–1942
A PURPOSE FOR WHICH TO SURVIVE

It's historically debateable if this military deployment was Prime Minister Churchill's worst disaster, but it was certainly William's.

That he was to be one of eighty thousand British, Indian and Australian soldiers incarcerated in prisoner-of-war camps after the fall of Singapore in 1942, was to be his undoing. A ripple effect, thundering through the generations.

The South-East Asian theatre of war was precipitated by the bombing, on American soil, of Pearl Harbour, Hawaii Territory, at 7.55am on Sunday, December 7th 1941. In 1939 nobody in Britain had paid much heed to American President Roosevelt as he'd ordered the US Pacific Fleet from California to Pearl Harbour. It certainly hadn't made headlines in the Fleetwood Chronicle. Some cocky general in Japan decided that this was to be his epic light-bulb moment.

Gordon had listened to the BBC radio after surgery had closed, and briefly pondered the outcome of Roosevelt's aggressive response to Japan's expansionism in the Pacific Ocean. His heart had beaten a little more wildly. Please no, he had thought to himself. His young son Douglas was fascinated with war, and longed to join the Navy.

In another house, at the opposite end of Fleetwood, a bitter, cough-laden old sea dog chewed his tobacco and ruminated. He had just returned home from the Victoria pub on Dock Street, where the talk had also been of Japan. He had received, that very morning, a letter from his son William. It was not easy reading. He was determined to marry Edith. An unlikely scenario to be sure. Perhaps it would be the Japanese General Tomoyuki Yamashita who would thwart William's desire to marry her and not, as William's father had thought, Gordon. He was to underestimate his only son.

After William completed his training and intelligence briefs, he set sail from the port city of Liverpool, on the west coast of England, eventually arriving in Singapore on the 29th of January 1942.

A journey to hell that lasted nearly three months.

William had sat cross-legged on board, composing love letters to Edith. He cared not for ventures into steamy Basra, Iraq's only seaport, or cool Cape Town in South Africa, he merely saw these ports as opportunities to post his anguished love letters to Edith in Glasgow. Along with all the other men on board, the rapidly changing war in South East Asia was little known to them. What would they have written to their loved ones had they known of the ordeal they were about to face?

The khaki drill and pith helmets they had been given to wear whilst they had been on acclimatisation in Deolali, in India, proved to be of little use to William, or the other Royal Engineers, once they disembarked in Singapore. It was insanely hot and humid. They saw few military and even fewer Singaporeans, spending most of their days trying to blow up bridges to halt the Japanese advance into Singapore.

The heat was relentless. The humidity of the tropics that had been tasted in Deolali now clung to them in Singapore, drained them and cloaked them in rivers of fetid sweat. They sat huddled of a mosquito-infested night in the hollows of huge tropical storm drains, the depth and width of a cow. These are the moments that test the courage and endurance of a soldier. Night after excruciating night, William huddled alone with his imaginings of what could have happened on his last visit to Edith. His mind soared as the heat of his thoughts echoed the temperature of his skin. His obsession became his saviour. As others whimpered and moaned when bombs fell scarcely a heartbeat away, William's only moans were those he dreamt Edith would make and his mind enveloped his being.

Often, his mate Paddy would look over to William and wonder where he was in his head. Not a taut muscle flinched as bombs fell all around. Only William's closed eyelids fluttered and Paddy envied him his imaginings. Paddy was so deeply scared that he feared for his life minute by minute. What the hell were they doing in this corner of an unfamiliar world?

Paddy heralded from Ireland. He often told folk he came from the North of Ireland rather than Northern Ireland, for he was a closet Republican, living in Belfast and dreaming of defeating the British. He did not belong in the British Army. He had only joined up because he had been obscenely drunk one night after a ten-hour drinking session in Berry Street, Belfast. They ended up in Maddens

Bar with others too far gone to say no to the recruiting officer cunningly placed as they piled out of the bar, mortally drunk and charmingly pliant.

He often sat back and watched William as he toiled daily to set the charges which would blow up the routes they thought the Japs might take to enter Singapore.

One monotonously steamy night, when others slept fitfully and the moon was cocooned in a cotton-wool cradle, Paddy took his revenge upon the army and in particular, the British recruiting officer who had thrown him into a van outside the pub and allowed him to roll in his vomit until they reached the barracks.

William was fast asleep, in his dreams, searching for Edith in Glasgow. He did not notice as Paddy crept out of the storm drain on all fours, his bare arse hanging out of his shredded khaki shorts, heading for a small ammunition dump in an adjoining storm drain. Paddy did not want to blow up his comrades.

Oh no.

Paddy, in all his crazed wisdom, was going to steal his own side's ammunition, wave a white flag and then hand the ordinance over to the Japs. He would then be hailed a hero, and given sound advice on how to defeat the British in Ireland and definitely be airlifted back to Belfast to complete his mission.

Paddy was suffering from his second virulent bout of malaria. That night he was shaking with the chills, yet simultaneously running a fever so high that he believed his crazy mission could actually succeed.

As he hid the grenades in his moisture-sodden pith

helmet he did not hear as William crept up behind him. William had woken suddenly, jolted alive from his dream of Edith pulling his hands away from embracing her face, then walking off without a backward glance. Unable to get his bearings for a split second he had imagined Paddy to be Edith and got up to follow her. The dampness of the inside wall of the storm drain, and the scurrying of the rats he had not been able to capture for his home-made bombs, alerted his fuddled mind to his present whereabouts.

Then, the wary soldier within became alive with suspicion.

Paddy had started to stumble towards the enemy lines. He stopped every few yards to shit through the ever-enlarging gap in his ragged shorts. The fierce abdominal cramps of malaria were accompanied by his moans, which guided William through the gloom to his comrade, had not the stench of his diarrhoea been enough. Following William were two other soldiers, alerted not just to the night's escapade but to the foulmouthed rantings that Paddy was often heard to be spewing when his mind rattled through the dark stages of malaria.

Following a summary court martial it was given to William the task of executing Paddy.

One blisteringly hot day, the remnants of the Royal Engineers and a few perplexed locals watched as William raised his American-made Lewis light machine gun and ripped into the hooded figure on the edge of Keppel Harbour, watching Paddy as he somersaulted backwards into the depths. The predatory bull sharks, normally in shallower waters, had enjoyed and engorged themselves on the human debris to be found there and were not disappointed, slightly gagging on the hood, but otherwise quite happy with the offering.

It was the day of the 12th of February 1942. Unbeknown to William and his senior officers, nearly thirteen thousand Japanese troops had made an amphibious landing further north of their position.

So much for blowing up bridges!

The final stage of the Empire of Japan's invasion of Singapore was rapidly unfolding. William's regiment was scrambled to defend the main ammunition dumps in the Alexandra area. The Malayan troops, given the bulk of the hand-to-hand combat, fought bravely but as each hour unfolded William could hear the battle approaching.

Following the regrouping of the last of the Malay troops, William finally sought refuge inside the Alexandra Hospital. His mind blanked off and he was with Edith once more. Her hand was in his as he walked her through the Glasgow wards, searching vainly for a safe place to hide with her.

The sound of his commanding officer being strung up on a lychee tree in the hospital grounds awoke his senses. The faces of the Japanese as they bayonetted and bludgeoned the British colonel to death reminded him of the hatred he had felt towards Paddy the day before.

He was ready to take out a hastily made white flag, torn from a bedsheet close to hand.

He would survive. He would marry Edith. A scared young lad snatched it out of William's hand and positively ran towards the advancing Japs. He was killed instantly, butchered within feet of William, the blood spurting from his bayonet wounds bathing William's eyes in the horror. William fell as

Japs trampled over him, racing into the hospital, and the ensuing carnage changed the course of history.

William played dead.

Then the Japs' thirst for blood finally abated.

He surfaced into the arms of the impatient Japanese and was hauled off with other fortunate survivors to be paraded as enemies through the streets of an ominously quiet Singapore. His was the war the British public have often watched, rather oddly, at Christmas, through such historically incorrect films as *The Bridge over the River Kwai*.

Lest perhaps we should ever be foolish enough to forget.

For William, the years in Burmese prisoner-of-war camps were a torture of the heart as much as the body.

As William marched endlessly towards the Kwae Noi River and years of deprivation, he was finally to be disgusted with himself for executing Paddy. Across the world, Sister Hart was also reflecting upon a death, her slaying of Violet.

Burying her misgivings beneath layers of flawed justifications and moral outrage at the injustices of her upbringing and looks, Marigold Hart reinvented herself in Glasgow.

Once there she had cut off all interaction with her family. A necessity born out of self- preservation. As she pounded the wards on night duty, desperate to block the sound of Violet screaming out to her sister as she was flung backwards into the dark and engulfing waters, so too did William pound the route to Changi, desperate also to rid himself of a drowning that might end up crucifying his conscience.

Whenever she knew that Jonathon and Edith were on duty together, Marigold would find hollow excuses in her own mind to shadow them and observe. She learnt about deep glances and soothing touches. The language of lust and love was played out in the most unlikely places and she drank it in, as a love starved prisoner would.

Somewhere best not investigated too closely, a link between the two tortured souls was forged.

A quick glance at an envelope suddenly found Sister Hart sweating. A letter postmarked from Fowey awaited her. She quickly stuffed its flimsy substance into her uniform pocket, where it continued to cause an ache in her heavy dimpled thigh all through the morning. By lunchtime she could endure it no longer and rather appropriately dashed into the sluice room to read it. She was horrified.

The gorgeous Gregory, who had been the object of both sisters' desires, had a brother. His name was Julian and he had always loved Gregory's wife.

On the night of the drowning, Julian, after consulting Gregory's wife Christine, had gone after Gregory. The route from Bodmin to Fowey was snake-like. Julian knew of Gregory's tryst with Violet as the two brothers shared their secrets. Except that is, the fact that Julian lusted after Christine. He had finally managed to spill his feelings to her as she had collapsed into his arms when Gregory had left to meet up with Violet. Julian had gone round to see Christine in the hope that he could give her some comfort. He was surprised to hear of her latest pregnancy and simultaneously disgusted in his brother. He had blurted out the truth to Christine, who insisted he followed her husband to obtain the facts. Without too much thought he had leapt back onto his prized possession, a Matchless Silver Hawk motorbike and shot off into the dark night through the treacherously high-hedged single-track routes to Fowey.

Hiding behind the very moored boat that Marigold had borrowed the oar from, Julian had seen it all. The horrific scene that had unfolded still danced hauntingly inside his head. As a brother, Julian was supposed to have been a sensitive and caring sibling. But did he care that his only brother had been carted away as a murderer?

No, not really.

Did he tell Christine the exact truth? No, he did not! He kept that secret for himself. It might come in useful. It apparently just had.

After the trial and Gregory's hanging, Julian had moved in with Christine. It had been but a dream though. The reality was far from romantic. A late miscarriage followed the hanging of her husband, then Christine sank into a depression so epically bottomless that Julian was left to raise his four emotionally damaged nieces alone. On that bike ride back from the murder scene, long after the police and ambulance crews had left Fowey harbour, Julian had fantasised about Christine.

She would be his. His mind had not been on the road as he hurried back to her house. Around one sharp, steep, hilly route he met his nemesis. He flew through the air as the lorry skidded to one side, his now twisted bike continued and sometime later, yet only seconds in reality, he made a harsh tumbling contact with its hot petrol tank. The bike and its rider then swerved at an angle and the force simultaneously welded his manhood to the tank and mangled his leg in the aluminium spokes of his front wheel. His leg flesh was partially shredded.

By the time the trial and the hanging were over Julian had mastered his crutches. Christine was grateful as he received insurance money from the accident. But she was not that grateful. He was secretly relieved. Nothing now seemed quite as it was before. It would all take time and patience, said the nursing staff at Bodmin Hospital. The nurses, however, had revealed disgust and pity in their not so professional eyes as they examined his genitalia. They suggested that healing would eventually occur. As they gazed at his balls the size of watermelons and his penis, a crooked stump hiding underneath, their hollow words did nothing to reassure him. In time the swelling reduced to a manageable, yet still distorted size and he preferred to stay indoors anyway. Laughing eyes were his nightmare. His nieces were far too young to be horrid, yet.

Like the constantly changed bandages on his leg, his mind festered. The staff at the hospital had not been able to mend him properly. A nurse in another hospital had been, in his twisted mind, the cause of it all. His brother had been elevated to an almost saintly status, the man tricked and humiliated by Marigold.

Bumping into the still grieving woman who was Marigold's mother, one Saturday afternoon, had been enlightening. After discovering where her daughter worked in Glasgow, Julian had decided to write to Marigold.

As Sister Hart read the words in front of her, veined legs buckled and she bumped into a bedpan, as she crashed to the ground in a fittingly foul swirl of putrid urine.

Who was this man who claimed he had evidence of her complicity in her sister's murder?

How dare he rock her tightly wound world so epically?

She would not meet him!

But she had to meet him...

Julian had stated a time and place. Noon, under Grey's Monument in Newcastle-upon-Tyne. He would be sitting on the steps facing down towards the train station. Be there! He had insisted.

In fact, he had discovered, when he had been to the local train station, that he only had enough money for a single journey to Newcastle. He was gambling with her guilt. He knew she would be there. He had revealed just enough to convince her he knew the truth.

Edith discovered her dishevelled friend on the floor in the sluice room. Their shifts were ending. It was a fortuitous moment for the pair. Edith hustled Sister Hart into her enveloping cloak and the pair of them hurried out of the hospital and thankfully the torrential rain dripped away the potent stink clinging to Sister Hart's legs. By the time they arrived at the Wilton Street flat they were soaked. Edith left Sister Hart in the hallway and retrieved the large towel from the side of the bath. She insisted that Marigold strip whilst she held the towel up high to protect her modesty. Hiding the letter beneath her pendulous, misshapen breasts, she grabbed the towel, which only barely wrapped around her large frame. She left Edith to pick up the sodden garments as she trod heavily upstairs to have a bath.

Emerging clean, yet not wholesome, she quizzed Edith over rotas for the weekend and begged her to take the Saturday shift that should have been hers. She said yes. Jonathon was also on shift that night. Marigold relaxed somewhat and feigned a migraine so she could rest alone on one of the two single beds in the one-bedroomed flat. On the bedside table in the middle was the black Bakelite phone that Jonathon had insisted on installing for them. Well, actually for Edith. She coughed and spluttered as she dialled the Bodmin number, trying to hide the clickety-clack of the dial. Julian answered swiftly like a coiled predator waiting for prey and they curtly acknowledged the forthcoming meeting. No frills, no fuss. She would be there.

Tick tock to fate.

In Newcastle, Julian vaguely recognised Marigold. She had become slimmer than he remembered yet she was still stocky. She, never having consciously set eyes on him, merely stared blankly at the milling, weary-looking shoppers. Men with soot-encrusted clothes and women with haunted expressions moved, often swiftly, between the treacherous tramlines and hurried into the Grainger market. Julian was amazed at the trams and nearly missed his meeting with Marigold because of this. He felt an empathy with the miners out for a Saturday shop in the city centre and he sympathised with their harsh realities. His father and grandfather before him had toiled in the copper mines on Bodmin moor. He too had worked for the Phoenix United mine but the talk was of closure. He found himself being stared at quite a lot. He stared right back into the eyes of many miners, unused to the weak Northern sunshine. He used a cane now and walked with a hunched kind of gait. Since the bike accident he had been given an easier job on the Liskeard and Caradon railway, which had been built to transport copper ore to the seaport of Looe. This was how he had been able to obtain a cheap travel concession on the railway journey to Newcastle.

His clothes were baggy to hide his deformities and Marigold caught his gaze as her trained nurse's eye started to wander down his body.

'Let's sit down, Marigold,' he insisted

'If you think that's best,' she retorted sharply.

It took Julian a good hour to reveal what he knew and what he wanted. She listened. She was captivated by his broken soul. To his absolute horror Julian found himself reacting to her as a woman. The dormant crooked lump he had despaired of was homing in on this woman he had set himself to hate and blackmail. Across Marigold's eyes danced stolen images of Edith and Jonathon making love in the most improbable of places. How unlikely would it be, if this man sitting next to her and demanding money could be thawing her heart?

They moved closer to each other on the steps. Their fingers traced circles in the blackish coal soot between them. Rhythmically the circles entwined in a tango of lust until they felt a tingling as they brushed close to one another.

Then it started to rain. That heavy coal-dust-coating type of rain that smears the face and distorts the view. The smell of sulphur from the slag heaps nearby hung in the air, mixing with the hops from the brewery. Holding their noses, their breath and each other's hands they hurriedly took the tram down to the Royal Station Hotel, booked a room and fucked.

No talking, just merging.

Afterwards Julian lit a Woodbine, threw his head back and laughed at the absurdity of it all. Marigold clutched the bedsheets around her and snapped at him. They faced each other from opposite ends of the bed. They agreed to meet up again. A secret plan was hatched. A way to make money from the rest of the perfectly formed human race they were both not a part of.

It was an outcome to a meeting that was so wildly disparate from its intentions that they were stunned. To cement their new-found venture, they fucked again and then they parted. Not before Julian had agreed to try and get a job in Newcastle.

Marigold travelled back to Glasgow thinking about this emerging partnership. Plotting and scheming all the way home.

Julian travelled to Bodmin, working out how quickly he could extricate himself from Christine's home and abandon his increasingly clingy and needy nieces. He would wait, the right time would present itself and money was to be made.

During this time, William languished for far too many years as a prisoner and saw far too many deaths. He survived by eating maggots and sucking precious protein from their core. As Marigold lay on her bed, she dreamt of Julian. Julian dreamt of Christine. Edith dreamt of Jonathon. Jonathon dreamt of his wife, Esther, and William dreamt of Edith.

Night after endless night as William lay on his roughly hewn bamboo bed he listened to the screeching crickets and the shrill, slow sounds of death. He became adept at closing his tortured soul and reaching out for an ethereal Edith. In his captivity he was thus freed and fantastic were his imaginings.

During the daytime he marched and toiled and marched again. Scurvy and beriberi are not just the curse of distant sailors. The lucky prisoners who marched through the lowlands and then the jungle, to get to the construction site of the railway, had enough chance to grab what they could to restrain this disease. Guavas were hidden for night-time sharing with those suffering back at the camp. The prisoners all operated on a three-mate system. One cleaned you up when you had dysentery, the second boiled the drinking water they caught following afternoon tropical downpours and the third shared the food stash. But juicy overripe paw-paws just had to be sucked dry as soon as they were found. Survival was an instinct for William. Edith was in his head. Under his balls were the hidden batteries for the camera stashed back at the camp. William was the only surviving Intelligence Officer from the Royal Engineers.

He tried to take as many pictures as he could for what would be a grateful Imperial War Museum in London. Long shots of Changi, a prison originally built by the British in 1936 to house six hundred prisoners. The overflow into Selarang Barracks close by contained, at its peak, over fifty thousand Allied prisoners of war. It all became infamously known simply as Changi. William's pictures were to horrify future generations.

Humour was important. A kind of devilishly wicked dance-with-death kind of humour, predominantly British but the Aussies had a good crack at it too. Morning roll call was a scene of such hilarity. The Japanese commanders knew no English, yet insisted Emperor Hirohito was hailed as the prisoners marched by.

'Up yours, Hirohito!'

Stifled smirks sustained the prisoner's soul.

'Wanker Hirohito!'

Teeth clenched the insides of their sagging quivering cheeks. It was a daily ritual. It helped. Then the new commander came. He spoke English. But to the prisoners, he looked like the last commander.

The first unit to march past that day was shot. All of them, for abusing the Emperor through speech.

The rest of the prisoners were made to stand all day and watch the life seep out of their friends, for not all had been instantly killed. A slow death is a pitiful sight. Nobody should ever see or hear such evil as this. After two hours in the tropical sun, a cadaver swells.

The flies settle.

The gasses pop.

Then the vultures arrive.

By the end of the scorching hot day the bones had been picked clean. Only then were the prisoners released from standing to attention and given the task of disposing of the bones. William traded this horror for a fantasy with Edith. He was nestled in her arms and that was all that mattered.

Edith had received a phone call from her parents.

'Missing in action, presumed dead', had read the telegram that William's parents had received. Knowing that his son had wanted to marry Edith and had even bought her an engagement ring with the cash he had sent, Jack had trudged reluctantly to Gordon's home and broken the news to him.

Two tired old men, combatants in the last war, stared at each other and wondered what to make of it all. Gordon thanked Jack but didn't invite him in. Then he called Edith.

Her relief was as monumental as her guilt and she buried her fear that he might still be alive just as deeply as William buried his love for her in his heart. William's engagement ring was well hidden in the bottom of her underwear drawer. An irony not lost on Edith.

Elsewhere there was one Jew having a reasonable war. Jonathon had all but forgotten his German family. Edith was his life, his lover and possibly his future. They dared not share a flat together, but as bombs fell and confusion rained down on all around them, who was to know exactly who slept where and when?

Only perhaps Sister Hart, and through her, Julian.

She kept her silence, though, and was rewarded with an empty flat in which she occasionally entertained Julian who was, by now, working for the railway in Newcastle.

It was a convenient arrangement for both Marigold and Julian and the times were those in which one acted for the moment. For who knew when a bomb might fall close by and shatter life for ever?

Edith wanted to marry Jonathon. If William had been a social shock to her staunch Presbyterian upper-class Scottish parents, then surely the Jewish émigré doctor with an obvious German accent would rock their lives to the core. She did not care. Her years of exile in Scotland had hardened her heart to her parents' wishes. Now she felt cared for and cosseted by Jonathon, in a way that frequently reminded her of her grandma's love for her.

One weekend not long after arriving in Glasgow she had decided to make a joyful bus journey back to see her grandmother. Only she found her in the coldest, most desolate cemetery ever, with a headstone that revealed yet more deceptive treachery from her parents.

The date of her death coincided with Edith's return from her embrace to the chilly reception back in Fleetwood. The day she discovered this she stormed round West Kilbride, venting her fury on the cobbles and finally coming to rest in the High Street. She bought the largest bunch of red roses and returned to the cemetery and kissed the headstone as she laid the bouquet at its base. She sat down with her back on the granite, catching the low late-afternoon sunshine, and closed her eyes. Campbell danced in front of her as she chased him round and round to squeals of excitement. Grandma Ruth opened her arms to her in the rose garden at the rear of her small cottage. She was jolted back to reality as the church clock struck four and she dashed to catch her bus back to Glasgow, leaving at 4.20 pm on the dot. On the journey home she vowed to live only for herself, to squeeze as much joy out of it as she could. What else was the point of life?

Edith also received a letter one Friday before going off shift. Her parents still believed she held a candle of hope for William's return. They had read about the prisoner-of- war camps, even seen some aerial footage from the American bombers, shown at the local cinema. It was well known that the Japanese did not acknowledge the Geneva Convention and therefore no comprehensive lists of prisoners were available. It was quite ironic really. Possibly the very American plane that had taken the aerial photos was the one that William was later to amuse his drinking buddies with tales of.

One evening, just as the sun was about to set, towards the end of the war in Asia, an American bomber flew low over Changi and released a bomb, as the pilot thought he was a safe distance from life.

He needed to lighten his payload so he could make it back to base on the Mariana Islands. Unfortunately, the bomb hit the camp's pit latrines. William astounded his friends with tales of liquid shit raining down on not just the prisoners but on the guards also. The bombed shit had flown up into the tropical canopy, stuck there only to fall every afternoon as the tropical downpours wept khaki-coloured hailstones upon them all.

In Edith's letter, her parents noted that William might yet be alive. She shuddered. They also commented on the fact that their health was deteriorating, arthritis had flared up in Gordon's finger joints, horribly mutilated to a shape into which the dental equipment was nestled. It could not go on for much longer. They needed her back to learn from her father and run the clinic. She convulsed. Her resolve hardened.

In June 1945 Jonathon took Edith to see a touring company at Glasgow's Royal Princess's theatre perform a play by Noel Coward called *Blithe Spirit*. Sister Hart had sent him the tickets as a secret present. He knew how close Edith was to her. Yet something about Marigold concerned him. She had a scheming far-off gaze at times and worse still, he sensed her constantly staring at his groin. He never had the chance to tell Edith who had joyously given him their tickets.

A play about the supernatural written by a spy. It spooked Jonathon thoroughly.

On stage, the invited medium, called Madame Arcati, roused a ghost from the past who turned out to be the first wife of the main character; Jonathon blanched. His grip tightened on the worn red velvet of his seat in the stalls. Instead of the spirit onstage, Jonathon saw Esther, mocking and competing for his attentions with Edith. The two women battled for possession of their man and when the curtain fell on the performance Edith noticed that Jonathon was drenched in sweat. Edith was aware of the play's themes, but she was confident that her relationship with Jonathon was perfect. He rarely mentioned his past. Their future was hers for the taking.

Back in his flat after the performance, they settled into a familiar routine, each feeling wildly different emotions following the play. They turned on the radio to hear news of the advances across France by the Allies following the D-day landings in Normandy. The war was bound to end soon. A cold finger of doubt and foreboding wormed its way up Edith's spine and she sat bolt upright and asked Jonathon to marry her as soon as possible.

Jonathon had not sat down again after turning on the radio but had turned towards his small makeshift kitchen to get himself a shot of Jack Daniel's to calm his racing brain. Inside his head he was in Esther's arms, so vivid had been the imagery from the play. He knew that Edith wanted to get married. He was plagued with doubts. Buried doubts that had somehow been released from their Pandora's box during the performance in the theatre. With a jolt he realised that he must marry a Jewess. Would Edith convert? Would she?

The slamming of the front door was the finality of it all.

Edith was shamed by his silence.

She ran across the road back to her shared flat, passing a stooped man with a cane exiting the front door just as she entered.

Sister Hart was there to comfort her.

Somewhere, not too far off, raucous laughter could be heard.

Then God told his devilish counterpart to shut up.

CHAPTER 5

1967
REMEMBERING THE CRACKS

It was the beetroot sandwiches that forever stayed in her mind. For years after, Berenice's go-to comfort food was pickled beetroot in soft, white, Mother's Pride bread with lashings of butter and Heinz salad cream.

The flashpoint had been the rabbit.

One sunny Saturday morning, Berenice had lovingly picked up her neighbour's baby rabbit, thus contaminating it with her innocent body scent. Then she had been told, rather sharply, to keep the rabbit, as the mother was about to eat it, because it smelt foreign. Wow... that was a learning curve. A mother's rejection because of an outsider's interference: interesting.

Berenice was four. Barely aware of emotional under-currents, but absorbing her surroundings and adjusting swiftly.

Exactly twelve Saturday mornings later, it seemed like Evil had been at work in her home. A door had banged, she had heard that. The kitchen door; it made a certain whining on closing and she had heard that, quite definitely.

Her parents' white stucco detached house, built with a

government grant for returning POWs stood out on a road of bow-fronted thirties semis. The road curved slightly upwards at the end to the sand dunes and the Irish Sea beyond. Rossall Public School was opposite, in the near distance. Fleetwood beyond, Cleveleys behind and an increasingly depressing Blackpool not too far away.

The radio was on and as she tiptoed into the kitchen, sounds of Harry Belafonte singing 'Island in the Sun' swirled around her mind and she realised someone had put the radio on. Somebody must have been up to do that. She found nobody in the kitchen.

As an only child, she often felt like she was abandoned on a remote island. Extreme fantasies were her escapes, even then, an exciting coping mechanism. Intuitively, she realised that her father understood this very well.

In her brushed cotton winceyette pyjamas, she followed her senses through the kitchen and into the adjoining garage. She then reached up to open the outside latch door-handle from the garage to the back garden. The cool salty air of an autumn morning close to the sea assaulted her and sent shivers down to her toenails and up to her hair follicles.

Berenice first saw the cloudy eyes.

Not two feet from her lay the once endearingly fluffy head of her pet rabbit, Snuggles. Her brain was trying to register how the body, some ten feet away from her, could possibly be there. In between was a tangle of bloodied small ropes.

His eyes, in his severed head, kept on staring. She was mesmerised and locked into his stare.

Her high-pitched scream rent the air.

Death had descended and enveloped her with its icy

chills and numbing realities. She pelted back through the cold garage, turned left into the chilly kitchen, scooted through into the freezing hallway, leaving vague wet patches, from the claret-coloured dew, on the fussily patterned carpet. She clung to the bottom banister to swivel right and propel herself up the stairs and into her parents' messy yet permanently frosty front bedroom.

Her father was getting into bed with her mother guiding him. She reached her mum, resplendent in pink ruffled nylon and she clung to the soft curves of her body and wept.

Her father was weeping too. But she didn't quite register that then.

William had been so very proud of Edith the night before. The Freemasons' hall in Fleetwood had been the glitzy scene of his Masonic Ladies Night and Edith had shone. Nearly ten years since the end of the war and William had almost buried the demons and sometimes even believed that he lived the dream. Teaching at his old school had propelled him right back to being an eighteen-year-old and that suited him just fine thank you. No need to delve into anything further. No need at all really.

In fine gold brocade, elbow-length satin peach gloves and a dazzling paste tiara, Edith had outshone the other females by a mile. Everything had started off so well. Grace had been said, the ladies had been allowed to take off their gloves and the evening ensued. Being at the head table with the Worshipful Master was breath-taking in its splendour and made William feel at least another foot taller. Everyone had waited for the Lodge Master to take his first bite, as was the time-honoured custom and then the meal had progressed.

So much classier than his parents' Ladies Night all those years ago. Oh, how he had ascended. His father would have been quietly proud, his mother might just have sighed.

Later on, the Rose Song commenced and Edith was presented with a solid silver rose bowl as a memento of the evening. It was her night too. She supported her man as he went about his Lodge duties and now, she was also in the limelight. What could be better?

By ten that night William was half cut. But only half. As he mingled, a flashing image from Singapore darted across his frontal lobe. At one table he saw the ravaged face of a comrade he had not seen since exiting Changi. The troubled façade raised an eyebrow at him. William tried to turn away, but froze. He saw the ex-soldier wipe sweat from his cracked brow and grimace at the pain; that was William's undoing.

Where were the guards? They must be present, they were always there.

He was trapped and surrounded by the enemy. His mind fixated on the rhythmical drumming of the band, as he relived the march pasts of the camp roll calls. His dress suit felt tight and restricting. His collar seemed to be strangling the air out of his throat. He pulled off his jacket and wrestled with his bow tie in a futile effort to rid himself of the tremors he knew were coming. They had invaded him so many times before, but never in such esteemed company.

Grabbing a full bottle of whisky from the open bar he raced outside, jumped into his sturdy Morris Minor, with the window wide open to the chilly night, and shot off to purge his thoughts. But his thoughts were desperately despondent. He was sucked back into unimaginable horrors too often.

Could he ever shake his imaginings? He wrestled with these thoughts as his driving became more erratic.

Then the answer came to him.

A chillingly sane voice showed him the way out. He swerved into the petrol station and drove towards a parked lorry. He would be free.

As soon as William had left the hall Edith had run to the telephone in the foyer. She knew the drill. Later on, the police hauled his wedged car away from the tailgate of the lorry and a jolted William, drunk and safe, was dragged from the footwell of the passenger side where he had slumped, seconds before impact. God save the fact that seat belts were not yet mandatory. Or maybe not.

By midnight he was bandaged and released from Fleetwood Hospital and Edith had called a taxi to take them both back home. Her clothes were stained with his blood. Her tiara and gloves nestled in the Rose Bowl. Berenice was oblivious to it all, tucked up in bed with the neighbour Francis as a babysitter. The nurse in Edith attended to her patient yet again.

In the early morning Edith awoke to an empty bed and rushed to the bathroom to check if William was being sick again. She heard the creak of the rabbit's cage door in the garden below. Opening the bathroom window, she stood on tiptoes to see the garrotting of Snuggles and the tussle William had with the entrails. She frantically called out his name. He turned in a resignedly weary move and came back into the house, still reeling from the thoughts of places faraway in the sun.

Back upstairs in their bedroom, she wiped his sweat and

the rabbit's blood away with the satin gloves from the rose bowl resting on the glass top of the kidney-shaped dressing table. She urged him back into bed. Once there he would be her charge and she could do what she did best. Nurse him. She beckoned him to join her.

Seconds later Berenice flung herself into the room and the farce of family life rolled forward once again. Edith swore she had heard a dog in the garden. The neighbour's poodle perhaps. Berenice plotted the poisoning of the dog and harboured a swelling hate for her neighbour Francis, telling her mum never to allow her to babysit again. How could she have allowed her dog to enter their garden and savage her rabbit?

Such hate at that young age.

Such hate at any age.

William seemed happy in his faraway head.

One more Jap had been killed.

Poor William.

Poor everyone really.

Later on, Berenice went downstairs as her mother tidied up the garden and her father slept. A whole loaf of bread was on the kitchen table. She ate it all, stuffed with pickled beetroot, butter and salad cream. It helped. Slightly.

After that, Edith tried seriously hard to convince Berenice that she was wanted and loved. New toys were purchased, a dog was brought into the house as a sturdier pet and companion. She named it Beth, a shortened form of her middle name, which was Elizabeth, after Queen Elizabeth the second, whose coronation, she was told, she had watched from her pram on June 2nd 1953.

By the age of eight Berenice was unaware of a time in her life that she had not known she was adopted. But she had never quite understood what exactly it was all about. She thought little of it until one night a new government advert emerged on TV. Next day at school the children were horrid to her.

They too had seen this on TV. Kids loved watching the quirky, recently invented adverts. Berenice's favourite was the one about toothpaste. It certainly had a catchy song which she used to sing inside her head when she brushed her teeth.

'You'll wonder where the yellow went when you brush your teeth with Pepsodent.'

But this new hurtful advert hadn't been catchy at all. It had been about fostering and in the 1950s the British government was urging the population to foster children who, once sorted out, could go back to their natural parents. Adoption and fostering, what is the difference when you are eight years old? Her classmates were so cruel to her. They laughed mercilessly at her, yelling that she would be moved on soon when her parents had stopped fostering her. Would she? Perhaps that wouldn't be too bad!

At home that night she enquired, quite innocently, when she was going back to her birth parents.

All hell broke loose.

Edith gasped and William shot off outside to have a fag. More beetroot sandwiches were eaten. After hours of explanation, the difference between fostering and adoption had been absorbed. At school the next day Berenice destroyed several young souls by insisting that she had been chosen, she was the special one, other children had perhaps even been a terrible and shocking mistake.

Her parents had wanted a cute dark-haired little girl and they had gone to the baby shop and got one. Children wept in the playground imagining themselves to be a terrible and shocking mistake and the headteacher, not for the first time, called in William and Edith to decide how to handle a trauma involving Berenice.

On the home front, there was a continuing war in William's head. As the years unfolded and demons sought their escape, he found it harder and harder to suppress his longings to lash out. Berenice was, by then, aware of the undercurrents that existed in the silences and she largely avoided unnecessary contact with her dad. He was a frightening and conflicted soul.

As her 11-plus exam drew close, he was always urging her on to excel. Times tables up to 15 had to be learnt. He would sit outside the bathroom door as she bathed and she was not let out until all the mathematical tables had been recited accurately. Such discipline. Her bath was often cold, but by God she learnt those tables.

Close to the exam her head was in a spin.

Verbal reasoning, Maths, English, so many tests done each night in an effort to be ready for this exam which would ensure a place at a grammar school. One night, her mind elsewhere, she walked into the bathroom already reciting her times tables, ready for her exam. She had been unaware that her father was right behind her, ready to sit with his back to the closed bathroom door and hear his daughter repeat her times tables once more as he smoked a fag.

Berenice closed the bathroom door with a backward flick of her heel, then faced into the bathroom. She was up to her nine times table in her head. Bending over to turn on the heavy brass taps of the roll-top bath, she narrowly missed being hurt by the door being flung open with such force it cracked the tiles and hung off one set of hinges by the time it rested. She never finished her ten times table.

All he said was, 'Don't ever shut a door in my face again.' She never did.

The next day she sat her final 11-plus exam. Maths. It was an hour and a half paper. She finished in twenty minutes and an astounded invigilator let her out of the room as she insisted that she had done it all.

She ran back towards her house and hid in the sand dunes at the top of the road. No need to go there until she had to. She later learnt that she had passed her 11-plus as one of the top students in the county.

Night after night, an optimistic William sat in the dining room and filled out application forms. Another job, another chance at life. Simultaneously studying for his Master's degree.

Stuck in academia he could survive. It was ordinary life that confounded him.

The kitchen was featured again.

An innocent remark maybe the start of it all, who knew? She had been ironing her school uniform. What had she said that had annoyed him? Would she ever understand his mood swings? He came at her with lightning speed. She was, by then, a good four inches taller than her father. William picked up the iron in one hand, pinned her to the wall with his free elbow and tried so very hard to burn her face off her skull. This was not her father. He was a monster, raging and gurgling obscenities. A force of adrenalin surged through Berenice and she ferociously fought him, until suddenly, like a broken branch he splintered and returned to his cup of tea, sitting down on his favourite red stool and lighting a fag.

The iron fell to the floor; she picked it up and continued ironing, chilled and drained, devoid of emotions as her mother entered and enquired if everything was all right, because she thought she had heard a noise.

'Everything is fine!' came the swift reply from the combatants.

Miraculously a Master's degree was gained. A new job followed. A move was made. Whitley Bay was the chosen one. A place to start over, coinciding nicely with a move from junior to secondary school for Berenice. It all seemed so perfect. It would have been if that pesky Jap general had not had his light-bulb moment about Pearl Harbour, decades ago.

Edith felt isolated in Whitley Bay. The treacherous Shap Pass that separates the east from the west of England also now separated her from her family back in Lancashire. Her support network was out of reach. Daily she dreaded being alone in the semi-detached house she just could not bring herself to love. Somehow the home they had left behind was linked to the war, their shared past and young love.

The government grant given to build it had been a sort of thank-you to all the POWs. If she was having a hell of a time with William, at least she had a comfortable home. But the new house in Whitley Bay was horrible in her eyes. Depressingly clad in sharp pebble-dash, and only a semi-detached. It had been a rushed buy when they had been forced to move in a hurry because school term was starting. A lovely detached house not far away had been their first choice, but they had been gazumped and as the purchase fell through, they only had two weeks before they were all expected to move. William bought the house alone and Edith gasped in horror as they drove up Grasmere Crescent in Whitley Bay and the dull house came into view, emerging slowly from a sea fret.

From then on, Edith retreated into the shell of her dressing gown and was often to be found clutching this rose-coloured sanctuary firmly around her. The very act of discarding it might mean launching herself into the abyss. She had been rattled by the move. The house was the problem. Within six short weeks of a summer holiday she had packed, unpacked, and seen Berenice and William start in new educational establishments. She was left exhausted and tearful. Her familiar points of reference had vanished. Nobody in Whitley Bay knew that her family in Fleetwood were important and frankly she no longer had the willpower to prove it.

The house had needed redecorating and she had phoned for Fenwick's Department Store in central Newcastle to deliver large clumsy books of decorating options. She chose an appropriate colour scheme. Metallic dustbin grey had been Berenice's private evaluation. Sanderson decorators called the colour Onion Head.

The new carpet in the front room was grey wool. The new fireplace was grey marble. The wallpaper was a grey silk stripe and the loose covers on the three-piece utility suite were beige with large pastel flowers. The net curtains that hung ceiling to floor in the large bay window were white, or more often than not grey. Her mother cursed the smoke from the coal-fired power station at Blyth, which clearly left its toxic residue in the folds. The fabric on the lampshade was quilted white and as there were no other curtains, it was like sitting in a goldfish bowl at night.

Perhaps deliberately designed that way by Edith. Easier to see inside should the need arise.

The back room, with its cosy gas fire and warm yellow carpet, left over from the previous owners, was by far the preferred room. A beautiful flowering cherry tree, in an otherwise overgrown back garden, framed the view through the double French doors to the outside. It was a small room that was rapidly turning as yellow as the inherited carpet. William smoked at least sixty cigarettes a day in there and Edith fried food in the adjoining kitchen, as she had precious few recipes to choose from.

The reason for this lapse in her housewifery skills was mainly because her mother had never shown her any. This was because a cook had been employed, as befitting her family's status in Fleetwood. Her Grandma Ruth in Scotland was so well liked that her neighbours often left food for her, especially after her husband had died and thereafter, she was regularly taken out to the High Street for tea-time treats.

So Edith had never really learnt any cookery skills. William lived on a rotating diet of fat and carbohydrate and Berenice ate more tins of Heinz baked beans and tomato soup than were probably good for anybody. She mistakenly believed that all of this was perfectly normal.

It was also normal for her father to fly into a furious rage. The trigger would often be unknown. His nicotine-stained hands would curl around Berenice's neck in a flash. She was constantly on the alert. Her life was stuck in a depressingly repetitive cycle of depression. She would return home from school to find her mother sitting in the same chair, in the same dressing gown. On a good day Edith would dress just in time for William to return from the university he now taught at. Most days she did not bother.

William was training teachers and the challenge of the job exhausted him.

He came home from work utterly spent. His now lacklustre wife was about as alluring as the decoration in the front room and he was as frustrated physically as he was mentally. Apart from the doctors, nobody else in the North East knew about his problems. Nobody must ever discover. He had had a good war. That was all anybody needed to find out. He had survived, hadn't he? He did not even have time to join the local Masonic Lodge. If he had, perhaps the boozy social nights would have helped to relieve the menacing tensions building up within him. His long spell in St George's Park mental asylum in Morpeth, for the entirety of a recent school summer holiday, was never referred to.

And still Berenice thought her family was just like any other.

Her new bedroom was large. She liked this and the fact that it had a walk-in wardrobe. When the family had first moved in, she'd tried to play house in the capacious, chilly wardrobe, but the wardrobe never wanted that. In fact, the wardrobe was a rather odd place. On the other side of its wall was the upstairs boiler, in the linen cupboard. The wardrobe really should have been a warm place.

But it was stone cold.

Berenice found that the sounds of the new house were taking some getting used to. The creaking and sobbing, vied with the rumblings of her father's deep snoring and her mother's quiet whimpering of despair. Berenice was often to be found eating beetroot sandwiches, with her faithful pet Beth quietly waiting for the crumbs as they cascaded to the floor.

Sometime later she learnt that the house had been swiftly sold through a firm of solicitors, the deceased previous owner having chosen to hang himself from the solid metal railing, fixed high into the masonry, at either end of her built-in wardrobe. He had done this apparently because his wife had run off to marry her lover, whom she had entertained in Berenice's new bedroom, stopping short of defiling her marriage bed, but not stopping short of anything else. Berenice knew that a tortured soul hung around in her wardrobe. Had hung around, quite literally. She understood his pain. She knew a fair bit about tortured souls.

Her father also haunted her home. Her mother was slight and physically scared of his frequent rages. Yet strangely there was no bond between the two females in the house who suffered through this. Emotions lurched from the three individuals caught in this maleficent tangle of a triangle, but as isolated as they were by the fury within William, they found no bond.

One winter, coming home from school, she had witnessed her father kick away the short ladder Edith was climbing, in order to rehang the freshly washed net curtains in the bay window of the lounge. Maybe his irritation with life had been the trigger that day. Edith had had one foot raised above the highest rung of the three-rung ladder. A precarious balancing act at best. William had flown into the room he tried most to avoid and whacked her across the back. She wobbled. He swore. Her finger had hung in a curtain hook and for a second, she had swung in agony, before the hook popped open and dropped her to the ground.

The pumping veins on his neck turned purple. William then kicked her hard, paused, looked around, then stopped.

He left through the dividing doors to the dining room. Peeking around the lounge door, Berenice surveyed the carnage she had seen from the outside through the window, then quietly closed it and crept upstairs. Preservation was the key. Edith's right hand was in an elasticated support bandage for months. No cooking was done. Various takeaways were called upon to fill the gaping hole where a mother should have been. Mother was AWOL in spirit.

Thrust into the unforgiving atmosphere of the large grammar school at Whitley Bay, she sank. From a position at the top of her class in junior school, she tumbled wildly.

No matter.

Nobody seemed to care.

Her parents presumed that she coped, as she never said that she didn't. It was doubtful they would ever have had the head space for dealing with her if she had revealed that she wasn't coping. But then she didn't really know that she wasn't coping either. She found an outlet in individual sports. She was totally unsure of what team work entailed.

It had all started off as a way of not going home till late, once after-school practice had ended. Perhaps, if she proved she was good at hurdling, her parents would like her and stop arguing and all would be well. Life can still be that simple when you are twelve years old. Well, it ought to be.

She trained every lunchtime and after school. Her body responded in an agreeable way and she became long and lean. But her mother never noticed what time she came home from school. For a whole year she dedicated herself to this discipline. Exhausting hours of stretches and leaps resulted in being chosen to represent Northumberland in the County Athletics Championships. She had told her parents all about it. They had, rather surprisingly, agreed to be there to see her.

She warmed up, noticed by others as a honed young athlete with a future ahead of her. She won her heat. She won her age-group race. She was elated. Searching anxiously in the crowds she could see every other student had their parents present. Hers were not there. It was now her turn to feel frustrated. The girls' races had ended.

Charging up the track she leapt at the hurdles that had been set out for the next race, for the boys.

These hurdles were considerably higher than the girls' and she suddenly remembered that on the first hurdle. She fell, awkwardly, straddling the solid metal bar. Pain shot up her body and she toppled, along with the hurdle.

The attention was the best part.

All of her coaches helped her to the Red Cross station. Her father was called to take her to hospital for an X-ray. A hairline fracture of her left hip was diagnosed, no more sports, then, for a while. Her mother was dressed by the time they got home.

Perfect.

Berenice convalesced in thought, spending hours looking at the flickering jets of the gas fire in the back room and at last she began to realise that things were just not normal.

There was a war in her house.

It had never ended in September 1945; it still lurked in the dark corners of 12 Grasmere Crescent, Whitley Bay. Her father would nod off on the sofa and his fists would clench tight, his joints would rattle and crack. She felt cooped up in his madness; just staying alive was a juggle. It became clear to Berenice, as she got older, that her father would never erase the deep pain that gripped him and he surely would never find that someone he needed to blame. Except of course when he blamed his wife and daughter.

Their lives were a bit hit and rarely miss.

Probably, because of feeling inadequate following his daughter's accident, William decided to end it all one morning by laying his much battered and illogical head to rest on the greasy second shelf of the gas oven. Then very resignedly he turned the gas knobs open. It smelt weird. It was all so simple. Then he passed out.

Berenice entered the chilly, foul-smelling kitchen and dragged her comatose father backwards. In doing so he badly cut open his forehead as he exited the oven and her screams brought Edith downstairs and woke up William. The red-and-white-squared linoleum kitchen tiles lost their definition as blood soaked through various sizes of slippers. The smell of fresh blood swirled through William's nostrils and he fought off Berenice and Edith as they tried valiantly to restrain him whilst waiting for the ambulance. It seemed like a very long wait, mother and daughter staring at each other over the wrecked soul of their husband and father. Locked, finally, in some grotesque unity of purpose.

Another spell in the asylum followed. Two weeks later, Edith, probably looking for support from her almost grown-up daughter, took Berenice to collect William from the mental hospital. Refusing at first to enter, Edith sat on a bench outside the hospital with the police officer who had accompanied them and had a fag. Berenice wandered in looking for a drink of water. Her mouth was very dry. As she entered the asylum the afflicted peeked at her from darkened corners. She was very aware of their presence. It felt like home.

A lady with white hair and an almost conical shape called her over, and hesitatingly, Berenice went. She followed the seemingly angelic, round-faced woman. She took Berenice into the laundry and asked her to taste the cake she was baking in the washing machine. Carefully she took out her creation; it was in fact a very soiled pair of panties and, in that moment, Berenice felt fear. She sensed, from experience, that she was surrounded by insanity.

The police officer took control and she was swiftly whisked past open doors, where people lay with what looked like dog toys between their teeth. She heard inhuman sounds and electrical zaps. Then she was suddenly thrust into a room with her father, who was sitting awkwardly on a chair in the corner. A small defeated and depressed man, perched on a large wooden chair. It all looked so very bleak.

William stared at Berenice with tired, bloodshot, aching eyes. His wrists were bandaged, his heart was bleeding and he knew not how to express himself. Neither did she.

In the escorted ambulance ride home, with her silently brooding father and mother, the beautiful countryside of Northumberland went unseen. It was a surreal journey back to a familiar hell.

When William came home, he went to bed straight away.

The sick then nursed the terminally ill.

The pills in the bathroom cabinet were copious. But there was nothing to heal a war-damaged family. A fog of despair settled over the household.

Another fresh start was orchestrated. A new school for Berenice. She would love it. A single sex school in Jesmond. Paid for by her grandfather. Gordon was not insensitive to the traumas in his daughter's life. Edith had phoned for help; this was seen as help. Keep Berenice away as much as possible from the house. A long journey to school and back on the train. It all seemed so perfect a solution.

William saw Gordon's intrusion as more evidence that he was failing as a father.

He would show them all. He would orchestrate the perfect failure that would release everyone from this existence because it certainly was not living.

He drove alone to the Lake District, parked on the slipway at Bowness, facing Windermere, where he had taken Edith on their honeymoon. As dusk approached, he drank the last of his whiskey and slit his fragile wrists again, not before releasing the handbrake.

The car slid silently into the water.

It was the first day of her new school. Berenice had expected her father to drive her there.

Instead, a flustered Edith called for a taxi.

Nothing was going to change. As she walked up the steps to her new posh school, she thought she heard laughter. She looked up but nobody could be seen.

She felt a chill run through her.

CHAPTER 6

1945–1946
LIBERATION?

William woke up suddenly one morning, not because the notches on his rough bamboo bed were digging into him, but because he could sense an unfamiliar silence. He had heard the camp rumours that peace was about to be declared late the previous afternoon, but nobody had quite believed it. Stumbling from the pain of a recent stint on the construction of the Burma railway, he levered himself carefully off his cot bed and staggered to roll call for 6 am.

Their amazingly professional British commander relayed the stunning events of the night before in absolute calm. All the Japs had run away and the prisoners were now on their own. Together with his mates, they raised the British and Australian flags and waited.

No Japs came to gun them all down.

It was a curiously empty sort of a day, hanging around waiting for action and gossiping in huddles. Soon William and his comrades began to believe it was true, especially after an American plane dropped cartons of cigarettes and a letter from the Queen for their British commander.

After that the bulky paratroopers arrived thick and fast and William found himself being shaved hairless and all his weeping or half-healed sores painted in rainbow colours denoting their type of infection. His clothing, bedding and hut were all incinerated, but in deference to his rank of Captain, he was allowed to keep his camera and film.

Once well enough, William was sent, along with his unit, to a now functioning Singapore city. They all received mail which had been backlogged for years. He found a corner of the harbour and sat on the infamous wall to read every letter, along with other soldiers.

Some men were openly weeping. Home would not be the fantastic reunion they had dreamt of. William was cautiously optimistic. Edith had continued writing, albeit briefly, but her last letter seemed more welcoming.

He sailed to India from a Singapore he never ever wished to visit again and once there flew back to England. He reached his homeland one day short of four years since he had left, weeping uncontrollably all the way.

The War Office Casualty Branch lists his reporting as 9 am on the 20th September 1945, when his mention on casualty list number 1863, previously reported on casualty list number 991 as a prisoner of war in Malaya, was now not as a prisoner of war any more. His rank was Captain, service number 113812 in the Royal Engineers of the British Army. He was officially alive, with an archived reference to such exquisite joy as merely WO417/9. But being officially alive did not mean he in any way resembled a living person. He needed his time in the infectious disease hospital to find his mind and rebuild his frame. The day he'd arrived back in

Britain he had been able to grasp his upper arm between his thumb and forefinger.

He sat on his bed in the ward, slowly recovering and gaining strength. Underneath was a package containing the lace he had purchased in India for Edith's wedding veil. His thoughts jumped from the future then tumbled wildly down to the horror and dehumanisation of his recent past. But there had been some small victories.

One notable highlight had definitely been one of the many night-time forays into enemy territory. William and three others had left the camp grounds to barter with the locals for food and medicine. It was always an extremely risky venture. On the return leg, even though he had used his secret button compass, they had veered a little off course and literally bumped into a Jap officer, leaning on a tree, having a cigarette. William had looked into the eyes of the startled young soldier for a fleeting second before he garrotted him with some jungle twine.

No remorse. Just relief. Nothing was going to stop him from surviving the war and returning to Fleetwood for Edith.

Upon being declared well, he, along with thousands of others, had been ordered to go to Whitehall in London, not long before Christmas 1945. Men from all corners of the United Kingdom, who had fought in one horrendous corner of the world, sighed and rallied themselves for what was to be the last journey of their soldiering life. There, these desperately demoralised young men were traumatised once more, stripped and examined, then declared fit and healthy, yet curiously told they were unfit for future service.

In their hearts they silently thanked God. A God they'd

feared had deserted them in South East Asia.

William's pay book, like all the others, was stamped with the fact that they were unfit for duty, and once issued with his civilian clothes he rushed out and stood in the pouring rain, kneeling down and thanking God for his safe return.

Curious shoppers, struggling with the few Christmas gifts they'd been able to hunt down in a post-war Britain and weighed down with brown-paper parcels and umbrellas, stopped and stared. Then they wove between the sea of young men piling out of Whitehall and worshipping the ground with fervour. To be alive and healthy almost seemed something to be ashamed of in that moment and the shoppers quickened their pace.

William was determined that he would not be married in his baggy, civilian, army-issue clothes. With his back pay in hand, he walked steadily to Firmin's military suppliers on Norfolk Street in the Strand. There he purchased one brand-new army uniform and four hours after demob he was on a packed train to Blackpool, followed by a short tram journey to Fleetwood.

He stared curiously out of the misty tram window.

They rattled past the promenades and he thought of Edith. He stared down at the walkways and thought of Edith. As the tram left the seaside behind and rode down into Cleveleys, he saw people walking hand in hand and lovers sitting in the cafés en route.

Tears began to pour down his lined and yellowed face, the camaraderie of the kneeling soldiers, soaked to the skin in Whitehall, a fading memory. To be relived later it seemed. Had life really been this normal whilst he was a prisoner? Had he been forgotten about? Would his friends and family even want to know the details? As the tram passed the outskirts of Cleveleys and the sand dunes approaching Fleetwood came into view, he realised that life had indeed marched on at the same time as his marching had been abruptly halted.

His parents were shocked, relieved and cross in that order. He'd informed nobody of his whereabouts since he had returned to UK. Mostly his mother could not understand why he had not called from the hospital.

On reflection his father understood and he watched his gaunt but outwardly healed son march off down Harris Street, in Fleetwood, his new, yet still baggy civilian suit flapping around his thin frame.

He was going to visit Edith's father and request an urgent date be set for the marriage. Gordon first saw William in over four years as he strode carefully into the surgery. He barely recognised him, due to his jaundiced colour, a remnant from his bout of yellow fever.

He did acknowledge the love he saw in William's eyes as he spoke about Edith and recounted their hurried engagement, of which Gordon knew nothing. The old war horse in him softened. Standing before him was a proud soldier who had been a prisoner for his country and never given up.

Gordon respected that.

Despite an inner unease as to why Edith had not spoken of the engagement, he promised this nervous shell of a man, wringing his hands in front of him, that he would call her back home immediately. As William left the house, he ordered May to start arrangements for the wedding, New

Year, January 2nd 1946. May looked at the crumpled brown parcel her husband had given her from William and as she opened it the most gorgeous wisps of lace tumbled out, hand-made in Nagercoil in India.

Edith remembered other tearful journeys to and from Scotland. Before she departed from Glasgow railway station, Sister Hart had taken her home telephone number and as soon as she had left, called Julian to discuss their secret plans.

Edith snivelled and was disconsolate for the whole of the journey from Glasgow to Fleetwood. She was out of sorts and still so very mad with Jonathon. Cross that he'd hesitated and kept his back to her when she'd asked him to marry her. Hurt that he had never rushed after her with an explanation. Furious that she'd had to work alongside him, with not a glance or a touch given to suggest she should still dream of a future with him. She was still passionately in love with him. The range of emotions she was feeling on the journey utterly exhausted her.

Her trip back home in no way reflected the hope that William had experienced on thinking of and planning this wedding during his journey. She had been expecting the phone call from her father. She had seen the news coverage of the returning prisoners of war and she'd searched the crowds for William's face, only to give up, there were so many sad souls. She had always known in the recesses of her heart that William would survive for her. What she had never been sure about was what her reaction to him might be following on from her affair with Jonathon.

She did not tell her father the exact details of her journey. She wanted as much time on her own as possible. She had, after all, resigned from her hospital in Glasgow, packed up her life and forwarded her possessions to Fleetwood. Now she wanted just to breathe. To make that transition by herself for as long as possible. She did not want to be met at Blackpool Railway station in a fancy car and instantly whisked back to memories she had still not fully forgiven her younger brother for.

Her parents were shocked, relieved and cross in that order too. But as her mother fussed over her and followed her into her old bedroom, Gordon rang William. He answered almost immediately, arranging a time, just hours away, and a place to meet his dearest Edith.

William ran to her as he saw her approaching and crushed her in a hug so fierce that she was left breathless. This time she was in some pain from his bony frame sticking in to her. She took him by the hand, first wiping away the tears from his eyes, and together they went inside a nearby café. The war had ended, but rationing was still in place. She managed to get them both cups of weak tea and one rather dry slice of fruit cake. She listened as she stared.

She reflected on the fact that so many men had left for war, only to return quite unlike they had been when they started out. Edith heard a stranger yet recognised the man she knew as William, hardly at all. The images buried so rarely below the surface of William's mind were never to leave him. They altered his psyche permanently. Edith as yet, like so many thousands of wives and girlfriends, did not understand this. To her the man before her was no different from the patients in the hospital. William needed her expert tender loving care, that was all, and it had been given to her the job of healing him.

The last few months in Glasgow had been unsatisfactory for both Edith and Jonathon. She had never received the answer to her question. At work he had never referred to the subject at all. She was not to know the turmoil he was in. Doubts over the whereabouts of his wife and family, ideas swirling around in the mist of his mind, especially after reading some of the newspapers, about whether it would be safe enough to return to Germany and find out the truth. All of this he needed to address before he could commit to another. That he never spoke of this to Edith was their loss. The sparks of passion that had brought them close to begin with instantly snuffed out by his veil of strangled silence.

Edith and William were married one snowy January morning, in the heart of Fleetwood. William proud and tall in his new army uniform, Edith resplendent in satin and lace.

The *Fleetwood Gazette* had, just a week before, published an article about William. In it he had opened up a bit about his time in the camp.

Edith had finally plucked up courage to read this article entitled 'First Jap Prisoner Home Tells of Python Christmas Dinner' the night before her wedding. The townsfolk had hailed William as their hero.

Sweating profusely, she tried very hard to block from her mind certain unwelcome memories. How could she not marry her William?

The night before her wedding she slept fitfully, remembering her buried truths. She also dreamt of the images the newspaper article had conjured up.

After his return to England and his first British Xmas dinner for years, William had written:

'I had python for Xmas dinner in 1942, followed by snacks of rat and lizard, so this year has been a bit different! In Singapore, following our capture, we were marched into Changi on the 17th of February. We were in the camp for about two months, then we were sent as work parties into Singapore. We stayed in these working parties until October, when we moved to Siam to help build the railway. It was a five days trip and we made it by cattle truck, with thirty-two men to a truck. We arrived at Bampong and marched for three days through the jungle carrying full kit. Ultimately, we reached Tasau. There we were allowed to rest for about a month. At the beginning of December, most of the battalion were moved up the mountains, just in time for the cold weather. I had to stay in hospital with a foot ulcer. Over a quarter of our battalion died on this journey. Next, they took us to Tonchang, where the work was building, first the road, then the railway, which was to connect Siam And Burma to Ye.

The country was secondary jungle and the locality mountainous. Both officers and men worked on the railway line. Our battalion spent about a year at Tonchang and during it we had 27% casualties. Most of the deaths were from starvation, malnutrition, tropical diseases and overwork. Our worst patch was at a jungle camp where our water was a stream. Above us, using the same supply was a Japanese camp, a Tamois camp and an elephant camp. We found these particular Tamois to be very unsanitary. We contracted cholera and had many of deaths from it in June, July and August 1943.

The medical personnel were fine, particularly Dr Bennet. He fixed up a saline drip from Kerosene tins through which the sterile saline solution, which he made from ordinary rock salt, was pumped into the cholera patients at the necessary rate. Dr Bennet saved about 40% of the men there. Everyone had malaria and tropical ulcers which caused the loss of limbs.

I remember last June. I got five days solitary confinement on rice and water for not standing properly to attention, during roll-call. I had one foot in a drain by mistake. After that, I knew the sooner I got out of the that camp the better. I knew I was in for trouble if I stayed.

I volunteered for the first party to leave. I was at Changi when news of the peace came.

However, during the whole time we were prisoners of war we had a fairly regular supply of news thanks to the courage of Major MacKenzie of the anti-tank regiment and two Malayan volunteers. They had a wireless set and ran great risk in conveying the news to us. If they had been discovered the penalty would have been death.'

Edith woke from her dreams, bathed in sweat.

The worn lightweight red curtains in her childhood bedroom mocked her as she awoke, the morning of her wedding. They had seemed so vibrant when hung ten years earlier. Now, with a newly erected street lamp outside, they gave the room a womb-like glow and she shuddered. Earlier in the year, before the awkward question she had asked Jonathon following their outing to the play, she had tried so very hard with him. They had made love often, she trying to convince him she would be a good wife, he trying to block out his guilt.

Sister Hart had watched from the shadows. She was

an increasingly malevolent force, as yet unsure how to manipulate Edith for her own warped satisfaction. One day in 1945 the time had presented itself. And oh, so deliciously.

Sister Hart had been awoken by the sound of retching. She smiled to herself in bed. Whilst Edith tried so very hard to stem the contents of her stomach from splattering the toilet bowl with force, Marigold Hart phoned Julian from the bedside table and he answered as soon as his landlady shouted to him from the hall that there was a call for him. He was told of the situation and he laughed.

'Oh good, more grateful clients!' he said, almost choking with manic mirth.

Indeed, grateful, possibly, if all went according to plan. Whilst Edith had been preoccupied with Jonathon, Sister Hart and Julian had seen a gap in the market, a way to make money from other people's misery and that excited them, not just from a business point of view, but sexually. Sister Hart had, along with Edith, specialised in midwifery. A specialisation which made her very much in demand in the latter part of the war.

As Edith spent sultry nights at Jonathon's, Marigold Hart spent nights wrenching unwanted small and medium-sized foetuses from inside the bodies of absent soldiers' wives and girlfriends. The Americans in Glasgow were mostly to blame.

To begin with she had performed this herself. In the cruellest of ways. No drugs, no explanations, just a sudden swift thrust of her sharp-nailed fingers into the core of the woman lying trustingly and pleadingly before her, the sudden, excruciating pain forcing the woman to shoot backwards on the bed and knock herself out on the headboard. The first time this had happened she was aware the subsequent screams might alert others in the flats around them.

Luckily it did not and as the woman had paid Marigold £25 beforehand, she was able to pay for the deposit and three months' rent in advance for Julian to live in a flat nearby, in Wilton Street. She wanted him close. Julian, lured by the business opportunity presented by Marigold, he'd been able to give up working on the railways altogether.

They were onto something here. Julian and Marigold were excited by the money they were making and the otherwise morality of their butchery never entered their self-absorbed heads.

Furthermore, Sister Hart was aware that on the ward there were sometimes women who miscarried naturally, yet were anxious to hide the fact, fearing rejection from their husbands. Julian's now shuffling, hunched back, abnormal gait and clicking walking stick became infamous sounds, like the heralding of evil.

So, a plan had been hatched. A company was registered and Marigold and Julian started an adoption agency. Before the war had ended, they had successfully matched babies to mothers who had miscarried, from women who had suffered the searing agony of unwanted births.

Sister Hart was grateful to Julian the second time she performed an abortion at her flat. He held his hands over the mouth of the woman as Marigold stuffed a crochet hook inside her and attempted to prise out the foetus. After she had ripped the woman's cervix to shreds, he gleefully gave the mother's tensed stomach a couple of hefty thwacks with his black walking stick. The woman had eventually fainted, but the eight-month-old baby was born alive. In that moment Julian had a dark, abhorrent idea.

His landlady was mourning the death of her only son and husband in the war. She had recently spoken to Julian about the loss of her family. Julian ran from Marigold's flat to his own close by and told her that a woman had given birth to an unwanted baby, with Sister Hart in attendance, at the hospital.

His landlady knew that Julian was in love with this nurse and had admired the fact that they had chosen to live separately until they could be married. He was obviously someone that could be trusted, despite his uncompromisingly malicious appearance. For his troubles, she told him she would not expect rent from him for the next six months, if he could deliver a baby to her with fair hair.

The soft down-like fluff on the baby's head was blonde. A perfect match. Just like Julian and Marigold. The very next day they had registered their adoption agency. Theirs would be a very special agency and the price of doing business with them would be high.

When Julian ran back to Marigold's arms after the first deal was over and done with, they made love viciously on the same bed the woman had suffered on and the smell of blood in the air suffused and excited them.

Often, Marigold would close her eyes and imagine a finally consummated welding with a gratefully giving Gregory, only to open her eyes to the urgent stare of his brother Julian on top of her. She would have been mortified to realise Julian was also far away in his head, back in Cornwall with succulent Christine finally succumbing to him. But it worked. Their union brought them a sadistically satisfying sex life and money in the bank as well. Perfect.

Edith had slumped to the floor in the toilet, her morning sickness finally abating. She knew what was happening to her body. The first tell-tale signs had riveted the consequences to her heart and she was in a quandary. Jonathon had not mentioned marriage. She must, more so than ever now. A child was on the way. But she did not want to trap her lover. She wanted his love, as badly as she wanted this unborn child within her. She imagined herself to be barely two months pregnant. As she recovered, she heard the telephone receiver click in the bedroom. Wiping her mouth and flushing the toilet at the same time she walked slowly into the bedroom.

'Do you need help Edith, are you pregnant?' enquired the doe-faced Marigold.

'No need, I am seeing Jonathon tomorrow, we are going to see a play. It's OK, we will discuss marriage afterwards and I will tell you the good news when I get home.'

Sister Hart was to relish the fact that she had secretly palmed off the unwanted theatre tickets onto Jonathon. Then it had merely been a chance to have Julian round one more time, as his landlady was rather prudish. The plot of the play was going to rattle Jonathon immensely. Goodie, she thought.

That day, Sister Hart was off duty. As arranged on the phone earlier, Marigold met Julian in a nearby café. She was a bit late and Julian had bought a copy of the *Glasgow Herald* to while away the time. The front page was full of the joyful reunions of exiled Jewish Germans and their families who had managed to escape. It was clearly time for some good news in a war- bombed Glasgow.

Just as Marigold entered the café Julian's mind clicked into gear and when she sat down, he already had half an idea in mind. Over tepid coffee and wobbly vanilla slices they cemented their plan. Julian would pop the newspaper into the letterbox of Jonathon's flat. Hopefully he would read the front page and pine for his family in Germany. Edith and Jonathon would then go to the play the following day, with vastly different thoughts in mind. The destructive plan would hopefully leave Edith without a clear answer from Jonathon. It was all so wickedly sinister in its conception.

Marigold and Julian laughed. Together, the newspaper article and the theatre outing would play, literally, right into their hands.

Edith and Jonathon's love affair had merely reminded them that their own union was not so wholesome. Time after time Marigold listened to Edith as she recounted her lingering love-making with Jonathon. What she described was nothing like the frantic couplings with Julian, often painful in their brutality, yet strangely satisfying. It niggled away at Marigold's stone- cold heart and chips of ice stabbed her each time Edith giggled and looked lovingly out of the window over to Jonathon's flat. It was like salt on a wound and Sister Hart festered through Edith's joy.

Edith remembered that awful pain she had felt in Jonathon's silence. How she'd stumbled from his flat and into the caring open arms of Marigold. By the following week, on Sister Hart's next off day, the reluctant decision to abort her pregnancy had been made, egged on by Marigold, and a veil of hate began to settle around Edith's thoughts of Jonathon. Images of William re-emerged in her confused head. She had seen his engagement ring nestling in her drawer. Somehow the box it was in had worked its way to the top.

Marigold clucked around, first running a scalding hot bath. Edith kept on thinking of William, who was at that moment, halfway around the world, getting up, ready for roll call, in echoingly steamy circumstances.

Edith was given a suspiciously bleach-scented drink to knock back quickly before she entered the bath. Marigold paced. Julian was hovering in the kitchen waiting for instructions. Edith hesitated to get into the viciously hot bath. As she gagged on the drink her foot slipped and she plunged in sideways.

William stood to attention at roll call, but, thinking of Edith and whether she was still wearing his ring, he misjudged his heeled click to attention and his foot slipped into a nearby storm drain.

Edith was enveloped in a pain like no other she had ever known. Steam rose from the bath.

In camp, William was hauled off to a pit for solitary confinement as he'd dared to disrespect the Japanese by not standing correctly to attention at roll call.

Edith was knocked unconscious by the fall into the bath and Sister Hart called out for Julian, as she struggled to prevent Edith from drowning.

William was dropped into a vat of putrid excrement with barely enough leeway to strain his neck up and prevent him from choking.

Spluttering awake Edith was aware of being hauled onto a bed with strange rough hands holding her shoulders, then

Sister Hart prised open her legs. Once more she passed out as painful foreign objects jostled around her unborn baby, which was instinctively trying to wriggle away from harm.

After some time, William was thrust into a rough cage, in which he had to curl in a foetal position, so tiny was the space. He closed his weeping eyes and dreamt of Edith and the babies they would have together once they were married.

Edith awoke herself as she screamed horrendously, when Sister Hart managed to wrestle her dead child from her wracked body.

For the next five days both Edith and William lay in pain. On the fifth day Edith arose and committed herself to never sleeping with Jonathon again. William arose glad of his feelings for Edith, which had seen him through the worst of Japanese punishments. Although late on in the war, Edith wrote to William, a gently optimistic letter, full not just of her work stories but also, for the first time, with hopes for a future.

The night before her wedding to William, Edith remembered that letter once again, as William had mentioned it, reminiscing of the hope it had given to him when others had received letters of abandonment. He had not talked much about his war. He had no need to. It was etched on his whole frame. She finally drifted off to sleep as she blotted out the awful images of her abortion. Sister Hart had told her of the tiny twin boys. She had also told her of the complications and contortions needed to extract them. Future pregnancies were in question.

So, Edith thought of none of this as she slipped into her simply stunning, satin wedding dress and gasped in delight at the floor-length veil of gossamer-like weight that floated down from her bobbed hair to the tartan carpet in her room. Her mother knocked on the door and came in with a trailing bouquet of winter red roses and ferns, kindly donated, in lieu of payment, from a grateful patient of her father's. The brilliant red of the roses contrasted poignantly with the pureness of her gown. An expensive gift from Gordon considering the austerity of post-war Britain.

Outside Edith's room Marigold stood in purple crepe and a mink wrap. She was her only bridesmaid and her boyfriend, Julian, was to be William's best man, as most of his friends were either dead, disfigured, or in recovery. His limp had prevented Julian from being called up.

After the service William and Edith stood side by side on the snowy steps of the church. William was equally resplendent in his full military regalia. They had fixed smiles on their faces, both looking down as petals from the bouquet were whipped away in the crosswind.

William got drunk at the wedding reception, which was held in the same hall where he had received his Bailey Memorial Medal, years ago. He desperately tried to block out his flashbacks to the intervening years. His mind was both tortured and tainted.

Marigold and Edith whispered secretly, far away from the wedding buffet. Edith spoke of William's desire to have children immediately. She was reeling from having overheard the women around her talking in muted tones about her age and William's ordeals and whether the two of them would ever be able to have children.

She was twenty-seven for goodness' sake, it would all be fine, wouldn't it?

As she and William prepared to leave for a brief honeymoon in the Lake District, she threw her bouquet towards Marigold who misjudged the catch and the guests watched the gorgeous red flowers torn to shreds in the bitingly cold North West wind.

The honeymooners departed, leaving a trail of red.

Like blood spatters on fresh white bed linen, the petals from her bouquet bled into the snow.

Then the honeymooners departed.

Edith and William, at last a couple.

Joined in matrimony.

Separated by the consequences of an emperor's ego.

CHAPTER 7

1941– 1946
DYING – THAT LONG PERSONAL PROCESS

As Douglas watched his newly married sister, Edith, departing for her honeymoon he turned to his anxious-looking parents and predicted that this marriage would never last. He was disturbed by William's cloying exuberance, which to his still youthful, yet experienced mind, seemed quite manic. Lurking just within earshot, were Marigold and Julian, who, after eavesdropping his comments, squeezed each other's arms, whilst maintaining a fixed smile on their faces for the other few guests.

Douglas had distinguished himself in the latter part of the war. But his service had been quite without official merit. As were other underage young men of his era, he had been desperate to join the war and defeat the enemy. He marched, quite jauntily, down to the Marine Hall in Fleetwood, one Saturday morning, having spent the night before altering dates on his birth certificate. Gordon and May found out, one Sunday morning, that he had left for war, when one of their maids brought them a letter which she had found in Douglas's bedroom. The maid, called Annie, had been hoping to find Douglas. He was a handsome young man and she, just two years his senior at the age of eighteen, was partial to his early-morning charms. May had entreated, but Gordon stood his ground. Proud of the fact that his young son, at only sixteen, had virtually run away to join the Navy, he was not about to call him back.

As the train full of conscripts and volunteers had pulled out of Blackpool station, Douglas saluted the proud structure of Blackpool Tower, and dreamt of epic sea battles he would take part in, to help Britain beat the scourge of the German U-boats. By the time he was actually onboard a warship, the cramped, noisy, smelly reality was hard for him to absorb, as he'd been brought up wanting for nothing, in a capacious house, with servants. Cooped up, inside the belly of a churning nauseous war-machine, far from the glamorous adventure he had imagined, he grew up hard and fast.

In early February 1941 he was part of the rescue mission of crew and casualties from HM Armed Boarding Vessel *Crispin*. Douglas had actually wanted to be part of the crew of this special anti-aircraft ship, but his request had been declined, due to his inexperience. Fate would intervene though. Douglas's boat and many others raced towards the sinking ship on February 4th. But as they did, departing triumphant U-boat commanders were already sending reports back of sinking the *Crispin*.

Douglas had seen blood before. He had, on several occasions, helped his father hold down merchant seamen as their teeth had been painfully extracted. He thought he was no stranger to gore. The stinking, burning oil, eating into seared skin, dripped into the shredded limbs of the rescued screaming sailors. This vision was etched into his soul. The sound of excruciating pain, as sea water seeped into fresh burns, had made his own flesh wilt and it was all he could do not to vomit over these poor wretches as he hauled, just a few, onto the deck.

After this disaster, naval wits sharpened and their determination to protect Allied merchant convoys strengthened. There was hardly any sleep. On board, vigilance was the watchword and in just one week in February, 649 ships were safely escorted with the loss of just seven in that period. It took one battleship, many armed merchant cruisers, 43 destroyers, 39 corvettes and sloops, plus one submarine to achieve this small but oft repeated type of victory. The Navy was chipping away at the heart of German strategy in the Atlantic Ocean. British Naval successes in this theatre of war would start to bring about the downfall of Nazi Germany.

Douglas basked in the admiration of the mature women he met in various ports. His was a charmed life and he was spared any injuries. Once the war ended in Germany on the 8th May 1945, he had spent nearly four and a half years at sea and he decided to apply to stay on and take a five-year commission in the Navy.

Within days of her marriage to William, Edith realised her mistake. The road trip to the Lake District was barely a couple of hours. William had said not a word. As they windingly descended the narrow, high-hedged, single-track roads to the lakeside, with all the majesty of the waters of Windermere ahead of them, he was still silent. His hands were welded to the steering wheel in solemn preoccupation. Parking her father's borrowed Morris Tourer close to the steamers, William and Edith walked the short distance to the edge of the lake to admire the view. A curious swan waddled close and Edith retreated to a nearby bench. The swan edged closer to William and Edith tried to alert her new husband. In his hand William held the remnants of a sausage roll, part of a picnic packed by his parents, to feed them on their journey. Edith watched in alarm as the swan swiped viciously at the food and dropped it to the ground to peck at it cautiously. All the while William gazed out across the chilly lake, with the mist descending and dark clouds heralding a storm. His hand was grazed by the sharp-beaked swan. No matter. William had stopped feeling pain years ago. His pain was left on the Burma railways, the routes he'd marched upon and the huts he'd been forced into with dying men around him. A swan? A damp wind crashed him back to reality; he was still not acclimatised to chilly winter weather and he turned, momentarily, to see Edith wiping a tear from her eye. Goodness! What on earth did she have to cry about?

'A wind in the face at the end matters so little. Dying is a long personal process inseparable from living.' William's macabre words would have gouged a deep hole in the heart of Edith. Had she known, perhaps she would have bolted then.

William's mind was momentarily stuck in Singapore. The cool majesty of Windermere was thrusting him back towards the harbour scene and the toppling figure he'd gunned down so mercilessly for King and country. Just as the Japs had slaughtered for Emperor and country. What did any of it really matter? 'Perhaps the fog in the throat is a way off yet, but it will be no more than that, I think, when it does come.'

Disease, dying and death had preoccupied William for so long now that its process utterly defined him. Disease he could fight off and in doing so regain some sanity, function and live. Dying scared him and he became sullen and withdrawn. Death was fought with tremendous strength and when all the adrenalin was spent, an empty body would slump and begin again the ever-continuing avoidance of the fog in the throat.

Edith, as she sat and stared at the rigid lines of the silhouette William presented to the world, wondered when he would turn and remember her, sitting alone at the start of their honeymoon, on a cold bench in Windermere.

Both newlyweds were concerned at how smoothly the transition from prisoner to person the journey would be.

William shook his head to rid those swirling thoughts and sweated with terror at what the reality of marriage would actually be like. Could he marry it to the terror he had felt when, in 1944, a Japanese soldier had searched the first six rows of his returning wood party and he prayed he would not find the two camera batteries swinging in his G-string? Yes, it would be just like that and he turned, achingly slowly, to face Edith.

Within days of her honeymoon Edith realised that her mistake was in imagining she could heal him. She would have to live with it all, love it all or leave it all.

On the fourth day she went, alone, for a walk down the hill into Windermere, as William slept on in their modest guest house of sodden slate and dark granite. Outside the post office she found an enduringly solid red telephone box and dialled.

Sister Hart had been expecting the call. But she had not been prepared for the news. Edith complained of morning sickness. She was scared that her family would know she had not waited until her honeymoon. Sister Hart thought she had scuppered all hope of Edith becoming pregnant when she had sliced and diced her the year before. After murmuring forced, yet encouraging sentiments to Edith, the phone was sharply put down. Edith's stomach lurched again, perhaps more so, as the rain pelted noisily on the outside of the phone box, whilst her fingers hovered over the dial. She so wanted to hear Jonathon's voice again. To what end she was unclear. The acknowledgment that she had made a mistake in marrying William was beginning to invade her. Her hand lingered in mid-air above the dial, only to come crashing down as the heavy door of the telephone box groaned open. She whirled sideways, breathing in the cold air, and saw the pale, sweaty face of William.

Last night, as William had lain with her, clammy from the exertions of a body unused to sex, yet desperate for it, she had wandered off in her mind. Her Grandma Ruth had appeared and hugged her in an embrace, so fierce she gasped at its closeness. Alas, she was not there to soothe the newly-wed. Edith desperately needed some sound advice.

Leaving the telephone box behind, William and Edith walked off in search of shelter from the rain as he reflected that at least this British water dripping down his face today did not sting his eyes with sweat. He was only ever a sliver of a second away from Changi, wherever he was to go, for the rest of his life. He was soothed by her explanation that Edith had merely wanted a girly chat with her mum.

Douglas was in a fix. He had done, predictably, the very opposite of what his parents had asked of him. Shortly after Edith's winter wedding he had been due to sign up for his commission in the Navy. Quite naturally he had made the most of shore time and had, for a number of weeks now, been dating a gorgeously curvaceous young Catholic girl from Kirkham. His parents would have been horrified.

Overly dressed and nervous, she had accompanied Douglas to his parents' grand house, barely ten weeks since she'd first enjoyed his company. Yvette was beside herself with happiness at the thought of ingratiating herself with this well-to-do family.

Until she was subtly turned away.

It had been a deeply embarrassing moment. She had been waiting with Douglas in the drawing room as the young maid had gone to announce their presence to Douglas's parents.

She had been staring around in awe. The mahogany cabinets with leaded glass doors held Murano figurines and objet d'art, edged in gold leaf. The late afternoon sunlight on that winter's day twinkled and winked its way inside, causing devilishly dancing patterns on the tartan carpet. The maid, Annie, the very one who had already experienced Douglas and harboured a fierce protective love of him, had recognised Yvette. Unbeknown to Yvette, whose eyes were dazzled in the drawing room, Annie knew who she was. They had met before at the dances in Fleetwood and Yvette was well known for her flirtations and loud mouth. Some months before, Yvette had managed to charm the young lad Annie had been dancing with and that was the last time he was ever seen, as he hurried around the back of the dance hall with Yvette. Enquiring who this dark-haired, creamy-skinned vixen was, Annie had discovered she was from a large family of Catholics who had quite a deplorable reputation.

'There is a woman to see you in the drawing room, she has come with Douglas,' said Annie.

'Were we expecting anyone?' had enquired Gordon.

'No.' said May.

'Who is she, do you know?' asked Gordon.

Annie had recounted, quite coldly, exactly how and what she knew about Yvette. Then she'd curtsied and left the room. Gordon looked at May. An unspoken hatred of Catholicism ricocheted silently around the staunchly Scottish Presbyterian room, then Gordon rang the bell for the maid again. A red-eyed Annie appeared and was told to send their apologies but they were not at home.

Douglas had been furious and Yvette downcast. To cheer themselves up, he dragged her around the back of his parent's house and took her roughly against the prickly red-brick exterior. Annie was watching from the back pantry window and laughed as Yvette yelled in pain. She was particularly pleased to see that her stockings were laddered and her new wool coat was badly snagged on the brickwork

Annie was relieved at the timing of the resignation letter she had given to Gordon and May earlier in the day. Time to leave this house, she thought. Time to better herself before she too got drawn into a situation that there would only be a painful way out of. There is a God, she said to herself. When she heard the four o'clock bell, in the back pantry, she returned to serve tea to a now outwardly composed Gordon and May.

Afterwards, Douglas and Yvette went to Clegg's chippy, on Lord Street, in Fleetwood. It was a familiar hideaway and they ordered their usual, a strong brew, white bread and oily margarine, plus a large portion of battered cod and chips. How ironic was it that William's father had caught that very cod?

Yvette could not stomach the grease of the fried fish but managed to hold down the bread and strong Northern tea.

Oh yes. She was pregnant.

She wanted to sing the news from the rooftops and she had a big urge to rush over the tramlines to the *Fleetwood Gazette* offices on the corner and place an announcement in the paper. That would show Gordon and May she had meant business. Then she might just pop down the road to the covered market and buy some baby clothes, for all to see and gossip about.

That Douglas had not been able to tell his parents and ensconce her in the home as he took up his offered commission with the Navy was a big disappointment. Douglas really had thought that he'd got it all worked out in his head. Opposite him a downcast Yvette perked up when she saw her three large brothers coming over to meet them both. A creeping fear made its way down Douglas's spine to his sphincter muscle. He excused himself hurriedly and dashed out the back to the privy. Upon his return the three towering brothers made their exit towards the port where they worked, with a thumbs-up to Douglas as they left. He was distraught. He had told Yvette not to mention anything yet.

'My brothers are thrilled that we are getting married and I will be coming to live with you at your parents' house,' she purred with sickly sweet viciousness.

Another dash to the outside privy. After sitting for a while, he hatched a plan, as yet again he emptied his bowels. With apologies to Yvette for leaving her alone for a short while, he hurried home, entering through the back door, in time to give his favourite maid a bum squeeze. He was breathless and nervous when he entered the reception room. His parents finished their tea. Gordon prised his gnarled arthritic fingers from the fine porcelain of the Meissen tea set, troubling over how much longer he would be able to do this without cracking the handle from the cup.

He was surprised to see Douglas back in the house so soon. May, less so. Only last week she had begged Douglas not to go to sea again and stay and help Gordon. Who knew how much longer her husband could continue? The medical conditions he suffered in World War One were catching up on him, nearly thirty years later. The combination of his irritability due to his partial deafness plus the pain from the arthritis meant he was beginning to lose his patients to a new surgery in Fleetwood. It had been recently opened by a qualified returning POW. Little did Gordon know that Annie the maid and his sometime dental assistant would also be leaving at the end of the month. She too would desert him for the position of full-time dental nurse in the new surgery and she was ecstatic about the rise in pay and social stature.

But May understood it all.

Douglas implored, over and over again. Gordon fought against it. May urged calm. With an hour of tense negotiations behind them all, a truce, much like the ending of a war, emerged. If Yvette kept her Catholicism quiet, married Douglas somewhere far away, then yes, she could stay with them and they were going to be happy about the soon-to-be-born child.

On one very pertinent condition.

Douglas had to renounce any thoughts of a forthcoming commission in the navy and return home to learn and take over the dental practice from Gordon. With the sight of Yvette's three burly brothers so recently stamped upon his mind, Douglas finally gave in and a lifetime of regrets began. He cursed fate and his stupidity. In particular Edith, for refusing to help out in his father's surgery.

Douglas returned to the chippy and the beautiful face of Yvette looked up so longingly at him. He was suckered back into it all, unable to break free of a mounting feeling of destiny which had been growing in intensity since the moment he had seen her across the dance floor.

Upon her return from honeymoon Edith reasoned that the baby she was surely carrying was the answer. William was teaching at Fleetwood Grammar School, working towards academic glory for his pupils and consequently he marked books late into each night. There was rarely any small talk. William had forgotten the art. Hardly surprising, as his head had been used like a battering post every time any Jap soldier felt the urge to lash out.

The Jap guards had also been prisoners of sorts. They had vented their frustrations at not being able to actively fight in the cruellest of ways. Reliving all of this was often a confusing predictor of nightmares for William. During the day he could stay focused on his work because it was all knowledge embedded from university. But to cope with the kind of skills he needed to juggle home and work was proving untenable.

He lay down each night, scared of what his dreams would dredge up. His lovemaking was rushed and unsatisfactory. He had never forgiven Edith, for when he finally entered her, just hours after leaving the café where they'd met upon his return, he'd known, without a doubt, that the promise she had given was a lie. This had made him plunge into further gloom. He often took her with an almost violent fury and breathed sighs of sadness when it was over. Like other unwelcome thoughts, he buried this one in the large grave inside his head.

Edith found herself living in a make-believe world of happy couples and she hated herself for this deception. She waved goodbye to her husband from the front door, as he rode on his black, rickety bike to work each day. Turning back to enter their small rented bungalow she closed the front door on her perceived existence and invented her imaginary one. It was then Jonathon, not William, she had gaily seen off to work and she floated through the small amount of housework before her, then headed off to the shops at 11 am, in a mood of fragile contentment

The neighbours saw a petite, neatly turned out, rather reclusive young woman and they hesitated to approach her. She smiled if smiled at, waved sometimes too, but never engaged in conversation. In many ways, much like William, reality was detaching itself quite conveniently from her daily routine. Close neighbours would recall the time that one had shouted out to her across the garden fence.

'How's your husband William today? He teaches my son, you know.'

Edith had dropped the washing she had been about to hang up and had run back into the house crying. It was William of course, not Jonathon that she lived with and her mood for the day evaporated. She'd waited over an hour to go back outside and hang up the washing. Next time in the garden she would ensure there were no neighbours out in theirs.

William knew nothing of this. He came back later and later each afternoon, exhausted from the façade of normality he had to exhibit for his peers, as he grappled with his mind to stay alert. It held a morass of muddled images layered over the ordered thoughts of pre-war normality.

Consequently, there was little that either he or Edith had in common. At night she listened to the radio, her favourite programme being the irreplaceable, It's That Man Again. She would laugh at the silly catchphrases of its stars, Tommy Handley and Dorothy Summers, giggling at their signing off, TTFN, ta ta for now. Often turning to glance at William, she would see him with a frown on his face. Thoughts he wished never to think of surfaced oddly and as soon as the radio character of Colonel Chinstrap started to speak, William was utterly lost, reliving moments with colonels he had fought to save and those who had died weeping in his arms.

Edith's pregnancy marched on. Further phone calls to Sister Hart urged her to do this and that to help things along smoothly. She trusted her good friend so much, more than William, she often reflected.

Sister Hart was enjoying the good life with Julian. During the day he touted in the seedier suburbs of Scottish cities and there was a never-ending queue of willing ladies, ready to give birth or abort, using his wife's skills. The money was pouring in, as fast as the blood ran out. They had been married in secret, neither families notified. Their life and its utter cruelty and depravity was a secret. They hurt women, some permanently, and they matched up the dreams of barren parents' longings to discarded babies they kept hidden in their cellar. At any one time there would be three or four waiting for adoption. More would have been hard to manage as Sister Hart hated the crying and mewling of infants. She kept the damp air in the cellar at bay, with gas burners turned on at hourly intervals six times a day. Babies were fed every four hours, never on demand. And she clocked in the cash.

It was risky. Julian and Marigold realised that in order to expand their business they must move. A secluded house, near a park, that was what was needed. Sometimes it was hard to adopt babies before they started to crawl or walk and the cellar was not ideal. Then there was the smell; Julian and Marigold hated the smell of innocent babies. It permeated through the walls and invaded their lost souls. Oh yes, a much bigger house was needed to keep the smell and sounds well hidden.

Only last week they had nearly lost a sale, as the parents, from the really posh area of Edinburgh called Bruntsfield, wanted a healthy-looking baby, with a ruddy complexion. This was hard to achieve when their stash of ill-gotten babies sometimes spent months in their cellar.

Their request had been very specialised. The father, a wheelchair-bound pilot with crushed legs, had been shot down by a U-boat whilst flying low over the English Channel in 1945. Returning home from a bombing raid over Dresden, he had been one of the 722 heavy bombers sent out to flatten factories and ammunition depots and he was proud of his efforts, which changed the course of the war. But it had been at a price for him. He lost many friends in the aircraft shot down next to him and he took several hits to his own plane's fuselage himself. Clever airmanship and ditched gear meant he could try to hop back to Bicester Airfield in the south of England, if his luck held. It only held as far as the English Channel.

The moon, peeking out from behind dark clouds, had felt his pain and quickly hid once more, so he could fly his damaged plane undetected and limp home. But it was not to be. A prowling U-boat had heard him minutes before. The loud throbbing sound of his laboured engine, reinforced by the heavily beating hearts of the crew, were pinpointed for a mere second by the glow of red from his damaged plane. One burst and the lucky German gunner hit the petrol tank. The moon had no reason to hide any more. Out she came. Now it was the U-boat's turn to run scared in the light and glow of the burning aircraft. One last burst of gunfire, aimed at floating parachutes. No sooner had the bullets fled like darts to the bullseye, than a British Navy warship shelled the U-boat. The moon smiled.

The crew of the aircraft were saved from the churning seas. The crew from the U-boat were never searched for. The aeroplane pilot was screaming in pain when he was roughly hauled on deck. He remembered a kind young naval ensign, Douglas he was called, who soothed him and held his hand as the medics cut away his uniform and blanched at the sight of his legs. Then, he had thankfully passed out.

His wife had been nearly full term into her pregnancy at the time. When she heard the news, she had been living with her mother in Glasgow, as the baby was due to be born. On receiving the telegram of her husband's horrific, life-changing injuries, she went into labour. But no fear. Sister Hart was on duty. The poor woman howled and sobbed as she gave birth late one night at Glasgow Royal Infirmary and, as Sister Hart was alone on duty it all went swimmingly, of course. She looked sad and held the new mum's hand as she told her of the death of her child due to complications involving the placenta. Julian was in fact outside the ward holding his hand over the new baby's mouth as the woman sobbed for her loss. That child was in fact sold the next night.

Their deceptions were frighteningly easy to deploy.

Upon discharge, two days later, Sister Hart gave the grieving mother a scrap of paper, on which was a phone number. Of course, the woman had been told that any future pregnancy was a risk to life, so adoption had been mentioned. A toddler it was suggested would be easier. A child who could walk next to a wheelchair and be instantly part of the family. Sister Hart and Julian had one such boy more than ready. They were desperate to get rid of him from the cellar. Another success was notched up and somewhere, somebody smiled.

Soon after, they found the perfect house in Paisley Low Road, a well-heeled suburb of Glasgow. The house looked so handsome from the outside, its white detached exterior boasting two double-fronted bay windows. One large reception room for Marigold and Julian, another for business meetings with prospective parents and a large brick outbuilding at the rear of the garden, ready to be turned into their version of a nursery. Most perfect of all was its large secluded garden, which meant crawling and toddling infants could exercise and stay healthy whilst waiting for adoption. Close by was Bellahouston Park. Oh yes, playtime in the garden, walks in the park, Marigold Hart could see where all of this was leading. Furthermore, she relished the idea of living in an area which was rich with large period properties. Maids and their male employers were a good source of revenue for the abortion side of their business.

Just off the kitchen was a large utility room.

Perfect.

The large drains led straight into an outside cesspit.

Wonderful.

No need to have the cloying smell of blood hanging over the main living quarters any more. Life was about to get so much better. But it was imperative that she kept her job at the hospital for the meantime.

One Friday morning, horror suffused Edith as she felt wretched stabbing pains not five minutes after William had left for work. They had only been in the rented bungalow for six weeks, married for seven. They were waiting for their house to be built, two roads away. Searing pain knifing into her belly took her breath away. She screamed and the force of it caused a great shooting-hot fire bolt to escape downwards. A wave of nausea and shock hit her as she realised what was about to happen.

Crawling to the phone in the hall she called Sister Hart. Distance prevented any meaningful intervention, for the moment. Next, she called for the ambulance. Once admitted, a guttural thunderclap echoed around the corridors of Fleetwood Hospital and the nurses in Casualty knew at once that they were about to deal with no ordinary miscarriage.

By the time William arrived, Edith was in surgery. Doctors were horrified at the carnage inside her womb, even though the foetuses had not made it that far. Yet more twins had inconveniently trapped themselves in the fallopian tubes. Time vied with blood loss and if not careful the doctors would lose Edith too.

As Julian got home that afternoon Marigold was in a wonderful mood.

'Edith phoned with some news of her pregnancy woes.'

'Indeed, what's the latest?' said Julian.

'We are about to make some more money from her misery, it won't take long.'

'Oh goody,' said Julian.

'I love our happy endings.'

CHAPTER 8

1958-1962
BURIED IMAGES

Berenice was constantly being judged by seemingly unattainable, silent, standards. She failed to brood. Escape was her defence.

She lived with her parents in what seemed to her to be an overly large detached house near Fleetwood, which was somewhat incongruously nestled next to doll-like bungalows on one side and older buildings on the other. She spent long hours on her bed making a den out of the heavy quilted eiderdown, with large wooden hangers in support. This invariably collapsed as soon as she'd crept inside. She graduated to the wardrobe, another hide-out. But as a single child's unit it was far too small to escape into.

The hours between her return from junior school and her parents' departure to bed were a cleverly crafted, intuitive dance of circumvention. Her mongrel best friend Beth, with her thumping stumpy tail and perpetual grin, was all that was needed to keep her company. She rarely thought about her rabbit, Snuggles, any more. A buried memory.

As she got older, she would often charge up to the sand

dunes at the top of her road; there, she hid and lazed, cuddling Beth and watching, just watching. Berenice loved to watch other people and wonder if their lives were just like hers. She hoped not.

People would pass by, really close. She was invisible and Beth was in on it too, as if she almost stopped panting. Ladies with reluctant spouses dragging their feet behind their bustling wives amused her enormously. Like, if it was that much of a pain why didn't they do separate things? Her parents never went on walks together. They mostly did separate things.

Berenice loved the sky. Staring up at it with her head on the bushy beach grass and her dog squashed in tight to her side, she marvelled at the amazing phenomenon above. Clouds raced, scurried or strolled along, but were never stationary. Berenice was happy in her private den in the dunes. Somehow though, the contrast between the clarity of nature and the complexity of her nurturing unsettled her. Away from home she felt at peace with herself. The gnawing reality of what lay in the large white box of bother down the road was suppressed until the very last moment, detached from her thoughts, until a wave of gloom enveloped her upon entry.

She would creep, oh so carefully, down the path at the side of the house, holding Beth on a short lead and try very hard to slide in unannounced, through the often open French windows, backing onto their large rear garden.

Rarely would her parents be physically close, except when fighting. Yet that day her mother was standing over the slumped form of her father sitting in an armchair, with her hand on his shoulder whilst he held a cloth to his mouth and groaned.

'If you just wanted to do this to make me mad, well you have succeeded!'

William, within his pain-filled thoughts, reflected that he had, at least, accomplished that. 'Well, I suppose we will all be living on mince and mash for weeks now!' sighed Edith; they had no other choice it seemed.

William had gone defiantly out to the dentist, one sunny morning. Not Edith's father, but an ex-POW who practised locally. For twenty-five pounds, he had had all his teeth removed. Annie, the dental assistant, had held his hand afterwards and mumbled that she thought he looked great in his soldier's uniform, she'd seen him in a picture on the mantelpiece when she had worked for Gordon and May. That had caused a flicker of a smile in William's eyes. She was a very pretty girl.

William had hated his pain-filled mouth, with rifle-butt-damaged, yellowing, weak teeth. Berenice thought his new shiny white teeth, with really bright pink gums, gave him a doll-like appearance. She liked her dolls, they never screamed in the day or night. They didn't do odd stuff. Irrational stuff. Her parents did a lot of that. Her dolls always looked clean and happy and creamy pink. Her parents often changed colour. Red then purple, green and yellow, she could never keep up.

Friction in the household was often caused when either Berenice or her father did anything that Edith did not approve of. There was a lot of cautious verbal tiptoeing around innovative ideas or suggestions and the slightest hint of censure caused sentences to hang, like trapped flies in a web. So, a lot was left unsaid. It was just easier that way. Like Berenice's escapes to the sand dunes, her father's escape to the dentist was a victory to be relished.

That night Berenice watched as her father struggled with watery mince and smoothly creamed mash. As the Prime Minister, Harold MacMillan, spoke on the radio about the introduction of Life Peerages, her father raised an eyebrow whilst wincing at every bite. His mind was still razor-sharp at times, when he had space to let it be, and he pondered the implications of this new path for the House of Lords.

Edith snapped, 'How's the mince?' Silence.

'Can't you reply?'

MacMillan really did deserve a better audience.

After an early dinner her father left the room and went upstairs. He did that a lot. Berenice popped out stealthily to her friend's house two doors down. She was called Janet. She was a bit older than Berenice and according to Edith, working class, whatever that meant.

Janet's dad worked on the docks at Fleetwood, hauling boxes of frozen cod and other North Atlantic fish into the mammoth cold-storage sheds. Janet's mother had red raw hands, chilblained feet and was forever pregnant or resting. Exposure to Janet was rationed by Edith. Outside Janet's kitchen was an outhouse with a gently sloping cement roof. Berenice and Janet thought it was a great place to sit. They climbed up via the metal dustbins below and observed all the neighbours, at the back, doing the things they should and should not be doing.

For years they would sit and giggle at the man who lived in

the bungalow backing on to the rear garden fence. They later learnt that he was in fact a Mason, just like Berenice's father and grandfather. The two girls thought it was hilariously funny that he stood, quite naked, waving his hands around in stylised gestures as he rehearsed the Masonic drill.

Fortunately, the windowsill cut off a view of anything more private!

At school, Berenice felt that she didn't quite fit in. She couldn't brag about the exploits of her older brothers and sisters. She had none. Nor could she talk about family fun. There was none. It was an unspoken agreement that nobody would be invited back to her house. She once tried to make friends with a girl who also seemed not to quite fit in. The girl had a hole in her heart. Cruel classmates kept poking her, trying to get their fingers to go into the hole. Berenice tried to protect her from that. Then the girl died. Probably what was left of her heart fell out of the hole; nobody spoke about it, so that seemed about right to Berenice.

Stinging from the glares of pupils who had been told not to talk to her about adoption, following the disastrous TV advert for fostering, she tried desperately to impress her classmates by doing handstands against the red brick wall of the junior school.

'Hey you!' shouted the schoolyard bully, Freddie.

Berenice looked up from the tangle she was in following the collapse of her attempted handstand.

'I saw that TV advert too and you can't tell me I'm not wanted 'cos my parents are always telling their friends how hard they tried to get me. They always smile when they say that. So, I was wanted. Not you. You're going to be sent away tomorrow. Your parents are going to get rid of you. You are useless. You can't even do a handstand properly, why would your parents want to keep you? And your knickers are baggy!'

Before that encounter, truancy had been unheard of at Berenice's school. The sand dunes were closing in around her and the sky was getting darker. She hunkered down and tried in vain to wrap up her trembling legs with beach grass. The square concrete anti-tank huts on the promenade above her blocked out the rays of the dying sun. She was totally confused. Then, like a soldier emerging from war, a shadow appeared between the World War Two naval defences. The familiar shape held out his hand to her. She went home with her father. At 9 pm various houses were telephoned and the police were informed that the missing schoolgirl, Berenice, had been found. After recounting what had happened to her at school, Berenice had a warm bath and fell asleep for the next two days. Edith was right put out.

The next day at school, bully Freddie held out his hand too. The head teacher, Mrs Snatler, was short, fat, ugly and fierce. Like a ginger cat she spat and clawed and her hair stood out on end when children were naughty. As she raised the ruler high above her head, the specially designed split opened in the centre, the ruler separated, and as it came down on Freddie's quivering outstretched palm, pinched his flesh viciously as it was snapped back upwards for another wallop. The talk of the school was that perhaps Mrs Snatler's husband had also been subjected to horrors by the Japs. She seemed to have picked up some nasty interrogation tricks from somewhere.

When Berenice returned to school, the stares at break-time were epic. So, she did what she knew in her heart she could do, a perfect handstand, showing off a pair of her mother's pink frilly knickers. Freddie the bully gawked.

'Your parents are going to send you to a home one day because you are such a bully and they can't control you. I heard my dad say that last night and he is a teacher so he knows these things!' blurted out a nervously confident Berenice.

Years later Freddie ended up in prison. A psychologically damaged child. Everyone suspected the problem started in his junior school.

The dreaded 11-plus exams were finally, thankfully, over, so the pupils were invited to go on a camping trip to Wales as a celebration. Berenice longed to get friendly with Freddie. He was such a handsome young lad. Even aged ten and a half he knew that too. He kicked Berenice's shins every time he passed her, a sure sign of affection when you're that age. Girls can be real idiots about boys.

Berenice's fantasies about Freddie were only eclipsed by her dreams about Cliff Richard. Every morning she greeted the world with a heavy heart if she hadn't dreamt of Cliff with his slicked back DA hairstyle and black leather outfits. Anyway, how can you kiss Cliff Richard if you have never been kissed before yourself? Perhaps camp would help, she thought.

At the coach station Edith fussed and William hung in the background, observing and retreating. Berenice was a little nervous, unlike the other children, who seemed less rattled. Perhaps they had all been on sleepovers or holidays together, thought Berenice. She felt very alone at that thought. The students giggled and thumped each other as they waited to board the coach for camp.

Often, she had wanted to stay over with her cousin, Irene. But there was an unfathomable tension between Irene's mother, Auntie Yvette and her own mother, Edith. Irene was two years her senior and, amazingly, born on the same day. Berenice thought about this a lot. It made Irene almost seem like a twin. It was such a pity that they didn't meet as often as the girls wanted to. Parents!

The school coach was leaving Cleveleys Bus Station. All the children were on board. Leaving behind her mother's faintly cloying hugs she stumbled up the steps of the coach. All faces stared at her and muttered. As she sat down the bus passed the police station, then the outdoor municipal bowling green. Aha, thought Berenice, this is where the elderly, male of the species escape to. Clearly dodging their other halves, in much the same way as when they had gone to work, male pensioners with knotted white hankies, or Northern flat caps on their heads, could just be seen over the high fence.

The men underneath the funny hats were bobbing up and down, as much as their arthritic joints would allow, picking up balls and rolling them towards other balls. A very daft game thought Berenice, who liked to play 'Jacks' and had a set with her in her cardboard suitcase, ready to beat everyone at camp.

As the coach moved off it passed close to the bowling green. The schoolchildren were rewarded with a riotous sight. Crinkle cut, nut-brown, sea-weathered skin, folds of it, drooping over saggy knees, wizened elbows and feathered eyebrows. Shrieks of laughter from the passing coach caused consternation amongst the bowling enthusiasts. A tear or two was shed by the bowlers, but that could just have been elderly onset Blepharitis. Berenice thought bowling was very odd and someone should definitely make the fence higher so the wind would not make the old men cry.

As she had been the penultimate person to board the coach, Berenice had to sit next to Mrs Snatler. It wasn't easy. Her large thighs squelched out and wobbled their way onto Berenice's side of the seat. She smelt of 4711 Eau de Cologne and sweat. She was too fat. It was too hot. Berenice was trapped next to the intensive heat of the window and the cloying sickly steam emanating from Mrs Snatler. For the six-hour journey to Wales it was compounded by the fact that her head teacher kept getting up and turning around inwards to talk to the other students. Her cantilevered bust swivelled sideways and nearly suffocated Berenice. Holding her breath, she just about managed not to faint until Mrs Snatler sat back down again, with a loud reverberating, squelchy thud. Berenice had had no idea about the hazards of travelling by coach and vowed then and there never to do it again.

They stopped at Wigan for lunch. All the children got off the coach to go to a public convenience in the centre of town and they were allowed to stroll around for ten minutes after that. Some sat on wooden benches noisily sharing Lucozade and Tizer. Some ran back into the toilets and were sick. More still were sick, some not quite so accurately, into brown paper bags, back on board the coach. So, the coach driver had to stop again on the outskirts of St Helen's for a mop-up. After that all the children went to sleep and finally woke up again close to the Berwyn mountains and not too far away from the Welsh town of Llangollen.

Sitting on the slight hillside, watching their teachers erect the tents in the green valley below, took up quite a bit of time. Mrs Snatler pulled out a crumpled list from her brown shiny handbag and proceeded to arrange her students by sex. Berenice in one tent, opposite another tent.

And Freddie.

With thoughts of Cliff Richard and Freddie swirling around her budding brain, Berenice slipped awkwardly on the hillside as she stood up. Rolling down the hill with increasing speed she ricocheted off a tent peg and flopped sideways onto the soon-to-be-lit campfire, impaling her left calf on a sharp piece of recently cut branch. Thank goodness she had her mother's pink frilly knickers on again.

The doctor, from Corwen, was not very sympathetic and the local anaesthetic was less than useless. Her romantic excursions were dashed, the reality was a nightmare. The eight stitches stung and pained her. In seemingly no time at all, her parents had appeared. She suspected they had driven down behind the coach, although this was never confirmed. She was whisked back to Cleveleys before she had time to christen any other part of her body with electrifying sensations.

So ended her time at junior school and her days in Cleveleys were soon to vanish too.

She hobbled through the next few days, healing, as children do, quite fast. One night, as she sat on the top of the stairs hugging Beth and waiting for her bath to finish running, she overheard her mother crying. Grandma May was dead. At 64. Her angina pills had been too far out of reach and she'd died in a tangle of clothes as she had struggled to get out of the locked bathroom and to her medication on the bedside table. The maids had been dismissed long ago. Yvette and Douglas lived in but had been out shopping with their daughter Irene, after picking her up from school.

Berenice crept away into the bathroom, forgetting to lock the door. She felt numb. She was supposed to cry. That's what happened in school when children came in red-eyed telling of their grandparents' demise. She perched momentarily on the edge of the bath, overcome with pent-up emotion, then passed out as she slid in backwards. Thankfully William was helping Edith up the stairs for a lie-down in the dark when he heard the sloshing of water in the bathroom. The stitches on his daughter's calf had split open like a descending zipper. William, immune these days to blood, hauled her out, wrapped her in a towel, then went, quite calmly downstairs to call for the doctor. Berenice woke up on the bathroom floor for just a second. She looked down at her calf; the layer of flesh was open and gaping, first yellow then red as the blood pumped out. She fainted again.

In the next few days her father dealt with her and her mother dealt with death. Berenice longed to 'go with everyone to the cemetery, to see Campbell's grave opened up so mother and son could be reunited, but she was only well enough to go to the funeral service.

Ghastly Sister Hart was called in to help in the home. She, recently bereaved herself, knew that Berenice hated her. Like a feral cat circling its prey, Sister Hart watched

Berenice out of the corner of her eye. Evil has a scent and Berenice could smell it.

The funeral service was ghastly. Edith marched down the church aisle, jostling mindlessly with calmer mourners as she headed for the front pew that would indicate her position in the family. Head of it. Her grandfather Gordon had gone senile as soon as he found his wife dead. Douglas and Yvette supported him into the church. Berenice and Irene sat holding hands at the back with Sister Hart in charge. The two cousins were united for a while, neither old enough to realise that the scene unravelling before them was an elaborate game of family chess. The elder queen was off the board and the king was surrounded.

A buzzing younger, new queen was circling and Edith hated Yvette even more than ever in that moment. William had sloped off outside for a fag. Edith had to settle for the second pew as Yvette and her Irish Catholic clan from Kirkham had hogged the front pew.

The battle had begun. Staring young eyes, from the back of the church, watched it all in relative innocence.

With the death came the Will.

With the reading of the Will came the quickening of the slow death eating away at William. Edith was now rich, her mother's estate substantial. Why had he bothered to pass his Master's degree, why was he applying for better-paid jobs? Like the Japs before her, May, in death, managed to snuff out William's purpose and render him impotent. Immediately following the funeral Edith started, with manic endeavour, to sort out her mother's possessions, before Yvette could lay any more claim to the family heirlooms.

Meanwhile Berenice waited for her exam results. Her mother had been a woman on a mission whilst training her for those tests. Every night, after her revision was completed, Berenice was given sixpence to go up to the top shops to buy a treat. She would race out of the house, turn left before the dunes and on to the small line of shops. She always bought three liquorice sticks with yellow sherbet centres. She ate them hidden in the dunes. As she wandered back to her house, she longed to see her parents embracing in front of the coal fire, with smiles on their faces and love in their hearts. Instead, her father, often as not in his red paisley designed wrap-over dressing gown, was invariably hunched in a chair smoking, as Edith stood in the kitchen frying something quickly or cursing the wringer for jamming again. Love didn't flow freely in that household.

Berenice remembered little joy in her father's face. Except for the day he got the letter. On the three-legged, mock rococo hall table, there waited for him a large brown envelope. Staring at himself, in hope, in the oval gilt mirror above, he prayed that this time there would be no returning CV and refusal slip. Berenice held her breath too. Just days before Berenice had received her 11-plus results and that had been a resounding success. Now it was her father's turn.

Through the banisters Berenice watched as her father slowly opened the post. With great care and precision, he extracted the large letter within. So much writing, so many pages of something, surely people didn't write 'thanks, but no thanks' on six or seven large pieces of typed paper. She looked at her father's face in the mirror. His eyes were closed as he reverently slid out the pages. His yellowed fingers felt the depth of the correspondence and he too started to smile. He could not feel a mental paper clip. He had sent his CV with a metal paper clip. His oh-so-white teeth and pink gums shone in the reflection of the mirror, which in its turn caught the early morning rays from the glass panel in the front door.

It was a sparkly moment. Berenice held her breath and closed her eyes as soon as she saw her father opening his letter. She heard a small gasp and something that sounded like 'up yours hero too', it made no sense, but her father often made no sense, especially when he was talking about the war and the Japs.

Berenice really, really hoped that her family could sort itself out. She was beginning to realise that her parents were not like others. She couldn't say why exactly. But there was a darkness that made her want to run away and hide. It was so unlike Janet's house. There, washing, babies and muck vied for attention and there was laughter and jokes. Jokes? Never, ever had she heard her parents make a joke and laugh. She laughed when she was at Janet's and felt guilty for doing so, as if she had somehow betrayed her parents. Janet's parents talked of trips to Butlins and Morecambe Bay. They came back sunburnt and skint, living off scraps from the docks until the first wage packet came in. And they loved it.

Every year, for as long as she could remember, she had either spent her holidays going to visit her grandparents' new home in the posh part of Blackpool, or a secluded cottage on a farming estate near Ullswater in the Lake District. Half terms were especially hated as she was dragged along to see the witch, Sister Hart.

It was a four-hour car journey in ever deepening silence. Marigold lived with her weird hunched husband, in a large smelly house in Scotland. Berenice would be paraded inside, Sister Hart's claw-like hands gripping her shoulders and whizzing her around for inspection. Her father never came inside. He sat in the car and smoked or went for a walk in the nearby park. Berenice couldn't understand these visits at all. No sooner had she been inspected, than she was told to go and play in the garden. There she felt trapped and breathless. Especially with the creepy human gargoyle watching her from the stinky utility room. High hedges blocked the sunlight. Occasionally she found the leg of a discarded doll or just a vacant head with missing eyes; it was all very freaky and she refused to touch anything in the garden. She just ran around in circles or sat on the damp path and waited for the ritual to end and to be called back inside. Sometimes she thought she heard screams from the building at the end of the garden. The gargoyle would make his way to that building, after which the muted screams usually stopped.

Through the back windows of Sister Hart's house, she could see her mother and the witch, heads together, talking and patting each other on the back or hugging. It was weird. Tea was laid out in the sunroom, which was an odd name, as there was never any sun in that room, especially when the creepy gargoyle joined them. Berenice was tasked with taking the used crockery into the back utility room, ready to be washed up at a later time. She especially hated that room. There was a pervading smell that caused her to retch and the old lino was stained a peculiar colour, dark brown. Berenice had seen that kind of stain before, on hankies when she had suffered a nose bleed and let them dry out.

It worried her enormously.

The large porcelain sink was chipped and dirty. The wooden work surface adjoining it ran the length of the room and had gouged-out marks like the tracks Janet's father made when he raked the leaves across the grass. Berenice would pile everything onto this surface, holding her breath the whole time. It was a game she played with herself, not to breathe once she entered that room. Upon returning home from these visits, it would be great. Her mother would be moody and silent and her father retreated to the bedroom or the back shed. Nobody bothered with her. So, she usually then scooted off to Janet's or hid with Beth in the sand dunes. Magic!

Being a teacher, her father had holidays just like she did. It was torturous. Christmas would approach and preparations would begin for the pilgrimage to Blackpool to see her elderly relatives. It kicked off with present buying. Her mother bought the presents. Her father carried them horizontally, in case the tissue wrapping paper in the expensive boxes creased, or God forbid, he broke whatever was inside.

Berenice never got to choose presents for her cousin Irene. Her mother insisted on doing that and Berenice was quite jealous about them sometimes. No matter, she loved Irene and the thought of visiting her made all the daft stuff beforehand seem to vanish. Smiles that never reached the eyes were plastered on all her relatives' faces at Christmas and thank goodness her maternal grandparents' house was large enough to find a secret hiding place and play with Irene and her Barbie dolls.

Aunty Yvette would get sillier as the festivities progressed, banning everyone from the kitchen as she attempted to prove how worthy she was to cook in such a prestigious household. She usually failed. Burnt roast potatoes were her favourite, along with dried-out turkey and salted Brussels sprouts. But tubes of chocolate raisins and Smarties sufficed and Irene and Berenice hid under the complaining table as the grown-ups bickered over the food and who sat next to her grandparents. The girls stuffed themselves with sweets and then they all flopped into the large lounge to watch the Queen's speech, invariably followed by the BBC airing, as it had every year since 1957 when it was made, the British-American war epic *The Bridge on the River Kwai.*

Her father would disappear at that point, and everyone would look tense, except her grandfather, who turned the sound up, as he was totally deaf in one ear, and yelled in praise as each Jap was killed and bounced up and down when the bridge blew up. At that point Berenice usually deserted the lounge and headed for the train wreck in the kitchen, searching for bread and beetroot. Many Christmas lunches were sweets and beetroot sandwiches, which was OK wasn't it? Didn't everyone do that?

But of all the holidays she could remember as a young child, the Lake District ones were the best. Her father rented a cottage on a private estate most summers and basically the drive up was the last she meaningfully saw of her parents for weeks. She was allowed to play with the farm workers' children and Sammy Snail the metal rocker was always out in the garden to have fun rides on. As she grew up, she would run wild in the fields to the backdrop of infinite beauty and the aroma of smouldering wet wood. She grew alarmingly each of these summer holidays and by eleven years of age was already nearly five foot six tall. Her friends there spoke in accents she struggled to catch but it mattered little, she just followed their lead and by the age of ten she was confidently driving the farm tractor around the estate. One of the strapping young lads worked the machinery attached to the back of the tractor, picking up and dropping off large fallen branches scattered over the huge, walled, farm estate. Walking back down the hill to her parents' holiday accommodation at the end of a busy day, she was always weary and spent, full of good wholesome food and fond memories. That these youngsters accepted her so readily was truly wonderful, she was glad they did. She hated going home after these holidays.

As William looked at the contents of the letter in the hallway, he turned around, aware that his adopted daughter was staring at him through the banisters at the top of the stairs.

'It's good news, Berenice, I have a new job to go to in Newcastle. You will love it, it will be like a fresh start.'

Father and daughter gazed at each other for a while, both trying to erase everything that needed overlooking in a fresh start.

'Can I take my dog with me, Daddy?'

'Yes, you can, now let me go and tell your mother.'

So, Berenice ran down the stairs before he could move, out through the French windows, grabbed Beth and scooted

off up the road to the sand dunes.
   She hid there until lunchtime.
   Would it be safe to go home?
   Would it ever be?

CHAPTER 9

1940s–1960s
MURDEROUS MOMENTS

William sat back onto the second-class railway seat, closing his eyes against the houses flashing by, junk-filled back yards and litter-strewn hedgerows. He was so very weary. It had been such a very difficult few days, full of subterfuge and deceit.

After this, he hoped his war would soon be over. His network of pals, men who he was completely in tune with. The work they had achieved. His right hand twitched, as was so often the case afterwards.

As usual, Edith and Berenice would be waiting for him. His train would arrive home in two hours, Scotland a fading memory. He composed himself. Well, he tried. Composure was an odd thing, you thought you had it nailed, then bloody hell, you found you hadn't. Odd that.

Once home his mantle of hen-pecked husband would be resumed again for the outside world. His confused inner core sometimes burst forth unexpectedly and hurt those around him. He could be overwhelmed by it all. Then he would be put out of action for a while. Doctors came and went, more pills in the bathroom cabinet. The war couldn't be undone that easily, that was the problem nobody seemed to get. He spent hours anxiously trying to persuade the experts all was well. When it so very clearly was not. If they'd not been there, then they would never understand. Would they?

Last Thursday he had set forth, full of eager anticipation. Leaving work early he had caught the five past one train and eaten alone in the dining car. Edith knew yet disapproved of his recent invitation to another ex-POW gathering, this time up in Scotland. It was a different location each time. She had always hoped the camaraderie would quell the darkness and help find him some peace, for all their sakes. It hadn't up till now; maybe this time would prove different.

She had watched him leave the house the morning of the reunion. A slight swagger to his gait, a quickening step. What was it that attracted him so much and left him literally counting the days before each such trip, she wondered? He'd promised that this was to be the last meeting. She hoped so. His returns were always much more subdued, a moroseness held him in its grip and arguments were but a heartbeat away. It had to end. Time to live for the future.

The morning before William had left, he'd watched young Berenice playing with her dog in the back garden. He observed her strong limbs and stubborn demeanour as she tried in vain to hook up her dog to an old sleigh. He laughed to himself at her resilience. She would cope. She had to cope. In a few years, his adopted daughter would fly free. He hoped so. God knows they'd burdened her enough.

As his country had burdened him.

In 1946, a first meeting had been hastily arranged. The

group of men who had found themselves kneeling in post-war Whitehall in the rain with William, that fateful day of their de-mob, had willingly agreed to meet up in six months, in the exact same spot. Not all had, but enough went and hastened to the nearest pub. Joyful once more, to be able to talk of things to others who understood, instead of shuddering, weeping, or worst of all, simply ignoring them.

Two common threads united them all. Pain and betrayal. William had watched men around him read their version of a 'Dear John' letter. At that time, he had thought he was the lucky one; Edith had waited for him. On that desolate harbour wall in Singapore men wept and some even took their own lives. Not content that they had made it through the building of the jungle railway that had taken a life for every rail laid. Not even thinking about the graves of nine thousand of their comrades and the luck they had had in surviving. No. These men had been kept alive with the faintest glimmer of hope and in some cases love. There was someone waiting for them when they were freed. When they read that this was not to be, a few slit their wrists and plunged backwards.

William had alerted the authorities and quickly this was stopped. Men crying, in the arms of other men. It had been a pitiful sight.

He had met some of those men again in the first meeting after demob. These men were to be the core of the new group. They had devised a motto, *Iungimus in dolore*; it was their password also. In pain we unite.

How apt.

Only those who had been there knew the excruciating

daily mental and often physical pain. They would be united by their shared understanding of man's inhumanity to man. And their women's betrayal of their men.

It had been an unusual start. Ex-servicemen drinking deeply, laughing loudly, each trying to outdo the other with tales of derring-do, depravation and despair. All to the incongruous backdrop of a packed post-war pub, dense with sweat, cigarette fog and humanity.

In the smoky haze, one of the group, a man he had held as he wept whilst hurling his fiancée's rejection letter into the estuary in Singapore, froze. His eyes glazed and one tear fell as his mouth curved downwards and his body tensed. William followed his stare. At the bar stood a tall, broad-shouldered American airman and on his arm a very petite brunette. They had an aura around them. They saw nobody. They flowed. Linking arms, they glided towards a seat at the far end of the pub, close the passageway to the toilets.

William put a hand on Peter's shoulder. He tried to hold down this adrenalin-infused man who had, in an instant, become quite another person. In Peter's mind he remembered the beatings, lashings, starvations and humiliating inglorious shame of captivity. Before him swam his memory of Sarah. Their engagement party in York. How they'd run hand in hand down the Shambles, he ducking his tall muscular frame to avoid the overhanging timber of the centuries-old framed buildings. They'd run giddily past the magnificent Minster and upwards, to the train station.

The timing was agonising, but he had to report for duty and go off to war. The Minster bells had rung loudly as he'd hurled himself onto the troop train. But his heart had beat louder when he turned to squeeze, for just a second, out of the window and see his fiancée Sarah, mouth that she loved him and would wait.

She had waved her left hand to say goodbye, with her new diamond engagement ring twinkling in the fading afternoon sunshine. Further down the platform a group of American airmen had just disembarked, they were milling around, waiting for their transport to RAF Clifton in Yorkshire. Sarah paid no heed to them, but as she left the railway station her silk scarf slid off her shoulders and one of the Americans bent to retrieve it and hand it back to her. She thanked him and rushing to take the scarf from him snagged it, catching it on her sparkly new engagement ring. One of the claws caught in the fine silk and suddenly her ring was pulled from her slender finger and fell to the ground. The American pilot still had hold of the end of the scarf. She gasped. The ring rolled. The next train was coming into view. As if in slow motion neither she nor the pilot could reach the ring before it skittered off the platform and disappeared under the front carriage of the train entering the station. Sarah fainted into the arms of the pilot. Stone cold passed out. The pilot was being urged to join his crew as their transport had arrived. The stationmaster, who knew that Sarah's father ran the pub close to the airbase, asked the American if he would be so kind as take her back since the pub was en route to the airbase. He agreed, but not before the stationmaster jumped down onto the rails and retrieved the mangled ring, minus the diamond. It seemed the diamond had nestled with the ballast in between the sleepers, hiding perhaps.

Peter's last memory of Sarah had etched itself within his

heart. It sustained and nourished him all through the war. To survive was to imagine. Men toiled and cursed, but in their head, they had to be elsewhere in order to survive. His 'elsewhere' was now sitting hugging someone else. She rose to turn and go to the Ladies'. Peter rose too. William followed, at a distance.

Sarah was unsure. Still unsure, after everything she had done and agonised over. So many tangled thoughts. The war. Her brief engagement to Peter. Her chance meeting with her American lover. The letter she had written to Peter. Now the war was over and she knew that he had survived, a voice deep within her nagged and ate away at her. No release though. Her new engagement ring was waiting for her in the box on the pub table. They had come up to London, especially to buy it, from a lovely Jewish jeweller close by. She walked on to the Ladies', simply to splash water on her face; she was sweating. Something felt not quite right.

Peter strode manically to the table where the American sat, then bent over him to whisper something in his ear. On the table was an open jewellery box. Inside, an engagement ring. A blood-red ruby. Fresh from a recent briefing by his superior, the airman partially stood up, leaving the box open on the table, and leant close to hear what Peter had to say, not wishing to offend the British man in any way at all. The pub was full, crowded and very loud. The Americans were beginning to annoy the Brits, politeness the watchword. Peter's move was electric and devastating. Holding the American by his elbow he lowered him back to his seat and wedged him upright into the corner. Then swiped the box swiftly from the table. Nobody had seen the deadly attack knife attack. A noisy drunk crowd careered between William and Peter. William hung back. For just a second, he admired Peter. He watched him as he snatched up the ring box, then made his way into the Ladies' toilet. As Sarah raised her head from the washbasin she gasped. Peter spun her round so fast. He kissed her violently, love and hate surging through his limbs. No hesitation though. He thrust the same knife in and up, till it reached the heart of a petrified Sarah. With his mouth enveloping her, no cries were heard. Sliding her to the ground, he laid the ring box on the knife wound, then left.

Standing, isolated by the swaying crowd, Peter and William, smiled at each other.

'Everything OK, Peter?' he enquired.

'All good now,' said Peter, rather remotely.

William urged the group to go outside into the fresh air, walk the embankment and chat. Distance needed to be put between Peter and the pub. They talked long into the damp evening and huddled close, sharing their secrets and forging their bonds. Peter had been drinking from a concealed whisky flask and after an hour broke down crying and confessing. His bravado spent, his conscience struggling. But he was to be surprised. To a man everyone agreed to keep his secret and stood listening when William said, 'Has the war ended for you all?'

They agreed to a man that it really hadn't.

'Peter fought demons, caused by the war, in that pub – do you blame him?'

They didn't.

Each man went home that night tasked with a decision.

By the next time they met, this time in York, in honour of Peter, their group was forged with a mission.

To right the wrongs of pain and betrayal.

Iungimus in dolore.

All of Peter's comrades had been captured at the fall of Singapore. Not one had seen more than a few months of active duty. Their war had been surrounded by second-rate Japanese soldiers in stinking hellholes. Now they would plan and execute with stealth and cunning. They would be victorious. They would get to fight their war.

Only at home in the silence of the night did their sweats start. As civilian life clawed them in, the tug on their souls deepened. Some men dropped out. William stayed.

The year before the most recent meeting, Peter had died, in a vicious attack, whilst undercover for William in Glasgow. William had a suspect in mind and Peter had been on reconnaissance for him at the time. Others in the group had melted away to suburbia by then, many having righted their own personal wrongs.

Their motto buried in their heads, but their victims were often left unburied.

One job left.

William was shadowing Peter's last known haunt, Glasgow central train station. Once there, a shape appeared that he recognised. In just the place, doing just what Peter had phoned him about. Standing awkwardly on the spot where Peter had been found with a fatal knife wound to his back, Julian was exactly where Peter had said he would be at this time of the day. Huddled in deep conversation with the station prostitutes, his walking stick, an ever-present evil.

Julian was wary. Last year, he had known that he was being followed and thought it was an undercover policeman. The stab that had ended Peter's life was in the shadows, in a poorly lit corner of the station. Peter had thought he was well hidden behind the coconut tree, he never saw the Jap sneak up behind him and when Julian killed him, he sank slowly, clinging to the station column and mouthing the name Sarah over and over again.

William knew Julian well, as the husband of Edith's friend Marigold, the people they had adopted his daughter from. Dear God no, he thought as he edged closer to try and hear what was being said.

Could Berenice have come from one of these women? He hoped not. The adoption agency they ran was private but doubts had arisen. He had sent Peter to find out the truth for him.

William now shadowed Julian, who walked painfully slowly. Fading into the brickwork, he overheard two of the women discussing Julian. He was appalled. What depths the adoption agency had sunk to were unravelled as the women spoke of lost babies, complications following abortions and the house near the park that Edith made William and Berenice visit each year. A year later, when Edith was ready to make the annual trip to Marigold and Julian's, William would be ready.

Then, as usual, he had dropped Edith and Berenice off at the door. He was never invited in. He didn't mind, patience had been learnt in Changi. Julian sat and smoked in the back utility room, so Berenice had previously told him. Edith and Marigold chatted in the sunroom, whilst Berenice played languidly in the rear garden.

Stealthily he had edged round the far side of the large house, focused and alert. The sunroom was a three-sided affair and an upper oblong window was open on his side. He hunkered down and listened. Afterwards he'd wished he hadn't.

'Do you ever think of Jonathon, Edith?' purred Marigold. 'I have his number if you do.'

It was a familiar conversation to Edith. She sat in silence, but not quite. A sobbing started and a low moan left Edith's throat.

'Edith, so many times I have told you. Leave this warped man you live with. Go back to Jonathon. He waits for you. He knows about the abortion of his child, I couldn't hide it from him, he quizzed me endlessly, he suspected anyway. He has been helping Julian and me on the side lines. He waits for you, Edith.'

In fact, Jonathon was to pay Marigold handsomely if Edith returned to him.

'Julian and I would love to have you and Jonathon living close by again. What fun we would have. Think about it. Leave that bothersome child with William. I should never have matched her up with you both, despite your request. She is trouble, loud and too inquisitive – she will bring you trouble, that one.'

Out of the corner of his eye William could see Berenice. She sat on a path in the back garden and picked petals off a flower. He loved her, even though she was not his own, but Edith and life prevented him from showing her very often.

Now he knew that Edith had been unable to carry the twins to term because of these two butchers. He had always suspected a prior intervention, miscarriage or abortion. From the stories Peter had reported to him, Julian was a callously eager partner in this duo of death.

The plan was formed. He would target Julian, simply because Marigold adored him. See how she would like it when a loved one was wrenched violently away from her. The idea had taken a whole year to ferment. In the end it had not been so very difficult.

But it had been risky.

Now, sitting on the train, racing back to Edith and Berenice from Glasgow, his beating heart started to slow down. He lifted his hand to wipe a bead of sweat off his brow and noticed, calmly, a spot of blood on his shirt cuff. No matter.

Julian's evening ritual of a slow, laboured walk through the park, after dinner, watching for prostitutes, had been his undoing. Passing close to an ancient oak he had paused to look down as he nestled his cigarette in the palm of his hand ready to light it away from the breeze.

He never looked up again.

For William it was just like the Japanese soldier he had garrotted years earlier. Julian fought little and gurgled profusely. As William tugged violently on the sturdy thin wire he had twisted around Julian's neck, he heaved once for the memory of his own twins, so cruelly wrenched from Edith. Julian wrestled in vain. The second violent upwards pull was for Peter, his death witnessed by a frightened elderly prostitute, unwilling to give evidence. The third fatal twist and tug on the wire was for all the women the reluctant prostitute had said would be glad to see Julian die painfully. It could have taken seconds, but William spun the ordeal out as long as he dared, finally sitting Julian down, leaning against a tree. William walked on, unobserved he thought, to the silent cheers of the women of the night. He had a train to catch.

Now, ready to greet his family again, he would tell Edith that the ex-servicemen's meetings were over. It was a shame; he had enjoyed this extension of the war with his comrades. Unsure of how he would cope, now that he did not have the planning and the sorties to look forward to, he pondered his immediate past.

Twenty kills in so many years. None ever detected, but some a very near disaster. Each kill a cleansing for the killer, a sigh, a tear, then an agonised moment or two before declaring that they would leave the group. Their work complete, mission accomplished. He had participated in twelve. Each time it was over, the remaining group would meet to reflect and plan ahead.

William had never questioned Edith's faithfulness to him since they had been married. But he reflected far too often on the first time he'd taken her. He had taken virgins whilst at university, he knew the feel. He had taken women who had given birth, he knew the feel. Inside Edith felt rough, as if scarred somehow. For the first few years he had no real inkling of her past. She gave nothing away. As he'd left her body that first time he looked down into frightened eyes, tears of shame welling up which she hid behind other emotions. The back room of a friend's house, close to the café where they had met after the war. Not ideal, both still mainly clothed, desperation mingled with shyness. Fleeting thoughts scurried to the far reaches of his mind, but beneath him was the woman who had kept him alive during his war. How she had kept herself alive was not for debate at the moment. As he looked forward to his imminent marriage, he buried his doubts just as shallowly as he'd buried the dead Japanese guard.

Indeed, these thoughts festered. Initially he'd blamed her totally for the miscarriage so early on in their marriage. Layers of blame heaped upon Edith which erupted into violence when his muddled mind could make no sense of it all. He knew he was ill in a way all other traumatised ex-prisoners of war were ill. But he was hurting from some as yet, unfathomable betrayal and he needed someone to blame.

As the years had progressed, he knew there had to be a link to Marigold and Julian. His very intuitive daughter always called Marigold Hart the witch; innocence can often be threatened by evil in no tangible way. At first, he joined with Edith in admonishing Berenice, who stubbornly refused to change her mind and was often to be heard whispering the word 'witch' over and over again, supposedly under her breath in the back of the car, as they drove up to spend time in Scotland with Marigold and Julian.

As he'd waited in the car for them both, outside the Harts', the trained soldier in him was alerted. Couples walked quickly by, eyes down, as if scared. Women dressed to invite comment paused under trees in the park opposite and pointed to the house, then strangely hugged each other, turned away and tottered off on their high heels. Dogs that had been quietly walking on the lead with their owners sauntering behind them suddenly rushed forward, barking crazily and straining to be let off the lead. With gums rolled back, teeth flashing and tails down they howled their discontent. Birds in the park swooped low and shot off in another direction, never ever flying over the Harts' house. The jigsaw of evil was complete in William's mind. It was then that he had decided to research their background and he had recruited Peter, who had stubbornly refused to leave the group after his own kill.

It was over.

Peter's death avenged.

Many deaths avenged.

William was alone now. On the train, fresh from his last kill.

Edith heard the phone in the hall ring and wondered if that would be William informing her of the time his train arrived. She hated the noise and smells of the station. William would get a cab, she hoped. She wanted to talk to him about a visit she had planned to wish her father happy birthday. She needed William to drive them. That was all. Once in Blackpool she felt at home and would circle her family with fierce drive and energy. Especially her niece, Irene. Like a deflated balloon Edith always returned home after each of these trips, simply to plan the next one.

In Scotland, Marigold still had the police poring over her house, looking for clues, no doubt. Julian lay, curiously straight-limbed now on the stretcher in the ambulance, waiting to be sent to the morgue. Blood dripped still from his severed throat and joined the drips of countless others beneath his now stone-cold body. Marigold could not easily look at his face. It was a rictus mask of surprise and horror. She had stared into his astonished eyes, wide open and frightened still. No deep image there of who had done this. Like the police, she concluded he had been attacked from behind. His neck had been broken at the same time as his throat was sliced by the garrotte. The ferocity was seemingly personal, not random.

She imagined any number of aggrieved men and husbands who might have done this. For the police she smiled, offered them tea and sought to pluck a name from her head of someone who might have wanted to murder the saint she called her husband.

Although the park had been dark, it had been busy. The police knew only too well the ladies who hung around waiting for clients. Strangely none had seen a thing. Bizarrely they had to stifle smiles as they recounted their innocent stroll through the park and horror at nearly tripping over Julian's dead body. Without real evidence the police had no leads. It would become a cold case.

As they left with Julian's corpse in the ambulance, Marigold called Edith. In shock she revealed the facts and despite Edith's soothingly calm efforts to comfort her, Marigold was rigid with disbelief. There was nobody else she felt she could talk to. Julian was gone. Their business was compromised. As Marigold fell asleep, she vowed to disband the adoption agency. She would visit church the very next day. She had to organise the funeral. Moreover, she needed to organise her soul. She did not want to join Julian in hell. But she suspected that if she did not atone very quickly that was where, most certainly, she would end up. A lost cause indeed. Lost years ago, in the one fact she refused to let surface. Her calculated slaying of her own sister.

By the time William arrived home that night, Berenice was tucked up in her bedroom. She had been alerted to Marigold's call by the urgency and intensity of her mother's replies. It was strange indeed. For weeks her mother would be almost comatose, curled up on the sofa or perched on a red plastic stool in the kitchen. Then her grandfather might call. Or a situation with Irene would be relayed to her. Then her mother took on another persona and was galvanised. A woman on a mission to sort things out. It was that kind of tone to Edith's voice that had caused Berenice to tiptoe to the top of the stairs and listen to the conversation. She heaved a sigh of relief when it became clear that it was not the emergency services calling about her father. She stopped rocking and holding her knees tightly to her body. Angst, blood and gashes were synonymous with her father's existence, had been since she first ever had memories of him.

No sooner than her mother had put down the telephone than her father arrived. By now she realised that the witch's husband had been murdered. Her father seemed only interested in murdering a cup of tea and having a fag. Her mother tutted and walked back into the lounge to watch her TV drama, somehow taking small comfort in the fact that other people's woes were worse than her own, hugging the rank dressing gown about her. Her father was heard to stifle a laugh and ended up coughing his guts out. Sometimes she really liked her dad. But not often enough. She just prayed this death didn't require a trip up to visit the disgusting house and the bereaved witch. There followed an epic argument.

Her father had said that if she wanted to go and support Marigold at the funeral then Edith could find her own way there. He wasn't taking Berenice out of school or having any more lectures cancelled because of this situation. Edith was heard screaming about his time off for ex-comrade meetings but William was having none of it. The glass-panelled dining-room doors slammed, then rattled alarmingly as they settled back into their frames. The kitchen door whooshed shut just as fiercely but less noisily. The doors from the kitchen and then to the back garden, through the garage, whammed in unison and sympathy with the other stressed household doors and Berenice ran to her bedroom window. Predictably, her father was pacing around the edges of the garden. Round and round he went till the purple veins on his neck subsided and he stopped running his fingers through his rapidly thinning hair. He reminded her of the two tigers from Blackpool circus that had been sent to Blackpool zoo to retire. Round and round the edges of their enclosure they paced, desperate now to escape, as they could finally see the sky. She wondered if her father longed to escape just as much. She guessed he might, because if he felt anything like she did in the house, he must be plotting escapes daily.

Her lovely dog Beth hid behind the garden shed until her father's veins disappeared, then sulkily followed him round the garden. When he stopped to stroke the dog, Berenice knew that all was OK again. She leapt back onto her bed and not long after heard her parents coming up to bed. They thought she didn't know that they slept separately. They never made the sounds that her friend Janet's parents had made when they were in the same bedroom.

Berenice and Janet had heard them often when they'd been perched on the outhouse roof, surveying the neighbours. Janet said they were making babies.

Berenice knew her parents would never make that noise because it seemed like a lot of giggling and fun was taking place. That never ever happened in her house.

She wished she could sneak out and talk to Janet now, or even to Irene.

Her mother was always slightly odd when she played or giggled with Irene.

Such a lot of weird in one family.

It was a miracle that she was sane.

CHAPTER 10

1946–1953
I NEVER SET EYES ON YOU

Edith did indeed have something in common with William. Her young soul was shattered into thousands of jagged pieces.

At the start of their marriage, she had pleaded with him to let her go out to work. But some men in the 1940s and 50s still expected to provide for their womenfolk and in this respect, William had still not been able to break free. Edith's quest for work symbolised all his repressed inadequacies and he lashed out at Edith in a way that was to set a pattern until his death.

Edith was bruised, angry and scared. She told nobody and battled on. She just did not have the physical strength to fight him. Especially after the gruelling recovery following the miscarriage of her twins.

Her father's poor hearing was a casualty of World War One and indirectly her partial loss of hearing was a casualty of the backlash from World War Two. William's right hand came into contact with her right ear far too often. He was comfortable with conflict, particularly of a marital nature and however politely Edith framed a request it was always received as a challenge.

Early in 1951 Edith used William's absence in London to invite Sister Hart down. The Ministry of Defence was mounting an exhibition of rare Changi pictures and William's were the centrepiece at the Imperial War Museum. Edith and Marigold would have the whole weekend to themselves. He did not ask her to go with him, this was his world. Edith never invited Marigold when he was home. That was her world.

They talked long into the night of exploits up in Glasgow. Edith was still virtually incapacitated by her secret desire for Jonathon. She longed to have an excuse to go to Glasgow on her own and see him. She was equally furious that she was shackled to a man she finally realised she mainly pitied. Sister Hart was to bide her time with this one. She could see an adoption on the horizon, but not yet. Edith was still far too consumed with grieving in general.

The timing was wrong.

On Sunday, Edith and Marigold walked the blustery prom from Cleveleys to Fleetwood, heads down against the ear-numbing coldness, dodging the spewed-up seaweed, and made it in one piece to the cemetery in Fleetwood. It was something of a monthly ritual for Edith. She gazed at the monument to her gorgeous, playful, brother Campbell and spoke, yet again, of her sorrow and regret over his death. She had long since forgiven her father for his cruel words. Marigold shivered, desperate to get out of the cemetery. It seemed like the occupants of the nearby graves were sending stabs of icy shivers into her shins and it spooked her. Both women's shoes were now wet from the perpetually soggy earth in the cemetery.

To prompt a reaction and thus get out of the place quickly, she blurted out a lie that Jonathon had left for Germany in order to find his family. Instead of marching off in a fit of pique, Edith crumpled onto the ledge around the grave. Holding her head in her hands she wept, out of frustration, lost hope and fear for her future with William. A darkness descended. Marigold was having none of it. She pulled her up roughly and marched her into Fleetwood, where they had tea and scones at Pablo's restaurant in Adelaide Street. The glowing red bars of the electric heaters had soggy shoes stacked all around. It was a popular café after Sunday pilgrimages to the cemetery.

The warm Lancashire greeting of the staff, many of whom still had their teeth fixed at her father's surgery, revived Edith, along with the strong Northern tea. Marigold found it difficult when surrounded by good wholesome people. It was hard to smile back into the eyes of genuine warmth, when your heart harboured such evil. The waitresses left the two women alone once they had been served. As if a chill surrounded them both. They might enquire if they needed anything else; but the waitresses did not like the look of Marigold Hart at all. She continually emanated almost tangible, toxic, negativity.

Shortly afterwards, Marigold left on the tram to Blackpool then back on to Glasgow. When Edith returned home that Sunday, William was already back. He knew she must have been to the cemetery. He looked shattered. He sat with his head in his hands crying. She was fortunate that he did not notice her own red eyes.

His father had died whilst he had been away viewing

the consummate absurdities of war, in a vividly sobering exhibition. The pictures had been well received, army generals and elderly Museum curators, both absent from the field of real war, had been savagely and piercingly reminded of what the young soldiers had endured. Thank God the pictures were in black and white. Nobody expected the exhibition to last too long; the nation needed to be cheered up, not constantly reminded of horror.

It was only hours ago that he was on the journey home from London, viewing the war-ravaged country and desperately trying to remain buoyant. He remembered Edith's extreme reaction to the first images of Nazi death camps. He'd seen similar looks on faces in the museum that day. That she could feel so much for the German atrocities yet so little for him baffled him. Trips to the cinema and the Pathé News reports in the intermissions had often horrified Edith, as she had surveyed the clean-up of the concentration camps and viewed the original horrific footage the Americans filmed during liberation. She wept for Jonathon. Wept for his pain. She wept for her lost love. She wept for her lost babies. Until finally, she did not know what she was weeping for any more and she staggered red- eyed and confused of soul out of the Odeon cinemas and back to her reality. And then she wept again. She never thought to comfort William for the flashbacks he must have had. He just silently wept inside, until it all got too much.

After Jack's funeral, Edith was tasked with supporting Faith as William mingled with the mourners in the back room, sipping tea and eating fish-paste sandwiches. Sitting in the front parlour, after everyone had left, Edith shivered.

The pervading sea frets that rolled in from the iron-grey Irish Sea had wormed their way into the terraced house. Edith surveyed Faith. She was partially blind from cataracts and had stubbornly refused home help, just as she now refused to go into an old folks' home. Edith stood up to pace around and stamp her feet in an effort to get warm. The hem of her black skirt caught the dried flower arrangement in the cold hearth, which crackled and seemed to Edith to have a similar texture and sound to Faith's skin and voice. She waited impatiently for William to finish cleaning the stains of death from the scullery floor, where her father-in-law had died. He had coughed himself dead from far too many Woodbine cigarettes. Faith had been too blind to see the stains and they were starting to rot and smell.

As a proud working-class Lancashire woman, Faith wanted Edith to know what she thought of her insistence on looking for work. It was often mentioned to Faith when she remarked on how peaky her son looked and he used it as an excuse to hide the real tensions in his marriage. Rarely did Faith get a chance to speak to her alone. Her son needed a good woman at home when he returned from his job as a teacher. Bread and dripping on the oiled tablecloth, six pennies' worth of tripe and some batter bits, a mug of steaming hot tea and a bit of a cuddle. To Faith her son looked thin and pinched. That William and Edith had clearly not been getting along was obvious to all at the funeral.

'What's wrong with you and my son? Are you too high and mighty to look after him properly? Did your posh mother not show you how to cook? Too many maids in your house for your own good, was there? Because if that's the case then he can come back here and live with me, now that me man's gone! You're no bloody good for him, everyone can see that!'

Edith's rather shallowly buried dislike of this fisherman's wife surfaced alongside all the other twisted messed-up thoughts. She did something she had never done before. She slapped Faith hard, very hard. Then she rose and excused herself quite politely. She left the house, slamming the front door so violently that her husband's childhood clogs danced on the mantelpiece in the front room as William was emerging from the back parlour with a perplexed look on his face.

Walking briskly along the cobbles in her smart black patent block-heeled shoes, she turned the corner away from the house and slowed down a bit. She was actually ashamed of her reaction to Faith. She walked along the cobbled streets, passed the Mount and with flagging adrenalin sank onto a wooden viewing bench on the prom. That she was frustrated and bitter was not in denial. The solution was elusive. Although Sister Hart had mentioned adoption, she was not convinced it was the right path at all. The shame of acknowledging to the world that somehow her body was corrupted, revolted Edith utterly. She barely dwelt on this reality herself; to discuss it with others would be excruciatingly difficult and embarrassing for her. William had looked so hurt as she'd left him in his mother's hallway. Of course, he would have heard the slap. This was not the day when it should have occurred.

William was exhausted from the funeral arrangements which had fallen upon him, the only child. His father had died of a coughing bout, so prolonged and intense that his lungs had collapsed as his heart had burst. He'd reached out for his Woodbines then subsided onto the stone-flagged floor of the scullery in a heap of vile green phlegm and dark brown blood. Sixty fags a day for forty-five years fairly much guaranteed as much.

Back in his Harris Street home, William had his arms around his mother.

'That woman of yours has some spunk in her after all. But I don't think you bring out the best in each other. What's the matter?'

William wrapped his arms around the mother he was supposed to be comforting and sought refuge in her thin brittle embrace. She was a cunning old bird.

'Come home, William.'

And he did, the very next day. Edith was later to accept his decision, as it was just temporary, until his mother had adjusted. They all had to adjust somehow.

Edith temporarily revelled in the solitude of her home. No guilt was felt, just relief, and peace.

Yvette and Douglas had been to the funeral, in support of William, and left early to get back to baby Irene. They missed all the drama with Edith and her mother-in-law. They had married in haste. Living with his parents, Douglas was trying, not very convincingly, to subdue his wanderlust and be the perfect son and business partner his parents wanted him to be. Annie, his first conquest, lived far too conveniently close. He often had to pop over and beg for last- minute dental supplies that he had forgotten to order, she was such a temptation. The surgery she worked in was three minutes away and stealing so much of his father's business too.

He would shout out to Yvette that he was off out for five. Yvette was a canny lass. One afternoon, whilst baby Irene slept, she followed Douglas to this new dentist's surgery. The sign said closed. She had seen the dentist leaving in his black Austin. It was Wednesday afternoon. Everywhere shut on Wednesday afternoon. But not, apparently, Annie's legs. Through the back-kitchen window Yvette saw them wrapped around Douglas's neck as he pounded away, screaming out the same incomprehensible moans he made with her. Fleetingly Annie locked eyes with Yvette and grinned. Revenge was complete.

Yvette rushed home, packed her bags and was back in Kirkham before the sun set. Irene was still asleep. As Douglas came back, very pleased with himself, he was appalled to find his child alone in the bedroom. Yvette's possessions were gone. His life came crashing down on him and still a mother's boy at heart, he ran to May and wept till he heard Irene wake.

'Mother, I don't know what to do with the child,' he beseeched. May knew exactly what to do with the child.

By nightfall baby Irene was asleep in Edith's arms. For once it seemed like heaven in her home. She'd called Sister Hart with the good news, who had initially flung a vase at the front door when she had put down the receiver.

Edith nursed Irene, a placid baby, with all the love and tenderness as if she were her own. William came home from his mother's, one month later and was amazed at what he found. Edith was alert and loving. A purpose to her day had arrived. A purpose to her life had arrived. Her destiny as a mother, snatched away from her twice before, was finally fulfilled. This child was now her own and nobody would remove it from her grasp. On outings, she never corrected the townsfolk who commented on the beauty of this dark-haired, doe-faced child. She adored being called mother or mummy as passers-by looked at sweet, innocent Irene.

Suddenly William saw a side of Edith previously buried. He was calmer because of it and Edith's insatiable appetite for all things Irene left him alone to work at night without comment, to visit his friends when there was an occasion for it and generally to spend time just existing without any interaction with Edith. This he could cope with. Just. Baby Irene was melting his heart too.

Edith was like a person reborn. From the moment she woke to gaze into the peaceful eyes of Irene she was in love so deeply that to imagine her not there caused her to physically ache. The toddler ate everything given to her and tottered beseechingly into Edith's arms at eleven months gurgling 'Mamma'.

Edith actually thought her heart would burst when she heard that. Outings to Fleetwood Market to buy new clothes for the growing Irene took all day. Often, she was stopped as women bent down and ruffled the dark straight hair of gorgeous, placid Irene. They commented on her fair complexion and told Edith how lucky she was to have such a small- boned, petite, bonny child. Edith floated from inside stall to outside stall and back again, buying far too much and spending her evening taking the clothes on and off Irene. Irene never complained. She smiled vacuously at Edith, her enormous brown eyes oozing liquid love, and Edith was transfixed by it all.

Unbeknown to Edith, one of the stallholders in the Market was baby Irene's uncle. He'd left the docks and set up a stall selling knocked-off tins of fruit. He knew who Edith must be because on one such outing to the market Douglas had been with her, buying baby clothes for his daughter, and had poked Edith saying, 'Come on sister dear, what should I buy?'

He'd remembered Douglas from the chippy when he'd first been introduced to him and the whole sorry situation. None of Yvette's relatives had been invited to the wedding, that had been an order from Douglas.

Yvette's brother would have jumped over his wooden stall and clouted Douglas then and there if he could have. But that would have got him evicted from the market plus another night in the foul-smelling cells at the police station and he could not go there again, thank you!

The possessive look, glued on Edith's face, both alerted and alarmed Yvette's brother. At lunchtime he popped over to the raised market café for a brew and a bacon butty and recounted the incident to a busty blonde he had designs upon for closing time. The waitress knew who he was talking about as she had served Edith many times and even heard her talking about her baby daughter to passers-by.

At home in Kirkham that night he speedily relayed all of this to Yvette. She was having second thoughts about her hasty departure from the luxury of Fleetwood anyway. The milkman she'd hitched up with shortly after her desperate escape from Douglas's deception was proving fickle. He had a reputation, and the closed cab of his milk float rattled in the back lanes of more than one household in the vicinity.

That night she called Douglas. He too was downcast. Gordon was rapidly declining with age related illnesses and Douglas was more or less running the surgery himself. To expand and beat the competition he needed to employ a locum and be a proper business manager. No more fooling around. May was relying on him. If he was truthful, Yvette had organised quite a lot in the household since the maids had left. He needed her. The man in him admitted that he wanted her too. A chance remark by Annie meant he was aware of the rivalry between the women and he had the feeling of being used as a pawn in Annie's mission of revenge.

He must put all this behind him now and win Yvette back, then Irene.

Edith reacted with horror as, later in the week, her mother told her the news that Douglas and Yvette were talking to each other again. Her heart beat wildly and she felt physically sick. She excused herself and Irene quickly from the weekly visit she made to her parents and pulled Irene along, uncomplainingly as always, till she got on the tram and went home for a lie-down and a think.

Upon reaching home that night and discovering the truth behind Edith's worries, William looked up Sister Hart's number in their red plastic flip-action telephone book in the hall and called her. A call she had been long waiting for.

Could they adopt? Well for sure, she purred. But it will cost.

Douglas saw William battling against the winds as he fought his way through the sand dunes that separated the top of his road from the pounding sea. They had agreed to meet in a hurry, hiding as they must from Edith. They walked in silence for a while and finally settled into the comforting warmth of a concrete viewing shelter. Neither had actually been completely alone in the company of the other before. Douglas told William that he wanted toddler Irene back, as soon as possible. William had suspected the nature of the meeting, once he had realised why Edith had been so upset the previous night. Douglas still had a lot to talk about with his father when he got home. He had made a costly mistake with Annie.

For William, the vision of the months of almost calm married life were melting fast. He was more frightened of telling Edith that toddler Irene was going back to her parents at the weekend than he had ever been of any moment in Changi. By the following Sunday Edith had been prescribed Valium for the day and Mogadon for the night. The result was a physically functioning yet mentally comatose female adult.

The handover had been beyond words. Irene looked back towards Edith and stretched out perfectly formed little arms and screamed melodically for her mamma, Edith. Yvette marched the few steps from Edith's front porch to Douglas's waiting car and sat down in the front with Irene on her knee. As Douglas drove off, Irene pressed her face against the window and tried to wave. William had to pick Edith up off the porch floor and carry her into the front lounge. She wept for her lost babies and she wept for Jonathon and herself. Then she just stopped with the exhaustion of it all and stared blankly at the sparkling leaded windows of her bay-fronted house, trying to imagine baby Irene in the room. When she was finally medicated and asleep William called Sister Hart again.

A baby was required. She knew that. She promised to call

Edith in the morning.

A replica of Irene was ordered. Marigold was unsurprised at Edith's request. With the same birthday?

Of course.

Marigold Hart had been contriving the moment for some time. There had been horrific failures. Near full-term babies plucked out on April 11th. She had tried this twice last year. The babies had died. One of the prostitute mothers also. Julian had thrown their bodies in the cesspit behind the utility room. Marigold looked on from the sunroom as he had done this. Human remains floated nauseatingly to the surface and the stench would have caused tumours if it had been inhaled too deeply. Nobody ever bothered with the scum of life anyway, they just disappeared and became, literally, scum

This year it looked more hopeful. She had three women in mind. Two were lined up and ready to have a caesarean on April 11th, just weeks away. In two weeks, Irene would be two. William needed this sorted...quickly. He was oblivious to the extent of Sister Hart's efforts to comply with Edith's specific requests. All William wanted was his life back again. He cared not about the actual baby, as long as Edith recovered, and left him alone with his work and reunions. She didn't even want sex right now. And for that he couldn't even thump her, as his mother-in-law was visiting far too often these days. No, he had to sort this out and he put all his faith in Sister Hart.

Luck prevailed. A youngster, an ex-beauty queen, had found her way to Sister Hart. She was working as an account assistant locally, having been banished from her family home by her stern mother called Sarah, who had told her not to return until the bastard baby had been born and given away. Her due date was April 11th. The woman was attractive, dark-haired, strong-limbed and desperate to give this child away and restart her life. Her cousin, who she was staying with, was a bookkeeper at Glasgow Infirmary and that's how she had made her way to Sister Hart and the adoption agency.

On April 11th 1953 this child was born naturally, screaming and kicking. A foul-tasting rubber teat was thrust into her mouth as she was torn from her exhausted mother, who turned away, desperate not even to look at this bundle of trouble that had blighted her belly for nine months.

Edith and William were there, pacing outside the birthing room. Sister Hart came out carrying the baby and placed her into Edith's open arms. The rubber teat dislodged itself on handover and baby Berenice, as she was to be called, screamed loudly. The mother inside the birthing room shed no tears as she heard that scream, but her body reacted and her breasts leaked. She looked down and stuffed hankies round her aching pumping breasts. She had given her baby away. Now she had to get on with her life.

Baby Berenice looked healthy, had the requisite dark hair, albeit curly, and was a trifle larger- limbed than Irene had been, but nevertheless she was acceptable. Edith handed over the cheque to Sister Hart, two thousand pounds, a fortune. Gordon had cashed in some family shares in ICI, following discussions with Douglas and William. He was not overly keen on it all but had been persuaded by May that it was the right thing to do. He was too old and weary to decline the request. A part of him felt sorry for Edith.

He was sorry that he had sent her to her grandmother's, all those years ago, but he was far too proud and old to tell her that now. Better to buy her the baby she wanted. At least the baby was of British descent, the birth certificate was to record that prominently. Gordon looked at May and they resigned themselves to another wee small intruder, into their aloof, Scottish family.

Julian was delighted with the adoption money and he and Marigold purchased a large Rover and bought new furniture, then went on an extended touring holiday of Britain. Still there was money left over when they got back home. It had been worth the wait. All those nights of listening to Edith and probing her family's wealth had paid off. All had been confirmed of course when they had journeyed down for the wedding of Edith and William. After that it had been a waiting game that paid off. William and Edith were never told who the birth mother and father were and that was just the best way forward at the time. It was all recorded but never spoken of.

In their eyes, Edith was always a potential money-earner. William was weak from the war. Mentally fatigued. He might not be able to hold on to Edith. Jonathon was still desperate for her, aware of the marriage and constantly alerted to its failures by Marigold, who still saw him regularly. Edith thought he was away in Germany and had put thoughts of his loving out of her mind. Now that she had Berenice all would be well. Sister Hart doubted it and worked the angles at every opportunity.

Nightly Jonathon prayed that Edith would make her way back to him, and he would even accept the child, a replacement for his dead son perhaps. He quizzed Marigold Hart about her often.

After the war he had requested to be sent copies of the newspapers and magazines that Hitler had proudly used to desensitise the public and gain their trust that his policies were the right way forward. Reading these, Jonathon was in despair about the sanity of his fellow Germans, repulsed at the thought of living and working with them again. It was only after Germany fell that he discovered the mind-numbing truth behind the Final Solution and the industrial-scale gas chambers probably used to exterminate his family. He could not believe that the ordinary German had had no idea of this. As post-war Britain revved up its industrial output, Jonathon could not look at smoke spewing out of factory chimneys without a shudder. He had no need to go to Germany now. All his fanciful thoughts of finding his wife and child hiding in the cellar of his bombed house were eradicated as he had watched the bulldozers flattening his street on an extended BBC report into the destruction and rebuilding of Germany. He had settled down in front of the television, hoping to forget for a while. Now he truly could forget and he realised that he wanted Edith back in his life whether she was Jewish or not.

But Edith was in baby heaven again. Reality, however, didn't take too long to intervene though. Every time Berenice cried, which was a lot, Edith's loosely bound fabric of truth unravelled. She was not the perfect baby.

Every time Berenice pushed rather than nuzzled, Edith tensed and sighed. Berenice was born and collected by her new parents, all on one Saturday. Edith and William placed her in a new shiny cream-coloured plastic carrycot, on the back seat of their four-door Ford Anglia 100E. They then set off on the long drive back from Glasgow to Fleetwood. Rationing was still in force in 1953. Baby Berenice would be issued with her ration card in due course. But new clothes were not easily available.

Edith nodded off for most of the journey and the rocking of the rudimentary suspension on the car lulled Berenice to sleep as well. William was just busy fighting his own wars in his head and glad of the quiet drive, if not the inner peace. They wanted to show off their baby to their parents. Upon entering Fleetwood, William had taken a roundabout perhaps too sharply, as he was getting tired and longing for a cup of tea.

The car windows were open due to William smoking, even though there was still an April chill in the air. It was Saturday and the traffic was quite heavy as shops were closing all around them. The noise in the car, mingling with the noise outside, meant neither new parent heard the back door swing open as William hugged the inner lane of the roundabout a shade too fast.

Neither then heard it click shut as William righted the car to travel straight on to Lord Street.

Edith turned around as he parked and screamed.

Her scream was high-pitched, forcing William quickly to put his hand over her mouth to instantly shut her up and stop the ear-piercing sound that reminded him of things best not mentioned. Her arms and legs flailed and when she was nearly choking William let go and looked around to the back seat to where she was pointing.

Berenice had gone.

The back seat was empty.

William catapulted his brain into the present, a rare ability he had, when he chose to. He roughly crunched the gearstick into first and sped off, just as May was looking out of the front window of her house, expecting to see this new baby. She thought nothing of it, as she found William to be quite odd at the best of times. Perhaps they would come by later.

Edith was gulping for air, whilst crying and blaming William for this catastrophe; what her reasoning was for this was not clear in her head, but William had a sneaky suspicion of what had happened.

At a petrol station just outside Garstang he had been forced to stop to fill up. Edith had got out too and opened the back door to tuck Berenice's lovely shawl, a present from Sister Hart, closely round her. Berenice had wriggled it loose once the car had stopped. William had paid the garage owner in cash, telling Edith to hurry up and get back into the car.

Now, he suspected that she had not shut the back door properly. No sooner had he processed these thoughts than he approached the roundabout into Fleetwood, the very one he had swung around five minutes earlier and there, sitting on the raised grass mound of the central roundabout, was a brand-new cream-coloured shiny plastic cot.

The shawl was already outside the cot and had blown on to the busy road. It was shredded.

Berenice had, even then, been desperate to put distance between herself and the witch.

William parked illegally on the central grassed area of

the roundabout and Edith jumped out of the car running wildly to the cot. Berenice was still inside, purple-faced and very indignant, with oozy green splodges exiting her badly fitting cloth nappy. The bump as she had landed had winded, then frightened her. She saw Edith staring down, with the dying afternoon sun behind, almost as if an angel had rescued her. Almost.

And thus ended the second drama of her life.

The first had been the birth.

And she was only six hours old.

CHAPTER 11

1970s MOMENTS OF CLARITY

'There's a call for you, take it upstairs on the bedroom extension,' shouted her husband, Jed. He had to shout, the 70s disco sounds blaring out from the hired DJ's speakers were making the wattle and daub in the listed Buckinghamshire cottage in Lane End shudder in protest.

Looking back over her shoulder, Berenice paused on the steep staircase. Jed was clearly loving his moment, a party to cement his career as partner in a prestigious law firm in Oxford. Senior partners had flown in from the Channel Islands and beyond. He stood tall and willowy in his new Moss Bros pin-striped three-piece brown suit with his jacket discarded early on over the end of the banister. She touched it tenderly, amazed at the feel of the fine wool, further amazed they finally had enough money to even consider buying such luxury.

He was willowy and edgy, with strawberry blonde hair that caressed the back of his neck. He had a lopsided endearing half-smile, not a smirk, definitely a smile and it had melted her heart the moment she had set eyes on him over six years ago. Tonight, though, his attention was all on a legal secretary with more cleavage than brains and a skirt with tassels on, a kind of Temple Church meets Soho look. Berenice looked away, her husband did not. Maybe she would give up teaching. Maybe not. More time to dwell and fester. Not good. Then she climbed the stairs to take the call in the relative silence of their pretty pink bedroom, with pine wardrobes and floral wallpaper borders.

Before picking up the heavy cream receiver Berenice caught a glimpse of her married self in the mirror. She had opted for slinky black. She had first flirted with this semi-Gothic style at Oxford, but then finally fell for the lovely florals of Laura Ashley. Tonight, she had reverted to a bleakly sexy siren look which, she reflected, at twenty-six years of age, might have been a mistake. Clearly was a mistake if she compared herself to the twenty-year-old wannabe downstairs currently flirting with her husband.

She noticed a run in her black fishnet tights. It started at mid-thigh and was beginning to snake its way downwards. She reached for the clear nail varnish bottle on the pretty dressing table to halt the run. Her hair was styled in homage to a Suzi Quatro meets Kate Bush epically coiffed halo. She had recently dieted to within an inch of her life and her hair actually looked weightier than her. Sadly, her cleavage had been flushed down the loo with the weight loss and so the mesh that traversed her chest revealed only ribcage and monumental collar bones. That legal secretary was preying on her mind.

Ah well, hopefully Jed would have moved on by the time she went downstairs. Probably not though. Her mouth twitched in agitation.

The light on the telephone showed the caller was still waiting for her to pick up.

She wondered. One past midnight, on a Sunday morning. Strange. Her parents never called her, she called them. She hesitated.

Last Easter, she had met them in Wales. Sharing a cottage with Jed, an extravagance of cash about to befall him, he'd booked it to surprise her. Her parents turning up uninvited had mildly annoyed her more than Jed. An intrusion when she'd just wanted to eat home-made melba toast and paté curled up in bed with Jed. What was it with Wales? Did they just like following her there?

The light on the telephone showed the caller was still waiting.

No sooner had her parents parked at the cottage, than her mother insisted that she go for a walk with her, alone. Her father looked relaxed and chipper, despite his racing-car- style slide to a halt on the gravel in front of the cottage. Small victories, Dad, small victories.

The yappy white Scottie dog, a present from her father to her mother, following the death of faithful Beth, needed to stretch his little fluffy legs. He seemed to be positively hopping up and down on the sharp-edged Welsh stones beneath his paws. So, after grabbing some wellies and a duffel coat, she slouched off down the lane with her mother, as her father entered the cottage with the familiar blue suitcase wobbling under his outstretched hands. He was attempting the narrow doorway with the horizontal case. Her mother was well out of his view by now, but he dared not break the habit. The consequences of her finding out were beyond thought.

The light on the telephone showed the caller was still waiting.

As soon as they had been out of earshot her mother had turned anxiously to her, complaining that she was at her wits end with her father and his behaviour was too much to bear.

This was somehow new?

Edith had sensed that Berenice was not grasping the essence of it all, so she just blurted it out. Her daughter was married now, she might understand. The problem was, continued her mother, during that stroll in the drizzle in Wales, her father never stopped demanding sex.

Berenice froze.

But Edith plunged on. As had her father, apparently. Having taken early retirement from the university, he had occupied himself in forgotten pursuits. Her mother clutched her geometrically patterned nylon headscarf wildly, as if it comforted her. Four or five times a day.

WHAT?!

Her mother seemed frail. No wonder. What advice could her daughter give her? As Berenice was breathless at the thought of sex four or five times a day, she was actually hoping that her father was giving her husband some advice, but she didn't mention that as her mother, rather uncharacteristically, tugged viciously at the dog trying to pee in the hedgerow. She was speechless as her mother said that she had initiated the drive across to Wales as she knew William couldn't have sex when he was driving and hopefully wouldn't have sex on the sofa-bed on offer in the cottage.

Really? Had her absence from the house rekindled their desires, or was her father just bored? Knowing her father, probably bored. Anything to block out the pain of life.

The light on the receiver showed the caller was still waiting.

She picked it up and listened to the voice on the other end.

'A what?' she shouted.

The noise from the party suddenly erupting through the ancient rafters. 'Wuthering Heights' belted out from the speakers, *Bad dreams in the night, they told me I was going to lose the fight,* sang Kate Bush.

Berenice closed one ear to the music and blocked green-eyed thoughts of whatever the legal secretary might be getting up to in the small confines of their walk-in pantry with her husband.

'Say that again,' and the caller did.

Berenice had but a moment to digest the information before she crumpled. A body blow of a message; air escaped from her lungs, but no sound came out. The party seemed on another planet and her world was spinning. She leant back on the plum coloured quilted headboard and splayed out, sagging, as if her bones had been crushed with the weightiness of the news.

She thought of her father's face the last time she had seen him. She and Jed had been leaving her cousin Irene's extravagant wedding just a few weeks ago. Berenice had thought how swamped Irene had looked in heavy satin and lace, a combination Edith had not entirely approved of, it seemed. Her cousin had wanted a simple ceremony, but her parents had insisted on paying for a grand affair. Perhaps crafting an event twenty-eight years too late for them, but necessary for their daughter. At the wedding, Irene had presented a contrastingly fragile image compared to large-boned Berenice. Edith noted that and said nothing other than pursing her thin lips, which spoke volumes. Berenice thought the herringbone three-piece wool suit from Jaeger had been a tad too stout for a wedding. She wished she suited floaty dresses and frills, but doubted that she ever would.

She longed to be the petite fragile soul that needed taking care of, but it was not her lot in life. Irene did that so much better. Berenice constantly needed to be strong and sturdy. It helped her to survive.

Her parting glance at the wedding had been her father whirling her mother around, very uncharacteristically, as younger dancers gyrated in their own space; her father had held her mother's hands and looked over to Berenice as she yelled goodbye and he had winked. That wink had tugged at her soul and she had wanted to go over and hug him, but Jed had propelled her out to the car. He had a five-hour drive ahead of him and a case in Oxford Crown Court the following morning involving a Jamaican man who had tried to smuggle a frozen chicken out of Sainsbury's under his woolly hat. He had subsequently collapsed with hypothermia and was intent on suing the supermarket!

'How?' Berenice yelled into the phone, but the caller was scant on detail. Her mother was heavily sedated, her father stone-cold dead on a metal slab in a Whitley Bay morgue, aged just sixty.

Jed erupted into the room wanting to know if she was coming back down, his boss was leaving and wished to thank her for the invitation and the party.

'My father died three hours ago.'

Jed froze. He wondered what to do. Did Berenice want to leave right now? There was no reply from her.

She thought of her father's last wink at her. He loved a party apparently. What more was there to learn of this man? Now she would never know. What would he have wanted her to do?

At Oxford, he had been the one to come down when she was curled up in bed in the Radcliffe Hospital, unsure of life, needing direction. She had only opened her upper-storey student-flat window to get air, she told him. The thought of her boyfriend, Jed, shouting and flailing his fists in her direction had made her gulp for air. Unclear how to voice her distress, she had needed to breathe. The sand dunes were far away but the shouting had been present and frightening. Of course, Jed had really no idea what torment he was causing her, what leapfrog to childhood issues his raised voice brought about.

No, she had not been trying to jump. Daft idea. She had just needed air. There had been nowhere to run to in that block of student flats. At home she would have grabbed the family dog, slammed the glass front door and gone for a long walk over the Links and onto the promenade, probably ending up in her favourite café, The Rendezvous. A coffee and a Wagon Wheel, comfort eating her way out of the chaos of home life and its recurring physical and mental abuse.

The college authorities had hedged their bets. A couple of nights' stay in hospital was required. Berenice had clearly been overwrought. Her father had held her hand as she lay in the hospital bed. Too quickly she blurted out the question.

Why had her birth mother given her up for adoption?

Suddenly, all of her life seemed connected to that thought.

Loosed from Edith's grip her father seemed quite normal. He sat beside her on a hard-backed folding metal chair and looked for all the world like a normal person. He smiled. Tension lines eased a tad on his still tanned, but large-pored face. The tropics had left their mark everywhere. He looked down, breathed in, moved on.

'Your birth mother just couldn't keep you – she wanted to, but the father had run off, he was from Armenia. Your mother was one of six girls. Originally from Sweden. That's all I know really. She did want you, Berenice, she did. She just couldn't keep you. Her mother wouldn't allow her to keep the baby. It was so very different then. If we'd had the pill, it, you, might never have even been conceived.'

Ah yes, the pill. A morning necessity for most female students. Her father was looking at her, and she was waiting for a response to information he had been forbidden to utter all those painfully fraught years. Secrets strangled people. He knew. So, he waited. Looking at Berenice he welled up. Would it really have been so bad for her if the surprise court case had returned her to her birth mother in July 1953? Maybe they had been wrong to oppose it? The court papers had arrived out of the blue. There had been a grace time, a pause for reflection for both sides, an unavoidable adoption formality, they had been told.

Then wham.

Her birth mother had wanted her back.

Back to a place she had barely been really. Unless you

count the nine months avoiding swiftly swigged gin and two bumpy, fast trips down a flight of stairs. Berenice was definitely sturdy. The other side had lost. Or perhaps Berenice had lost. Afterwards, Edith had started to sleep again and he had gone back to his contrived normality. Actually, she might have been better off. He shut down those thoughts, the silence had been broken.

'Well, thanks, but it doesn't help that much. Are you going to tell Mother you've told me all of this?' He replied swiftly that he thought it was a good idea not to. It would forever be their shared secret. The first really adult conversation she had ever had with her father. And it was their secret.

She had actually been wanted, for who she was, not who she replaced. That thought healed her somewhat.

And now her father was dead. A swift death, she hoped, not too torturous a fog in the throat.

So, she replied to Jed that no, she was not going to abandon the dying stages of his tremendously successful party of partnership for the already dead, she would be down in a minute, nobody was to be told. She would journey up to Whitley Bay at first light. She had already told the neighbour who had called her of her intentions. Her mother was sedated. She would never know. It felt the right thing to do. In her mind, she saw her father dancing and he smiled at her. She descended the stairs moments later, and stood on the third step watching their late-night revellers dance to the final song of the night, the Bee Gees' hit 'Night Fever'. She joined in, eyes shut, and took the outstretched hands of her father.

'Here I am, prayin' for this moment to last, livin' on the music

so fine, borne on the wind, makin' it mine.'

The music ended. The party was ending. Like a woman possessed, she tidied up for three long hours. Glasses and crockery were stacked in the trays the caterers had left, to be collected later in the day. She found Jed's suit jacket on the back-door hook. She would not think of why it was there right now. Furniture was rearranged and windows flung open to the misty fog as cigarette smoke clung to the curtains which, she reflected, must go to the dry cleaners as soon as. She bathed, ducking under the lather in their smart brown bathtub and emerging fresh and ready for the angst.

At 6.30 am she caught the Oxford to Newcastle train alone and as soon as she sat down, she slept.

Part of the history of her life had died.

Arriving in Whitley Bay, much later in the day, she was met by the neighbour who had called her and he made her a strong cup of tea. Her mother was still asleep upstairs.

After three days of arrangements, her mother emerged from the fog of a drug-induced sleep and turned to face her daughter, who was quietly insisting that she be told the details of her father's massive stroke.

Perhaps, at that point, Edith was glad that she had broached the subject of sex with Berenice in Wales. In whispered embarrassment she admitted that William had been on top of her when he died. As he came, he went. A rigid arched form, convulsed jointly in joy and pain. She had been forced to wriggle out from underneath. In a thin cotton Marks and Sparks nightie she stumbled in the December drifts, barefoot and weeping, to the neighbours. She had rung their bell then collapsed in the arched shelter of their doorway until a sleepy face in a winter dressing gown opened the door and hauled her distraught frame inside.

The ambulance had been called.

The police had been called.

The family doctor had been called. Yes, the same one! Berenice was thankful to miss a face-to-face with him.

After all of that, apparently perhaps as an afterthought, she had been called. Berenice stared at her mother. Her father was dead. He died a lovely death, she thought. She dared not say a word. Cautiously she put an arm around her mother. It was a strange feeling. Frankly she could not remember when she had last done this. Edith felt like a fragile bird, thin-framed and brittle to the touch. Memories of Berenice leaving the house for teacher training popped into her mind. Surely, she must have grown up a bit since then. She had been so harsh. A backwards glance, her mother at the frosted-glass front door looking unsure. Her father absent, again. Being zapped at the loony bin. Again.

'You can rent my room, I'm not ever coming back to live here.'

Yes. Harsh. But heartfelt. She meant it. After her studies she would fend for herself, she was quite sure about that.

A present from her grandfather, to her mother, had been a burial plot close to wee Campbell's grave. So, in order to bury her father, the pilgrimage to Fleetwood commenced again. Her mother sat slumped next to her in the train, her fingers clenched tight, her legs crossed and her lips pursed. Her father was in the goods van, resplendently cosy in cream plush satin and solid oak. Berenice had, earlier, been forced to beseech the Barclays Bank manager in

Whitley Bay to honour a cheque her father had, apparently, signed two days before his death and was for exactly all the money he had in his account, £19,347. Edith had sat at home twiddling her fingers until Berenice came home, cash in hand. Handwriting experts were not called. The bank manager's daughter was a student of her father's. Yes, he would honour the cheque, even though the signature did not match terribly well. The coffin had been purchased and the arrangements were made. Edith was hanging on to her money, safely stashed in another account.

Jed met them at the station, having been alone for the last few days, doing God knows what. They went to the undertaker's chapel in Fleetwood first. To her amazement, many distant relatives, old students and apparent friends were there. She sat and watched her mother glided around the room inviting funeral guests to pop next door for a viewing, something her mother had not even been able to do yet. Berenice had not been in either. Her mother came over and asked her to accompany her in. She refused. A collective gasp ricocheted inaudibly around the room.

'No, I won't go inside if you don't mind, Mummy, I want to remember Daddy with a smile and a wink on his face.'

Her mother froze in mid-step, as if she had been expecting Berenice to follow her automatically. Such insolence from her daughter. Irene would have done as she was told. Her mother marched off, as if determined to confirm the death of this man who had been so very different from the young boy whom she had thought she'd loved.

Everyone looked at their feet and held their breath. From inside the small room, Edith screamed. Jed jumped up to rescue her from the room. Still Berenice refused to go in and see her father, lying in the coffin. Her mother came out, indignant and hysterical. The undertakers had put his false teeth in the wrong way round and the make-up and cream frill around his neck made him look comically effeminate. Thankfully the hearse arrived.

They then went straight to the church.

At the end of the ceremony, Berenice got up to sing the Lord's Prayer. A vision of the last time she had sung in front of her parents swam menacingly into view. She controlled her voice. Her hand shook. Her vocal tribute to her father ended and the coffin was carried out of the church as the last notes hung in the air.

From there, they progressed to the burial, in bitterly cold conditions. On the slow progression through the twists and turns of the cemetery, in the hired black Rolls Royce, they were stopped by a knock on the window. The hearse slid graciously to a halt. Her mother, dressed in her own mother's short mink jacket and a newly purchased Fenwick's French burgundy suit, leant over Jed and wound down the old window, with some difficulty. Outside was the family lawyer, Roger.

Bizarre.

He popped his hand in and managed to avoid Edith grabbing the envelope, saying it was for Berenice from her father. Edith nearly sliced through his arm with the sudden ease she found in winding the window back up again.

The verbal abuse was disturbingly volatile. Edith ranted and foamed as Berenice slid open the stiff cream envelope and extracted the formal notice from the insurers, informing her of the legacy her father had left her upon his death.

Edith's language descended as her tone rose. How could he, she screeched, the number of times she had had to borrow from her own father and all the time he was paying the insurers for Berenice and not for her. She was within inches of a heart attack herself until Jed slid a protective arm around her and, as if suddenly deflated, she responded to his grip and calmed down. Jed turned to wink at his wife. He was quietly estimating how far that cheque would reach. Cars to be bought and home improvements to be made were whirring through his head. Just as Berenice was having similar thoughts. Well done Daddy, thought his daughter, her mind had been taken off the awfulness of the burial.

The hearse stopped and Berenice shoved the letter, which she had refused to show her mother, into the pocket of her black velvet jacket. It was December. It was bitingly cold and desolate. Alarmingly she saw a rip in the back of the ancient mink her mother had thought appropriate to wear. It pleased her. She felt guilty that it pleased her and plodded on to stand next to her mother at the edge of a very, very deep hole in the dark soggy ground.

'I've booked for three,' said Edith.

Three what, thought Berenice idly? She had already told her mother that she would be staying at the house with her until the weekend. So why did they need a hotel booking for three?

'Your father, then me, then you. Booked for three, that's the reason the hole is so deep.'

Berenice took an involuntary step backwards and as she had been holding hands with her mother to her right and her husband to her left, all of three of them wobbled, and alarmed the vicar at the head of the grave.

'I'm not going in that hole, no way, not happening EVER!' she shouted shrilly and the vicar wisely started the short ceremony without delay. Mourners clutched their coats around them as the sharp wind whistled its desolate tune and the sea fret enveloped them all in its deathly damp chills. The coffin creaked and wobbled as it slid on slippery ropes down, down, down. The sods of dark intertidal earth fell, splodged and amassed until finally, after at least thirty minutes, the epically deep hole was filled and her father was obliterated from her mother's view for ever.

A wake had been organised. The £19,347 was being put to very good use. Berenice watched as cousin Irene, freshly returned from her honeymoon, put an arm around her auntie and Edith looked lovingly into the vacant brown pools of love. Sausage rolls were consumed. An enormous amount of alcohol was downed and Edith became giggly and flirtatious. Berenice's uncle Douglas suggested that Berenice and Edith should make their way to the train station and he offered them a lift. Goodbyes were said. Jed decided to leave too, rather too sharply, back to their empty house down south. Berenice sat on the train and watched the calm smiling face of her mother as she slept on the journey back up to Whitley Bay. This time without her father in the goods van.

The next day Berenice found her mother manically rummaging in the front bedroom or office as it was known, which her father had called his domain. It was unclear to Berenice exactly what was being searched for, but academic papers were mixed up with house insurance documents and bank statements, the detritus of death that awaits the unwitting. All round her mother, who was sitting cross-legged on the floor, was this arc of paperwork. Her hysterically urgent sweepings through these papers were slightly unsettling. When Edith leant forward for a closer look, she spied a black metal security box lurking, mostly hidden beneath the chest of drawers.

Berenice was asked to extract it as she was nearest, and with some difficulty she slid the heavy, extremely dusty box out of obscurity and into the light. Edith leant forward, a surprisingly agile move for a woman of sixty, and grabbed the metal handles on the long end of the box. The other papers shrank back out of the way of this obviously important container. The dust flew up and was caught in a winter sunbeam that dared to challenge the solemnity of the occasion by peeking through the hastily closed curtains. The dust, with an unnerving life form, sparkled its way up through the slit in the curtains and sped its way upwards. Berenice was hypnotised in the moment, seeing her father smile and wink once again.

'The bloody box is locked, have you got the key by any chance?'

Edith was beginning to question the depth of the true relationship between Berenice and William. Certainly latterly, after that trip to Oxford when she had been a student, they had seemed to be in contact more. The smile and wink as Berenice departed dear Irene's wedding party had not gone unnoticed and Edith recalled the sadness in his face after their daughter had left. His hands had turned cold, even though the night was hot and he sat down after that dance and never got up again. She had danced with other men then. He had looked relieved.

Trance-like, Berenice moved swiftly to the deep chilly walk-in wardrobe she had left behind in her childhood bedroom. There, on a high shelf above a sturdy rail was a small, pigskin document case. She'd left it behind after she'd visited her parents just before her twenty-first birthday. She pulled it down. It had been a gift from William's father to his son for the same occasion. William had re-gifted it to Berenice on her own twenty-first. She remembered him giving it to her. It had seemed such an oddly archaic present, especially as she and her friends were travelling to London to the Talk of the Town nightclub for a glittering meal and cabaret. She had thought maybe money for a new dress would be given. But no, an old-fashioned, pigskin writing case with various little hidden pockets and secret places. She hadn't even looked inside. She had left it behind at her parents' house.

The Talk of the Town outing with two other couples plus Jed had been fascinating. A glimpse into a London scene she perhaps could be a part of. A glimpse, for Jed, of a lifestyle he definitely wanted to be a part of. The headline act had cancelled and at the last minute, been replaced by Rolf Harris, the Australian performer. He got out his didgeridoo and proceeded to amaze everyone with his rendition of a Stones classic, 'I can't get no satisfaction', followed by the most lurid and sexually explicit jokes Berenice had ever heard.

The stunned audience had tried to line up who they were watching with what they had seen of Rolf Harris on children's TV, and it was proving difficult.

Berenice's group ordered coffee to recover from the shock of the disgusting jokes and they were stunned at the end of the night when the waiter asked them for sixteen pounds. Her parents had paid upfront for the evening. But not, apparently, for the coffee. She would rather have had some cash in her pocket than that stupid pigskin writing case, she had thought at the time. Coins were searched for, and the sixteen pounds was finally found. The memory of the overt sexuality of Rolf Harris's act hung around the edges of all their minds for years to come.

Now, with dawning clarity she began to fumble excitedly into the hidden spaces in the pigskin case. She found the key and knew exactly where it would fit. Perhaps he had left her with the best gift of all, the means to unlocking who she was, where she came from and with that information, freedom to choose. With a steady adult hand, she unlocked the steel box on the floor between her mother and herself.

Edith was lighting a cigarette as the lid sprang open and the details of Berenice's birth and adoption lay bare to the air for the first time in over a quarter of a century. Edith lost her mind, flung the still-lit match into the box and the room filled with smoke.

Berenice walked calmly away and on a scrap of paper in her childhood room she wrote down what she had seen in that split second of clarity.

She looked out of the window, up to the laden sky and thanked him. Edith was to be heard screaming, choking and sobbing in equal proportions.

Berenice started to pack.

Well, actually, Louise started to pack.

That had been her birth name.

The search was on.

CHAPTER 12

1923–1953
THE ARMENIAN CONNECTION

Yeltsy Tevadaze was born one chilly, starless night near Yerevan, the capital of a conflicted Armenia, in 1923. His grandparents had been slaughtered there during the Turkish-led genocide in 1915.

This baby's proud, nationalistic parents, Madak and David, both worked long gruelling hours in the treacherous gold mines close by. They were fanatical about the possibility of a true independence for their strangled country. They had both been brought up by relatives, following their parents' massacre, in the same mountainous village. Listening, night after night, as they grew up, to the tales of horror, rape and mutilation heaped upon them by the invading Turks. Their path was hewn round the fading embers of a dying nation and their fervour was matched by their ferocious belief that they would one day prevail.

Despite their desperately long hours spent at the sprawling mine complex, both parents would walk home, with a spring in their step, hand in hand through warm summers and freezing winters. They would stop, when the view overcame them, either the majestic scenery, or the love mirrored in each other's eyes. They held each other and dreamt of the future, their depth of feeling only rivalled by a fierce love for their country.

Before baby Yeltsy was born, his mother, Madak worked in the mine canteen and her job was to keep the broth hot and hearty for the miners as they stumbled out of the dangerously deep shafts and damp, cramped tunnels, into her steamy hot kitchen. They sat, exhaustedly, on rough wooden benches, to rest their aching limbs for a short while. Her *Harissa* was the best beef stew the miners would often tell her. They felt revived after finishing this food. Her secret ingredient, one of the local *urts*, or herbs. She used thyme. As a young girl, her mother had taught her how to cultivate this to lower the blood pressure of the miners as they were under tremendous pressure each shift. She would always try to ensure that David got extra-large slices of bread to soak up his broth, recharge himself and have strength to complete the backbreaking shifts.

Madak was the sort of woman who cared for them all; she was greatly respected for this, her kind smiles, her devotion to her husband and to the cause. Once home, they would sit with others in the small village, drinking steaming hot herbal tea and eating local lamb, followed by their flatbread, called *lavash*. David reared, caught and butchered the sheep in his precious spare time and Madak, he was often heard to say, made the best lavash in the region. Once replete, they would discuss with other activists the true liberation of their beautiful country, their role in this and how and when it could reasonably be achieved. As the evenings slipped into night, they cuddled each other close and fell into an exhausted sleep.

One night, Madak's only brother, Serge, aged just fifteen, secretly ventured, very recklessly, across the nearby Turkish border, in a raid to try to amass more arms for their struggle. He had heard the many inspirational plans to right the wrongs of 1915 and his impetuous youthfulness blinded him to caution. About him he had secreted the small nuggets of gold some revolutionary miners had stolen and with this he was going to pay for the arms. The barracks close to the border were rumoured to store many guns and ammunition. He would be a hero. His dead parents would look down upon him and keep him safe, of this his innocence assured him. Madak and their extended family would be so proud.

He never returned.

His young, naked, butchered body was tied to a rope and hung at the border crossing for the crows to pick clean. The howling wolves, jumping and ripping at his flesh, as he swung in the wind, alerted the nearby villagers on the Armenian side.

The news filtered through to Madak and she sought comfort in David's arms. She blamed both the Turks and her family; there had been a vulnerability about Serge that only she had seemingly noticed. They all should have held their tongues in front of him. The talk of revolution was subdued. Increased Turkish raids, searching for activists, haunted their movements. Even venturing onto the mountain to search for herbs was restricted. They were crippled by doubt. The vicious rumours that he had run off with the gold were rampant. All false. David had made the trek to the border one night and seen the haunting eyes in the savaged corpse that had once been Serge. An honourable death had not befallen him. Upon his return, David sought comfort from Madak in a way they had refrained from before. Liberation first, babies later.

That was before Serge died.

Afterwards the couple clung to their love, as a raft in which to navigate their grief.

For years their comrades had admired their political drive. But the death of Serge had drawn the couple physically closer, dented their resolve and ability to function rationally should they meet the Turks or Russians on their soil. Madak became introverted, she spoke of Serge in her sleep even, whilst cradling her blossoming belly. Family became everything and most of hers had been felled. Irrationally she reasoned that she would replace her dead brother with this baby. Her friends watched from afar, scared for her mind and concerned for the couple's increasingly vulnerable existence. The Turks paid for information and no amount of broth or lamb would be enough to deter a weak, hungry man faced with a hefty bribe. Their immediate friends could keep them safe for the moment; it was the future that everyone feared.

Between 1914 and 1923, over three hundred and fifty thousand Armenians fled to escape the terrible economic hardships and genocide in their country. Meat became scarcer as various Byzantine, Persian, Russian and Ottoman raiders stole their livestock. Some Armenians fled to live a new life and forget, others to establish a pipeline and channel funds back to Armenia. The Armenian diaspora fuelled the fury and financed the fighters as often as they could. Yet still, Armenians felt like a landslide was permanently about to divide or engulf their country.

As Madak's pregnancy grew, possible separation lay ahead for the couple, as mothers were forbidden in the mine complex. They had to decide what to do and quickly; neither could bear to be parted from the other. From the Black Sea to the Caspian, across mountainous regions in between and to the very extremities of the Armenian borders and beyond, it was decided that groups of sympathetic activists would meet and shape the destiny of this couple and their yet unborn child. And his future generations.

One freezing night, on the wooded hillsides of Lake Seven, Madak and David's unexpected future was sealed. Driving sleet began to splatter them and the group they were meeting up with. They all huddled in the shallow curve of the mountainside, waiting. Fingers of sharp iced rain cut into faces, strong, thick dark hair clung to them and even the sturdy took to shivering uncontrollably. The leader of the group, who planned these escapes, was a fearsome-looking man of at least five decades' worth of battle scars. He stood six and a half feet tall, his face carved with deep lines, beneath which was buried each conflict he had fought and escaped from. He stood up and the sleet stopped, perhaps in awe of his raw power. His ruddy face was topped with monolid eyes that revealed his ancestry. Huge, rough, paw-like hands gripped David's as he assured the couple, he could plan a successful escape for them. He had done it so many times before. Both Madak and David had been faithful and fearless for the last fifteen years, had given of their time and youth. They would leave Armenia and his group would help.

In two weeks, a cargo ship was sailing from the Black Sea port of Batumi and certain sailors on board were sympathetic to their cause. The couple would sail under the cover of darkness from there, through the Bosporus, into the Sea of Marmara, down the tapered waterway called the Dardanelles, which would then connect them to the Aegean Sea, offloading at Rhodes.

From there another ship would pick them up and transport them to the English port city of Hull.

A new life in England. A new name and citizenship papers. The couple cuddled each other as they heard the news, daring to smile as Madak caressed her ever-enlarging belly, which had started to lie low. Droplets of light rain fell off their eyelashes onto each other as they kissed in joy at the news. Watching them, the monolid eyes seemed to shut for a second as a memory of love flitted across this warrior's brow and he was envious. His own wife and baby had died in childbirth, following a winter of near starvation. His motivation to free his country, an emotional reaction to that event twenty years ago. He stamped his feet on the freezing hillside. The moment, the memory, gone, buried, but never forgotten.

This couple would have the life he had never had and he was glad to be able to organise this for them. They represented fresh hope to the activists. By the same reverse route, David would send back arms and funds to free Armenia. The leader toasted the couple with a whisper of stolen Russian vodka, just as an exhausted runner arrived breathless, with news of the enemy, the Bolshevists. They were gaining ground and soon all pretence of an Armenian independence would be shattered, as one of the growling bears next door established a truly cowed Soviet Republic of Armenia. Russia had cunningly lent a helping hand to Armenia, who also feared the sabre rattling of the Turks on the other side. But Russia was shaping up to be a far worse bedfellow. There had been riots and demonstrations aplenty when Armenia started to accept support from Russia. Was it now too late to turn the clock back? Not if the monolid eyes could avert it!

He had been fighting and subverting the Russian effort for years. The Armenian people had two enemies, Russia and Turkey, and more than ever before help was needed from overseas. There could not be a better time for the couple to leave and court the outside world into helping. David and Madak were both proud to help in this way, yet nervous of leaving their homeland and starting afresh. The monolid eyes were darting around. The runner was insistent that he came. The Bolshevists needed dealing with.

David and Madak slowly made their way home. Two weeks were left before their departure.

It passed swiftly.

Their baby, christened Yeltsy, was born into the arms of David as they lay hidden in the woods above the port, waiting for their rendezvous with the ship. David had been forced to suppress Madak's screams with his hands. The birth had been quick, but there had been so much blood. Madak was slight, the baby heavy. It had not been easy. Straddling over river edge, Madak cut the umbilical cord, with the same knife she had been used to cutting up strips of cured meat in the kitchen. She watched part of her body float away with the current as the water swam red about her knees. Next to her David held their child and baptised him quickly, the cold water making his sturdy new-born lungs yell with surprise. David and Madak held their breath.

Had they aroused slumbering enemies? A whistle alerted them to the rough cart, drawn by a weary-looking donkey and driven by a man whose face they could not see but whose help they had been assured of. Dripping wet and stunned by the birth, the new parents stumbled hastily up the grass verge to the cart. David collected his dry coat from a branch and with that wrapped around them all, his wife and new son snuggled up to each other and kept reasonably warm. David shivered next to them. The birth had been too early. He had expected to be on board when this occurred. It was not a good start.

At the port, many carts were offloading, it was dark, and in an instant, with the captain's attention diverted by a staged dockside brawl, the couple made it up the gangplank and into a tight, cramped space under the oiled tarpaulins of the cargo section. Here the slow four-week journey was to be spent. David was in a tight embryonic embrace with his wife and child. He wondered if they would make it, he was cold and hungry. The dry bread and cured meat in the various pockets of his coat barely enough to sustain them for the journey. Sympathetic crew would help when they could but then David felt his forehead; it was boiling, yet he shivered. He expected it was just nerves. As the rolling old cargo steamer left port David sighed, he was so very, very, weary, and he slept.

As David lay shivering he dreamt of warmth and freedom.

During the second week of his journey, his fever consumed him utterly. Two days later, the stench beneath the tarpaulin alerted the captain when he was doing his rounds and as he stripped back the heavy cloth, he nearly fainted at the desolate sight that greeted him.

Once Madak had realised David was dead, she had removed his coat and added it over hers, for within the lining were sewn their new identity papers. As Madak was helped to stand upright with two sailors either side of her, clutching her baby in stinking rags, she said a silent prayer as the body of her dead husband was rolled overboard, on the orders of Captain Srinikan. Her eyes rolled back and it seemed as if she would falter, but the sailors caught her. Madak and baby were taken to the captain's quarters. They were led to a steaming tin bath, the only one on board. Madak and baby Yeltsy, named after David's father, were slowly released from the stench of birth and death. But not before Madak had ripped away their identity papers and hidden them under surprisingly clean towels. Just in time it seemed, as their clothes were taken away to be vigorously washed.

Once clean, in one of the captain's over-large nightshirts, Madak slept for two days and nights whilst excited sailors, especially the cook, found ingenious ways for the baby to suckle warm milk through clean muslin cloths. The journey to Rhodes was completed as Madak awoke and nursed her baby to the backdrop of excited activity surrounding them in the belly of the lurching ship. The sailors were all keen to help, even to the point of small fights breaking out over who was to tend to the baby and his mother. The voyage had not been without its scary moments, as the old wooden hull bucked and twisted through the rough seas. Days flowed into nights until the sun finally rose to greet them all with that most spectacular of sights. Rhodes.

The captain had insisted that Madak start using the English names that had been arranged for them. She had shown him the new identity papers, scared as she was that they might not look right. He had been impressed with their apparent authenticity. So overnight, she became Mary Thornton and her baby was called Jeff.

She wept for the memory of David baptising him Yeltsy.

She wept for Armenia.

She wept for no reason at all.

The captain was beginning to lose patience with the situation. He had been furious at the complicity of some of his crew. He was unsure who the owners of the boat pledged allegiance to, but, he reasoned, he was not a heartless man and so he had helped.

Once docked, the pair were swiftly delivered into the cart of an Italian merchant who was known to the others back in Armenia and who had promised to take the family to the correct ship, further down the bustling port. As they wove their way through the crates and confusion, he pointed out their steamer, berthed at the very end of the quayside. He parked his cart in the shadows of a small side street, as Mary attempted to shed her stained, rough, peasant garments and put on the soft, new, unfamiliar clothes he had brought for her.

She tried to do this without drawing too much attention to herself. It was not to be. The Italian, pretending to be on watch, joined her next to the cart and demanded more than he should have. There was a tussle. She fell back into the cart, her watchful baby next to her head, starting to scream. Without a moment's hesitation, she withdrew the familiar knife from under her discarded coat and she slit the rapist's throat as swiftly and efficiently as she had slit the throats of Russians and Turks before him. She looked down at her knife, memories swimming before her, but her crying son jolted her into the present. The Italian slumped sideways to his death, rolling under his own cart, partially hidden. She stepped away quickly to avoid the pumping blood from his carotid artery. She wiped his warm blood on her old clothes and dumped them on top of his scraggy form. She felt nothing for him, totally devoid of emotion. In his calico bag, hastily thrown on to the cart before his assault on her, she found their food supplies and with only minutes to spare, Mrs Thornton and her young son sped along the quay and stepped aboard the steamer for Hull. As the boat pulled away, she was to be found at the rail, gazing vacantly down into the sea, seemingly searching for something.

She shared a cabin with other women, hopefuls, miles and lifestyles away from their memories, bound together with excitement and fear in equal bucket-loads. She felt like her whole life had been suspended in disbelief and confusion since David's death and she had said very little to anyone. The price of her pent-up grief and anxiety was exhaustion and a suspension from reality. The various families around her did their very best to keep her fed and baby Jeff comfortable. They took pity on this sad, thin woman. Mary had shed not only her baby weight but a third of her body weight in the last, gruelling, few weeks. She had her strong jawline left, but her handshake and smile were weak. For the remainder of the trip to Hull, the people around her became her lifeline. As they sat, dreaming of their new futures in England. Mary dreamt only of David.

Upon disembarkation, she attached herself to the strongest woman in the group and together they endured the questioning and tepid welcome from the British authorities. She followed others on the march through Hull and they all camped in makeshift tents between Beverly and the main town, on the banks of the river Hull.

Mary was weak and still in shock.

Getting up from her camp bed, on that first night, in the grip of a fierce fever, she left baby Jeff sleeping, as she heard a voice calling her and she made her way to the banks of the river estuary. She pulled up the now dirty new skirt, so as not to catch it in the long grass, as she hurried along, a voice persistently echoing around her head.

The moon was in a teasing mood, showing itself, then diving for cover behind the scurrying clouds. For many minutes she stared at the fast-flowing river. She felt David's touch on her arm; they had often sat next to the river close to their home and talked of their future. It was by one such river her baby had been born into the arms of her husband. Tonight, Mary felt entranced by the rhythm of this water. She conversed with David, who enfolded her within his current. Once more she was swept along in the cradle of his embracing love.

Her body floated downstream, joining the Humber estuary close to the docks.

The captain of the boat she had just left had swiftly

taken fresh provisions on board and was casting off, reverse thrust, to escape the confines of the estuary and head out to sea. Leaning over the port side of the boat as the steamer negotiated the narrow channel, he felt a faint thump and thought he saw debris and a hand rise from the churning froth made by the propellers. It disappeared in a second and he doubted what he had seen. He was sure he doubted it. He had a tight turn around if he was to get back to Rhodes on schedule. He walked back to the warmth of his wheelhouse and obliterated the doubt from his mind as efficiently as his propellers obliterated Mary.

The British Authorities dealt with the baby boy. He had been dumped on them by a woman from Armenia who also handed over papers she had found in Madak's coat, which she had left behind on the night of her suicide. She had been seen wandering towards the river; they presumed she had drowned herself. She had seemed unbalanced for the whole sea journey. Subsequently, baby Yeltsy, or Jeff as he was now known, was delivered to the nearest orphanage in Hull, which had not long been rehoused at Hesslewood Hall, a mansion five miles away on the outskirts of the city.

Once he was old enough to walk, Jeff had to follow the rules the same as everyone else. His sturdy little legs raced around, jumping on the window ledges to open the windows, come rain or shine, as soon as the boys were out of bed. This was a rule. After prayers at 7.30 am he would, until the age of six, help the girls in the laundry and he had to stand on a stool all day and turn the handle on the mangle. This was a rule. At seven years of age, he went to school twice a day and as soon as he was nine, he was allowed to stay up with the older boys, one whole hour later, till 8 pm. These were the rules.

But by the age of nine and a half he was more than ready to break the rules. He was fed up of prayers for this and that, beatings for the silliest little things, and he was especially fed up of the older men. It had started once his dark curly hair started to dance around his neckline and his rosy cheeks were noticed to contrast with his faintly, ever so permanently tanned features. Fat men, old men, smelly men, rough men, urgent men, careless men and mainly just hurtful men all found their way into the boys at the Home and not one word was uttered outside the linen cupboard, permanently set aside for such atrocities.

At evening prayers, the boys who were to be abused that night were singled out by salivating men pretending to pray but who were secretly whispering their orders to the matron. She sighed, grimaced, then dutifully directed the young lads as they left the chapel. In the shared dormitory, seemingly hours later, these same boys would walk awkwardly yet silently back to their bed and instinctively role over on their sides and cry themselves to sleep. It was simply part of their routine. No other routine was known. The girls fared no better, their lives forever stained by the outrages against them and the resultant births of even more unwanted children. It was just the never-ending cycle of life in many a children's orphanage in the 1920s and 30s.

By the age of sixteen Jeff had started to rebuff the advances of many of the men, threatening them with violence and causing the Home's authorities much relief when he asked to be allowed to join the army in 1939. They could not wait to get rid of him. His name was often written in the large, black-bound punishment book for all to see. He just laughed at this and for the last six months had even refused to do the punishments meted out to him. The Home was anxious to offload this troublemaker.

To speed up his release into the army the Home had organised a British passport for Jeff Thornton. For this alone he was grateful to them. As for the rest, he would rather forget. When he left, in an army jeep, he turned his back on this home of his for the first sixteen years of his life and smelt proper freedom for the first time.

Or so he thought.

He leant back against the hard metal supports of the bouncing jeep, closed his eyes and dreamt of killing men everywhere. Whisperings in the orphanage had caused him to believe he may have come from Armenia and he had built a fanciful story in his mind around freedom fighters and returning there one day to search for his real roots. Often when imagining killing men, it became all mixed up with killing Turks and Russians too. Basically, he just wanted to kill and erase the rage that coursed within him.

Due to a debilitating tendency to develop pneumonia, which had actually been with him since birth, but re-emerged with force during his basic training, he spent most of World War Two working in the NAFFI. This was created by the British Government in 1921 to run the canteens and recreational establishments needed by the armed forces and to sell goods to servicemen and their families.

He was ultimately to attain the giddy heights of Store Master. His inadequate war was fought through listening to the exploits of others and his deeply carved resentment towards humanity and his current inability to kill anyone manifested itself in an abuse of the system. It gave him enormous pleasure to rip off the army majors, some of whom he remembered from his childhood days in the Home.

When such vividly painful memories consumed him, he took even more daring risks and within five years he had amassed quite a small fortune from his black-market dealings. He had nearly been caught a few times, though. One such time he recalled one of his previous abusers popping in to the stores, early on in 1945, looking for ingredients for his wedding cake.

The Major had been bending over a sack of flour, scooping it up into a waxed bag, ready to take home for his soon-to-be mother-in-law to use. Jeff stealthily crept up behind him and in a flash, pulled down his trousers and underpants, and the ladle he was holding had disappeared into the Major. A sickening scream emanated from the bowels of the flour. The whimpering Major made it all the worse by trying to squirm away. With a vicious twisting move Jeff extracted the ladle as the Major lay slumped next to the flour bag whilst it shed its contents all over his back. Then the flour turned claret. Finally, the handle of the ladle was thrust down the Major's familiar throat and twisted with vengeance till his body moved no more.

Jeff surveyed his handiwork for a second too long. The Major's eyes fluttered open for the last second of his debauched life. He had recognised Jeff. Revenge, the sweetest moment that ever was cooked in hell.

One day though, Jeff imagined that he would fight a real

war. He would return to Armenia and help free his country from the grip of Soviet death. When Germany invaded Russia in 1941, he had rejoiced, only to weep in 1943 over the Soviet victory at Stalingrad.

He had no real friends but everyone was his chum. He could find nylon stockings for soldiers' wives and girlfriends faster than it took a bouncing bomb to hit its target. A cylinder head for the Major's old Austin, not a problem. Cash first though, always.

Tall, dark-haired and athletically handsome, he was well liked but cautiously feared. He had a tendency to cough a bit on damp days, but otherwise he was the picture of good health and vitality. Sometimes the women offered themselves instead of cash and sometimes he obliged them. It was impersonal and rough, they never asked twice. But it served a purpose. He never went to the NAFFI dances; once he had finished work, he went home. He never bought his own black-market clothes or shoes. He was saving. He lived frugally for one with shed-loads, literally, of stolen goods. He mused on the day when he could escape himself, as a caterpillar sheds its cocoon, and steal into the mountainous regions of Armenia, form his own army and liberate his country. He had tasted the thrill of the kill. As with many repressed fantasies, this was now his obsession. David and Madak would have praised his resolve.

Rationing continued in England, in a half-hearted manner, into the 1950s. His profits changed from a fast-flowing river to a sluggish stream. So as a result, he said goodbye to the army and bought himself an old Humber van. Under the floor he hid his black-market takings and for a while the van became his home as he tasted the post-war freedom of the Midlands and slept upon his profits.

During his first few weeks in civvies Jeff obtained not only a van but a girl called Hazel.

A birth mother and father had met and the result of their union, only a passionate few sparks away from creation.

Like him, she was drifting.

Waiting to explode upon that first caress.

CHAPTER 13

1950s
THE SWEDISH CONNECTION

The second of six girls. What a fate!

In 1949 Hazel's whole family had emigrated to England from Sweden to live with an aunt, whose family name was Hankansson. She had changed her name to Ansson, and Hazel's whole family adopted the last name in a bid to hide their Jewish origins.

Hazel's father, an engineer in the copper mines of Falun, and her mother, an accountant there, had both been dismayed at Sweden's neutrality in World War Two. They knew only too well that to hide their origins was a good ploy in order to survive. It was a Jewish family trait in the 1940s. Auntie Jessica, with whom they went to live in Britain, had actually left Sweden in the first wave of immigrants in the 1920s.

Jessica had married well, a rich industrialist who had lost his first wife in childbirth and who basically just needed a housekeeper for a convenient fuck and a nanny for the motherless baby. They had met at his first wife's funeral, when she had been hired to help with the waitressing. Grief morphed into consummation for the heartless industrialist.

All would have been well if Jessica's best friend had not walked in on them in the ladies' toilets and screamed. Jessica had insisted upon marriage or shaming him. It was his choice. He was rich enough to own a big property but too mean to pay for hired help. He married her. In December 1940, her husband and young stepson had gone to watch the Christmas pantomime 'Aladdin', at the Palace Theatre in Manchester. She had not been invited.

That night, the Luftwaffe, orchestrating the Manchester Blitz, dropped a doodlebug from 2500 feet above, seemingly with her husband's name on it, at a speed of 400 mph, directly on top of 97 Oxford Street, in the heart of the city. Or so she told her relatives from Sweden, when she was a little drunk.

She had been sad about the boy. Not about the man.

She was delighted to find she was the sole owner of his six-bedroomed house and she proceeded to take in Jewish refugees, even before they had delivered the scant remains of her husband and stepson to her front door. She turned the cart away. A pauper's grave, if you please. The door was firmly slammed shut.

So, when another knock on her door revealed her own uncle Jakob, his wife Erika plus six adorable little girls, Elizabeth, Hazel, Sonia, Freida, Martha and Joanna she was delighted that they had finally answered her plea to join her. The bombing had been for a purpose and she joyously led them inside to start their new lives in Britain.

Jessica soon found jobs for Erika and Jakob at Manchester United football ground, where she worked as a clerk. Jacob became a jack of all trades and Erika an accounts clerk. Life was going well.

Hazel was sixteen and envious of Elizabeth who, being a whole year older, was allowed out with boys. Hazel sat on the inside window ledge of the upstairs bedroom she shared with Elizabeth in Lapwing Lane and watched her walk out down the road, holding hands with her admirers. She was so very jealous. She struggled, purposefully, to learn English. As soon as her sister had turned the corner at the end of the road, she leapt off the window ledge, hunkered down under the blankets and turned to her Swedish/English dictionary to help propel herself into British society.

If she could actually speak to boys instead of blushing and stammering, she might get somewhere. Hazel was pretty, far prettier than her sister; she only encountered problems when she couldn't reply, though she was not short of admirers. Of medium height, with unusually rich, dark, glossy locks, she stood out in a household of blondies.

In her aunt's home she was always so very cold. There were no open log fires in all the rooms, as she was used to in Sweden. High ceilings and draughty sash windows seemed to invite chilly air inside and allow it to hang around. She found it hard, very hard, to learn anything when she was so cold. The only fires burnt downstairs and sometimes even they went out, when Sonia and Freida forgot to fetch in the heavy coal bucket from the damp shed out the back. Then Martha and Joanna would cry and whimper and Freida would blame Sonia and in return Sonia would smack Freida and their aunt brought it to a close with slaps all round and no tea, just bed. A cold, damp bed at that.

Hazel missed her school friends back in Sweden. Especially Kerstina, who was a beauty; all the boys had admired her and Hazel had often basked in the residual glow of her aura as she dismissed more hopefuls in an hour than Hazel had in a week.

The dynamics of her immediate family changed for the worse when the seemingly mature Elizabeth was around the clearly adolescent Hazel. Tensions in the family grew. Auntie Jessica was concerned. Hazel had not found a job yet and she was also expected to find a husband. Until her English improved, she could do neither. But marriage was finally in the air for someone. Elizabeth had managed to snag herself a widower who worked as a clerk in the tax office and was considered a good catch. Hazel was beside herself with frustration. She wrote to Kerstina about it all, pouring out her woes in Swedish and seeking help.

Post-war Britain was grim. So, something very special had been organised in order to propel the country and its population into the recovery mode and positivity needed for growth. An amazing event was evolving. Kerstina wrote back to Hazel that she was actually coming to Britain to take part in the very first Miss World Competition, then known as The Festival of Britain Competition. Hazel was stunned as she read this. Fluttering out of the envelope was a backstage pass to the Royal Albert Hall in London, to act as chaperone for Kerstina. As part of the huge Festival of Britain celebrations there was to be a beauty pageant that her very best friend had been chosen to take part in in order to represent Sweden. Hazel was beside herself.

She flew into the kitchen clutching the letter. Elizabeth was jointly jealous and flustered as Hazel was the centre of attention now and she hated it. Her mother and father reluctantly looked on, as, not for the first time their two elder daughters spat and clawed at each other. Aunt Jessica intervened with precision. The bread knife was wielded dangerously close to the two girls, who calmed down, Hazel slumping next to the range, on which bubbled the morning's porridge and Elizabeth taking the huff and going out the back door to have a fag next to the coal shed, which looked as bleak as she felt.

It was eventually decided by Aunt Jessica, who had a distant relative living in South Kensington, London, that Hazel would travel down and stay for a couple of weeks, in order to be with Kerstina, as had been requested, and help with her backstage preparations for the competition.

Hazel gloated. Elizabeth sulked.

Elizabeth was finally subdued when she realised that the ever-emerging gorgeousness of Hazel would not eclipse her summer wedding. Hazel would be in London that day!

Peace was restored in the house.

Hazel was breathless with anticipation. Without her parents' knowledge she had been learning about hair and make-up from her Aunt Jessica who still, despite her age, liked to turn a head or two when she visited the local pubs. She mixed with the football fraternity and had an eye for the young players, especially Stan Pearson and Brian Birch, but she usually ended up chatting to Matt Busby's mates and that led to trouble fast. On a few secret occasions Hazel had accompanied her auntie and was beginning to learn how to hold her drink, as well as chatter in English. With all of this, plus her beauty knowledge, she felt she was well equipped to face London.

She barely remembered the long, austere, train journey down, she was so excited. She was met by Kerstina, who had arrived herself three days earlier. They were whisked away, by taxi, to the headquarters of the pageant at The Gainsborough Hotel in Queensbury Place, just around the corner from the Royal Albert Hall. She never would stay with her aunt's distant relative, who had thankfully been swiftly silenced by the promise of two complimentary tickets. And so, the adventure began.

Eric Morley came personally to the venue every day. His role was to supervise the girls on the catwalk and ensure the professionalism of the event. He had been tasked, by the British fashion industry, with promoting a new swimwear sensation, called a bikini. At first Kerstina, a tall leggy blonde, was as astounded by the briefness of the bikini as was every other girl in the competition, but egged on by Hazel, and all the other chaperones, the girls donned their bikinis and strutted their bare stuff in rehearsals, as if they had been wearing these skimpy, frilly outfits all their lives. The male staff, watching whilst trying to clean or arrange banners, just gawped. Then the female staff went on a diet.

Hazel worked magic with Kerstina's eyes and the thick black eyeliner just accentuated her natural beauty. Every night for two weeks Hazel washed and ironed Kerstina's clothes and gazed at the wisps of seductive bikini she discarded on the floor, wishing herself as svelte as her friend, so she too could fit into and look stunning in those bikinis.

Hazel had been dieting. By the time of the actual competition, she could squeeze into Kerstina's clothes and she chose a stunning red gown to wear to the Royal Albert

Hall for the night of the pageant. Like some kind of royalty, the girls and their chaperones walked along a red carpet with flashbulbs popping in every direction. Hazel heard the press call out,

'How does it feel to be in this first Miss World Competition?'

Hazel had never heard this term before, it had been made up by the press, but it had stuck. And yes, Hazel liked it very much. She turned to one seasoned reporter and answered his question. 'It feels lovely and I am very privileged to be here, thank you.'

He was from the North and worked for the *Manchester City News*. It was very auspicious.

Once backstage, time flew by. The chaos, the tantrums, girls bitching and bikinis going lost. It was mayhem. Hazel kept Kerstina's outfits close. A contestant from Australia was especially one to watch, she had a vicious streak, as if believing she should be the favoured one. Eric Morley, though, had no favourites and no time for such nonsense. Words were had. Tensions were running high. All the girls respected him.

By the time it came to announce the results nearly three hours had gone by. The girls were shattered. All on stage, standing tall and proud in next to nothing, they plastered on their smiles and waited for Eric to announce in three-two-one order, who the winner was.

Hazel had been sitting with the other chaperones in the Green Room backstage, but at this point they crowded into the wings and yelled their support along with the watching throng. It was tense. The stage lights were beating down and droplets of sweat ran down the girls' bodies, into their belly buttons and out again, to form rivers dripping down their inner thighs. The insides of their shoes were getting soggy and some feared they would squelch out of them and stumble if their names were called out.

Kerstina was the one.

She was number one.

The first ever Miss World.

And she came from Hazel's birth country, Sweden.

Hazel thought she would pass out in a dead faint when her best friend's name was announced.

After that everything moved at speed. Kerstina exited with the entourage swamping Eric Morley and it was left to Hazel to tidy up backstage and gather all her friend's belongings together. Back at the hotel Hazel saw the notice on the ballroom door and it read, 'Private Party, for Pageant Participants only'.

One day she thought, one day soon. The next day she travelled alone back to Manchester. She had not been able to speak to Kerstina since she had won. Her whereabouts were unknown to Hazel. In the carriage she sat opposite a reporter, who was looking through some pictures he had taken on his camera, the night before, at the Royal Albert Hall.

'Excuse me, but weren't you the chaperone to the winner at the Festival Bikini Pageant,

or as we like to call it, The Miss World?'

Hazel was snapped back to reality. She stared at him. Too old, and definitely too downtrodden. She remembered him as one of the reporters from the night before on the red carpet. But as her Auntie Jessica had always said, it's best to work the angles when they present themselves. So, she did. By the time they arrived up in Manchester the reporter, named Burt, had agreed to forward her picture and name to the newspaper bosses with a view to sponsoring Hazel for the next Miss World Competition, which would start with regional heats. Hazel acted suitably surprised at the suggestion but agreed graciously, inwardly a bubble of excitement.

Burt had her address and intended to be there as often as he could. On the second night back in Manchester he called at the door with a hand-delivered letter. Jessica answered; Hazel was still asleep from the exhaustion of the pageant and the house was quieter as Elizabeth was away on honeymoon and everyone else was watching the BBC in the large sitting room.

She took Burt into the kitchen for a chat. Opening the letter, even though it was addressed to Hazel, she gasped at the girl's good fortune. Burt was given a large whisky and as they both dwelt on the letter, a plan was hatched. Burt's newspaper had agreed to stump up fifty per cent of the costs involved in trying to get Hazel to the next Miss World. Jessica thought that with a bit of persuasion, Matt Busby could be touched up for the other half. What was good for Manchester was good for Manchester United and Matt Busby. Burt was beginning to warm to Jessica. Age was put aside as the whisky flowed. The deal was sealed in the most time-honoured fashion between a man and a woman. Hazel stumbled blearily into the kitchen at around nine o'clock as Burt exited the back door and her rather flustered auntie showed her the letter as she buttoned up her frilly nylon blouse. Hazel was sure she could hear it crackling with static.

She flew into the sitting room. Her family was watching

Come Dancing, a large show on a very small TV screen with women in huge frocks, dancing with slick-haired partners and being judged on their performance. Nobody wanted an interruption. Erika and Jakob leant forward to see the moves. Sonia, Freida, Martha and Joanna were all out of bed watching also, sitting on the floor at their parents' feet. Collectively they screamed, 'Shush' as she walked in. The results were about to be announced. So, she walked out again.

Auntie Jessica dragged her sulky crying form into the kitchen. The range made it warm and cosy. In no time at all, with a stiff whisky inside her, Jessica assured Hazel that she would get all the help she needed to promote her in the world of beauty competitions and it would be their secret until the time was right. Hazel was subdued and rather in awe of her auntie. Her father had not really learnt English so well. Her parents kept themselves to the house mostly, once work ended. To the relief of Jessica, they kept the large house in perfect order. The smaller girls were at school and often at other friends' houses. The younger girls spoke perfect English now and found it frustrating that their father often misunderstood them.

Firstly, Jessica convinced Hazel that she had to get a job. That way her parents would not be nagging her day in day out. At night, Erika was persuaded to teach her daughter the basics of bookkeeping and Hazel, with an end goal in sight, suddenly learnt very quickly. Through her mother's intervention she slipped into a very junior accounts position at Manchester United Football Club. Just as Matt Busby's team strode to further fortune and glory.

Her parents were delighted; their first daughter was

married and living in a council flat close by in Trafford Park. Their second daughter might even catch the eye of a footballer. Erika was enormously proud of her family. Despite not speaking English one hundred per cent, she observed keenly. Hazel was noticed. But because she worked in the same office as her mother she was off limits, a very frustrating turn of events for Hazel, but she savoured the secret she shared with her aunt and it sustained her. Every night as her family sat mindlessly watching the endlessly repetitive programmes churned out by the BBC, Hazel would be in the kitchen practising her catwalks, swivels, replies to her aunt's questions and all with three large accountancy ledgers perched on her head!

Christmas and the New Year passed in a blur, and 1952 dawned as did Hazel's eighteenth birthday and her right to enter beauty pageants. The *Manchester City News* paid for her entrance fee to the Miss Manchester regional competition and Manchester United Football Club paid for the outfits. One day, working late to finish the backlog of accounts, Erika spotted her daughter's name on a receipt. She was startled. She went home with a copy of the receipt in her pocket.

After high tea of fish fingers, tinned peas, chips and tomato sauce the family moved to the sitting room, as was usual, to watch an early episode of the hilarious show called *I Love Lucy*. Usually Erika would sit transfixed, laughing a second or two after her young daughters so as not to embarrass everyone that she had not quite understood. Tonight, she moved to the kitchen, opening the door to find Hazel in her bra and panties with three ledgers on her head and Jessica holding a spatula to her mouth as Hazel answered her questions. Hazel dropped the ledgers onto the floor and grabbed her mother's pinny from the back door to protect her modesty. Erica sat down open-mouthed and looked to Jessica for answers. Hazel beseeched her mother to stay silent and not tell a soul.

Erika looked from one to the other and said nothing for what seemed like ages.

Secretly Erika was proud but in equal measure worried. She had seen the looks of the young footballers as they increasingly traversed the management block from entrance to team room through the accounts section. Of course, they had all been staring at Hazel, who held herself with grace and poise even when she was merely flashing her heavily made-up eyes around the office.

She gave her consent. The kitchen erupted and a bottle of bubby was produced, just as Lucille Ball and Desi Arnaz could be heard screeching at each other from the living room.

Matt Busby got personally involved and declared that the mayor had promised him his purple velvet robe, edged with ermine, to clad the winner in. The whole football team was at the pageant cheering on Hazel and wolf whistling at all the girls.

Hazel's whole family was there also. Her bikini was the very same one that Kerstina had won in at the first Miss World. When Kerstina finally arrived back in Sweden she had written to thank Hazel and enclosed the bikini for good luck. What else she had to say about what happened immediately after she had won the competition startled and excited Hazel.

She had remembered the night she had stood at the

door whilst her elder sister Elizabeth had recounted the joys of her honeymoon to her mother. In whispered Swedish Hazel could just about make out what was said, despite the two women's giggles, and relished the day she could have just such a conversation, but probably not with her mother. Aunt Jessica would be the one to hear all about her first sexual encounter. It was increasingly dawning on Hazel that maybe she should discuss these issues with her aunt anyway, as Jessica certainly seemed to have a never-ending stream of male admirers, despite her age.

Holding in her stomach and willing the judges at the Manchester Regional Miss World competition to choose her, Hazel smiled to the audience she could not see beyond the footlights. The red bikini was so skimpy it made the judges gasp with admiration. Hazel's young, proud body glistened with sweat, which, when caught in the lights, twinkled at everyone. She was so very happy. And innocent.

Jeff thought the most beautiful girl he had ever seen in the world was smiling right back at him. He wanted her, urgently. His van was parked outside, ready for just such another rendezvous. He'd been given tickets by a grateful council caterer who had been tasked with providing food and entertainment for the party, following the pageant. Jeff had been able to sell him, at vastly inflated prices, sugar and butter for the winner's cake, and cooking fat and bacon for the hearty butties the men would expect before the drinking began. As all of these were still rationed in 1952, Jeff made a tidy profit and the council caterer hoped they could do business again, when even more events like this came his way, on the back of this night's success. Unbeknown to the contestants, a betting ring had formed and Hazel was the number one to win. As the mayor announced the winners, in true Eric Morley style, Jeff and many other men held their breath.

Hazel was the one.

She was the number one. She would be the first ever girl from Manchester to enter Miss UK and then, hopefully, the summer pageant to be known as Miss World 1952.

As the mayor plonked the regally styled crown on her head and whisked off his robes to drown her in stinking ermine and sweaty velvet, the audience erupted and Hazel heard only the beating of her heart as she attempted to walk off stage with all the grace and poise she had learnt in the kitchen.

Her legs buckled. Her emotions caved in on her. Jeff was there in a flash, his front-row seat a heartbeat away. With strong athletic arms he lifted her up to whoops and cries and Hazel fainted just after looking into his strong brown eyes and feeling the tautness of him beneath her.

Flashbulbs popped, she felt like the queen. When she had regained her composure, she had pictures taken on her own, with her family, with her sponsors and with every one of Matt Busby's boys, all trying to kiss her cheek and squeeze her bum at the same time. She was toasted with champagne. She ate little and drank loads. She was ready for this. So ready for this. Jeff watched it all from afar. Propping up the bar he drank wisely, Villa Sap, or Sarsaparilla, as the non-alcoholic drink was known. He'd paid for a crate from the pop man and sold it on to the barman for a profit.

Jessica and Burt danced and laughed the night away. Erika, Jakob and the younger, very jealous sisters, left early, beseeching Jessica to keep an eye on things and bring home

Hazel safe and sound. Jeff too was keeping an eye on things.

As Hazel stumbled out of the room, with just a bikini and the mayor's robes around her, Jeff struck. He pushed her roughly into the ladies' loo and locked the door. Hazel moved to strike him but, as she raised her arm, he ripped her bikini top off. She tried to clutch her heavy breasts but he caught her hands and whizzed her around so her head was dangerously close to the toilet bowl. Bent over as she was, it was easy for Jeff. He slid past the frilly bikini bottoms with lightning speed and as Hazel screamed and tried to arch backwards to get free, he leant over her, forcing her forehead to smack against the toilet seat. She screamed, he moaned and it was over.

He released her arms and she slid to the floor. After wiping himself off on the ermine edge of her cape he left. He was driving towards the outskirts of Manchester before Jessica found her and bundled her into Burt's car for the journey home.

Thank God the pictures had all been taken said Burt. Jessica clouted him on the head and that nearly caused an accident. He was not invited in.

Jessica guessed what had happened as Hazel curled up on Jessica's bed in a foetal position with the cape wrapped firmly around her. In her head she replayed the seconds it had taken the strong man to rape her. This had not seemed like the tender caring embraces she had heard sister Elizabeth discuss with her mother, nor the hours of agile manoeuvres Aunt Jessica had alluded to when she had had one or two too many whiskies with Burt.

Hazel knew her rapist was called Jeff, as he had introduced

himself to her at the after party. She had been aware that he had been staring at her, but then so had all the other men. Her breasts spilling out and her starved stomach caving in had been such an alluring duo. Accentuating as it had the pertness of her youthfully high bum. The slight curve of her thighs as they brushed past men had them in such a dither that she had been heady with the power of her allure. She would put it all in the past, lock the thoughts away and never ever refer to them again. And with that thought she got off the bed, left the ermine and velvet cape on the floor, ripped off the remnants of her bikini and strode into the bathroom to rid herself of all traces of what had just happened to her. Aunt Jessica did not ask, she was too scared to know, didn't want to get the blame.

As the weeks marched on Hazel stayed at work and could have had any man around her. But she chose not to. All her efforts were focused on the Miss World. She started to go to the gym, unheard of for most women in the 1950s. They all did so much physical work in the house anyway, trips to the gym were quite unnecessary. But Hazel wanted to flaunt her looks and tease the men. It was her kind of revenge.

Then the sickness started. She knew what it was, her sister Elizabeth had had morning sickness before she had miscarried and this was exactly the same. Hazel was in denial.

Totally.

She went to work, she came home, she stopped going to the gym and she got a bit rounded. One night she tried on the bikini she had won in and screamed when it would not sit flat on her stomach. It curled downwards to avoid her baby bump. She ran along the upstairs landing, towards the stairs; this could not be happening to her. Reality was in the present. She wanted it in the past and she threw herself down the stairs with painful twists and turns on the way.

Erika and Jacob left Dixon of Dock Green smiling into the camera on TV and ran to their daughter in a heap at the bottom of the stairs in a bikini. Jessica came out of the kitchen and the looks that passed between the two women spoke of an understanding of Hazel's situation.

Erika had seen her daughter's tummy, but thought she was just getting a bit chubby. Now she knew otherwise. Jessica cradled Hazel's head in her arms and rocked her back and forth whilst crying for the pair of them. Jakob took charge and with his still strong miner's arms lifted Hazel over his shoulder and carried her back up the stairs to her bedroom.

The doctor was called. The examination proved their suspicions. Hazel wept and wept for her lost chance at Miss World. She hated her body right now. Hated the alien growth within. Hated all men. Hated herself mostly. She was sent away to Glasgow, to work in the accounts section of a hospital until her confinement.

She wore a brass washer that fooled nobody.

She was introduced to Sister Hart, who might be able to help.

She made two other attempts to rid herself of the curse within her, but failed.

Fine she thought, you stubborn, sturdy little bastard, be born, but don't expect me to love or like you.

Sister Hart circled as Hazel finally rid herself of the growth within on April 11th 1953. Hazel refused to look at or touch her baby. She had to name her for official purposes so she chose Louise, the name of her rival for the 1952 Miss UK.

And then her baby daughter was gone, with a scream and a twist of her dark brown curly head, as she attempted to look backwards towards her stubborn birth mother.

Hazel was unconcerned. She was never going back to Manchester anyway. The hatred and disgust she had seen in her family's eyes as she had left for Glasgow had crushed her heart utterly. The shame and fear showed openly as they bundled her into the taxi to take her to the station for Glasgow. Hazel remembered her mother telling her not to come back until she had got rid of it.

Well now she had got rid of it.

Instead, she would be returning home with a nice chap she had met on her long lonely walks in Glasgow. He had not minded her situation, especially as she was to have her child adopted. He had waited patiently outside the ward when she was delivering. He had seen the anxious faces of the adopting parents as they scuttled away with their new charge, Sister Hart in tow.

If her parents had objected to an illegitimate child just imagine how thrilled their Jewish selves would be to find their daughter married to a Windrush Jamaican immigrant. The next afternoon they were booked into the registry office in John Street, Glasgow.

Hazel laughed to herself. She could not wait for the wedding ceremony. She could not wait to see her parents' faces. Miss Ansson was soon to become Mrs Ebanks.

She just hoped her breasts would stop leaking during the wedding ceremony.

They didn't.

Somebody,
Somewhere,
far off,
laughed.

CHAPTER 14

1972
LIFE, NOT LIVING

Edith closed the front door with extreme caution. She last remembered being truly alone on train journeys up and down to Scotland. The feeling unnerved her dreadfully. Berenice had just left to train to be a teacher, with an acid-tongued back comment. No, she was not going to rent her daughter's room, but hey, thanks for the advice, Berenice. Wearily she closed her eyes.

Edith was determined to sort out her life.

William would be home from the asylum in one week.

Maybe Berenice would ring to let her know that she had arrived safely. Probably not. After the second day she knew she would not hear from her headstrong daughter.

She decided a spring clean was long overdue. Berenice's room was a complete and utter shambles. She had left her A-level notes, discarded school uniform and dried-up make-up behind. A sorting-out was needed. Then Edith would tackle her own room. She felt an air of rebirth and moved with some vigour. Up, down, up, down the stairs with bin bags for collection. By lunchtime, she had only the icy-cold walk-in wardrobe to sift through. She decided to let it wait until later and sat down to enjoy *Lunchtime with Wogan* on ITV and a salad sandwich.

When she finally opened the double doors of her daughter's wardrobe, she leapt back, wary of entry. It was dark inside and still had a strong smell of her daughter's perfume, called Charlie. She stepped falteringly inside and heard a crackling under her feet. She had stood on a discarded handbag-size make-up mirror, and being barefoot, cut herself deeply. Reversing out of the space, she landed on her back with her foot in the air dripping blood downwards. She tried to save the carpet and managed to hobble to the bathroom with a handy pair of old tights wrapped around the cut. By then she was feeling woozy, and she was losing a lot of blood. Once bandaged she skittered down the stairs on her bum and managed to make herself a cup of sweet tea before collapsing into her wing-back chair. She dozed for the rest of the afternoon. The throbbing in her foot woke her up. She probably needed some antibiotics to curb infection and made her way painfully back upstairs, to the medicine cabinet in the clinically tiled bathroom. She chastised the nurse in her for being so forgetful of procedure.

Whilst rummaging around the deep cupboard she wobbled slightly, as she was balancing on just one foot. Tumbling out of the cabinet were familiar friends from the past, some in dark brown bottles, others in packets. She sat on the edge of the bath, still scummy from the bubble bath Berenice had luxuriated in before she left. It simply reminded her that her own bathing schedule was overdue and once again she reflected on her own shortcomings. Looking around she could see that the collection of angry plastic bottles was simply a dated marker for various stages of her married life.

In a combination of haste and horror at the sheer volume of drugs, she started to throw them away and with them she shoved their memories into the wicker bin of life. Finally, she came to a very old eye-dropper with *Baby Louise* written on it. It had been given to her by Sister Hart, as Berenice, then Louise, had been born with sticky eyes. Why had she kept it? She knew why. Every time she had opened the medicine cabinet in the last eighteen years, she had known it was there. A testament to the fact that Berenice was not actually Irene, as evidenced by the pipette. It had been a painfully slow dawning for Edith. Sometimes she would go for months without swiping away pill bottles in front of it and finding its reassuring presence in the back of the cabinet. Then Berenice would do something loud and annoying and, is if by remote control, she'd spy the eye bottle and assure herself that none of this was her fault. The child was someone else's, but worst of all, she was not Irene.

As a small child Berenice stomped as Irene glided. Berenice shouted as Irene whispered and most alarmingly of all, Berenice challenged as Irene just accepted. Berenice was happiest away from the house. This was clear to Edith. She had no skills to remedy this. Food was cooked and the child ate. Clothes were washed and the child was clean. Eventually simple homework was helped with and the child seemed grateful. Alarmingly Berenice did not read fluently until she was eight years old. Every night William and Edith beseeched and every night Berenice closed her eyes and hummed her own tune. She was so very belligerent at times.

Then one morning, as William put down the *Daily Mail* newspaper, Berenice picked it up and started to read the lead column. William had dropped his spoon into his tea causing a splash and a brown stain to seep in to the white embroidered tablecloth his mother-in-law had given him for a wedding present. Edith patted Berenice on the shoulder, who just shrugged and said she had been able to read all along, hadn't they known that? Then she had risen from breakfast to get her Brownie uniform ready to take to school in her heavy, brown leather satchel. Which annoyingly matched her heavy, brown leather, Clarks buckle sandals.

Berenice had been a disappointment to Edith until she started to show some academic ability. At that point Edith had given up the obvious comparisons with Irene, as it was really just a farcical waste of time. Instead, she started to boast to her brother and his hateful Catholic wife that Berenice was going to go far. Irene had failed her 11-plus exam miserably. Berenice sailed through hers and in the judgemental climate of the 1960s, Berenice was lauded as she entered grammar school and Irene slid into muted depression as she was surrounded by loud-mouthed children at a local secondary modern school. In her defence, Irene looked gorgeous every day. Berenice was wild and rumpled, always lugging sports gear around and rushing home breathless and dishevelled, only to rush out again five minutes later, leaving the detritus of her daily life strewn from landing to hallway and beyond.

Edith begrudgingly admired her daughter's bid for individuality. She wished so very much that she had followed her own heart, as Berenice seemed intent on doing, all those years ago in Glasgow. Jonathon loomed in her daydreams.

Over the decades of upheavals, with William's persistent descent into depression, Berenice's wilful pregnancy and her own obsession with her family she had merely retreated more into herself, hugging her slight body on the chair and rocking sometimes to quell the dithers. The last two years had been tough.

She was ageing. No hope now to rekindle her love affair with Jonathon. William was becoming more dependent. He needed her now more than ever. As that need rose, Berenice's fell and suddenly, here she was, alone in the house, her husband due to be released from hospital soon and hopefully a fresh start around the corner of life.

William so did not want to leave the structured daily routines of the asylum. He had recourse to any number of chats and therapies and felt calm and at one with himself there. Other men his age, war-weary and cowed, knew his pain and they shared their stories for those who wanted to hear.

He knew, through Edith's phone call, that Berenice had got away safely, down to Oxford. Good God, how would he cope alone with Edith in the house? She neither cleaned nor cooked adequately. He knew now that she had not been ready to marry him when her father had plucked her from her nursing training at the end of the war and propelled her into this marriage. He too should have bided his time. The war had warped them both. Skewed their vision of what was required of them and caused them to look back for comfort instead of ahead. The future had seemed so mystifying then. It had soothed him to reach out for the familiar. Then he had not needed any new routines. He had needed his past to become his present. That it did not, it could not, had been a downward spiral of depression for William for the last three decades.

William sat on the bench, his duffel bag at his feet, the angry red suicide slits on his wrists fading and thankfully just above his cuff. A male nurse sat with him. The ambulance was due soon. He had been told that it was going to take him home. Where was that, he pondered? He felt a cold icy finger of fear worm its way into his soul. He really did not want to go. A crunching on the gravel and the old ambulance slowly rounded the corner. William wanted to bolt back inside. The male nurse sensed his discomfort.

'Relax, William, you can cope.' Could he, though? What experiences had led him to believe he could?

Was it the mind-numbing brutality of war?

Or the mind-numbing emptiness of his seemingly sterile marriage?

Perhaps it was the waspish retorts of his acerbic daughter testing her skills on her parents? A door grated open and the male nurse escorted him into the back of the parked ambulance. Home appeared to be waiting for him.

He closed his eyes and pretended to sleep. It was just easier than trying to converse. A pain darted through his eyes, straight to the back of his head; it usually heralded a memory. He started to sweat. Heat rose from his core to his extremities and a twitching started in his fingers. William gripped his hands together, desperate to silence his screaming limbs, trapped as they were in his shell of discontent. He started to breathe more easily. The tremors subsided and he opened his eyes as the ambulance churned on past Blyth, Seaton Sluice and along the coastal road to

Whitley Bay. Through the small square windows, he watched the late holidaymakers swing their buckets and spades, push their red-faced infants in prams and actually just do the things that so often he had missed out on with his own family. A tear started to form. Further on they approached a small roundabout close to the Rendezvous Café and as they turned right, away from the coast, the male nurse awoke and looked out the window too.

'Man, these are nice houses on these streets. Do you live close by, William?'

He did. But not close enough for Edith. Nothing he had ever done was quite right for Edith. A tear fell.

'Don't cry, William, it really will be all right this time,' and he handed him a paper tissue.

William knew that it would never be all right but he smiled, said 'Thank you' and made as if he was calm again. He was dreading home. He would do anything not to go home.

The ambulance stopped and reversed up his drive. Edith came out and ignored the twitching of the neighbours' net curtains on Grasmere Crescent. She held out her hand to William and he almost stumbled out in surprise at her offer. They greeted each other in an awkward hug, shielded from the prying eyes of others by the open doors of the ambulance. He took her face in his hands. A flash again, a memory. Her body tensed. He leant forward to kiss her and the nurse, still inside the ambulance, smiled. Edith turned her cheek when William sought her lips and her cheek was warm. Her familiar scent of 4711 hung around in his nostrils and he fought to keep his need for her at bay as she held his hand and took him inside. Once the paperwork was signed the ambulance moved out of their sight, already a buried memory, as the reality of their home overrode the pain of his last failed suicide attempt.

The acrid lingering of a thousand cigarettes hung in the furnishings and sprang out at every footfall. They went into the kitchen and the plastic seats and frilly café curtains wafted a greasy hello to them both. As they turned right into the dining room an intense dry heat grabbed them as they sat opposite each other and the gas fire spat its welcome noisily.

Arched outside over the French windows, the fading blossom of the dying Japanese flowering cherry tree waved a fragile goodbye. Beth scampered in and licked ankles in delight, then subsided as neither William nor Edith moved either to greet or pat their faithful dog, who was missing her real mistress, Berenice.

Edith spoke first. 'I've had a bit of a clean-out whilst you were away for so long, maybe there's more to do. I made a start on our bedroom then I gave Berenice's room a good solid shake-down. She left such a pile of rubbish. Lots has gone in the bin. The rubbish was collected yesterday. Would you like me to order a Chinese takeaway for tea?'

William remembered, from his childhood, how his father had returned from hospital once, following a bad accident on his trawler. One of the winches had snapped and lashed its flaying wires across his father's arms. The crew had thought they were going to lose their captain as they fought the bucking trawler all the way back into port in the rough churning Irish Sea. After two weeks in hospital his father had been well enough to return home. His mother had spent all day cooking. It was only Friday, but they had feasted on a roast and all the trimmings and his father had looked lovingly at his mother, and even when his arms felt almost too heavy to lift the spoon for bread-and-butter pudding, he battled on and admired the hard-working woman he had married. They had left the table and gone upstairs. Adolescent William did the washing-up and tried not to make too much noise clattering the crockery in the porcelain sink of the scullery. Above him the floorboards creaked in contentment. William had never forgotten that day. He could have watched all the romantic films ever but nothing stood out more in his childhood memory than that declaration of love by his mother to his father.

Through clenched false teeth he sighed that a Chinese would be OK. More rice, more memories; he was going upstairs to rest, he would be back down at six, was that all right? Edith nodded and he thought she sighed, he could not be so very sure, it might have been a groan. He stood up and the dog scuttled away. Edith was left on her own.

The house had a different feel to it once he was upstairs. He started to panic. His notes, his memories, his letter, had she touched them, found them even? He darted into his study, where the normal film of dust was gone. This was a bad sign. He bent down and checked deep under the chest of drawers. It was still there. He could breathe again. He looked quickly into each drawer and nothing had been touched. She had, as she said she had, merely dusted, the real sorting of his room left for when he came home. His heart rate returned to normal. He felt weary with the stress of all those secrets and lay down on the small cot bed in the corner, used in part as a sofa couch, but mainly as his refuge. He pulled his old army demob blanket around him and drifted swiftly into a troubled sleep, where slaying Japs and avoiding death was the thrust of it all.

Edith paced around downstairs. They had not had sex since Berenice's abortion. Somehow the events merged, as if to commit the act would mean to remember the abortion. Their daughter could get pregnant but Edith could not. Nightly she shied away from William's touch, until he simply stopped asking and slept alone in his office. The fertility of their daughter, and the dawning threat of jail should their hasty intervention in her pregnancy be revealed, seemed to strangle Edith. She had let Berenice roam far and wide once she returned home after the debacle in Bristol. Edith would not talk about it. William could not bear thinking about it. That he had been persuaded to murder his first grandchild abhorred him utterly and he too lost his lust for life. Berenice had matured enough to accept that work was the way out. She studied hard and when she had space she played hard too and nobody stopped her. Her parents were so very scared that one day soon she would march up the drive with the police in tow and accuse them of being party to the murder of her child. She had been just seventeen when it happened; they should have known better. But Berenice felt the guilt. She believed she should have had the strength of character to stop them. She had nearly succeeded. The syringes were perhaps to blame. So, misunderstood, yet again, by her parents, she blocked out all references to the abortion, told nobody and marched on into life as if a slice of it had been cut out from her. As actually it had.

Edith came in from the takeaway just around the corner

and called up to William that their dinner was ready. William stirred and the pungent aroma of sweet and sour chicken made its way into his head and woke him up to a fierce hunger and thirst. Downstairs, in the darkening gloom of a northern early autumn they ate on in silence.

Then the bombshell broke. 'William, I found some jumbled notes from a guy called Peter hidden under your demob blanket when I was making your bed.'

The air was sucked out of the room. William's hand lashed across the space between them and Edith toppled over backwards on the dining-room chair, cracking her head on the floor, and she passed out. William stared at the enemy. He had to get out of the jungle. He raced through the forest until he found his tent and he crashed inside, hiding under the blanket.

The phone rang and rang. Slowly Edith slumped sideways, then grabbed the edge of the dining table for support. There was a bloodstain spreading outwards on the carpet. Her hair felt damp. She had to answer the phone. It was Berenice. Apologising for not calling sooner, the start of term had been manic, and she enquired if her father had arrived home safely. Edith spoke in a fog of pain and at the other end Berenice just thought her mother was being distant and weird again and rang off as soon as she could. Edith sat on the bottom step of the stairs and wept. Much later, looking at herself in the hall mirror, Edith gasped. The back of her blouse was blood-red. Her grey hair was matted and congealed. Dried blood fell like angry words onto her shoulders. Attempting the stairs was almost impossible, her feet seeming uninterested in going there. Clinging onto the stair rail she tried to climb slowly up, with her head down and her whole body sweating and screaming in disbelief at what had just happened. The pain was just too much and she sat heavily on the bottom stair again, looking out of the dimpled-glass front door. Memories of Berenice marching stridently out, dragging her enormous trunk to the taxi, swamped her vision. The door mocked her. She could see the outside world but it was distorted through the mottled glass, as if trapping her inside her hell. Her daughter had escaped, why could she not? The street lamps were on but the houses on the crescent outside seemed silent; her attack must have occurred hours ago.

She staggered back into the scene of the crime. Congealed lumps of viscous pink cold chicken assaulted her nostrils and sticky sweet and sour sauce dripped resolutely onto the legs of the upturned dining-room chair. The pungency of the aroma mixed with the acrid smell of her blood in the same room made her nostrils flare and she sank backwards into the only easy chair in the dining room. The chair sat silently in the corner, often a refuge for William when he could not take the underlying tensions of the living room any more. The scene of Berenice and Tony's tryst and now a comforter for Edith as she wept once more for herself. Leaning forward, head in hands, she prayed for death. It must surely be coming soon. It must come soon.

The floorboards creaked. By now it was 3 am. The roots of the dying Japanese flowering cherry tree had snaked their way under the foundations of the back room in this troubled house. Outside the clouds darkened as the wind curled round the edges of the eaves and rattled the roof tiles. The tree moaned and buckled in the wind. Beth started to whimper in the confines of the draughty garage. In sleep, Edith was rocking in the chair. Sitting on the lap of her Grandmother Ruth it felt so warm and safe. She was squeezed tighter and tighter by her grandmother, beseeching her to stay.

Outside the room a large branch snapped off the tree, smacking into the French doors as it fell. Edith woke with a start. The clear glass of the door was splintered and the temperature in the room had dropped to Beth was barking madly in the garage. Edith hauled herself up and tried to see beyond the cracked pane. There was nothing to see. It was dark. And then the wind dropped and a stillness descended. There was a malevolence in the air and her heart beat faster. Turning painfully, she left the disturbing room and behind her the door slammed shut with a vicious whack. The stairs took away all her remaining strength as she climbed.

Sinking back into the bath she doused her head in diluted Dettol and cried out when it sank into the rawness of her wound. She could imagine what the back of her head looked like. In 1943 an air-raid warden had staggered into her hospital in Glasgow just as she had been about to leave, as the all-clear had sounded, a similar bloody gash across the back of his head. She had been rushing to get to Jonathon's flat for a tryst and did not want to be late. She had showered at work and changed into her own clothes, dousing herself with the remaining droplets of her mother's birthday gift to her, from a treasured bottle of *Joy* perfume.

Ironic really as it mattered little what she was wearing because Jonathon would strip her naked within five minutes and stare at her in wonder by the light from the flickering gas fire before he slowly moved to her and lifted her into his arms. The air-raid warden had halted her as he fainted at the doors of the hospital, his head raw and angry. She had stopped, hesitant to help, desperate to get to Jonathon, then Sister Hart had appeared and taken charge. Edith wished for her now. With an old towel wrapped around her head she climbed into bed, swallowed two Mogadon tranquillisers and drifted fitfully into a deep, trouble-free sleep.

In the morning she sensed William standing over her and offering her a cup of tea and a Jaffa cake. Cautiously, he lowered the mug and biscuit onto the glass-topped bedside table, not wanting to wake his dearest wife. He left for his first day back at work following the summer break and she was alone.

She emerged from the pile of bedclothes and drank her tea. The Jaffa cake sank sweetly into her mouth, dissolving almost without chewing, saving her the pain of that action. William had gone. She had the house to clean. The blood to erase. The memories to forget. It was another day.

William had no recollection of thumping his wife. In the early morning he awoke, a habit from the camps he just could not break, and as usual searched for Peter's torturous notebook he kept badly hidden under his blanket. One of Peter's relatives had sent it to him following his death. It had been sealed in brown paper with William's address on it in case of Peter's death. Now it was gone. He leapt out of his small bed and glanced wildly around his domain, until he saw it on the dresser. He could not remember putting it there. But then he could not remember many things very clearly. His habit was to read over Peter's journal of their daring post-war escapades and feed his soul with those long-forgotten events, as a way of spurring him on each day. He had finally quenched his thirst for war. He was a killer. It had all been worthwhile. With this mantra in his mind, he felt he could face the day.

At work his colleagues saw a small-framed wiry man, sallow-skinned and deeply furrowed of brow. A man not to be cornered or challenged. A man who had a brilliant yet unpredictable mind. He lectured, he rarely taught. Interaction with his students was limited in the extreme. They listened and he spoke. As the years progressed, who the students were in front of William mattered very little. What was of great concern to him was his continuing ability to teach the same history, year in, year out, as an affirmation of his years before the war and concrete evidence that there was actually a purpose to his existence.

He clung on to his academic posting. His students knew, through the inevitable back chat of university life, that their lecturer had been a prisoner of war. They respected that. They listened in silence. They worked hard for him and attained high marks. But to stop him mid-flow, to ask a question other than in the session reserved for that at the end of the lecture, was disastrous. He would become confused and aggressive, female students cowered and the tension in the lecture hall was palpable. As his reputation grew, so the less his students interrupted him. It was just safer all round not to.

From his window in the lecture hall William could see into the staff car-park. Of late he was beginning to see unfamiliar cars parked there, rumoured to having been made in Japan, by the Japanese. His heart rate doubled at the sight of these small Civic hatchbacks. As he churned on with his lectures he wondered if any of his captors, or their offspring, had been part of the production line at Honda. What hands, hands that had tortured and tried to kill him, had touched that car? It was an insult that assaulted his eyes, causing flashbacks to his incarceration. He had spent a lifetime repressing any such thoughts. It disturbed him greatly. Yet only a glance away from the structured existence he had carved out for himself lay the very needle to puncture his mind and draw out thoughts he barely had locked away. He continued falteringly with his lecture. A tell-tale vein throbbed in his neck. Underneath the lectern his hands twisted and tensed. Students stared at their lecturer. He had stopped talking.

At the back of the lecture hall stood the Head of Faculty. There had been a similar incident earlier in the year when one of William's students, an aspiring figure skater who had trained at the Whitley Bay rink, returned from the Winter Olympics in Hokkaido, Japan. He had not gained any medals but rather a cute little Japanese girlfriend who, desperate not to miss out on Valentine's Day with her new lover, travelled back to Britain with him. On February the 14th, she had hung around outside the lecture hall, when the student had restarted university.

It had not taken long for William to notice her, he had virtually touched her as he had rushed late to the lecture hall, with all the students already seated inside. His hand had faltered on the heavy handle of the hall door. A sweat had formed on his brow. His pulse had raced. He had turned around and spat words of Japanese at the first Japanese he had seen since the night before he was liberated.

'Nidoto watashi ni furenaide kudasai... Don't ever touch me again' rang in her ears as William's distorted face yelled the words at her, just inches from her skin. The look of her, the smell of her, the words she screamed back at him:

'Watahi wa mo tekide wa arimasen... I am not the enemy any more'

The problem for William was that she was and would always be and that thought would just not leave him. The students had piled out of the hall when they heard the ruckus outside. As the door flew open it knocked William sideways and he staggered back against the wall and slid to the ground with his head in his hands. The girl was standing over him, glaring. Remembering.

Her father was a disgrace in Japan. A failed Kamikaze pilot who had fled back to the aircraft carrier *Akagi*, citing engine problems. The rest of his comrades had successfully bombed Pearl Harbour. Consequently, branded as a failure, her father led a life of misery and regret. She hated the war. She wanted to heal the wounds of war. The man before her had the haunted, desolate look her father often had. She was scooped up into the arms of her boyfriend, who was perplexed as to what might have occurred. There were mumblings, rumours of this and that.

She had returned quickly to Japan. William had been sympathetically chastised. Some students dropped out of his class. William had been told not to let his past impinge any more on his work. How on earth could William do that?

As his personal life slid menacingly, once more, into his

professional life, decisions would have to be made. The Head of Faculty made a mental note to follow up, when the time was right, on this incident. From experience he knew that William would resume lecturing again once whatever demon thought had passed. William had been unaware of his presence.

Minutes later, outside the lecture hall, a small red Honda Civic pulled out of the car park and vanished into the heart of Newcastle.

Then the large red vein in William's neck vanished too. His words returned. The lecture continued.

His class of '72 looked around at each other.

And breathed again.

CHAPTER 15

1970S
WEDDING FEVERS AND FATE

Gordon was sick to death of it all. He wished May were alive to help. In truth Douglas was fed up too. That it was out of control was a mild assessment. Yvette was loving it. The shallowly hidden gypsy blood of her Irish ancestors came to the fore and Irene's wedding was completely sabotaged by excess, large frills, flounces and sequins. Irene smiled sweetly and agreed to everything with a rather irritating sideways nod of her head in deference to her mother's suggestions, before any alternative ideas had even caught the wind.

Coming from rural Kirkham and living in touristy Blackpool, Yvette knew that the height of serious good taste was be found in Poulton-le Fylde, a small market town a mere ten minutes' drive away. Women in Poulton never shopped in Blackpool and for Yvette, if Irene was to rise in the world, Poulton was to aid her renaissance.

Edith sat on the side-lines, anxious to help, anxious to be even asked to help. Cursing William for his job and their relocation to Whitely Bay, as it was so very far away from the centre of things right now. It was all so very different from Berenice's wedding a couple of years ago. A phone call, asking them if they could come. Of course, they would bloody come, she was their daughter, wasn't she? William had chuckled inwardly at Edith's discomfort and silently praised his daughter for just getting on with it. Berenice had bought her wedding dress jointly with her husband, a lovely Empire-style gown that Edith had fretted over, lest guests thought she was pregnant.

Again.

She had not been.

With a Juliet cap, of all things, there was not a hint of a suggestion that she needed a veil. She'd been unveiled years ago in the comfy chair in the dining room. Berenice had phoned her father at precisely 7.35 pm one night, to ask him about her reception. At 7.35 pm Edith would be sitting in her shrine to Sanderson furnishings, by then in desperate need of re-decorating, and she would have been glued to *Coronation Street* since 7.30 pm.

This soap opera had transported Edith out of many a gloomy evening since December 9th 1960 when it was first aired on ITV. She had watched it through suicide attempts and abortions, domestic abuse and post-traumatic stress disorder and that was just what was happening in her home, not on screen! She felt a connection to the storylines.

William had gone to answer the phone in the hall, as he had been having a quiet smoke in the kitchen. Aware that Edith would not stir and holding a fag in one hand and the heavy black receiver in the other, he had been delighted to be asked to pay for the reception at the Bull Inn, Woodstock, in Oxfordshire. A small wedding had been chosen, family, no friends, then a quick escape to the Lake District for a honeymoon. He had agreed instantly, silently hoping the honeymoon would be livelier than his had been.

What joy, William had thought, and he had gone to pour another cup of tea, then rebelled and had a large Harvey's Bristol Cream to celebrate. He had kept the news to himself for weeks until Edith had snapped at him one day, saying that Berenice needed to consult her about the reception and the cake. The cake just had to be square and two tiers. He quietly mentioned that she had organised it all and the reception had been paid for by him. Berenice had ordered everything; it would be just fine.

Edith had been aghast. She was to be denied the planning and the joy? Apparently so. How could she tell her relatives that she had nothing to do with this wedding, other than turning up, and even then, she was never sent an invitation. William ducked and dived his way out of it all as if on manoeuvres. He insisted he had mentioned it to her, but she had been watching 'Corrie'.

Deep down Edith knew that this was Berenice's attempt to forgive and bond with her father, a process that had started in the hospital whilst Berenice was still in college. In a rather reflective mood, she wondered when it would be her turn. How could a mother stand by her daughter's bedside during an illegal abortion and spit out 'Bastards beget bastards' and expect ever to be forgiven. The nurse's pledge sprang in to her mind.

'I solemnly pledge myself to the service of humanity and will endeavour to practise my profession with conscience and with dignity...'

Where was her nurse's conscience when she had begged

their local doctor to sedate her daughter for the drive to Bristol?

Where was it again when she had pleaded with the scoundrel of a doctor not to perform a caesarean, thus risking her daughter's life? Had that fleeting thought of better a dead daughter than a pregnant one really whisked across her brain?

Where had her nurse's dignity been, in the hospital chapel, screaming at her daughter to pray to rid herself naturally of the child within her?

Berenice's father had never, ever, looked her in the eye during the whole debacle in Bristol. He had a conscience. It had worried him enormously. But apparently not Edith. So maybe, thought Edith, she would keep quiet and say nothing to Berenice about her forthcoming wedding. It seemed like Berenice was spoiling for a fight. Edith's fight was wearing thin.

However, Edith reached further dizzying heights of parental torment when William also revealed that he and Berenice would stay in one hotel the night before the wedding and she would stay with her family elsewhere. Berenice wanted another moment of her Daddy all to herself. Edith had excused herself at this comment and gone upstairs to the bedroom. She pulled the quilted nylon bedcover over her mouth and screamed loudly. A muted guttural moan escaped into the chill of the lifeless room. Edith sank sideways onto the bed and she saw a reflection of herself many times over in the three-sided table mirror atop the dressing table. A small, grey-haired woman, too many lines on her fifty-eight-year-old face. Her crumpled twinset ageing and dull. Her life held together by the thinnest threads of deceit and confusion. By 2 am she had given in and called Marigold. Who had, herself, seemed to wither considerably after Julian's death.

Marigold had been up, sitting in the scullery at the back of the house, a place she was drawn to time and time again when she wanted to think about Julian and the life they had shared. She lived on her savings now and did occasional temp work for a nursing agency. William heard the muted telephone conversation through the thin walls between their bedroom and his study. He knew who Edith would be chatting to. He rolled over, hugged his frayed demob blanket around him and wondered how he and Edith could free themselves of their past in order to have a future.

The day of Berenice's wedding dawned. Irene was the only bridesmaid, the matron of honour too, or in this case the matron of dishonour as Berenice liked to joke self-deprecatingly. Irene wore a tranquil moss-green long-sleeved, full-length gown that she looked glum in all day and it pissed off Yvette, as it matched Edith's wool suit perfectly. She suspected they had bought their outfits at the same time. Secretly, Edith had indeed purchased Irene's outfit at Fenwick's French salon in Newcastle, on the same day as she bought her wedding clothes. The reason for Irene's lack of energy at the wedding had nothing to do with that, though; she was watching her whacky adopted cousin, Berenice, get married and so far, she had not found a husband herself and she was two whole years older. To the day. Odd that.

The night before her wedding, Berenice dined with her father and asked him, perhaps inappropriately, considering her marriage was the next day, why he had not divorced her mother. She felt mature enough to ask; she wanted her father to be happy. Perhaps too readily she blamed her mother and the separate bedrooms. Berenice had a happy knack of burying bad memories. Her father's aggression towards her as a teenager had been blocked out.

William had been speechless at the question. He took his time and sighed. Why should he do that? he queried; they were getting along just fine now, he lied. It was the wrong answer for her, confirming what she had speculated on earlier. She had been the problem. No matter, she was getting married and would be out of their hair permanently now. Her secret triumph was a heart-shaped wedding cake. She knew Edith would hate that.

All that had been wrong with Berenice's wedding would be erased and rectified by Irene's. For that reason alone, Berenice nearly didn't accept the lavish gilt-edged, hand-tooled invitation that arrived a year after her own wedding. Berenice had simply called all her guests up and invited them to jot down the details if they wanted to be there. They'd all turned up, hadn't they?

Irene found time to call Berenice one evening as Berenice was marking exercise books and Jed was reviewing case notes. Of course, she would be there, miffed slightly but understanding that the gaggle of bridesmaids from Kirkham had been arranged before Irene could catch her breath. Berenice felt she was like a sister to Irene, the old childhood resentments buried as both cousins saw the limitations of their mothers and talked about this often.

The wedding date was an issue though. Jed had an

unusual case on in Oxford Crown Court and needed to be back on the Sunday to work through the police file before he defended. Sadly, she informed Irene they would not be able to stay long after the reception, she might miss the dancing. Irene and Berenice giggled at the thought of dancing next to their parents on the same dance floor. How weird would that be? Berenice was glad she was going to miss that.

Irene's husband was six feet four, a body-builder and deep-sea diver. He was known as a tough yet vain piece of work on the Blackpool circuit, working angles, never missing the short cut. He appealed to Irene because of the sheer strength of him and she thought that he would always be able to protect her. Irene knew very well that she struggled academically, she smiled too often, never understood anything deeply, but she knew she wanted to be loved and leave behind the cloying, suffocating love of a mother that swamped her.

Not long before his niece's wedding, William heard Edith on the upstairs phone talking to Irene about bridal stuff. He dared to sit in Edith's chair, the one facing the TV. The only one facing the TV. He watched the Winter Olympics and delighted, as he knew his daughter would, that John Curry was set to win in the figure skating for England. His habit had been to take Berenice to the Whitley Bay Ice Rink every Saturday for many years and unbeknown to her had slunk in after half an hour to watch her adolescent antics on the ice.

Berenice was tall and graceful, but at fourteen years old she had looked nineteen. She whizzed past the ice-hockey players who tried to go faster on their double blades. Some tried to trip her up but she jumped out of the way. Watching her master going backwards was wonderful to watch. She just would not give up. One time she had fallen badly, cutting the length of the inside seam of her herringbone flares apart as she landed with one leg bent in to the other.

He had made no pretence of his presence then. In minutes he had bounded down the wooden seats and had lifted her off the ice and into the car with Herculean strength, considering she was three inches taller than him. She had pleaded with him to go and buy her a pair of jeans, all the other girls wore jeans, jeans wouldn't split, they were for tough girls. She was a tough girl.

She couldn't understand why her mother objected to them. So, he had. In the back seat of the car, she had swallowed her wounded pride at falling in front of her heroes of the ice hockey team and arranged herself so she could be back at the rink within the hour, with her newly bought jeans on. This time William stayed close by. Berenice kept half an eye on him as she attempted the 180 degrees jump to enable her to skate backwards; she stayed upright and skated backwards just for a few steps then crashed into the barrier, laughing with her dad as her body expelled all her nervousness and fear. They went home after that. William had no doubt that his daughter would succeed, just as he had no doubt that she, right now, was watching the Winter Olympics down south, as he was, up north.

Irene could not get out of a visit to the bridal shop with her mother. She wanted a simple wedding dress. She envied Berenice having been able to choose and buy her own gown herself. Her mother didn't do simple, ever. Living with her grandpa and her parents was so very claustrophobic for

Irene. She had agreed to marry the first man who asked her, such was her need to escape. In this respect the two cousins mirrored their feelings exactly. Her grandpa, being slightly deaf, was slightly annoying, but as he bankrolled almost everything in her parents' house, she sat quiet, smiled and watched on as her mother used her feline skills to win him over. It was hardly difficult; he too was growing increasingly dependent upon Yvette, so he had little choice.

The bridal shop in Breck Street, Poulton was the place to buy her gown, Yvette had gushed. It was close to the church of St Chad, dating back to Norman times, which meant nothing to Yvette beyond the fact that it reeked of good taste, unlike herself, and was the church in which her daughter would marry handsome Steve. A Ronald Joyce gown was bought. Irene hated it. Yvette loved it. Douglas just wrote the cheque on his and his father's joint account. The dress had lace. Irene had wanted heavy satin. It had layers. Irene had wanted a simple, A-line fit. It had beading and looked busy. Irene had wanted a calm look. Worst of all it had a twenty-foot train which might possibly snap svelte Irene in two if it snagged on anything. Steve visited the shop the following week and bought himself a grey wool flared suit with a waistcoat of lavender silk and a white silk tie, sturdy enough for a full Windsor knot. This was his first suit. His casual, open-shirted, medallion-man look, which he used in the Blackpool nightclubs, would have to be shelved for the time being. Steve had plans. He wanted to open a dive shop in South Shore, Blackpool, convinced it would succeed. He had no business sense or common sense but plenty of ambition. Irene understood none of it. Their main wedding present was a cheque from her parents and grandfather to start up the dive shop. Steve enjoyed spending the money pre-wedding on stylish fixtures for the shop and all his mates from the Manchester Pub on South Shore egged him on.

One particularly nasty piece of work, an ex-con', who trained with Steve in a local gym, suggested to Steve that he probably should take out life insurance on Irene. Steve had not thought about this but conceded it might come in handy. The deed was done, for three hundred thousand pounds. Irene signed in agreement. Or rather Steve's friend at the gym did on her behalf; he had practice in these shady matters. Steve felt well prepared for the wedding.

William and Edith travelled in near silence to Irene's wedding. Edith was hoping that her daughter would not turn up in the hippie look she had favoured for the past few years. Most of all she just wanted to get as close as possible to Irene in the wedding pictures. She wanted a trophy for the mantelpiece, one that would eclipse the picture sent to her by Berenice of the cake-cutting at her wedding. She blanched every time she saw the triumphant look on Berenice's face as she drove the knife into the centre of the love-heart-shaped wedding cake that had appalled her so. If she could, she would confine the picture to the dining room, but perversely, William insisted it stayed up, in Edith's sight, in the living room. Even though he spent many hours alone in the dining room.

Berenice had bought a wool suit for this wedding. It was still chilly in April that year. It would come in handy for parents' evenings at the girls' boarding school she taught at. It was a departure from her normal bohemian, cultish look and as Jed looked at her, he said, 'Your mother will like that.'

He had a hard job keeping it on her after that but she was finally persuaded to get in the car with it on and they too, like her parents, drove to Irene's wedding in near silence.

Steve towered above Irene. Berenice felt a disquiet as he strode back down the aisle with her cousin in tow. She was glad that they were not staying for too long. Her mother and father circled, mainly her mother angling to be at the heart of the photographer's shots. She looked at her father, hanging back in the shadows, slight of build but looking very dapper in his morning coat. She had insisted on plain double-breasted three-piece suits for her own wedding. It may have been a mistake. She would die rather than admit that, though.

Irene sat on the bridal table with as many of Yvette's family around her as they could get and Steve's mother and cousin holding the fort on his side of the family. There was no father in sight. His mother was enjoying the free booze. It was set to be a typically dysfunctional wedding.

It was getting late before the dancing started. Irene had gone upstairs in the hotel to change into her going-away outfit; she too would not be staying long if she and Steve were to catch the midnight flight to Benidorm from Blackpool airport. She was so very pleased that she had chosen the Shard Hotel at Hambleton, on the riverside, with its enchanting terrace overlooking the river Wyre. She and her Aunt Edith had often lunched there when she was down from Whitley Bay and in fact, it had been this that had made her choose the venue. She always had a great time with her aunt. From the window of her room, she saw her cousin leaving, wiping a tear from her eye and being hugged by Jed. She opened the window and called out to them to wait. She ran down the stairs. Outside it was freezing, the two cousins clung to each other and Berenice whispered in her ear the Shakespearean parting they had made their own, 'Good night, goodnight, parting is such sweet sorrow, that I shall say goodnight till it be morrow.'

Looking back at Irene as she stood watching her, with what seemed like a tear in her eye, Berenice had a similar feeling to the one that had upset her so much minutes before, when she had glanced at her father dancing with her mother.

It was that feeling that had first assaulted her when she had opened that wardrobe door, in her childhood house in Whitley Bay.

Evil.

She caught her breath again, rushed back and hugged her cousin fiercely. She wished she had done that with her father. Then, before Irene could see her tears, and she spoilt her wedding, she ran to the car, where Jed was revving the engine, and she sped away, far too quickly.

Irene could see her new husband through the window. Ten minutes earlier he had been in the bedroom with her, he too changing for the flight. She had asked him to step aside so she could see herself in the full-length mirror. She was three steps behind him. His height and weight utterly eclipsed her. He had turned around and scared her with his look. Then he'd left. Later that night, Edith asked Irene if Berenice had actually left, as she hadn't seen her for a while. Irene confirmed that she had. 'Shame,' said Edith, 'I think her father wanted a word with her.'

He was never to have that word with her.

Irene sighed and moved inside to find Steve dancing with a blonde who worked on the reception desk at his regular gym. He ignored his new bride. Yvette was too drunk with her family to notice. Gordon looked on and wondered at it all. Perhaps it had not been such a good idea for his son to take his wife back, all those years ago. They would have survived. They all would have survived. It was too late now. How he missed his dear wife May, and sitting awkwardly in the corner, without a companion in the world, he shed a tear and nodded off to sleep, despite the music. Being deaf was such a help at times he thought, as he shut his eyes on the modernity all around him. He drifted off to sleep and found himself in the trenches with a head wound and thick green smoke all around. It was only the dry ice machine from the disco, shouted Douglas into his better ear, as he had woken up screaming and shouting.

He longed for death.

Edith and William drove back from the wedding the next day, across Shap once more. She had been worried about the state of her father, he seemed to be getting very confused. She had suggested to Yvette, at the wedding breakfast, that maybe she should stay over and help with her father for a while. William's mind had been willing Yvette to agree and looked on eagerly as Douglas and his wife exchanged furrowed looks. It was decided that no, thanks all the same, they would manage for the time being; if not, they would give her a ring.

Gordon had been lip-reading the whole conversation. It

puzzled him that for the most fleeting of moments he simply could not remember who these disparate people were sitting around him having breakfast. He looked down at his toast, it was just easier. Then he buttered it for a second time. Nobody noticed.

Irene saw little of her new husband at the Hotel Don Juan in Benidorm, a shabby two-star affair with water stains on the ceilings and even worse stains on the bedding. School-style meals were served institutionally at regular intervals, plus chips with everything.

She shuddered. Steve had paid for the hotel. Somehow, she had just expected better. Outside of their room a small balcony overlooked an industrial complex, which housed the hotel laundry and a noisy metal works. Steve made no apology and simply said that cost-cutting now would ensure a better business model later. Irene longed to be back at work with her friends. Familiar faces. At night she cried for her family and especially Aunt Edith and Berenice. She was unused to change, depressed at the lack of closeness to Steve. She wondered if she had made the right decision. He seemed to have made a contact in the area, something to do with a joint venture in relation to the diving business she was told. So, after dinner, she actually saw very little of him.

Edith and Berenice, strangely united for once, were each having the same thoughts about the mysteriously menacing Steve. Talk of the honeymoon had spurred William on to ask, once more, if he could enter their bed and thus Edith. She claimed all manner of illnesses to repel his advances. He would wait. But not for much longer.

Then finality of life came down the telephone once more.

Edith called up to William in hysterics.

Irene was dead.

Steve had come back to the hotel room to find the balcony doors open, his wife's body crumpled four storeys below, skewered on discarded metal from the factory opposite. He was naturally distraught, flying home with Irene's ashes as soon as. It was too expensive for him to bring the body back. He had not taken out any travel insurance. The British Embassy in Spain had offered to fly the body back and retain Steve's passport in Britain until he had paid them back. He had refused. He intended to complete the paid for holiday.

Upon his arrival back at Blackpool airport, he shed more light onto his new wife's death. She had been drinking heavily, indeed the Spanish authorities had found large quantities of whisky in Irene. Tellingly they also found many Temazepam. It was ruled as a suicide. She had been cremated within three days of her death. The season for British tourists was kicking off again in Benidorm. The police there had no real desire to deploy any further resources looking into her death. It had all seemed so clear to them.

Douglas noted the scratches on Steve's arms as he heaved the suitcase into the car boot. He said nothing. He'd also observed the shifty way his eyes had searched the arrivals, a few minutes earlier and the speed with which he'd offloaded the urn containing the ashes into Yvette's arms. Douglas had further noticed a familiar face with her head down, a few feet back from Steve, with a cap on her blonde head and her eyes firmly facing the floor. He could not be quite sure. He would check the wedding pictures when he got home. It was not over for Douglas. That night he called William with his suspicions.

Yvette was huddled on the sofa with the green plastic urn cradled in her arms. She seemed to have shrunk. All around were the wedding photos waiting to go into the gold-leaf-embossed album. Douglas stared hard at one of them and saw it straight away. He called William back.

Edith was wailing so hard that William could hardly hear Douglas on the phone, and said he would call back. Up to the medicine cabinet he flew, found his tranquillisers and crushed two into a sweet cup of tea that he urged Edith to drink.

She missed *Coronation Street* that night.

Douglas was struggling with a recent diagnosis of cancer that he had been keeping from breaking to the family until his daughter's wedding was over. The pills he was on made him feel weak. Could William help? William had wondered how. Douglas was unclear, too scared to speak of the revenge his father's heart was bursting to exact. William told him to calm down and take a step back; the police would be at his door first thing if anything happened to Steve right now. Reluctantly Douglas put down the phone on the idea that his brother-in-law, with a very subdued but evident ruthless streak in him, was unable or unwilling to help.

William was neither.

To steer his pent-up fury at being denied sex by Edith, he sat alone in the kitchen as she slept on upstairs and he decided to act. No more than he had done many times before over the years. By acting, he hoped Edith would see the justice of it all even though she would never find out that it was William. Maybe then she would invite him back into her bed.

William wanted to act fast but his clever head told him to wait.

In fact, he waited until he was in Blackpool, the following Christmas, with Edith's relatives.

As Edith and her family sat around following a very subdued Christmas lunch, all still obviously mourning Irene's passing, he popped out. He needed to find a shop open selling cigarettes. Nobody tried to stop him. He had done his reconnaissance. Steve still lived in the Blackpool South Shore house that he was supposed to have been living in with Irene.

William pulled up outside. The late afternoon was darkening and a sea fret had rolled in. Steve's new Range Rover sat in the drive, with diving gear heaped in the back. Proceeds of the insurance claim handed to him two weeks after Irene's death. It had been hard to restrain Douglas when he'd heard about that; only his increasing constraints as a result of his prostate cancer prevented him from action.

William skittered underneath the high end, off road vehicle. Easy for one so slight. He nicked the soft brake tubes leading to the back wheels. That way, when Steve started the car, it would seem like the brakes were still working, as some of the fluid would still be in the system. William was back in his car in an instant. Nobody noticed the muck on the back of his jacket when he got back. Well, Douglas did. He just prayed and his thoughts were evil.

And evil was duly done.

The breaking news on the TV, a few days later, just before New Year's Eve, silently cheered everyone up as they sat in stunned silence, looking at the wreck of Steve's car and the mangled pair inside. A treacherous stretch of black ice on the hill by the airport was thought to be the cause.

Douglas glanced over at William.

William stared blankly back.

Above, Irene's happy face lit up the skies.

Edith smiled over at William.

Things were looking up.

CHAPTER 16

EARLY 1970S
BEFORE WILLIAM'S DEATH

To Gordon, it seemed as if he was often in two places at once, sometimes even three. This perplexed him greatly. His dear wife had died. He knew that. He remembered her funeral well. The months and years after were not at all clear. Years later, in the dental surgery, his final major incident could have certainly cost him his licence. It had frightened him terribly. Looking down into the gaping mouth of an elderly patient he had momentarily frozen: why was he here, who was this person, what even was his own name?

Douglas had been but a step behind him, sensing that not all was well. His father was ageing rapidly. A gaunt stretching of the skin over now seemingly fragile bones. A lost look in his eye that Douglas put down to his father grieving still, for his mother. But in that moment, standing behind his faltering father, he too panicked. A trickle of sweat ran down the back of Douglas's shirt as he reached out to touch his father's shoulder, ever so gently.

It had been enough. A familiar touch, a reawakening of the senses that alerted Gordon to his surroundings. But he had jerked slightly at the touch. He was holding a small dental scalpel; he had been about to scrape off the plaque from the base of the patient's teeth, where it had adhered to the gum. With that jerk came a contact that never should have happened.

The patient, a seventy-year-old, with a surprising number of his own teeth still intact, thanks to Gordon's care over the years, had seen the vacancy in Gordon's eyes and had been about to speak. His tongue had made sharp, painful contact with the scalpel. Blood poured from the slash in the tip of his tongue and the dental surgery erupted into chaos.

The patient sat upright and screamed.

Gordon took an involuntary step back, dropping the scalpel. It skittered under the chair, leaving a trail of blood in its wake.

Douglas escorted his father out of the surgery and sat him down hastily in his own waiting room. He then rushed to the freezer for some ice and wrapped it in surgical gauze, insisting that the patient ceased screaming, and sat calmly applying pressure to the graze, at the very tip of his tongue, until the bleeding stopped. Within ten minutes it had and the patient was told to go home and rinse daily with salt water. There was a nick in his tongue, not a deep cut.

Fortunately, this had been the last patient of the afternoon. As he stumbled out of the surgery, past Gordon in the waiting room and out to the taxi, which Douglas had called, Gordon had sat with his head in his hands. He never spoke, not sorry or one solitary word. Once again, he was unsure of his surroundings and he closed his eyes to the white walls and strip lighting, far too bright, far too modern for a soldier. But he recognised the trail of blood.

There was confusion all around him. Choking smoke in the air. Barbed wire, with shreds of life flapping furiously in the breeze, as if gruesomely waving a macabre farewell to arms. He rolled over in the mud and something dug into him under his left leg. Reaching down he held the hand of another fallen soldier and tried to pull him out from underneath him. The soldier felt light, wasted by war. It was only a hand.

To his right there was machine-gun fire, to his left the occasional bursts from Lee Enfield rifles that whizzed over his head. He hunkered down low in the crater; it was surprisingly comforting to hold the hand of the dead soldier beneath him, it was still warm. Dusk was approaching as the French moon descended over the edge of the huge crater and Gordon waited. He had dropped the hand once it became icy cold and ripped ragged strips of somebody's shirt around his throbbing head and acutely aching ears.

His ears felt sticky. Sounds became muted as they filled up with mud, his own blood and the slivers of others blown to buggery in the blast that had rocked his fighter plane and caused him to roll out of the open cockpit and land where he was. The quagmire of decay surrounded him in his purgatory. No-man's-land was surely just that. A land where no man should reside. The smells swamped him as his senses returned once the shock wore off. Rotten, it was all rotten, even the blood turned brown as it sank or swam in the rain-filled puddles that became indistinguishable from slaughterhouse slop. Dear God in heaven, he prayed, save me for May. 'Save me!' he screamed.

From not too far off came an urgent whisper. 'Be quiet, we are close, we will save you.'

Gordon never returned to war.

He was sweating as he looked down at his hand, covered in blood.

'It's OK, Dad, it's the patient's blood, not yours.'

For a heartbeat Gordon thought he was still holding the soldier's dead hand in no-man's-land. Then he fainted.

Douglas looked down at this crumpled shell that had once been his mighty father; he could not cope with this by himself. His father was ill. He should not be allowed to practise any more. There would have to be substantial changes.

Whilst Douglas organised all of this, Gordon was sent to live with Edith, as, rather conveniently, she was alone. William was in the asylum having respite during the summer and Berenice was living down south.

This galvanised Edith. She was up, dressed and functioning within fifteen minutes, and caring for her father became her lifeblood. She let him sit, every day, in her precious wing-backed chair. She had no time to sit. It was a race with her proud father to find where he had hidden his soiled underwear and his urine-stained trousers. Thank God, the central heating was not on, as tucked behind every radiator in the house was the evidence of her father's decline and his distress.

Edith needed more energy to deal with all of this and suddenly she began to cook and eat more.

Her energy levels were high and needed nourishment. From a slice of toast at breakfast and perhaps a leftover chicken wing for lunch she graduated to three square meals a day. Her father ate languidly. He often looked at food that he had started to eat ten minutes earlier and proclaimed it not to be his. He wouldn't touch food that others had started to eat. He would shove it away violently, spilling it on the floor. Edith had a hard job with the stains on the ageing worn yellow carpet in the dining room. Her father withered before her and his eyes became rheumy and distant.

At night she would put the TV on and sometimes she would turn to look at him, but then he would pick up the newspaper to hide his face from her.

In those moments Gordon was panicked. Utterly panicked. He did not recognise the woman sitting to his right. He did not recognise the room he was sitting in. He looked down at his arthritic fingers and age-spotted hands and wondered who they belonged to. Where was his wife? Why was she not next to him as she always had been? It was easier to hide behind the paper until his panicked, contorted mind subsided. After an incident like this he would just stare blankly or snap requests at Edith.

After six weeks of this Edith was exhausted. Thankfully, Douglas had called. A dentist had been hired to run the surgery and replace their father. A home help had also been hired and he felt all was in place to have his father back in the home he was familiar with. Dementia patients need familiarity, he had been told. Douglas's assertiveness was also born of the fact that he was now in sole charge of his father's finances and he very much felt that he called the shots. He was unwilling to continue sending money to Edith; he and Yvette would deal with it all themselves. Thank you very much, Edith.

A special downstairs bathroom had been installed for Gordon. He would no longer share the upstairs bathroom with them. He had a bed made up in the smallest of the downstairs rooms and this freed up space in the house so Yvette's relatives from Kirkham could stay over. Douglas bought himself a lovely white Jaguar, one that his father simply could not get in to or out of. He was going through a delayed adolescent indulgence, one that had been partially robbed of him by the war. In December the ritual Christmas and New Year family gathering was cancelled. Edith was distraught.

William more so. Berenice and Jed were in Italy for Christmas. What would her parents do? The rhythm of their life was flaky at best. Edith suggested ringing Marigold, she was all alone now, perhaps it would be a kindness.

William was having none of it. He called Yvette. He had always had a special affinity with her. She was a survivor and so was he, they shared the commonality of outsiders within this proud family. Well perhaps just New Year, she suggested. She was having her Kirkham clan over for Christmas, but New Year would suit if Edith and William could make the journey over the new Shap motorway, at that perilous time of the year.

Edith did call Marigold, but fortunately for William she insisted they come up to her for Christmas, which William refused to do, far too much driving, he complained. And so, it was settled. They would be by themselves for Christmas. They stared at each other over an indifferently cooked Christmas lunch. Neither of them could ever remember cooking one before. It was a grim and shudder-inducing vision of their future laid bare before them. They did not like what they saw, and were unclear in their heads as to how to alter their lifestyle.

Old Shap pass was perilous. A stretch of the A6, which links the north to the south and often becomes hazardous in winter, had by now been replaced by an equally treacherous stretch of motorway. This 36 mile section of road linking Lancaster and Penrith was, and still is, the highest section of motorway in England, at 1043 feet high. For William, it was still unfamiliar. He was used to driving on the old Shap pass. Ridges of reinforced ice, blown into drifts by bitingly cold easterly winds, surged onto the motorway. In much the same way as they used to on the old A6 road. The difference being, motorists were lulled into thinking they could now travel faster, as it was a real motorway. This meant extra vigilance was required.

William had started driving just after noon on New Years' Eve. The car's heater packed up at 3 pm and they were still miles short of traversing the width of England in order to get from Northumberland to Lancashire. Edith gritted her teeth, as much out of frustration with the journey as with the effort to stop them from chattering. The cold was intense. By 3.30 pm she had lost the feeling in her fingers. William's hands gripped the steering wheel as he fought the car for control, straining forward as the wipers struggled valiantly with the flurries of snow that blinded the windscreen every minute or so. As he drove, he pondered how much longer this could continue. They had been making this pilgrimage every year for nearly three decades. What had to happen, in their household, for a change in routine to occur?

He had no time to think, as something suddenly fell off

the lorry ahead of them, across the hard shoulder and the slow lane, but far enough ahead for them to stop safely. The other two lanes were already blocked off for maintenance and thick with virgin snow. William needed Edith's help.

He pulled over into the hard shoulder and parked. In patent leather Clarks block-heeled shoes, she was woefully underprepared to be trudging in the snow. William's leather brogues fared no better. Together they bent down, her mittened hands brushing against his leather driving gloves. They turned to stare at each other. United in effort. Perhaps for the first time in decades. They pulled and rolled the escaping piece of scaffolding to the side of the road and stood up. William hugged Edith. She was so stiff with cold it felt like heaven and she arched into him in a way forgotten for years. She looked up into his eyes and they were both startled by the hoot of a car horn, barely a couple of yards away. They had been lost in their own world for a second.

'Do you need any help?' shouted the driver of the car.

'Well thanks, but I think we have everything sorted. You don't have a wee drop of whisky, do you?' asked William. It was nearly New Year after all.

They reached Blackpool by six. Shoes were discarded, toes steamed next to the coal fire, but far enough away to avoid chilblains. A strangely silent William and Edith stared at each other, as if seeing themselves afresh.

On the radio they listened to a Scottish New Year with bagpipes and songs and Gordon sat in the corner, dozing in his chair. Yvette had served a late dinner, waiting anxiously for William and Edith, who had had no means of contacting them until they reached a phone box an hour outside

Blackpool. Thankfully the phone had been working.

Time for bed. It was 1 am. Whisky had been consumed. They had opened the curtains to watch some noisy fireworks. Yvette had first-footed the home. She had cried throughout the experience. As Berenice was not there, it should have been Irene. It was a grim affair, but at last it was time to stop putting coals on the fire, turn out the lights and head for bed. Douglas went over to his father. Gordon slumbered on, slumped on the sofa with his head peacefully resting on the low wide arm of the comfortable brown leather Chesterfield. No point in moving him thought Douglas, and Edith and William had already gone up to bed. Yvette was upstairs, asleep fully clothed, slightly sloshed, again. So, Gordon was left where he was.

As Douglas made his way to bed, across the landing he could hear Edith and William arguing. It seemed that Edith was refusing her husband. Douglas despaired of the ill-matched couple. That they had not divorced years ago was a mystery to him. Then he heard a clout. He moved to put his hand on the bedroom door handle, then thought better of it. He stayed outside the door for at least ten minutes. Silent, waiting to burst in and confront William. He heard a kind of laughter, then snoring. It was only then he went to bed, slipping in awkwardly, trying to get under the candlewick bedspread and sheets, which was tricky as Yvette was on top of everything. Then he too started to snore.

Downstairs Gordon struggled to sit upright. The dying red glow of the sun as it finally descended over the crater plunged him into near darkness. His head hurt terribly and he could not be sure what he was hearing. Suddenly there were flares everywhere; through the opaque darkness he saw them as they whizzed high into the sky, arching downwards far too close to his position. He attempted to move but sank further into the crater. He clawed at the brown earth around him but made no headway. He lurched to the side and seemed to slide down a further embankment. The flares rose again and Gordon curled himself tight in a foetal ball to avoid being spotted by the enemy. In the silent space he heard low rumblings, like a heavy engine trying to move forward. He felt a rising panic; what with the flares and the sounds, he was sure his position would be compromised shortly. His left arm pained him terribly and his throat went dry. Then he saw the clear white light moving towards him and his chest pain totally subsided.

May's embrace was so very tender.

Edith stumbled, literally, into Gordon as she rose early and went to resurrect the fire. She lay on the floor with her stone-cold soldier father and started a moaning which awoke Douglas. He rushed into the room and surveyed the tragedy. His sister and his dead father on the cold carpet and the rising pungency of death pervading his nostrils. There was no doubt. The doctor was called and by the time he arrived Edith was being comforted by William who, strangely, was sporting a very red cheek. Last night, Edith had refused sex, yet again, not in her father's house if you please, she had said. She had slapped William at the thought, but he had merely laughed. It wouldn't be long he had thought, then he had fallen into a deep sleep.

A numbingly wearisome round of procedure and form-filling ensued and then Gordon's funeral was finally planned for the end of the week. Edith was rocked to her core and moved cautiously as if her limbs would drop off if she made sudden movements. Re-visiting her mother's grave, so close to her small brother, spun her back in time and she was largely supported through it all by William who stood stoically by in the numbing January coldness of the cemetery. The gravediggers had waited until the last minute, they had to be persuaded to chip off the cement round the marble and slide back the heavy slab. It was not work they relished at this time of the year. Douglas had offered them some extra cash but even then, the funeral party had stood around for far too long in the chill.

Everyone was relieved when the white marble slab was hoisted back into position and they could arguably leave the cemetery without undue haste. How lucky was Berenice to be enjoying Italy?

Actually, she wasn't. There had been arguments in her household too. Go to Blackpool for Christmas and New Year or go to Jed's parents? The decision was taken to tell both sets of parents that they were going overseas. They actually stayed at home and the landline had been unplugged. It had been brilliantly indulgent. Berenice could just not face the Blackpool scene with no Irene to share jokes with. They had mentioned to everyone that they were arriving back on January 8th. One day too late for her grandfather's funeral.

When she finally reconnected the landline, it never stopped ringing. Jed's mother was waiting to see the holiday snaps. Awkward. But her own mother was simply distraught.

Berenice felt rotten guilty. She had found her grandfather difficult, due to his deafness. But the war stories he had told her when she was a youngster had always been fascinating and now, in adulthood, she guessed that it had been his way of reaching out to her. He would probably have preferred a grandson. Her whole life was trying to second guess what her immediate family would have preferred instead of her. But he was gone and next time she went with Jed to Blackpool, they would pay their respects at the cemetery.

To remedy her guilt and reach out to her mother, she vowed to take her away at Easter, on holiday. She spent a long time flicking through the various brochures that were there, on her hall floor, when she came home from work. A Fly Drive holiday to the Loire valley was chosen.

Perfect. Just her and her mother.

Time to make amends. Time to connect and forgive.

As an adult, she reflected that a baby may not have been the right thing to acquire in her teens. Should she thank her mother? Well, no, that would have been a step too far.

Edith was anxious. She had never flown before and was faced with an internal flight from Newcastle to Gatwick in order to meet Berenice, fly to France, then collect the car for the holiday. She was excited, nervous, sick then bossy in a round of emotions that William was exhausted by, and which only ended when she marched along the companionway and on to the aeroplane. Edith looked admiringly at the red, white and blue stripes of the air hostesses who greeted her aboard the British Airways Trident. She had insisted on travelling by British Airways for her first ever flight.

William had not gone to the airport viewing lounge, as he was asked to by Edith, instead he had rushed to the car park and scooted off home. Unused as he was to the house all to himself, he intended to smoke in every room and only tidy up the morning of Edith's arrival home. He too was suffering from a delayed adolescent surge of defiance that had been lodged so deeply he had previously feared it might never surface.

Berenice had parked in the twenty-minute-only pick-up bay at Gatwick. She knew what time her mother was arriving. Inside she watched the display board reveal the arrival times. Birmingham, Manchester, Edinburgh... hang on a minute, Newcastle had been scheduled to arrive before Edinburgh!

Edith had been seated next to the window, overlooking the aeroplane wing. In her smart blue suit and matching hat, she looked more like she was going to church than on holiday. But then she rarely went on journeys. Her leather-gloved hands gripped the sides of her seat as the plane began the short taxi to the end of the runway. The businessman next to her had sighed and hoped he would not be involved with a middle-aged lady having a panic attack. The passenger behind Edith was trying to stop giggling at the mesh on her ridiculous hat, which kept getting caught on the back of her seat.

As William pulled into the driveway he smiled. He was still smiling as he lay on what was essentially Edith's double bed and smoked. He meandered downstairs and made himself an enormous fry-up that stank the house. He was enjoying this holiday of his. It was not just Edith on holiday he thought. With a cup of tea in one hand, a fag hanging out of his mouth and a bacon and fried-egg butty sliding worrying around a greasy plate, he plonked himself down in Edith's wing-backed chair and switched over to BBC as soon as *Coronation Street* came on. There was a thankful sigh from the region of the TV.

As the plane gathered speed, Edith started to scream. The plane was on fire. Well, actually not the whole plane, but there were a few worrying licks of red emanating from the engine attached to the wing, attached to the plane and therefore, surmised Edith in blind panic, attached to her! She screamed, the businessman's pen jolted and smudged his precise notes for his London meeting. The lady behind Edith stopped smirking and started grimacing; she too could see the smoke billowing from the engine. With take-off speeds of nearly two hundred miles per hour, the resulting engine failure from the bird strike had caused the plane to make an emergency stop and Edith, along with all other passengers, had been hurried down the chute on the other side of the plane, whilst the still smoking engine was doused with foam.

As she hurried away from the plane, shoes in hand, the swishing of her nylon stockings as they rubbed against the nylon of her petticoat nearly caused secondary sparks. She heard the staff talk of the mute swans that lived on the nature reserve, just beyond the end of the runway at Dinnington. As she ran away from the chute, she stopped and looked back for a moment. The plane by then was being attended by five fire engines and was busy being cordoned off, the sight of which caused her to faint into the arms of the irate businessman who had previously been sitting next to her and who felt the bloody woman had cursed the flight with her nerves. He dumped her into the arms of an air hostess and the emergency crew picked her up and drove her back to the airport.

Berenice heard her name echoing out of the airport passenger locator system. Report to customer services desk 43, it politely asked her. She trudged the length of Gatwick. What on earth could have gone wrong with her well-made plans? Hidden behind a bank of offices was desk 43. She was informed of the delay, her mother's reactions and her current situation. Was her mother all right, she had enquired? Oh yes, quite fine, if a little speechless. Following an agreed 'get back on the horse' type of policy, they had escorted her to the next available flight and she was now on her way to Gatwick where she would be arriving in exactly one and a half hours. She was already airborne. Berenice called her father at home who took a little while to answer, as he was listening to sports on the BBC, but he confirmed that Edith was fine. He hadn't even gone to the airport; he had, of course, agreed to the staff placing her on the next flight to Gatwick. She had apparently been reluctant to make any such decision. He had been insistent. Berenice congratulated her father for this swift and decisive action and rushed to the café to sit still for a moment and check the ferry timing and if all would still work for the Channel crossing with the car on the ferry.

The car!

Shit shit shit!

Berenice rushed to where she had left it, but it was gone, hauled off to the airport pound. A long, long, walk later plus a stern talking-to by the authorities had not improved her mood and she just about got it all completed, finally parked in the long stay car park and had a reviving coffee when the arrival of her mother's flight was announced. When she emerged through arrivals, the two dishevelled women glared at each other at the start of their epic 'get to know each other' holiday.

Edith watched as Berenice took charge. Upon reflection, it seemed to her that Berenice had always, in her own way, been in charge. Perhaps not when she made her get rid of the baby, but that had seemed very wrong afterwards. Because of it, Edith was haunted by guilt. Her dreams constantly sapped her strength and her morale was low, for so long afterwards. It had been as if William blamed her too. How many babies had she lost? These thoughts and more swirled unceasingly around her until at times until she could no longer function. She knew she should not sit all day long in festering inactivity but she knew no clear path out of it. Except now, looking at the resilience of youth, how Berenice had seemingly put it all behind her, she marvelled and wondered if she too could erase the demons and resurrect her joyful self.

For once she was glad her daughter had an independently bossy streak. She just needed to be told what to do right now. There was no denying she was in shock from the plane debacle, but the no nonsense approach of Berenice and the urgency of the sea crossing propelled them both quite swiftly to the bowels of the ferry. Once in the upstairs lounge, they looked at each other and laughed. Perhaps the holiday would not be a disaster and to Berenice's surprise her mother ordered a glass of wine. Good – the wine-tasting holiday would be a success, despite the inauspicious start.

For three whole weeks the pair of them giggled and gasped at too many wine tastings, in fairy-tale French chateaux, resplendent with Disneyesque turrets. Montsoreau,

Langeais, d'Amboise, Chambord and Fontainebleau swam into dizzying sameness as Sauvignon Blanc vied with Merlot and Cabernet Franc to cloud their horizons and fill the boot of the car with tinkling samples. Berenice and Edith variously drove, admired, supped, laughed, clinked then slept their way through the whole holiday as if they were the very best of friends having a blast. To Berenice, it was as if this creature she was sharing this holiday with was not her mother, but a similar-looking person who bore no resemblance to Edith and drank far too much and even, dare she say it, flirted with the French guides hosting the wine tastings.

William was feeling slightly guilty. Guilty for rushing away from the airport so speedily. Guilty also for the awful mixture of nicotine and grease that hung in the air in every room of the house. Berenice had promised to call once they were both safely en route home.

He could not wait any longer for Edith to be the wife he wanted her to be.

The first day of Edith's holiday was the day his letter confirming early retirement arrived. He had not discussed any of the implications of this with Edith. The negotiations had started months earlier. He could be free of it all by the time the Easter holidays expired. He signed with relish, a weight from his heart, and a lightness appeared in his step. No more pretending he really understood the modern world, no more hiding behind his façade of academia. In retirement he could really be himself, and himself wanted, just as he had wanted all those years ago in Changi, to be a proper husband for Edith.

Edith's holiday was for three weeks. He had two weeks left.

He cleared the heaped ashtray from the fireplace hearth and switched off the TV. He knew how to start planning this. There was an inevitability about his decision that had been brewing for years. He started the preparations for what must be done before he retired.

Once that was done, there would be a way forward with Edith.

It really wouldn't take too long.

He smiled.

CHAPTER 17

AN ENDING AND A BEGINNING

Marigold was ageing poorly, having literally shrunk following Julian's death. Rudderless and confused, she dared not leave the house to make the connections he had made. It was bad enough going to the shops. She had never learnt to drive, so he had done it all for them both and following his death she had sold the Mercedes he had treasured.

The adoption agency floundered and with new, tighter, government procedures, she felt it best to give it up and not be the subject of scrutiny by curious faces from Social Services. The only two people she kept in contact with were Jonathon and Edith. William had sussed her, she felt sure. On visits over the years, he had stared at the house malevolently and refused to come inside with Berenice and Edith, claiming that he needed to smoke and didn't want to clog up her lungs with his fumes.

She knew that had been a lie, he knew she knew that it was a lie, but the game was played out. They had stopped coming years ago, though. Berenice had always hated her too. A precocious child with a strong will and a stare that sent shivers into Marigold. Surely, she couldn't know too?

That she suspected something was evident, and as the years rolled on it came to the point that Marigold suggested to Edith that it was better simply to meet up on their own, whenever the chance arose. It seemed that Berenice would divine the truth with her stare and Marigold just could not cope with her manner any more.

Just as tenaciously as Edith hung onto her secrets regarding her true feelings for Jonathon, she continued to contact Marigold at every bump in her life. Hearing Marigold's voice would transport her back into Jonathon's arms and for Edith it was the respite from the horrors of her life with war-ravaged William that she needed. Marigold never wished that she had conducted herself otherwise. She had no remorse, no understanding of what she had done as wrong. Her lust for power for its own sake, above the common needs of decency, never appalled her. Jonathon had long since privately diagnosed her as a psychopath and a very dangerous one at that. Her superficial charm and grandiose sense of self-worth were matched one hundred per cent by her pathological lying and manipulative ways. Her need to dominate was only eclipsed by her need to intimidate and be cruel. She believed, utterly, in the fact that she was better than anyone else around her. Her amorality escalated her madness to a messianic belief in her actions. Only when Julian had died did she pause.

Walks to the local shops alarmed her. Women stopped in their tracks when they saw her, such were the rumours, then walked on the other side of the street rather than have to cross her path. Shopkeepers rushed to their doors to switch the 'open' sign to 'closed' if they saw her walking towards their shop. If they were too late and she got a foot in the door, then they insisted goods had run out, when they were in plain sight. She had to walk farther each shopping trip. Her bones were aching, her muscles were weak, she had never walked far. Julian had done all that, despite his afflictions. But everywhere she went she felt the eyes of others bearing in on her and she scurried through her shopping trips, rarely fulfilling her needs and consequently wasting away quite alarmingly over the years.

One day, Marigold was walking past a local Catholic church when she encountered a priest. He was on the steps leading down from the double main doors. He looked at Marigold and instantly he remembered one of the Catechisms of the Catholic Church, which clearly reads,

When the church asks publicly and authoritatively in the name of Jesus Christ that a person be protected against the power of the Evil One and withdrawn from his domain, it is called exorcism.

The priest was adept at sensing the Evil One. There is an unholy aura which surrounds people in the grip of the Evil One. Marigold had that aura. The priest had followed her, she had hurried, sensing his flapping robes gaining on her. She had stumbled. He made a grab for her, but found he was repelled from touching her and she fell to the ground. He stared into the face of the Evil One and his body shook with the power of repulsing the strength of the Devil.

Marigold pushed herself up off the ground and stumbled away more quickly than she thought she was able. The priest was left, resolute in his belief that his faith had been tested. He shook his head and reached for a handkerchief to wipe away the sweat from his brow. On the pavement, an old-fashioned shop receipt lay glued by the morning drizzle. He picked it up. Marigold's address was on the receipt.

Charging back to his church he was halted by the splendour of the nave, as he looked up to the domed area above the altar. He was then felled to his knees in the deepest of prayers. Crawling painfully forward, he reached the altar where not hours before he had performed the Eucharist. Sunlight flooded down through the stained-glass windows and the statue of Mary, holding the infant Jesus, was bathed in light. The priest felt, with all of his being, that he was being sent a sign. The busy city roads outside, usually audible, even in some muted form, at this time of the day, were silent. No birds above, no traffic below. Just peace. A tapestry hung on the wall above the altar. He read the intricate, ancient weaving,

Put on the whole armour of God, that you may be able to stand against the schemes of the Devil.

This priest had trained for four years locally, in Bearsden, near Glasgow, at the Roman Catholic college of Scotus. He had been lucky enough to be offered a year as a transitional deacon in Rome. There he had specialised in exorcisms. It had fascinated him. Marigold did not scare him. The act of driving out demons from her home would surely take place. Maybe he could save her. All souls should be saved.

He stood up, feeling reinvigorated. He would search for his hidden, handwritten book on exorcism. The ancient phials, containing the liquids he needed to purify her home, were hidden in the basement of the church, along with a special thurible, normally used to swing incense. All of this he had brought back from Rome with him. In his thirteen years as a priest, he had never opened the package given to him by a dying priest in Rome, who felt it was important to pass on to the younger generations of priests, the mysticism and wisdom of the old ways. No pure incense had ever touched this thurible. Which would be destroyed in a furnace after the exorcism. He walked down to the basement to retrieve the liquids, mixing them according to the traditions of the church. Special liquids to be brewed in line with the strength of the present evil. The process was intricate, time-consuming and exacting. He would have to be vigilant. Wait for Marigold to leave her home. Then he would enter and cleanse her house of the Evil One.

That was the plan.

On one of Marigold's trips out she had bought a newspaper and seen that the government was launching a major recruitment drive for nurses to combat what they said was a grave national shortage. An inquiry was to be set up, to ascertain why so many nurses were quitting the profession. Marigold had known the answer to that. Nurses were skivvies for the most part. In the meantime, nursing agencies had been set up, and rather appropriately there was an advert for one inside the newspaper. Marigold applied and was accepted. Despite her age, she was given fairly regular work. For a time, this gave her some satisfaction. She was sent farther afield. This meant she could shop in places she was unknown and despite the bothersome bus rides home, she felt that life was getting a little easier for her.

When she had initially filled out the application form for the agency, she had used Edith as a referee. Edith had posted the effusive personal reference without William's knowledge. The thought of that priest's face, as he had stared deep down into her soul, had unnerved Marigold for the time being. Perhaps it was time to do some good.

Perhaps.

However, Marigold's true skills lay in being a killer.

This was justified, in her mind, as she felt that her parents had always favoured her sister. Marigold had been neglected and abused emotionally, to the point that when she killed her sister, she was completely desensitised and she had never looked back. Every relationship she had ever embarked on, had to work on her level. Her manipulative, wicked level, devoid of empathy and humanity.

She was often sent to the homes of the elderly. The weak and vulnerable souls who organise their days around the visits of the kindly district nurse. Sister Hart with her smile and firm hands. Sister Hart who made the tea and listened whilst she dressed their weeping wounds and listened to their weeping hearts.

After a short while, she was sent to look after an elderly man called Stan. He was eighty-nine and frail and before the nurse was assigned to him by Social Services, his eating habits had been sparse and his bathing irregular. He stank and he was thin. Something about this combination appealed to *kindly* Sister Hart. He lived alone in a large house; his wife had died fifteen years ago of a brain tumour and he had nursed her for the last five years of her sweet life, praying daily that his love and devotion would be enough to cure her.

It hadn't been.

Following her death, he accepted that his children had wanted to emigrate to Australia. They urged him to follow them. He promised he would in due course. He had been lying to them. Yet he searched the post each day for airmail letters with the familiar blue-and-white edging.

Within two years it was reduced to Christmas and birthday cards, which were usually late. Stan cried a lot and eked out his wife's remaining meagre stash of outdated Oramorph painkillers. He took these both to remind him of his wife and to dull the ensuing pain of his memories.

His house was weighted with fifteen years of neglect. His soft eyes blinked tears of joy when Sister Hart first entered his home through the ever-open front door. He saw his saviour. She saw her saviour and the finality of the outcome was set in stone; the only variable would be the when and the how.

For three weeks she came and went from his home. Her routine was always the same with Stan. She ran his bath, medium hot, no bubbles, and helped his scrawny frame in, gently sponging his often red and angry sores from the sedentary life his diabetes and heart surgery dictated.

His home was filled with photos, no people, just memories his poorly eyes could barely focus upon. Many of his pictures were black and white, entombed in ancient albums in meticulous chronological order, which crinkled with the tissue paper used to separate each page. He snapped at Sister Hart when she moved a picture frame when dusting, or put his heavy albums back on the shelf.

This irritated her enormously.

For all that she did for him, including the very most personal of care. Washing the stinky, sticky yellow dribbles from his arse and thighs. His near liquid diet and endless cups of tea ensured constant diarrhoea. After all of that, how dare he shout at her?

In the end it was easy.

It was a shame that the priest was still busy fermenting.

Stan's back was to her in the bath; he was complaining again. She really must stop moving his things around. She let the sponge slide slowly into the water as she placed her hands on his skinny ageing shoulders. Shoulders from which had hung proud medals in war. Shoulders, which had helped carry his wife over the threshold, into this very home. Shoulders upon which he had carried his children across the sand dunes. Shoulders that had helped carry the weight of his wife's heavy oak coffin.

A swift downwards thrust and the deed was done. Before she left the house, she moved every picture around and filled her bag with nearly all the provisions he had in his cupboards. No need to go to the shops again soon, she thought, as she heaved the heavy tin-laden bag onto the bus. She ate tinned steak and kidney pie that night followed by tinned fruit cocktail. She felt good in herself, in a way she had not done for a long while. This agency thing might be godsend, she thought.

God was singularly absent, as it happened.

She called the police a week later when she returned to Stan's house. Accidental death was the verdict. Of course, he had been alive when she last saw him. Why on earth had he tried to bathe himself? How foolish, she had said. She smiled inwardly as his bloated body was carried out of the front door and she assured the police she would tidy up and call his son and daughter in Australia. With the door closed and the house to herself she sat for a good two hours watching TV, then she disconnected the phone and left. She bought fish and chips on the way home to celebrate. She was beginning to feel like her old self again.

She waited a while but the blood was coursing through her veins again. She felt alive as she never had for years. The following December Edith had called asking her to join them for Christmas in Whitley Bay. Edith had felt she was neglecting her and had pitied her. Marigold laughed to herself; she had her patients and her plans, but to placate Edith somewhat, suggested that they all come up to her. Of course, William would refuse. He had, and to Edith's regret and Marigold's relief, the moment passed.

An old lady Marigold nursed for the agency had serious senile dementia and was becoming a burden. Every day she had to visit and listen to a tirade of abuse, cups of tea were thrown, accusations of the most ludicrous type were hurled at Marigold. From the recesses of her mind Marigold heard the tone her mother used for her and the bile rose in her throat. Her heart beat fast and she had to escape upstairs, where the ageing woman could not reach her. Her hands firmly over her ears she pushed so hard on the side of her head that she began to get a migraine.

She was waiting for the excessive dose of morphine to immobilise the ranting patient downstairs. She would just keep her ears covered until the bitch had drunk her tea. That was her plan.

The priest still had his plan, but a bad bout of the flu had held him up.

William had another plan.

During the second week of Edith's holiday with Berenice, he had taken the train from Newcastle and paid for a cheap guest-house only a few hundred yards from Marigold's house. He had been observing her. Keenly. Noting down her movements and waiting.

He had been forced to delay until the second week as he had been waiting for Berenice to call that all was fine in France. In fact, she called in the middle of the first week. Her mother was getting tipsy every day, she moaned. William laughed at this and told Berenice to keep an eye on her but let her have fun. Berenice marvelled at her father's sanguine approach. He clearly had depths she knew little about. Next time she would take her father away by himself. That was her plan.

William stood opposite the house where Marigold was attending to the old lady. He had tried to enter Marigold's home, but found he just couldn't bring himself to do it. He had watched her leave, but the wickedness of its past barred him from entry. So he had followed her to work.

He was waiting for his chance. Traffic whizzed by on the busy main road and it was a good five minutes before there was a lull and he could cross over. He crept into the front garden then down the side path to the back garden. Through the kitchen window he saw the old woman sipping tea, but he couldn't see Marigold. His foot knocked the metal dustbin and the old lady spilled her tea, broke her cup and scalded herself. She screamed so loud that even Marigold heard and rushed downstairs, fearful that the neighbours would hear and come running. William crouched down and hid next to the dustbin, a move made awkward by an army-issue bayonet stuffed down his left trouser leg.

From inside he could hear Marigold rough-handling the

old lady. He was itching to intervene. Suddenly the back door opened and Marigold marched fiercely out to put the broken cup in the bin. There was no escape. They locked eyes.

This time it was Marigold's turn to feel fear. She dived down the side path with William in pursuit. She shot through the gate.

Job done. Almost.

William paused behind the high laurel hedge. The screeching of the tyres, the screams of Marigold, the smoke from the lorry that had swerved but hit Marigold then pinned her to the garden wall opposite, must mean she was dead. Surely.

As neighbours gathered on the other side of the road he slipped away. Back to the guest- house. On the early evening news that night, as he was having supper with the other guests, he heard a report of the accident and how a district nurse had been taken to her old hospital for treatment. He cursed inwardly, nearly choking on a very dry piece of lamb chop. At night, when most of the other guests were in their rooms, he went to Glasgow Royal Infirmary, a late visitor, a beloved brother, he said. They had let him in; it was only 9 pm, but he would have to be out by 9.30. They would close the wards totally at that time. He carried a bunch of flowers. He smiled and said it was not a problem.

In a side ward, just big enough for one bed, was Marigold. A quiet room for an old colleague. It had not always been a ward, it used to be the office of Dr Jonathon, but he had retired and it had been converted some years ago.

William slipped inside with the flowers. She seemed asleep. Battered, with endless tubes emanating from her thin evil lips. He approached her bed cautiously, scanning the tubes. He had been in hospitals enough to know which were the ones that delivered the air. He put the flowers on the tube and lent down fiercely, enjoying the moment. Marigold's eyes flew open, but she seemed incapable of speech. He pushed down on the flowers and said, 'For ruining the womb of my wife... for ruining the lives of so many women and their children... for being evil and treacherous and the most manipulative of friends... but finally for just being a fuck-ugly bitch!'

Marigold choked, gasped frantically and just before the machine started to beep its warning, William turned it off. She clawed at the air, swivelled her head from side to side, attempted to sit up, then flopped back down. In the distance she heard her name, called in harsh and unforgiving tones. She clung on, wheezing and choking. William pressed down harder, his face so very close to hers and in that yellowing sallow skin he saw the enemy and twisted her head round with a vicious snap.

Job done.

The air stank. The room was icy cold.

William levered himself away from her very slowly, savouring the distress in her eyes, the gaping mouth and splayed fingers. A harsh death.

He placed the crushed flowers in the bin. Petals dropped to floor. He thought he heard a distant weeping as he watched the petals swirl around in the draught. One for every soul Marigold had destroyed.

As he left, he passed a priest, someone paid for by the hospital to come in and give spiritual strength to the weak, especially at night-time, when most were fearful the Grim Reaper would appear. The priest coughed slightly and William stopped to ask him if he was in need of help, because, surely, he was in the right place. The priest had smiled and thanked William, but no, he was fine, just in the last stages of recovering from a bout of flu. He even admitted to having spent too many days in the damp cellar of the church. Be careful, William had said.

Both men stopped talking to look ahead at the commotion in a nearby side ward, as nurses were gathering around a bed.

William then left very quickly.

The priest rushed ahead to look in on the patient, now dead, who was causing all the kerfuffle on the ward.

He gasped. God does indeed move in mysterious ways, he thought. Indeed, he does. Sometimes.

After leaving that section of the hospital, William took off his leather driving gloves and slipped out of the hospital in the crush of visitors being asked to leave so the doctors could do their final ward round.

He went straight to the guest-house and gathered his belongings. He felt so light, so young, so in control. He would wait for Edith's return from holiday.

Edith had never felt so happy. She was enjoying the wine, enjoying meeting and talking to the other group members on the wine-tasting holiday. Berenice was attentive and together they shared some special moments, she thought. The elephant in the room was never referred to, ever. The holiday had no time for that, their itinerary was exhausting. Berenice loved the Renaissance residences, especially Chenonceau; she was captivated by the beauty of the architecture and as her mother got merry, she got high on historical treasures. Their little car was filling up with boxes of miniature Sancerre and Muscadet, plus Edith's favourite, Vouvray. There was no time to talk at night as Edith collapsed into bed, slightly squiffy each evening. Berenice was left to reflect on it all herself and wondered how such a once pretty woman could have turned so dour in the company of her husband.

The final stop was Joan of Arc's resting place at Rouen and it did not disappoint. The pretty four-storey buildings painted in sunny pastels were as enchanting as the story of Joan of Arc was riveting. In the old market square Edith and Berenice stood in awe at the place of her execution, the monument itself a very low-key affair. Berenice said to her mother that she thought it was all about the way she lived her life, not the way she died, and this resonated with Edith. She reflected that she had spent too much time trying not to live her own life, to wish her past into her present without regard for William. Maybe when she got home, she would be more attentive.

She was so scared though.

It had been far too long.

On the ferry home both women were pensive. Berenice, fearing that her holiday had not helped her confused mind, still yearned for some truth about her adoption. She had not been able to discuss it with her mother at all. Edith was wondering how to approach William. She wondered what he had been up to?

As William waited at the arrival gate at Newcastle airport his heart was pounding. He had planned it all with exacting military precision. His wife walked through the doors dragging what seemed to be a very heavy bag behind her. She smiled. He smiled.

That night he showed her the cutting from the newspaper that he had been saving. He held her tight as she read, aghast at the horrors of Marigold's suspected murder. The murderer had vanished into the night. A priest who had had a conversation with the alleged killer could not remember a single feature of William's face. Edith slumped into William.

'You never did take to her, did you?' she whispered.

'She served a purpose, we have Berenice, but no, after that I found the pilgrimages to see her futile. Her husband was just as bad. The pair of them were very weird, didn't you ever feel that?'

Edith had been so very wound up in her own past with Jonathon that she reflected that she had never really seen beyond that in her dealings with Marigold. Yes, she had felt sorry for the woman, with no children of her own, and thus she had traipsed up each year in part to share her own good fortune with her and let her enjoy Berenice. In truth Edith knew that this was a lie. She had, more than anything, just wanted to hear about Jonathon. Edith looked at William. Perhaps the trips should have never happened. Certainly, the phone calls had not helped, just raked up old wounds and unsettled the air.

Edith would not have wished a murder to end Marigold's life, though. Yet, curiously her death freed Edith.

In the end the wine helped enormously. As William descended the stairs the next morning, he stopped and shouted back up, 'I'll bring you a cup of tea up in bed, shall I?'

'Oh, yes please.' answered Edith, basking in a glow of sexuality hitherto unknown in her marriage.

'Would you like some toast and marmalade too?'

'That would be lovely, thank you.'

William skittered round the kitchen; he did not want to be too long, he had a want, too, and it had nothing to do with tea and toast. He smoked as he hastily prepared Edith's breakfast. It would sustain her, because she would need her strength. He had years to make up for.

After months of this Edith was exhausted. A trip to Wales did nothing to calm William down. Berenice was staying in a lovely little cottage with Jed and from the moment Edith arrived she felt that she was intruding. William had to make do with the sofa that night. He was not pleased. They left the next day. At home this new and somewhat energetic phase of their married life continued for another six months.

William was beyond joy. He would close his eyes and imagine he was twenty again.

He imagined taking Edith in the cemetery, under the pier, in her father's dental chair, on the dance floor of the Marine Hall, Fleetwood, in the air-raid shelter in Glasgow and especially in his mother's front parlour. He dreamed of devouring her in his foul hut in Changi, under the bridge over the river Kwai and in front of imaginary handcuffed Japs, the ones who had tortured him.

He saw the face of his captors and pounded his sex into Edith.

Again and again.

He felt a sudden pain and pressure in his chest.

Those fucking Japs, were they trying to squeeze the life

out of him?

He arched his back still further and his arms flew to his chest.

He collapsed upon her.

Utterly dead.

CHAPTER 18

AND SO IT ENDS?

William knew, from the moment he spoke alone with Berenice in the college hospital and the conversations the night before her wedding, that he needed to do something profound, to cure her curiosity. She had spoken to him of a student she was friendly with and how when she had found out she was adopted late in her teens, it had destroyed her. They had not gone that route but Berenice needed to make that agonisingly treacherous journey of discovery and he felt it was his role to orchestrate that.

She was grateful that she had always known. But what, apart from a word, did she really know?

Adoption.

Didn't tell *you* where your eye colour came from.

Didn't tell *you* where your mannerisms came from.

Didn't tell *you* what inherited medical issues might arise.

Didn't tell you the nature of *you*.

Adoption focused on the nurturing of *you*.

And when that fought, headfirst, with the nature of *you*, the sighs, the roll of the eyes, the whisperings at family gatherings, all of these and so very many more, then, *you* knew, *you* were destined never to be *you.*

Upon his return from the visit to Wales, when he had observed her, with all his emotions now finely tuned and his mind on fire, what he had seen had hardened his resolve to allow her to find out truths for herself. She was married but never calm. She smiled, but rarely seemed happy. Outwardly she functioned. Her husband seemed oblivious to the signs, except when cracks filtered through to his carefully structured world and then he would sit back, look around and seemingly mock the moment that had caused distress.

So, William had gone out and purchased a black metal storage box. He'd managed to sneak it into the house when Edith was on the upstairs extension chattering to Marigold. Perfect timing. He had tiptoed up the stairs and into his small office. He'd pulled back his small sofa-type bed with great care.

There had been a knock on the door.

'William, I'm popping next door for a chat, will be gone for a little while, is everything OK?'

Well, it would be, he'd thought, but he'd replied with something bland and she had left. Left him alone. Underneath the bed, underneath the carpet, underneath the ancient underlay, in fact, layered so far down they were invisible, lay the 1953 documents of adoption.

They existed, but were rarely dwelt upon by the signatories.

Hazel. Edith. William. Marigold.

And other minor bit players.

He held the documents, carefully. Time-bombs of facts. He would be gone when the explosions occurred. A week earlier he had been to the doctor, who had diagnosed an irregular heart rhythm. He was advised to treat life cautiously and not overdo things. Well, that wasn't going to happen. Not now. Now that he'd found his Edith again.

He locked the paperwork away and shoved the box, far back, underneath a deep set of drawers. Then he went into Berenice's old bedroom and opened the fateful wardrobe. He knew that she had not taken her twenty-first birthday gift from him with her when she'd moved. But in time she would think about this gift and when the moment was right, he hoped, she would search the tiniest and most awkward secret compartment and find the silver key. He kissed the key, placed it carefully within and sighed. His final manoeuvre for Berenice.

He needed a moment to himself.

He went back to his room, reorganised, then lay down.

This is where Edith had found him, two hours later when she came home. She quietly left the room, not wanting to wake him.

Berenice was also reflecting. She knew that the holiday to France with her mother had been just that. A holiday. It had been a mistake to believe it would stifle the questions that increasingly haunted her. Her disjointed relationship with her mother had been reverted to as soon as the holiday was over. Giggly lunches in picturesque chateau settings, in the sunshine, with too much wine for safe driving, were just that. Time out, not reality. She despaired. Her mother had clearly once been a joyous soul – had life been so cruel as to change her for ever? She would not let her life be like her mother's.

Upon return from holiday, she decided to make contact

with her birth parents. Such a simple thought. Such an agonisingly treacherous journey.

She had an address and surnames, thank you Daddy.

Directory enquires were a great help, no issues with protecting identities then; if you had a name and an address, of course, the very helpful lady would scroll through her enormous phone books and without hesitation give you the phone numbers of people you might want to speak to. Bugger their privacy.

Berenice sat and looked at the numbers for hours. Her hand reached out to the receiver then jumped back on contact. Her brow was sweaty, her heartbeat fast.

Then she dialled into her future.

As soon as the lady answered, she asked the unknown person on the end of the phone to sit down. Obligingly, the female declared that she had. A good start. Berenice proceeded to lay bare her soul and enquire if the woman listening so attentively knew who Berenice's birth mother might be? Particularly as they shared the same family name.

Well, laughter had not been the expected response. The woman hooted and hollered and went through a roll call of hated aunts and weird offshoots of the family who might be the guilty party. Berenice was aghast at the frivolity the seriousness of her request had generated. This went on for at least ten minutes. It was hard to shut her up. She declared that she had married into the family and they were horrid to her and she couldn't wait to get the dirt on one of them. Berenice's phone call had made her day. The conclusion was that Berenice might not get far. This was a rich Jewish family who might think she was just after the money.

MONEY? It had never occurred to Berenice. The woman concluded that she would do the digging and for sure she would come up with a name. Berenice thanked her, gave her their contact number, then hung up.

She was in a lather of sweat.

It had not been a good start. It took months before she dared to try another call. This time she tried to trace her father. Well, it was a similar story. One man was asked if his name was the same as on her father's notes. He replied that it was. Good start. That's how she found him anyway, so he must be telling the truth. Then he was asked if he knew Hazel. Oh yes, he had replied. Excellent, thought Berenice. Her heart began to pound. Did he by any chance know of a child born to Hazel? Yep, he did... wow... this is simple, thought Berenice. Well, she had thought, a trick question might confirm the veracity of the conversation. She politely enquired if he had smoked a joint on the moon last night. Yep, he had... wow... she put the phone down.

At that time, a popular woman's weekly magazine was running a section called *Where Are You Now?* Indeed, where was she now? Stuck firmly in the limbo of life between one *you* and another *you*. She submitted a grainy picture of herself, a short biography. Bam, looking for you, mother, it screamed. Clearly reflecting the heartache of her existence, *Where Are You Now*, yes, exactly.

Wherever her birth parents where, whatever their circumstances, they were not responding to her nationwide plea. Maybe there was a good reason.

Berenice clearly needed professional help. It took a long while, real life intervened, but eventually she made what she thought at the time was the savvy choice.

One half-term she marched boldly into Glasgow Social Services, following a six- hour drive up the busy motorways. She asked to see the person in charge of adoptions and she was escorted to a sterile room on the second floor. She didn't even sit down, no time. She had to say it all now, right now. This moment now, which had been decades in the making.

'I know where I was born, what my birth name was and who my birth parents were, I know the name of the adoption agency and the woman who ran it. I want a birth parent contact number. All the information I have is here on this sheet of paper. Take it. I am not walking out of here without a contact number. I need a contact number today. I can't function without this. It's this moment now, here, today, with you... please, please help me!'

Then Berenice crumpled into a chair and broke down and cried, for ages. For another age, another life she might have had, for herself, her adopted parents and all who had suffered through this agony called adoption.

The mature social worker looked at the information, handwritten in neat almost constipated compactness. Across the table, she saw a crumpled, proud woman who clearly was imploding. She gently pushed the box of tissues across the barrier of impersonality her desk was there to ensure. She stood and walked around. It was to be her undoing.

Berenice clung to her and implored. Professional resolve weakened. Against all her training and strict rules, the breaking of which could cost her a future in social work, she caved utterly. Very quietly she asked Berenice to leave and meet her at 1 pm in the café across the road. It was

10 am. Berenice floated through the ensuing three hours, suspended between one life and the expectations of another. It was as though she was experiencing a rebirth. The hope in those words.

'Meet me at 1pm in the café opposite.'

There was a silence within Berenice's core, the moment after the thunder in the office, calmly waiting for the lightning to strike.

It came in the guise of a short scrap of paper.

Her life on a short scrap of paper.

A telephone number, last known telephone number of her birth mother. The Social Worker slipped it under a plate on her table in true Bond style and walked on without hesitation, no backward glance. A dead drop. Just as well she was retiring in a month's time. Just as well!

For minutes Berenice just stared at the numbers; it took a while for her to focus anyway. And then came the downpour. She should have heeded the biblical response. She did not. Walking out into the lashing rain she felt spiritually cleansed, ready for the reconnection, cut previously with the slash of the umbilical cord by Sister Hart. The red telephone box was hardly visible in the storm. Pulling open the heavy door Berenice fumbled in her purse for enough change. How much would you need to talk to your mother for the first time? There were no guidelines. With quivering fingers, she dialled and waited. She was there, in the present, but somehow not, like the life had been sucked out of her and all time was standing still, waiting to move on again.

'Hello, I would like to speak to Hazel.'

'But she hasn't lived here for years,' came the cautious,

somewhat faltering reply.

Berenice whizzed through various responses.

'I know that, I am an old friend.' Seriously, that was the best Berenice's addled brain could come up with after all the rehearsals in her mind, to all the responses such a call as this might create.

'Really, well why don't you have her number?' This woman was not going to roll over and hand out a number. Berenice started to panic.

'I lost my address book, but I have been to your house years ago, I seem to remember your voice, you are her mother, aren't you?' Wild guess. Then there was quite a long pause. Like someone was weighing something up.

'Yes, I am.' Thank goodness for that.

'I've forgotten your name, I'm sorry, it's been such a while,' replied Berenice. Indeed, it had. You could say that it had been a lifetime.

'It's Erika. How did you say you knew my daughter?' What? Think on your feet, girl, come on.

'I worked with her for a while and I am trying to organise a reunion.' Vague enough to be sort of true. There was another long pause and a sigh, she sensed the older woman was getting tired.

'Well, give me your number and I will get her to call you back, she is very busy, you know.' Oh God, Oh God, she was in a public call box, far from home.

Berenice hurriedly recited the number on the phone, thanked the woman and hung up. She had spoken to a blood relative.

Her grandmother.

The clouds cleared.

The air was muggy.

She stepped outside the call box and sat down heavily on a bench close by with her handbag propping open the telephone-box door. A pensioner came asking to use the call box. She was told she would have to wait. She asked for how long and Berenice just shrugged. The pensioner walked slowly away. Time lost itself.

The phone rang.

Berenice leapt up.

'Is this the number for a long-lost colleague of mine?'

'No, actually no, but I do want to talk to you,' Berenice replied.

Berenices's life hung in the pause.

A very long pause.

'Then I know who you are, I've been waiting a very long time for you to call.'

These were the first ever words she heard her birth mother speak, as if the both of them had been waiting for this moment. Berenice slumped against the side of the call box, whilst outside the pensioner had returned and was pointing at her watch.

Hazel agreed for Berenice to call her on Monday night and read out loud her own home number. Berenice was scrabbling to write it down, using a red lipstick on the reverse side of the paper given to her by the social worker.

Right now, Hazel explained, she was at work, as a busy funeral director. Berenice whispered that she understood, she was just so very glad they had been reunited. Hazel did not respond to that.

After repeating the smudged number, to ensure she had it written down correctly, Berenice hung up. She walked slowly out of the telephone box; it was only the pensioner brushing roughly past her that bumped her back down to earth and she sat on the bench close by, held her head in her hands and wept.

A good hour later, and countless people coming and going from the call box, she felt a tap on her shoulder. A policewoman was enquiring if she was, OK?

Berenice smiled and replied, 'I will be now, thanks.' Then she stood up and made her way back to her car.

A funeral director, she could have done with her birth mother's help recently, there had been too many deaths in her family.

Her family?

She recoiled at the thought. Who was her family? Finding her birth mother had been the end game, but she began to realise the enormity of the journey she had launched herself into. As if punch drunk, she made her way home. The journey back down the motorway was slow and cautious. Once home, long after midnight, she sat in peace, whilst not being at actual peace, and wondered what the hell she had started. But it had started.

Oh yes it had, thought Hazel. She was unsure of her feelings. As she put down the work phone, following her mother's and her firstborn's intrusion into her working day, she reached in her drawer for her EpiPen. It had been nearly four hours since it had all started and in that time no drop of sustenance had passed her lips. Her staff had been watching the mercurial change in her mood, noting the lack of food and watching the clock till they knew they must intervene and suggest she used her diabetic medication.

Her upper body was beginning to shake, there were beads of sweat on her brow and her general anxiety levels were off the chart. As discreetly as she could, she lifted her skirt, exposing the top of her thighs. Her knee-high, sturdy stockings were a necessity of work, her skirts, being funereally long, hiding the fact that she didn't wear tights. She couldn't, the EpiPen injections were as regular as clockwork.

After ten seconds of holding the pen firmly in place on her thigh, Hazel felt the epinephrine coursing through her body. The shakes subsided and the sweat dried to a cold feverish band encircling her forehead and the back of her neck. She looked up and all of her office staff looked back down at their work.

She sighed.

Wild thoughts were entering her head. Please do not let this child have the mannerisms of her father, please no. Not the smile, nor the walk, the tenacity and the balls. The looks, well yes, she'd seen a hint in the magazine's *Where Are You Now?* article. A strong jawline, a steely stare. She remembered lying on the adoption form. Were the birth parents both British, she had been asked. Not exactly. Wrong answer, she had been told. British? Yes? Excellent!

With that last thought she locked her desk drawers, collected her handbag and bade farewell to the staff. They would have to manage without her for a few days. She was taking some unscheduled time off now. She was the boss, so she could say that. But in the last twenty years she never ever had. This was a first.

This was her first.

As she drove home, she debated telling her boys the truth.

In another house her mother's anxiety levels were similarly heightened. She suspected what the call had been all about. What now? she thought.

What now indeed?

The following Monday, Berenice made the call at exactly 7 pm. Of course, she wondered if she had been given a misleading number. She hadn't.

Hazel answered briskly and launched into explanations. Quite curtly she told Berenice that she lived in her own metaphoric castle and she drew the drawbridge up tight. People were rarely allowed in. Berenice listened and knew that the drawbridge had been lowered a chink, otherwise the phone call would not have been answered at all.

Hazel confirmed that she had seen the advert in *Woman's Own* magazine. In fact, a colleague at work had shown it to her and asked if this was her, the young woman had been searching for? She had, of course, been intensely embarrassed, denied it with a quick laugh and a 'get back to work' bark. But they knew. Hazel had tried to sue the magazine. Berenice gasped at the story, being recounted so factually, so chillingly factual. Hazel waited for what she wanted to hear.

'I'm so very sorry, I didn't think.'

Exactly, had been the reply.

Hazel had been forced to leave work early once she had taken the call from Berenice. She had certainly been expecting such a call but had hoped for a period of mediation, social workers calming nervous parties, reflection and then decision making. This had been like a barrel hitting her and rolling right over her. It was her, though. This child was certainly hers. She knew it in her soul.

The fabric of her neatly coiled, tightly woven life, unravelled slightly and she shuddered. Where would all of this lead? What did this young woman want of her? More exactly, what was she able to give? She had to take a step back. She had picked up the phone at seven and had intended to be curt and matter of fact. Put her off, she will be depressed and then leave her alone again. She found she could not. She started off clipped and sharp, but somehow Berenice touched her with her insistent yet softly spoken questions.

So many questions. Spilling out, spewing forth.

Of the father Hazel could give scant facts. She had no intention of telling this woman that she was the product of rape. Anyway, she had been made to feel so very dirty and cheap by her family that she had grown to believe that it actually had been mostly her fault for parading herself around so tauntingly. Hazel had, over the years, grown stout. She was solid and stern, a look that inspired confidence in the workplace as a funeral director.

Berenice ploughed on with the questions.

Hazel admitted that yes, there were half-brothers. There had been three, now there were two.

'What happened?' asked Berenice, elated to know she had three siblings then, in the same breath crestfallen on hearing that one had died. Hazel told it straight. He had died when he was thirteen, hung himself from a tree. Berenice was silent on the phone, knowing not how to respond.

Hazel was swept back to the moment she looked out of her bedroom window to see his lifeless teenage body swinging in the breeze, his brown skin merging with the tree bark, his orange shirt flapping around his slender frame and his enormous flares mocking his skinny legs. She had screamed, oh how she had screamed. Her two other boys had run to the tree at the back of the garden and looked up. Their father was home and he cut his boy down. Shortly after that he had left. Her boys went to stay with her mother.

She thought it fitting to train to become a funeral director. She specialised in children's funerals. Nobody did it better in London. She had a reputation. By excelling at this job, she partly buried her fear. A fear that she had not been there for her dead son. A fear that she had pushed them all away too soon. A fear that they would find out. She daydreamed often. What had happened to her baby? Was she right to let her go? Would others forgive her now if she told them the truth?

She never told the truth about her past. Her family never ever referred to it. They even forgave her for her hasty marriage afterwards. All Hazel knew was that to keep it all inside had slowly soured her soul and now she was faced with the living proof that this had really happened to her and she felt that she had no skills to deal with this onslaught, this thing called Berenice.

Berenice was amazed to discover she had aunts and uncles, some academic, some in the footlights, she knew now where she got her love of the arts from; her eldest half-brother was a musician, and she asked for his telephone number.

'Later,' had been the reply. Berenice's future was rolled into this moment. Mother and daughter agreed on another day for another phone call. There would be no meeting yet and Berenice hung up, high on adrenalin, whilst Hazel crumpled onto the floor of her two- bedroomed flat and wept. The weeping went on for hours.

Next day Hazel went to the doctor. Stress was diagnosed. She was in a limbo land of self-doubt, rudderless in a churning broth of emotions that peaked at elated and plummeted without warning. Knowing that the woman, she could not yet, would not yet, call her daughter, would want to meet. There would be no reverse after that, an apocalyptical decision was fermenting. Such agony.

She recalled the moments after the child was plucked from her. She had not been able to look at her. She had turned her head, yet swiftly turned back again only to see the door finally close and hear the child screaming. The pain. The screaming caused sharp stabbing pains in her heart and her breasts. Milk had trickled down, a river of guilt staining her borrowed nightgown, there was nowhere else to look, no escape from the throbbing pain of her actions. A silent gasp wrenched open her heart and she felt as though she was being torn apart, ripped asunder for the world to see how wretched she felt. She had slipped down under the covers. A soft brown hand had eventually pulled back the sheets, kissed her wet eyes and held her in his strong arms. It would be OK, he had said, there will be more children, we will have them together and you can love them just as much, he had said.

She did have more. She was rarely able to love them as

she should have. How could she? She was a tainted mother, undeserving of children. Guilt-ridden and rotting inside. With each passing year, the yearning to know, yet not to know, wrestled deeper with her.

Now this. What should she do? For herself, for this woman?

Berenice was stunned. Functioning on the surface of life felt as if she was floating on an incredibly thin sheet of ice. Time was marked as either before or after 'that phone call' and even she recognised that a period of reflection was required. As the days and weeks progressed, she yearned for more. She became impatient, intolerant of others and self-obsessed to the point of paranoia, fearing no further communication would take place. It was down to Hazel now. Respect that, please, had been the request. She would call Berenice when she was ready. For a woman bursting with more questions and searching for her own truth, the wait was unbearable. It clouded every aspect of her life and dulled her.

Then it came.

The call.

They would meet.

On Berenice's next birthday.

After all these years they would meet.

Thankfully her birthday coincided with the school Easter holiday.

Berenice's blood pressure shot up, she danced around, dithered around, changed her outfit six times and checked the hotel location twenty times. They were to meet and stay over in an out-of-the-way, faceless hotel. Halfway between the two homes. It seemed appropriate. They would check in and meet on Berenice's birthday.

The day of her birth.

It was happening.

And so there she was.

There they were.

Finally, Berenice understood the depth of meaning to the words that time could stand still, because indeed it did.

Before her stood a smallish, stocky, grey-haired woman with no smile, tense shoulders and a hesitant demeanour. She dressed to camouflage and she wore sturdy rubber-soled comfort shoes.

What had she expected? Perhaps not this. She was momentarily stunned. Had she been so naive to expect a younger woman, a female who looked like she had recently given birth? Perhaps so, in the fantasy that had been her existence since opening the black metal security box.

She hesitated ever so slightly.

It was noted.

Hazel saw a tall dark-haired young woman and instantly saw the face of the man who had raped her. She gasped inwardly; it had been one thing seeing it in a grainy magazine picture, quite another in the flesh. Berenice stood tall, as he had. Was clearly as insistent as he had been and had that same lopsided grin as he had. It rattled her. She set her mouth into a tight grimace, almost before she could stop herself. It was noted.

Hazel was alarmed to see Berenice stepping forward. Before she could stop her, she was hugged and finally, at arm's length Berenice asked her if she had had a good journey?

A journey?

Hazel's life rattled through her soul. A journey indeed.

And still no mention of the word mother in the greeting, or daughter.

Berenice was surprised at the coolness wafting back at her. Unable to cope she gabbled on inanely and the two women wove their way through the reality of the hotel check-in whilst the bubbly blonde behind the reception desk asked if they wanted a double, or twin beds.

With no hesitation, they settled on two rooms. It hadn't been the plan. But now it was.

Staring at Berenice and recalling her moments with Jeff, the hope, the kiss, then the rough handling and the hasty departure, Hazel was feeling physically sick. She could not stay in the same room as Berenice. Nor could she tell her of any of this. She was truly sorry, yet fiercely sure she could not, would not, share too much time with this woman.

Berenice had told nobody of this meeting. That they would be in separate rooms threw her momentarily, yet strangely she felt relieved, and there was nobody she could discuss this with. Fleetingly, she thought back to her discussions with her father, the night before her marriage. She could do with a friendly face.

The two strangers adjourned to the coffee lounge before going up to their rooms. Berenice sat down and turned sharply as a waft of cigarette smoke caught her nostrils. He was here.

Berenice's strangled soul screamed inwardly yet she calmly ordered a cup of Earl Grey tea, lemon, no milk. Routines might help, she thought, as she sipped her tea and

Hazel drank her espresso. What now?

There was an aura of do not disturb surrounding the two women and the hotel staff kept their distance.

It was Berenice's birthday.

The day of her birth.

From her functional handbag Hazel pulled out a thin, oblong jeweller's box. She asked Berenice to open it and inside was the most exquisite diamond and ruby bracelet. Hazel had bought it out of guilt perhaps; it had cost her thousands. Thousands of tears. Diamonds for Berenice's birthstone, rubies for hers.

Berenice picked it up and Hazel put the bracelet on her child's wrist. Skin on skin and she hated the feel of her. She was reminded of her conception. Hazel started to sweat. The two women glanced fleetingly at each other as the intervening years and the world whizzed and they shot back in time. Still Hazel could not tell her of the rape. Still Berenice could not call her mother. But there was one question Hazel was burning to know the answer to. The right answer would absolve her of the guilt of giving her baby away.

'Did you have a good upbringing, were you happy?' In a heartbeat, Berenice flashed through the episodes of her life and tried to make a decision which, whilst not being disloyal to Edith and William, would in some way be accurate.

The reply, a fraction of a second too late, was her undoing.

Berenice felt trapped. To admit she had loved every minute of her young life would have been a lie.

'They did their best,' she had responded.

Hazel gasped and stood up, as if to leave.

Berenice lifted her arm, heavier now because of the

bracelet, to reach out and hold Hazel back from leaving. At her touch once more, Hazel fell back onto the chair and sobbed. She could not have Berenice touching her again.

'I have one question – why did you let me go?' Now she could ask this. Face to face with the woman who had given birth to her, and on the very day, years ago, that she had done just that, let her go.

Hazel, now ramrod-straight in the chair, with no hesitation, devoid of all emotion and staring Berenice square in the eye, replied, with a tautness to her voice, 'I never wanted you. Never held you. Never looked at you. Didn't want you.'

The final morsel of oxygen in the room imploded. Berenice gasped, searching for air to breathe. Her hand flew to her throat. Quite without warning, she remembered finding her adoption papers. Her father's face swam before her eyes and she knew, in an instant, that he was at her side. How very clever of you, Daddy. You knew this all along.

Then she felt the break.

The bracelet slithered down Berenice's arm in two separate pieces one half next to her, the other in front of her birth mother. She had worn it for exactly the length of time she had been alive with this woman on the day of her birth. And then they had cut the cord and they were separated. Hazel saw blood, not rubies, tears, not diamonds.

Both women gasped. Hazel quickly gathered up the two splintered sections of the bracelet and looked down abjectly at her broken attempt to say sorry.

Bernice got up, suddenly anxious to leave, feeling no emotion at all. Her heart still, her mind empty, a force willing her to be somewhere else, quite overwhelming.

When Hazel looked up again, Berenice was gone, and she let out a shuddering sob.

Berenice heard it and this time, as an adult, she turned around.

Their eyes locked for the merest of moments.

Then the front door to the hotel slammed shut in the wind.

Berenice on one side.

Hazel on the other.

Their bond splintered.